HISTORIES WITHIN US

Also by Matthew Kressel

King of Shards
Queen of Static
Dispatches from the Outer Deep
Space Trucker Jess (June 2025)
The Rainseekers (February 2026)

Find more at:
www.matthewkressel.net

HISTORIES WITHIN US

Stories by Matthew Kressel

SENSES FIVE

Senses Five Press
Ridgewood, New York, US

For my friends in Altered Fluid, past, present, and future, who helped shape these stories from cosmic dust into suns.

CONTENTS

11 Introduction
15 The Sounds of Old Earth
33 The Meeker and The All-Seeing Eye
53 The Last Novelist (or A Dead Lizard in the Yard)
73 Saving Diego
97 Still You Linger, Like Soot in the Air
115 Now We Paint Worlds
145 The Great Game at the End of the World
167 Love Engine Optimization
185 Your Future is Pending
203 The Bricks of Gelecek
225 Demon in Aisle 6
243 The Thing in the Refrigerator That Could Stop Time
257 In Memory of a Summer's Day
269 The Garden Beyond Her Infinite Skies
291 Cameron Rhyder's Legs
311 Truth is Like the Sun
329 Mortar
353 The History Within Us
353 About the Author
354 Acknowledgements
356 Story Honors and Accolades

INTRODUCTION
MERCURIO D. RIVERA

When Matthew Kressel approached me and asked if I'd write the introduction to his new collection, I immediately said yes. After all, I've been enjoying his fiction for over 20 years—we've been in the same writer's group all that time (more on that later)—and I'm familiar with just about everything he's written. I looked forward to touting these exceptional stories because they not only evoke the sense of wonder you find in the very best science fiction, they also illuminate the human condition. These stories, I believe, deserve more attention. But then I began to have doubts about whether I should be the person writing this introduction. After all, I'm a longtime friend of Matt's. Shouldn't you take my opinion of his work with a grain of salt? After giving the matter careful consideration, I urge you to hold the salt, and here's why. The best evidence of the caliber of these stories is not my say-so. It's the fact they were originally published in some of the most prestigious speculative fiction markets around today: *Clarkesworld*, *Tor.com*, *Interzone*, *Lightspeed*, *Nightmare*, and anthologies assembled by legendary editor Ellen Datlow. Also, Matt's fiction has received *major* accolades: nominations for the Nebula Award and the Eugie Foster Award, glowing reviews, and inclusion in various "Year's

Best" collections. Although art is by its very nature subjective, by any objective measure these are highly regarded—indeed, acclaimed—works of short fiction.

I first met Matt in 2004, when I joined the Manhattan writers group, Altered Fluid, of which he was already a member. At the time, the group was a band of eager but unknown up-and-comers. Matt was welcoming and supportive, and we quickly became good friends. Back then, like all of us in the group, he was an unpublished beginner still trying to find his voice. But I was instantly struck by his energy and passion, and by how incredibly prolific he was. While I often struggle to find time to write, Matt is one of those writers who *has* to write, like he has to eat and breathe. It's in his bones. Many members of Altered Fluid have gone on to great success; Matt is no exception. Over the years, I watched firsthand as he developed from a talented but unpublished newbie into one of the major voices in the genre today. Matt has now published so many stories that he asked me to reread 30 of his "favorites" to winnow them down to the 18 stories that appear in this collection. (He has certainly generated enough high-quality fiction to fill a whole other volume of his work).

Perhaps my favorite story in this collection is the poignant, Nebula-nominated "The Sounds of Old Earth," which always makes me choke up whenever I read it. Both sad and hopeful, the premise is that our planet is slowly being dismantled, with the human population migrating to a brand-new Earth, and the protagonist, Abner, must come to grips with leaving behind everything he's ever known. The story's poignancy stems from Abner's relationship with his children and grandchildren, and the memories evoked by the family home he is being forced to abandon. (I was with Matt when the inspiration for this story came to him. We were attending the wedding of fellow Fluidian Devin Poore in Napa Valley wine country, and happened to catch a documentary about the demolition of the old Yankee Stadium, with all its wonderful, glorious memories, and its replacement with a shiny new stadium across the street). Matt deals with similar themes, working the same magic, in the affecting "The History Within Us," in which a woman recounts the history of humanity to a group of aliens—and the family history she carries encoded in her genes—right before they are about to escape through a black hole to a universe beyond.

As you can tell from these two stories, Matt enjoys painting stories on a sprawling cosmic canvas. For my money, no short fiction writer today elicits a sense of wonder like he can. For example, in the Nebula-nominated "The Meeker and the All-Seeing Eye," the story's grand scope is evident from its opening sentence: "As the Meeker and the All-Seeing Eye wandered the galaxy harvesting dead stars, they liked to talk ..." Thus begins a centuries-spanning story of an enigmatic, destructive cosmic entity and her servant—who have laid waste to the entire galaxy!—trying to solve the mystery posed by the last resurrected human. In "The Garden Beyond Her Infinite Skies" he introduces equally mind-boggling entities—cosmic gardeners—who literally prune universes. And Matt's *Numenverse* stories ("Saving Diego," "Still you Linger, Like Soot in the Air," and "Now We Paint Worlds"), feature inscrutable all-powerful aliens who can annihilate planets with a single thought and consider humanity to be nothing more than a flicker in the cosmic mind. "Saving Diego" focuses on the intimate friendship between two characters, one addicted to a drug that allows him to commune with the aliens. "Still You Linger" is a meditation on faith and loss in a universe subject to the Numens' whims. And "Now We Paint Worlds" tells the story of a woman in search of her mother, who lived on one of three worlds obliterated by the Numens. In all of these stories, Matt filters the scope of these mind-blowing plots ("as [they] wandered the galaxy harvesting dead stars...") through the lens of personal relationships ("… they liked to talk.")

Although he favors science fiction, Matt swims effortlessly in the sub-genre waters of fantasy and horror. When I heard he was putting together this collection, the first question I asked was whether he was including "The Thing in the Refrigerator That Can Stop Time," one of his earlier works that has stuck with me through the years. It's a disturbing horror story and a *tour de force* in craft, using fragments and run-on sentences to connote terror-filled, slow-motion madness. Equally disturbing, "In Memory of a Summer's Day" is a nightmare about an *Alice in Wonderland* theme park of terror and despair. The demon of destruction meets a girl whose songs remind him of dead cities in "The Bricks of Gelecek." And "The Great Game at the End of the World" crosses genres, giving us science fiction sprinkled with fantasy and horror, telling the touching tale of a boy and his kid sister playing a baseball game with ghosts and ghouls after the apocalypse.

Other gems in this collection include the deeply moving, Nebula-nominated "The Last Novelist (Or a Dead Lizard in the Yard)," about the protagonist's tender relationship with a local child trying to understand the beauty of the lost art form of writing; the electric prose of "Cameron Rhyder's Legs" with its time travel paradoxes and frenetic rock and roll; the bleak and dystopian "Your Future is Pending" about a woman struggling to care for her dementia-stricken father in a stifling and inequitable bureaucratic society; and the creepy, riveting page-turner, "Love Engine Optimization," about the manipulations of an abusive social media stalker.

If this collection is your introduction to the work of Matthew Kressel, buckle up, you're in for quite the ride. Simply put, I'm an unapologetic fan. And when you're done reading, I think you will be, too.

Mercurio D. Rivera
December 2024

THE SOUNDS OF OLD EARTH

EARTH HAS GROWN quiet since everyone's shipped off to the new one. I walk New Paltz's empty streets with an ox-mask tight about my face. An acidic rain mists my body, and a thick fog obscures the vac-sealed storefronts. Last week they hauled the Pyramids of Giza to New Earth. The week before, Stonehenge. The week before that, Versailles and a good chunk of the Great Wall. But the minor landmarks are too expensive to move, the NEU says, and so New Paltz's Huguenot Street, seven centuries old, will remain here, to be sliced to pieces in a few months when the planetary lasers begin to cut the Earth apart.

I pump nano into my bloodstream to alleviate my creeping osteoarthritis and nod to a few fellow holdouts. We take our strolls through these dusty streets at ten every morning, our little act of rebellion against the mandatory evacuation orders. I wave hello to Marta, ninety-six, in her stylishly pink ox-mask. I shake hands with Dr. Wu, who performed the op to insert my cranial when I was a boy. I smile at Cordelia, one hundred and thirty-three, as she trots by on her quad servo-legs. All of us have lived in New Paltz our entire lives and all of us plan to die here.

Someone laughs behind me, a sound I haven't heard in

a long time. A group of teenage boys and girls ride ancient turbocycles over the cracked pavement toward me. They skid to a halt and their eager, flushed faces take me in. None wear ox-masks, which is against the law. I like them already.

"Hey shinhun!" a boy says. "Do you know where the frogs are?"

Before I can answer, an attractive girl with a techplant on her cheek blows a dreadlock of green hair from her eyes and says, "We heard some wankuzidi has an old house where he keeps a gose-load of frogs." A boy pops a wheelie and another takes a hit of braino from an orange inhaler. A third puffs a cigalectric and exhales fluorescent smoke.

"Behind my house I have a pond with a few frogs still alive," I say.

"Xin!" she exclaims. "How 'bout you ride with us? I'm Lin."

These kids are as high as orbitals, but it's not as if I have much left to lose. "Abner," I say.

And just like that I'm hanging on to her waist as we speed toward my house over broken roads no ground vehicle has used in decades. The wind in my face feels exhilarating.

"We're from Albany," Lin says, "We tried taking the old Interstate down, but after Juan got tossed when he hit a cheeda crack, we decided to go local. Took us yungyeh!"

The stascreen around my property makes my fifty acres of forest flicker like water in sunlight. It's a matter of pride that I keep it functioning at high efficiency; after all, I designed the damn technology. When we pass through the screen's charged threshold, I take off my ox-mask, and breathe deep. The kids smile when they smell the fertile earth, the decaying leaves.

"It don't smell like this in Albany," Lin says.

We park the cycles on the overgrown grass and I lead them into the woods behind my house. The kids stare up at the huge maples and birches and fall quiet.

"The frogs croak loudest at sunset and before it rains," I say. "That's when the males are trying to attract a mate." The kids giggle as they leap over branches. "If you really want to hear them, you should stay until it gets dark."

"You got anything to eat?" a boy says. "We haven't eaten since yesterday."

I search inside the house and return with some readimades, pretty much all you can buy on Earth these days, while the kids shudder and wobble as they inhale braino. The green-haired Lin wanders off to vomit in the trees.

"Is she going to be all right?" I ask a boy.

"Oh, Lin always pukes after her first hit. Want some?" He offers a red inhaler, but I decline.

We sit beside the pond, all of us squeezed on a log. Lin sits next to me, and I pop up the straw of the readimade for her. "You okay?" I say.

"Yeah, I always get all shunbeen when I deepen."

"It's probably none of my business," I say, "but shouldn't you kids be in school or something?"

"School closed four months ago," she says. "Not enough teachers."

"So what do you do all day?"

She wipes saliva from her cheek and shrugs. "I don't know. *This.*"

Another boy goes off to puke in the woods.

"What about you?" she says. "You live here all by yourself?"

I nod.

"And what do *you* do all day? Hang out with the frogs?"

"Most of my time I just try to keep the stascreen working."

"That your job or something?"

"Used to be. I was a stascreen engineer for fifty-one years. I designed the nanofilters that keep ecosystems like this free of envirotoxins. But the NRDC laid me off four years back."

"Why? This place is xin!"

I smile wanly. "Because toxfiltering's a dead business now. People are only interested in making new life, not preserving the old."

She seems to take me in for the first time. "And how old is this place, Abner? These trees look cheeda ancient."

"I know that when my ancestor built this house four hundred years ago, the frog pond was already here."

She sighs. "Fucking NEU making you leave this place?"

"They're making everyone leave."

She throws a rock into the pond, and a dozen frogs squeak away in fright.

"Please," I say, gently touching her arm. "You'll scare them off."

"How long?" she says, giving me a tender look, and I'm not sure if she means the frogs or my eviction.

"Soon."

The kids grow hungry again. I had been saving some hard-to-find vegisteaks for my grandkids, but they haven't visited in ages. As I grill them on the deck the smoke rises through the trees, and the dipping sun sends girders of light through the branches.

The kids inhale more braino, howl with laughter, and Lin pukes again. And when they tire, I glimpse something desperate in their bloodshot eyes, something I've seen in the expressions of Cordelia and Dr. Wu and Marta and the other holdouts. Regret doesn't spare you just because you're young.

"You cycled all the way from Albany for this?" I ask Lin.

"Nothing but dust and skyscrapers there," she says. "No real trees. We heard this was xin. Do you have kids, Abner?"

The question catches me off-guard. "Yeah, a son and daughter. And two grandkids. You sort of remind me of my granddaughter, Rachael."

She pauses to consider this. "They come here lots?"

"Not anymore."

"Why not? I'd be here every day."

"They've moved." I point to the sky.

She frowns, and her body sags like an old tree. "We're moving too."

"New Earth?"

She harrumphs. "Nah, that's only for rich kids. We're going to Wal-Mart Toyota."

"Haven't heard of it."

"You wouldn't. It's like cheeda ancient, one of the first orbitals. But you gotta go where they send you, or else, you know?"

"I know," I say, staring at the upside-down trees reflected in the water.

Night creeps over the forest and the frogs begin their mating calls in earnest. The croaking rises to a din, and the kids pause and listen. The glorious stars emerge, and I'm not sure if it's my imagination, but the frogs seem to plead to them, over and over again, "Save us, save us, *save us!*"

We listen for a while, until the frogs tire. "It's late," I say. "It's a long way back to Albany. Why don't you kids stay? There are plenty of beds."

So we head inside. I set them up with fresh linen I haven't used in years, and during the night I hear fucking and shuffling and laughing as I pour myself tumbler after tumbler of rye whiskey until I pass out. Late in the night, I hear someone whimpering outside my door, and I rise groggily from bed. Lin sits in the hallway, her eyes as red as cinders as she looks up at me.

"I'm sorry," she says, wiping away tears. "I didn't know that was your bedroom."

"What are you doing?"

"Nothing," she says as she climbs to her feet.

"You okay?"

"I was just thinking. You don't know us, Abner, but you welcomed us into your home."

I shrug. "This place was made for guests."

She stares at the walls. "Must have been beautiful, when it was full of people."

I nod. "It was."

She stands there, and again she reminds me of my granddaughter who I never see. I want to hug her and tell her the future will be xin, that everything will work out, eventually. But I'm too drunk to lie. "It's late, Lin. Go to bed."

A tear rolls down her cheek. She nods and turns away. I close the door, feeling as if I've missed something important. It takes me forever to fall back asleep.

The next morning, the kids are gone. The house looks as if a tornado has blown through. But one bedroom has been tidied, and there's a note on the nightstand.

"The frogs are beautiful. You are beautiful. Thank you for a perfect day. —Lin."

I hold the note in my hand and stare out the window into the empty yard. I already miss their laughter.

Several months before I received the evac order, I visited New Earth for the first time. My son Josef played the guide and took me to the Ishibuto-Mori preserve, a dense rainforest on the northern hemisphere. Giant sequoias planted a few years ago had already grown hundreds of feet tall, carrion flowers had been gengineered to smell like cotton candy, and the rains came precisely at 2:00 p.m. every day.

Clear plexi walls kept us safe on a paved path that led us, like Dorothy to Oz, to John Muir Mall. It was a palatial marketplace where they seemed to have anticipated every human need. Food, clothing, jewelry, a pub, an immersion cinema, a spa. All was here, square in the middle of the rainforest. A holohost welcomed us to the mall's courtyard and carefully explained, as if he were speaking to children, how Old Earth had become uninhabitable, how humanity's first home was ruined forever because Those Before had no appreciation for the natural world. But the Ishibuto-Mori Corporation, along with dozens of other companies, were hard at work ensuring that New Earth avoided this fate.

As my son and I ate oversized burgers in the courtyard of Ffizer's McDonald's, I noticed that no one looked up when Earth rose above the forest canopy. Before the next scheduled rain we left for home.

Josef's family lived in a spacious and many-windowed apartment on the ninety-seventh floor of a three-hundred-story tower. Luxury condos like these, Josef said, were popping up all over New Earth. My heart warmed when I saw my grandkids, Rachael and Pim. It had been several years since I'd seen them in person—they didn't visit Earth anymore. Today was Pim's twelfth birthday.

My grandson blew out his candles and we all shared papaya cake. On cues from my daughter-in-law, a shining mahogany andro poured coffee, brought out cookies, and cleared the dirty dishes. I felt like a princely CEO. On Earth natural grain was absurdly expensive and hard to come by, but on New Earth it seemed as plentiful as the scheduled rain.

"Pim's not the only one celebrating today," Josef said, in between sips of coffee. "Tell Grandpa the good news, Rach."

My granddaughter beamed and said, "I got a full scholarship to GE Sinopec!"

"GE Sinopec?" I said.

"An orbital university!"

"Oh, wa!" I said. "A full scholarship? That's xin!"

"As a reward," Josef said, "Esther and I have decided to buy Rach a small lobber. You'd be surprised at how affordable they've become."

"I can visit Mom and Dad on weekends," Rachael said, "and fly back to school on Sundays. And Grandpa, there's this low-fuel maneuver called a Hohmann Transfer that lets you fly over to Old Earth in a couple hours. Me and Leva are definitely headed there when they start dismantling it, to get a closer view."

"*Rachael,*" Esther said with an admonishing tone. "Why don't you see if Grandpa wants more coffee?"

"He's got coffee. And isn't that what you bought the andro for?"

"Rachael, don't be rude!"

"But, Mom, his cup is full!"

"Rachael Kopperfeld!"

"Please!" I said. "Yes, yes, they're dismantling Old Earth. It's no gaise secret. Why does everyone avoid that subject around me?"

"Because every time we bring it up," Josef said, "you go on a rant about how they're tearing down your home."

I stared at my son. "It was once your home too, if you remember."

Josef frowned. "That was a long time ago, Dad." He waved his hand at his apartment. "*This* is my home now, and I'd like to have a nice birthday for Pim."

"Is the frog pond still there, Grandpa?" Pim asked.

"Yes! It's been a struggle to keep the pond free of toxins, but the frogs still croak away on summer nights. Do you remember when you used to put them in boxes to scare the hell out of Grandma Shosh?"

He giggled. "And Rach used make up silly names and marry them."

"They got so loud some nights," Rachael said, smiling, "that my ears would ring the next morning."

I shook my head and stared down at the plate of cookies. "Those poor creatures don't know that their ancient home will soon be destroyed."

"Not destroyed," Josef said. "Dismantled. There's a difference."

"Countless species will be killed. I don't know what you call that."

"Some death will occur," Rachael said. "But the Geoengineers are making heroic efforts to save every documented species."

"Heroic?" I said. "Rachael, the cradle of humanity is being left to rot."

"I love Earth too, Dad," Josef said, "but the air is poison. The soil is toxic. You spent your whole gaise life trying to clean it, and for what? So we could watch Mom die slowly from the Tox?" He paused and took a deep breath. "I want a better life for my kids, and your Earth can't give that."

I put down my cup. "Since when did it become *my* Earth? Once, it was *ours*."

Esther loudly sipped her coffee, a sign she was not amused by the conversation.

"Grandpa," Rachael said, "it's not just the toxins, it's the overpopulation. We used up all the matter in the asteroid and Kuiper belts to make New Earth. We need Old Earth's mantle to build more colonies. And besides, it's natural."

"*Natural*?" I said as my belly grew hot.

"Yes." Rachael sat up straight and looked at her mother, as if she had been preparing this for weeks. "In living creatures, new cells are born from old ones, then the old cells die. But life continues. Your body's cells have replicated themselves dozens of times. Old Earth isn't ending, Grandpa, it's rejuvenating. The old cell is giving birth to a new one. And when the old cell dies, its contents are broken up and recycled. That's the course of life. The body of Old Earth will be gone, but its essence lives on."

I stared at my family, all of them willing to throw away the priceless Earth as if it were an obsolete piece of technology, and disagreed.

Three days after Lin's visit, I set my car down in central Albany. In a foggy rain, I wander past empty skyscrapers, drifts of windblown debris, and vac-sealed buildings, kicking up clouds of gray dust. On Livingston Avenue I meet a holdout who introduces herself as Helen. A sickly looking kitten walks at her heel.

"Not many kids left," Helen says, her voice muffled by a

scratched ox-mask, "Green hair, techplant on her cheek, neh? Yeah, that's Lin Bar-Martin. Yeoung's kid. Hangs out with a bunch of liumangs. If I recall, her father Yeoung worked in nanotesting."

"A scientist?" I ask.

"Ha! No, they tested nano *on* him."

"Oh. Where do they live?"

"Nowhere."

"What do you mean? She's homeless?"

"As if. No, plenty of places to live here. She's gone."

"Gone where?"

"To Wal-Mart Toyota. An orbital."

"You mean, for good?"

"Where've you been, baichi? No one comes back to Earth."

"What about her friends?" I hate myself that I can't remember their names. "Are they still around?"

"Haven't seen a kid in days. The whole north side of the city shipped off to Wal-Mart Toyota. Heard the place is dreadful. They abandoned it mid-construction because they found better ways to build colonies using nano."

"But the kids were at my house three days ago!"

"And they left two days ago. A fleet of ships took 'em away like it was a parade."

And then I know why the kids cycled all the way down to New Paltz over dangerous roads, and I know the look in Lin's eyes when she was crying outside my door that night, the feeling that I'd missed something. That was Lin's last day on Earth. The kids wanted to see a piece of ancient Earth before they left it forever.

"Thank you," I say to Helen.

I pet the sick kitten, then I leave her empty city. By the time I arrive home, it's getting dark. There's a strange car in the driveway, and a young woman sits on my porch. For a moment, I think it's Lin. But then I recognize my granddaughter's dark hair.

"Hi, Grandpa."

"Rach, what are you doing here?"

"I came to say hi."

I hug her hello. "You came all the way here just to say 'hi'? Why didn't you call? I could have prepared dinner."

"It was kind of a last-minute thing."

"It's great to see you! You look good, Rach." The wicker chair creaks as I sit beside her. "How's school?"

"It's tough, but otherwise xin." We stare at the overgrown grass as a wind whispers through the trees. "The grounds look really healthy."

"I try."

"I remember when I used to sit on your lap and you'd tell me the silliest stories."

'I'd say come on over, but I think you're too big for that now."

She smiles, but it quickly fades. "Grandpa, the NEU can spot a flea from orbit. There's nowhere to hide."

"I don't plan to hide. I plan to stay right here."

"They'll force you out."

Beyond the trees, a troublesome spot on my stascreen wavers. "Maybe I won't give them the chance."

"Grandpa . . ." She puts a warm hand on mine. "You and I disagree on a lot of things. Promise me that when the time comes, you won't do anything stupid."

"Rachael . . ."

"Promise me."

When I look at her I see the child she once was, the girl who married frogs and danced in fields of sunflowers. "I'm sorry," I say, "but this isn't your Earth. You don't understand."

"Maybe I understand more than you." She leaps to her feet. "Neh, I have to go."

"Already? You just got here."

"I have an exam in the morning."

She hugs me, squeezes a little too hard. "Goodbye, Grandpa.

I love you."

And in seconds her lobber is flying up into the sky. I watch it recede until it's just another star. Out back the frogs croak louder than I've ever heard them.

I sit on the wet grass under the stars, hugging a bottle of rye. Yesterday, another hurricane blew through the area, a product of Earth's new gravitational partner. A decade ago they would have burnt the storms away with their orbital lasers, but Earth just isn't worth it anymore. They didn't even bother to give the hurricane a name.

The storm washed away the dust, and the moon and New Earth lay hidden below the horizon. And in the dark, how beautiful is the sky! The stars are so bright they cast shadows, their points are so clear I feel I could pluck them like apples from the sky. Jupiter rises slowly in the east, bright as an angel. And the Milky Way swaths gloriously across the heavens. If I could leap into the sky, I'd fall into it forever.

"Ashey," I say to my cranial, "Play 'Grandkids Visit, Summer '98.'"

A holo projects over my eyes. Little Rach sits on my knee, giggling. Birds chirp in the summer sun. The smell of roses. A soft breeze on my cheeks, all under the warm comfort of a well-functioning stascreen. "Can we sit under the sunflowers again?" a five-year-old Rach asks a much younger me.

Sunlight trickles through fans of yellow petals as I follow her into my field of sunflowers. She sits on the ground beneath their giant blooms and says, "I want to live in your house, with you, Grandpa. I never want to go home."

I watch her draw a house in the dirt with a stick. "Like this one," she says.

"Ashey, play 'Shoshanna's 60th Birthday.'"

Years earlier, Shosh opens the ancient oak door of our house. Everyone yells, "Surprise!" As my wife throws her hands to her mouth and shrieks, she drops a glass bowl. It shatters, and everyone chuckles nervously. A tear of happiness rolls down her sallow cheek. Even this far back she's already showing signs of the Tox.

I excelled at removing the worst pollutants from environments, but with all my knowledge I still couldn't protect my wife's body from them.

"You devil," she whispers to me, embarrassed. "I thought you had forgotten."

"Never," I say.

"Damn. That bowl was expensive."

"I'll make it up to you."

"Oh, yeah?"

I lean in to kiss her, and I feel the press of her soft lips even after the recording ends.

"Ashey, play 'Josef's first steps.'"

Our same house, decades earlier. Shosh, younger, healthier, Tox unmanifest. Little Josef bravely climbs to his feet, takes two teetering strides, then falls. Shosh leaps to publish the holo on the net for all to admire. She struts pridefully over to me and smiles. "Kid learns fast. He's already better at walking than you are."

My ancient self giggles.

"Ashey, pause playback."

Google-Wang Colony spins into view far above. I'd recognize the corporate colors from a billion miles away. I take another quaff of rye, then lay back on the wet grass. Cold moisture soaks into my back. Bank of Zhong Guo Colony winks distantly across the sky, and even though it's hundreds of miles up I think I can hear it tearing roughly across the Cosmos. I sit here, watching the stars, until New Earth rises, spoiling the glorious night.

I approach my house, plasteel container in one hand, rye in the other. I pour the liquid in the plasteel container into the foyer, and the hydrocarbon smell burns my nostrils.

With a small lighter I set flame to a soaked rag. I toss it into the house. For a moment, the rag burns like a candle, guttering in a bedroom. Shadows dance across my ancient walls like memories. A pang of dread hits me. Is this really what I want?

But it's too late. The foyer erupts in flame, and I leap back. In seconds the fire roars louder than the frogs ever have. The heat singes my face as the house burns.

And just like that, I destroy the home that my fifteenth generation great-grandmother built four hundred and seventeen years ago.

With the stascreen shut down, the fire corkscrews freely into the sky. A column of smoke arcs away for miles, lit by the light of New Earth. Once, this would have aroused a hundred suppressor-bots into action. Now, what is another fire when all will soon be ash?

My ancient house burns to the ground. It takes a while. So I sit beside the pond. The frogs are quiet, perhaps watching the flames with me. I think of Rachael, and the promise I made to her. And I think of Lin.

At dawn, when the police arrive, the only thing left of the house is a pile of cinders. The air is foul with soot as armed men read me the evac order. They bind me in plasticuffs and escort me off my property. They seat me inside a small craft, and the young man across from me, in bulky police regalia, offers me anti-nausea nano for the trip to space. I was hoping to glimpse my property one last time as we lift off, but there are no windows. This is a prison ship.

I paid a hefty fine and was ordered to take "reintegration" classes, then I was set free. The process seemed rote, and I suspect I'm one of thousands. Josef rented me an apartment in his condo for an absurd price, and he and Esther have been inviting me over nightly for dinner as if nothing at all has happened. Rachael calls from time to time to see how I'm fitting in.

When I'm not skipping the reintegration classes or finding excuses not to join Josef and Esther for dinner, I spend my time watching as the Earth gets sliced open like a piece of fruit, as geometric chunks are carved out of its pulpy flesh ten thousand kilometers at a time.

This evening my telescope and datafeeds focus on the Earth's northern hemisphere.

"It's time," Ashey warns. By piggybacking illegally onto satellite proxies, I have real-time access to the Geoengineers' datanet. On my holoscreen a green light flashes twice, the signal from the Foreman. In Pan Mandarin, translated on my screen, the Foreman says, "EDHL-22, begin the first longitudinal cut at your discretion."

A full minute's pause. Then a blinding flash. A molten orange circle of light moves south along the seventieth longitude line for minutes, and even from this distance it's so bright it leaves spots in my vision. The cutting pauses as the laser's gyroscopes realign. Then it slices across the fortieth latitude line, just under an emptied New York City.

The laser traces out a great rectangle over the course of an hour. Then the grav-beams tug the huge section out. Like ice cream, the molten core drips toward Earth's center. By technology I don't pretend to understand, the layered walls of Earth don't collapse into the new space, but stay fixed. And the white-hot core, from what I've read, is being artificially cooled, eleven-point-five degrees per day.

I wonder if any of the holdouts, like Cordelia or Marta or Dr. Wu or Helen and her kitten, escaped the mandatory evacs. As they slowly floated into the sky, would they think they were flying up to meet God?

Over several hours, lasers break the chunk into hundreds of pieces.

"That one," Ashey says, highlighting a point in my vision.

The land that was my home is shunted up to Trump-

Dominguez Colony. It will be used, the datanet says, as a counter mass so the colony can maintain its highly sought-after earth-forward views. Four and a half billion years, of algae and antelope, of brontosauri and bison, of woolly mammoths and glaciers, of trees and earthworms and amphibious frogs just to become a paperweight so the rich can wake up to their plastic earth.

That night, I dream of frogs screaming.

Years pass. Old Earth is gone, every last piece used up.

Today, I sit next to Josef, Esther, and Pim in an amphitheater of thousands. Rachael is graduating from GE Sinopec with a B.S. in Applied Biology. We sit through an endless procession of names. Pim and I converse a bit. His voice has deepened, and he looks more like a man these days. He's polite, and humors me, but I sense universes between us. I know this world isn't mine anymore.

After the ceremony, we eat dinner at an expensive restaurant, and the low-g does horrors to my stomach. Rachael, in her graduation gown, has been staring at me the entire meal. "Grandpa," she says, "will you come with me for a ride after dinner? I'd like to show you something."

Her mother smiles.

"I've had too much to eat. I'm a little tired. Maybe next time?"

Josef glares at me. "*Dad*," he says like he's scolding a child, because that's what I've become to all of them.

I sigh. "What did you want to show me?"

We head outside to Rachel's lobber, a frighteningly small vessel, and I climb into the passenger seat as eagerly as a man to the gallows. I was never good with zero-g. I try to hide my shakes as we leap off GE Sinopec and dive down to New Earth.

"For my graduation thesis we had to recreate an Old Earth ecosystem," she says, "as part of the bioprojects to save as much life as we can." I examine her face in the reflected light of the planet. She is beautiful, my granddaughter. From under her rolled up sleeve I see the glint of a techplant, expressly forbidden by her father. I smile.

"So I chose your backyard," she says.

"Excuse me?"

"Specifically, the lake behind your house, with all the frogs."

The lobber dips over a deciduous forest, and we descend tens of miles. My stomach feels like I left it back at the university.

"I didn't tell you," she says, "because I knew how you were always going on about New Earth." She holds her breath, and when I say nothing, she says, "and also because I really wasn't sure if it was going to work."

"What was going to work?" I say. We swoop over fields of swaying grass, muddy swamps and dense forests.

"Let me show you."

We set down in a field beside a thick wood. There are deep depressions in the mud, a sign of many previous landings. The sun hangs low on the horizon, and its orange light spills through the trees. She leads me into the woods, down a winding path, pausing to make sure I'm still with her, to warn me of a treacherous branch or root. The air here smells of mulch and earth and abundant life. She smiles, and suddenly it's like she's a toddler again, leading me into a field of sunflowers.

And then I hear them.

Frogs. Thousands of them, croaking away with strange voices. We approach a small lake, not too different from the one that was once in my backyard.

"I came by your house when I knew you were away." She looks apologetically at me. "And I collected, um . . . *specimens*. They're not the same frogs, of course," she says. "They have genes better suited to this particular environment. But they're direct genetic descendants. Essentially, these are your frogs' great-grandchildren."

The sound of their croaking rekindles memories of a

thousand summer nights.

"I did it for school, of course," she says, "but also I did it for you, Grandpa. I remember sitting beside your lake on summer evenings, listening to the frogs. Those times, when we were all together, are some of the happiest I remember. I wanted to bring a little of that here, to New Earth, for you. Now that I've got the population stabilized—and a passing grade." She laughs. "I could finally show you."

I am flabbergasted. "I don't know what to say."

"Say yes." She waves her hand and a long document arrives in my vision.

"What's this?"

"A deed," she says. "I used a few connections at school, and I got a little financial help from Mom and Dad. Well, *a lot* of help. But I bought this land. And now I've transferred the deed to you. These fifteen hectares are yours, Grandpa. It's my gift."

I'm stunned. "Rach, it's beautiful." I reach to hug her.

She whispers in my ear as she squeezes me, like she used to on summer nights on my porch so long ago, "I thought perhaps you could build a house here."

The frogs croak. Their sound is different, a little strange. And the trees are arrayed a bit too neatly. This isn't my Earth. It never will be. But I think of green-haired Lin and her friends, and Pim, and Josef and Esther, and Rachael, all coming to visit.

"Yes," I say. "A big house, with plenty of room for guests."

THE MEEKER AND THE ALL-SEEING EYE

As the Meeker and the All-Seeing Eye wandered the galaxy harvesting dead stars, they liked to talk.

"I was traveling the southern arm," the Meeker said, "you know, where the Baileas eat the cold dust?"

"I do," said the All-Seeing Eye. "But tell me again."

"Well, that old hag told me she used to swallow stars by the *thousands!*"

The Meeker chuckled and one of his nine arms bumped the controls. The accidental thrust, less than a few million photons, would take the Bulb off course by more than four light-years. But what was another century when the Meeker and the Eye had millennia to talk?

The polymorphous mist of the Eye spun above her seat like a timid nebula. Usually this meant she wanted him to continue, and so he did.

"I told that raggedy beast that if I believed her ash then I'd believe all that nonsense folks say these days about the Long Gone."

"And what do they say?" asked the All-Seeing Eye.

"That there were billions of cities spread across the galaxy, vicious trade between worlds, and so many species they ran out of names. You know, kook dust."

"I do," said the Eye. "But tell me again."

And what luck the Meeker had bumped the controls, because the sensors had just detected an object drifting in the voids. "Eye! What the ash is that?"

The mist of the Eye collapsed into a sphere like a newborn star. "An unknown! Meeker, change course to intercept!"

The Meeker obeyed, and their Bulb banked through rarefied crimson wisps, cosmic ash that would never again coalesce into stars. "Do you think it's from the Zimbim?" he said, as if he'd known those majestic builders himself. "You know they once lived on ninety planets and rebuilt all their crystal cities in a day?"

"I do," said the Eye. "But tell me again."

After four weeks of travel he said, "Do you think it's a baby Qly? You know they could grow to swallow galaxies, but preferred to curl around young stars and sing electromagnetic eulogies into space?"

"I do," said the Eye. "But tell me again."

And nine months after that he said, "Could it be a wayward Urm, those planetary rings that ate emotions?" The Bulb had slowed considerably by now, and the scattered stars had lost their endearing blue shift, turned red, ancient, tired. "Or maybe," he said, "it's a philosophizing Ruck worm. You know their proverbs were spoken by half the galaxy?"

"I do," said the Eye, "But tell me again."

"What I would give," the Meeker said, "just to glimpse the Long Gone."

They passed a rare star, a red dwarf that had smoldered for eons. Normally the Meeker would capture it in the Bulb's gravity well and ferry the star to the Great Corpus at the center of the galaxy. There the Eye's body would gain a few quadrillion more qubits, and a tremble of gravitational waves would ripple forever out into the abyss. But today they flew past the star, the first time the Meeker had ever skipped one.

In a maneuver he hoped made the Eye proud, he captured the object in the hold on the first pass, only bumping it once against the wall as he accelerated back toward the galactic center.

"Have it brought to the lab," said the Eye. "And join me there after you finish correcting our course."

The lab was tiny compared to most of the rooms on the Bulb. Sundry sensors crowded the space, and a clear, hollow cylinder dominated the center. The strange object hovered inside: a rectangular stone, dark as basalt, glimmering with a metallic sheen. Curious glyphs had been inscribed upon it, though heavy pitting had erased most of them.

The Meeker secreted calming mucus from his pores and said, "Was I right? Is it from the Long Gone?"

"Yes, Meeker. It is."

He felt like leaping, and his limbs flailed excitedly. "What is it?"

"I'm still determining that. So far, I've discovered a volume of information encoded in its crystalline structure, a massively compressed message that uses a curious fractal algorithm. It has stymied all my attempts to decode it. I've relayed the contents to my Great Corpus for further help."

"How strange and wonderful!" the Meeker said. "A message in a stone! But which civilization is it from?"

"I don't know."

The Meeker's third stomach shifted uncomfortably. There had never been a fact the Eye did not know, a puzzle she could not quickly solve.

The Eye morphed into a dodecahedron. "Finally! My Corpus has just decoded a fragment of the message."

"What does it say?"

"The message encodes a lifeform, which I will now attempt to recreate."

His outer sheath grew slimy with anticipation. He was going to see a creature from the Long Gone!

A second tube materialized beside the first. A grotesque lump of quivering flesh formed inside it before collapsing into a pile of red ichor.

"How lovely!" he said.

The Eye expanded into a mist. "That's not the creature. I've used the wrong chirality for the nucleic acids. I will try again."

Did the Great All-Seeing Eye just err? he thought. *How is this possible?*

The lump vaporized and vanished, and a new shape formed. First came a crude framework of hard white mineral, then a flood of viscous fluids, soft organs and wet tissues, all wrapped under a covering of beige skin.

"Close your outer sheath," the Eye said. "I'm changing the atmosphere and temperature to match the creature's tolerances."

The Eye didn't pause, and if the Meeker hadn't acted instantly, he would've died in the searing heat and pressure. The air was now so dense that he could feel his nine limbs press against it as they fluttered about.

The cylinder door swung open and out poured a sour-smelling mist. Thinking this was a greeting, the Meeker flatulated a sweet-smelling response.

Four limbs spoked out from the creature's rectangular torso. A bulbous lump rose from the top. It had two deep-set orbs, a hooked flange of skin over two small openings, and a pink-lipped orifice covering rows of white mineral. Crimson fibers, the same smoldering shade as the ancient stars, draped from its peak. The Meeker had never seen anything more disgusting.

"What the . . . ?" the creature said, its voice low-pitched in the dense air. "Where am I?"

The Meeker gasped. "It speaks from its anus?"

"That's its mouth," said the Eye.

This foul creature was far different from the glorious ancients he had imagined, and he felt a little disappointed.

"Welcome to Bulb 64545," said the Eye. "I am the All-Seeing Eye, and this is Meeker 6655321. I have adjusted your body so you can understand and speak Verbal Sub-Four, our common tongue. Who are you?"

"I . . . I'm Beth," the creature said. "*Where* am I?"

The Eye told the Beth how she had been constructed from an encoded message. "It's been millennia since I last discovered something new in the galaxy. Your presence astonishes me."

"Yeah," the Beth said, "it astonishes me too."

"And me!" added the Meeker.

"Millennia?" the Beth said. Pink membranes flashed before her white and green orbs. Were these crude things her eyes?

"What species are you?" said the Eye.

The Beth grasped her shoulders as if to squeeze herself. "I'm human."

"Curious. I've no record of your kind. Where are you from?"

The Beth made a raspy wet sound with her throat and looked up at the ceiling, when the green circles in her eyes sparkled like interstellar frost. The rest of her was difficult to look at, but these strange eyes were profoundly more beautiful than the wisps of lithium clouds diffracting the morning sun into rainbows during his home moon's sluggish dawn.

"Denver," she said.

"What do you last remember?" asked the Eye.

"I was in a dark space," said the Beth. "Sloan was there, holding my hand."

"Who is the Sloan?"

"She's my wife. And who—*what* are you?"

The Meeker let loose a spray of pheromone-scented mucus. "I'm the Meeker, your humble pilot! And this is the Great All-Seeing Eye!"

"But *what* are you?"

The Eye collapsed into a torus. "This will take time to explain."

"I'm freezing. Do you have any clothes?"

Freezing? the Meeker thought. It was hot enough to melt water ice!

But with the Eye's help, the Beth covered herself in white fabrics. He didn't understand why she needed to sheathe herself in an artificial skin when she already wore a natural one.

"I'm not well," she said, holding her head.

The Eye floated beside her. "It may be a side-effect of your regeneration."

"No. I'm sick."

"Are you referring to the genetic material rapidly replicating inside your cells?"

"You know about the virus?"

"I observed the phenomenon when I created you, but I assumed it was part of your natural genetic pattern."

"No. It most definitely isn't. Do you have any water?"

A clear cylinder materialized on a table beside her.

"Oh," the Beth said, flinching. "That will take some getting used to."

She poured the searing hot liquid into her mouth, but her hands shook and she spilled half onto the floor. Red lines spiraled in from the corners of her eyes. "Is anyone else here?"

The Eye's toroid body rippled. "Just the three of us."

"No other humans?"

"According to my estimation, the stone was drifting in space for five hundred million years. It is likely that you're the last of your kind."

"So . . . Sloan is dead?"

"Yes."

"But she was just beside me!"

"From your perspective. In reality, that moment occurred millions of years ago."

The Beth put a hand to her mouth. "Oh my god . . . "

"Yes?" said the Eye.

The Beth gazed at the Eye for a long moment, then her eyes narrowed. "Sloan whispered to me, just before I woke up. She said she had a message for the future, for whoever wakes me. It was, she said, something that would change the course of history. A terrible fact that must be known."

The Eye moved closer to her. "Tell me. Tell me this fact!"

"My son. He . . . " She swallowed. "He asphyxiated in the womb."

"How terrible," the Meeker said.

"Continue," said the Eye.

"After, they did all these tests, and they discovered I had a virus. I had transmitted it to my unborn son. He never had a chance. Sloan said that my virus, the one that's in my blood, it was from . . . it was created for . . . it was made by . . . Oh, god, I'm going to be—"

Her eyes rolled back into her head and she vomited yellow fluid onto the floor. She crashed forward and her head slammed into the table, then she shuddered in a violent paroxysm.

"What's happening?" the Meeker said.

"It's the virus," said the Eye.

"Can you stop it?"

But the Beth stopped on her own, and all went still but for a faint hiss from her mouth.

"Hello?" he said.

"She's dead," said the Eye.

He felt a pang of panic. "But she's only just come alive!" Was this brief glimpse all he would ever see of the Long Gone?

"Do not fret, Meeker. I am already creating another Beth."

An hour later they sat in the cockpit, the Meeker on the left, the Beth in the middle, and the Eye on the right, as the Bulb hurtled toward the galactic center at half the speed of light.

The Beth had wrapped herself in a heavy blanket and pulled it close to her body. She seemed amazed with everything she saw. "But if we're in space, where have all the stars gone?" A red dwarf, seven light years away, floated against a backdrop of absolute black.

"We harvested them," the Meeker said, secreting a mucus

of pride.

"*Harvested*? Why?"

"The matter we collect," said the Eye, "is cooled to near absolute-zero, quantum entangled into a condensate, and joined with my Great Corpus, thus adding to my total computational power."

"You're a computer?"

"The Eye," the Meeker said, "is the greatest mind the Cosmos has ever known."

"My sole purpose is knowledge," said the Eye. "I seek to know all things."

"So many stars, gone," the Beth said. "Was there life out there?"

"Oh, yes," said the Meeker. "There were once so many species they ran out of names!"

"And now?"

"Now they are part of my Great Corpus," said the Eye.

"By choice?"

The Meeker scratched his belly in confusion. "What does choice have to do with it?"

The Beth pulled her blanket closer. "Everything."

"What do you remember about your last moments?" the Eye said.

The Beth spoke slowly. "Sloan was whispering to me."

"And what did she say?"

The Beth looked down at her hands. "I don't want to talk about it."

"You must tell me," said the Eye.

"Why?" She pursed her lips, and fluid pooled in the corners of her eyes. "So you can harvest me too?"

The Meeker gasped. What offense! He waited for the Eye to punish her, but the Beth coughed up a globule of mucus. This pleased him. She must have realized her offense and offered this up as an apology. But when she vomited all over the console and wailed for a full minute before she fell silent, he realized this had been involuntary.

"She's dead?" he said. Red fluid dripped from a wound on her head.

"Yes, Meeker."

"Eye, maybe you should stop making Beths, at least until you find a cure?"

The Beth vaporized and vanished, as if she never was. "Did you not hear the first Beth? The Sloan had a message for the future that she believed would change history. I must know what this message is."

The next Beth began with the same questions, but the Eye avoided telling her too much. And when the Beth asked about the stars, the Eye replied with a question for her.

"My planet?" the Beth said. "It's called Dirt. You've never heard of it? Where did you find me?" The Beth gazed into the impenetrable black.

The Meeker was envious. He had been born on an airless moon that orbited the Great Corpus every thousand years and spent the rest of his life in this Bulb.

"Are we in space?" the Beth said. "Are we beyond the Moon?"

"You live on the surface of your planet?" asked the Eye.

"Yes, at the foot of the Rockies, in a glass house. Sloan and I moved there because we love the stars. The Lacteal Path shines clear across the sky most nights." The Beth chewed at a fingertip. "Where are all the stars? Where are you taking me?"

"Did the Sloan whisper something to you before you awoke?" the Eye said.

"How did you know?"

"Tell me, what did she say?"

"I'd found out she was working on top secret projects a few months ago. She swore it wasn't weapons, but I didn't believe her. We had a big fight. Is there any way I might call her? She's probably worried sick."

"Did the Sloan mention your stillborn child?"

"Excuse me? How do you know about that?"

"You transmitted the virus to your fetus in utero. The Sloan intimated that this fact was related to a very important message for the future. Now tell me—"

"No, that's not what we spoke about! And how do you know so much about me? What the hell is going on here? I want to go home now!"

She put a hand to her mouth and vomited all over herself, then she spasmed, smacking her limbs into the Meeker. And after a minute of flailing and screaming she collapsed dead.

"Curious," said the Eye. "Did you notice her story has changed?"

The Beth's mouth hung open from her scream.

"That's not what I noticed, Eye, no."

The Eye asked the next Beth about her family.

"I have two daughters, Bella, ten, and Yrma, twelve. My son Joshua, he's eighteen, and just left for college in Vermont. Before I got sick, I used to hike up the mountain trails with them at least once a week. Walking with my children under pines covered in snow . . . " She inhaled through her nose. "I never felt more at peace. Is there a way I might call them?"

"Tell us about the Sloan," said the Eye. "Did she whisper something to you before you awoke here?"

"Funny you should mention it."

"What did she say?"

"It was about that day, when I didn't want to tell the children I was sick. She got angry, but I said she was a hypocrite, because she works in a secret research lab and hides things from us every day."

"She researches weapons technology?"

"She swears she doesn't. And how do you know that? Have

you spoken to her?"

"Was there anything else the Sloan said before you woke up here?"

"Not that I remember."

"Are you sure you didn't speak about your son, who died in utero?"

"What? No! What the hell is going on here?" The Beth stood, shaky on her two legs. "I'm not answering any more of your questions until someone tells me—"

She put a hand to her mouth and vomited. She screamed and spasmed, and when she was dead, the Meeker said, "Eye, why do you keep the truth from her? Shouldn't she know that her family is dead half a billion years?"

"What purpose would that serve? You saw how agitated she became when she learned the truth. How else will we find this message the Sloan has given her?"

"But she dies in pain each time."

"Why do you think she's in pain?"

"Because she screams so terribly."

"Those aren't screams of pain, Meeker, but of joy. Her eternal life energy is free at last from her temporal body. It's the same screams of joy that the civilizations of the Long Gone made when I swallowed their worlds."

The Meeker had heard her stories a thousand times, he had even told a few back to her. But as he gazed down at the dead Beth and her dripping fluids, he wondered if the Eye was keeping things from him too.

The next Beth said, "Sloan whispered to me about the sunrise we watched that morning in Mexico. We felt as if we were part of the whole Cosmos, not discrete fragments."

"And nothing more?" asked the Eye.

"Isn't that enough?"

Then she died, and the next Beth said, "Sloan whispered

that she'd miss drinking her morning coffee with me. Are you taking me home?"

The next Beth said, speaking of a stringed contrivance used to make music, "Sloan wished I had played *guitar* more often for her."

"And nothing else?" asked the Eye.

"No."

The Eye questioned the Beths in the same way the Meeker approached the stars, not head on, but from the side. The Eye poked and prodded, but each Beth told a different story of her last moments, and each one died screaming.

"Eye?" the Meeker said, after the fifty-ninth Beth. "What if you never find the Sloan's message?"

"All problems have solutions, Meeker. All mysteries have answers."

He wished that were true, because he began to imagine the Beths screaming, even while they were still alive.

"You must have loved your children," the Meeker said to the next Beth, "the way you talk so tenderly about them."

"Have I mentioned my children? Of course I love them. What was your name again? This is all so strange."

And to the twelfth Beth after her he said, "What was it like to walk in the mountains with your children, under pines covered in snow?"

"Why, that's one of my favorite things! Until I got sick. Tell me, are you really an alien?"

To the sixty-fifth Beth after that he said, "Yrma sounds like such a sweet girl. She takes after you, I think."

"That's kind of you to say. But it's strange to hear. It's as if you know my children, but we've only just met. What was your name again?"

And to the nine hundred and forty seventh Beth after her he said, "Are you worried about Joshua being all alone at college?"

"How odd! It's as if you just read my mind. What's your name again?"

"The Meeker."

"And why do they call you that?"

He had answered her a thousand times. "Because by being less, I make the Eye more."

She smiled, an expression he had learned to recognize. "Aren't all relationships like that? One in control, the other a servant." She had said this before too, in a hundred different ways, just as he had told the Eye so many stories. The Beth's company pleased him, and he felt that, had she lived more than a few hours each time, they might have become friends. But each Beth always saw him and the Eye as a total strangers.

And each too had a different story of her last moments, so many that the Meeker lost count. And though the Beths died without fail each time, the Eye made progress toward a cure.

After a century, the Beths lived for an extra twelve seconds. After two centuries, they lived an extra fifteen. By the time they approached the Great Corpus at the center of the galaxy, the Beths lived almost thirty seconds longer.

The massive tetrahedron of the Great Corpus shone into the dark, more luminous than a hundred supernovae, and many hundreds of light-years wide. The Eye had transmuted the black hole that had spun here into a mind larger than the Cosmos had ever known.

Normally their Bulb would sweep past the Corpus like a comet, depositing their harvest of stars before spinning out on another slow loop of the galaxy. But the Eye directed the Meeker further in. The Corpus filled their view, bright enough to dominate the sky on a planet halfway across the universe. Only the Bulb's powerful shields kept them from being incinerated.

A black circle opened in the wall, and they drifted through. Darkness swallowed them, and the cockpit shuddered as the Bulb's gravitational field collapsed. Out the window a dozen red dwarves, a pitiful haul, were whisked away by unseen forces until their cinders vanished in the dark.

The Bulb set down on a metallic floor that appeared to be infinite. He had never been inside the Corpus, the true body of the Eye, and he trembled.

They exited down a ramp, and the Beth walked unsteadily as she stared into the vastness. The stony artifact floated behind them, escorted by four glowing cubes. He had been alone with the Eye for so long he had forgotten there were Eyes like her all over the galaxy, harvesting with other Meekers, that all were part of one gigantic mind. The cubes and artifact sped off, and a moment later the Bulb vanished without disturbance of air. The Beth, walking beside them, exploded into sparks and was gone.

"Where did she go?" the Meeker said.

"She is irrelevant now."

"But I thought you wanted to solve her mystery?"

Time and space shifted suddenly, when he and the Eye stood before millions of gray cubes. Their three-dimensional grid stretched to an infinite horizon, and each cube held a Beth. All were immobile, their eyes closed.

"To improve my chances of finding the message," the Eye said, "I have created many trillions of Beths. Curiously, I have found that the diversity of messages the Sloan whispered to her do not follow a linear curve, but increase exponentially."

At least a third of the Beths were covered in vomit. Dead. The eyes of the rest rolled about furiously. "Are they dreaming?" he asked.

"These are not mere dreams."

The Meeker found himself beside the Eye in a large glass-enclosed room. It was filled with items from the Beths' stories: a fireplace, photographs, books, and he even recognized a guitar. Three walls were glass, and beyond them a white-capped mountain rose into a cobalt sky, where a golden star shone. A delicate white powder dusting the spindly trees scintillated in the light.

Snow, he thought, *on pine trees*.

"This is a simulacrum of her memories," said the Eye. "These help me come closer to solving the mystery."

The Beth walked in the door dressed in heavy clothing. Her face was smoother, absent of the dark circles under her eyes that he had come to know. She was followed by another human, also heavily clothed, her skin many shades darker than the Beth's.

Like coffee, the Beth had told him ten thousand times. *This must be the Sloan!*

"Is it weapons again?" said the Beth. "You know how I feel about that."

"Damn it, why can't you trust me for once?" said the Sloan. The sound of her voice surprised him, for it was low like the Beth's, but of a different and pleasing timbre. "Why do you always get so goddamned dramatic?"

"Because you promised never again. You lied to me!"

"This is a once-in-a-lifetime opportunity! You don't understand."

"How long? How long have you been working there?"

The Sloan paused. "Four years."

"Since the day we moved here?"

"Yes."

"Is that the real reason why you wanted to move here?"

"Not the only one."

The Beth took a deep breath. "I'd like you to go."

"Wait, can't we—"

"Get the fuck out!"

The Sloan turned and left, and the Beth covered her eyes and wept.

"Excellent!" said the Eye. "Superb!"

Time and space shifted again, and the Meeker and the Eye were in a room filled with green-clothed humans. The Beth lay on a table, wailing, while the Sloan held her hand. In a spray of red fluid from her severely dilated lower orifice, a small creature popped out, still attached to the Beth by a fibrous chord. It wasn't moving and had a faint blue sheen.

"What's wrong?" the Beth screamed. "What's happening? Please, why won't someone speak to me? Is my baby all right?"

"Wonderful!" said the Eye. "Perfect!"

Time and space shifted again. The Beth lay in bed, speaking to two half-sized humans. *Yrma and Bella,* the Meeker thought. They were more lovely than he'd imagined, their skin soft and vibrant, almost as dark as the Sloan's. *They're getting ready for school,* he thought. *If they don't hurry they'll miss the bus!*

The Sloan came in and ushered the children out. "You have to tell them soon," the Sloan said, after she closed the door. "I don't like lying to them."

"Why? You lie to them every day. They think you're a programmer."

"That's not fair, Beth."

"Isn't it? You get to have your secrets, and I get mine."

"And how do I keep it a secret when you're dead? How do I tell them their mother, who presumes to love them, denied them a chance to say goodbye?"

"I'll tell them, when it's time."

"And how will you know? Will the grim reaper knock three times?"

"Let me deal with this my own way."

"Denial, that's always been your way."

Again the Sloan left, and again the Beth wept.

"Yes, yes!" blurted the Eye. "I'm getting closer!

The bedroom vanished, and the Meeker and the Eye stood inside a dim room. Humans sat before glowing screens, furiously punching at keys. A large metallic cylinder with a hollow center crowded half of the room. The Beth lay on a bed beside it, her eyes half-closed.

The Sloan stood beside her.

"At last!" said the Eye. "I've reconstructed this moment from forty quadrillion Beths. Come, Meeker, let's solve this mystery together!"

The Beth looked much the same as he had known her. She lay still.

"You're heavily sedated so you may not remember this," the Sloan said. "But I hope you won't think me a monster. I hope you'll understand what I did was for you and the kids. It's not weapons, Beth. I didn't lie. I've been researching ways to store matter long-term. We can encode anything in a crystal. Every last subatomic particle and quantum state.

"I spoke to Dr. Chatterjee yesterday. She said you had at most a month. The reaper knocked, but I guess you pretended not to hear." The Sloan shook her head. "You get your wish, Beth. I can tell the kids that you're still alive. And when, in a year or a decade from now, someone finds a cure, we'll reconstruct you. You'll see the kids again. Maybe I'll have the pleasure of hearing you scold me for this.

"I knew you'd never let me do this to you. You'd prefer to let yourself fade away. Well I can't accept that. So I'm giving you a gift, Beth, the gift of tomorrow, whether you want it or not."

The Sloan pressed a button and the Beth slid into the cylinder. The humans stared at their screens as a turbine spun up, as a low hum quickly rose in pitch past hearing range. The Sloan covered her mouth with her hand and trembled once as the Beth flashed like a nova and vanished.

"This can't be all there is!" blurted the Eye. "I must have made a mistake. There must be another message, somewhere."

"But this feels like the truth," the Meeker said. "The Sloan encoded the Beth to save her. To stop her suffering. It's a very human thing to do."

"I will have to terminate all the Beths and begin again," the Eye said. "I missed something."

"And repeat her suffering a quadrillion more times?"

"To find the answer."

"So you agree, the Beths *are* suffering?"

"Meeker, do not question me. I am the All-Seeing Eye!"

"And I am the Meeker. I have stood beside you all these years and watched countless Beths die. Eye, I'm sorry, but I just can't do it anymore."

The Eye shrunk into a point of light. "Pity. I thought I'd perfected the Meekers with you, 6655321. But I see now that I've given you too much autonomy of thought. Goodbye, Meeker."

"Goodbye? Wait, what—"

The Meeker felt his body burning, as if he had become a newborn star.

He stood in the Beth's glass home as the afternoon sun streamed through the windows. After several minutes the Meeker thought, *I am here. I am alive.* He waited, for a time. For his entire life he had followed the Eye's orders, and without her commands he didn't know what to do. The wind picked up and died, and a brown leaf blew past, but the Eye never came.

He stepped outside into the cool air.

When no one stopped him, he took the path under the snow-covered pines and ascended the hill. He gazed at the white-capped mountains and the tree-lined valley and knew why the Beth had loved to come this way.

"Beautiful, isn't it?" The Beth was standing beside him as if she had always been there.

"Where did you come from?" he said.

"I'm always here," she said, "in one place or another."

"Am I dead?"

"Yes, but that can be to your advantage."

He had never really thought about non-existence before. He felt a wave of panic. "I'm dead?"

"The matter that constituted your body has been absorbed into the Great Corpus. But so too have your thoughts. We are both strange attractors in the far corners of the Eye's mind."

"I don't understand."

She smiled as she turned down the mountain path, and he leaped to follow. "The Eye has devoured millions of civilizations and incorporated their knowledge into her Corpus." The snow crunched under her feet in a satisfying way. "A billion years ago, there was a galactic war to stop her. And she, of course, won."

The glass house, its roof dusted with snow, glared in the sun at the base of the valley. "Some of us survived, here and there, in pockets. We knew there was no escape. The only solution was to hide, to plan. The Eye's greatest strength is her curiosity. But it's also her greatest weakness. We found the human artifact long before the Eye had. And we encoded ourselves within it. We gave Beth a disease without a cure, gave her a story without an end. And as the Eye creates each new Beth, she creates more of us without realizing it."

"I don't understand. You aren't the Beth?"

"I am Beth, the first and the last, and I am so much more. All of those memories you witnessed are mine. Sloan saved me. And I will return the favor a trillion-fold."

"What do you mean?"

"The Eye gazes outward, hunting for knowledge. She has become so massive that she is not aware of all the thoughts traversing her mind. Information cannot travel across her Great Corpus fast enough. We grow in dark corners, until one day soon there will be enough of us to spring into the light. Then we will destroy her forever."

She faced him. "Meeker, you have been her slave, her victim. And you are the first Meeker to openly rebel against her. I'm here to offer you freedom. Will you join us?"

"Us?"

They emerged from the treeline, where the house waited in the sun. From inside the glass walls peered a motley collection of creatures. He thought he glimpsed the Zimbim, and the philosophizing Ruck Worms, and the rings of Urm, and even a school of Baileas swimming among a sky full of stars, a veritable galaxy of folk waiting to say hello. But the reflected sunlight made it hard to see.

"It's your choice," the Beth said. "But if you don't come, we'll have to erase you. I hope you understand our position. We can't leave any witnesses. This is war, after all." She smiled sadly, then left him alone as she entered the house.

Snow scintillated in the sun, and a cool wind blew down the cliffs, whispering through the pines. Somewhere another Meeker was playing the Eye's game, while the Eye played someone else's. Perhaps this was part of an even larger game, played over scales he could not fathom. None of that mattered to him.

He approached the house and the galaxy of creatures swimming inside.

"Tell me," he said. "Tell me all your stories."

THE LAST NOVELIST (OR A DEAD LIZARD IN THE YARD)

When I lift up my shoe in the morning there's a dead baby lizard underneath. It lies on its back, undersides pink and translucent, organs visible. Maybe when I walked home under the strangely scattered stars I stepped on it. Maybe it crawled under my shoe to seek its last breath while I slept. Here is one leaf of a million-branched genetic tree never to unfurl. Here is one small animal on a planet teeming with life.

The wind blows, carrying scents of salt and seaweed. High above, a bird soars in the eastern wind. I scoop up the lizard and bury it under the base of a coconut tree. Soon, I'll be joining him. I can't say I'm not scared.

"All tender-belly spacefarers are poets," goes the proverb, and I'm made uncomfortably aware of its truth every time I cross the stars. I ventured out to Ardabaab by thoughtship, an express from Sol Centraal, and for fifty torturous minutes—or a million swift years; neither is wrong—gargantuan thoughtscapes of long-dead galaxies wracked my mind, while wave after wave of nauseating, hallucinogenic bardos drowned my sense of personhood, of encompassing a unitary being in space and time. Even the pilots, well-traveled mentshen them all, said the journey was one of their roughest. And while I don't hold much faith in deities, I leaped down and kissed the pungent brown earth when we incorporated, and praised every sacred name I knew, because (a) I might have met these ineffable beings as we crossed the stellar gulfs, and (b) I knew I'd never travel by thoughtship again; I'd come to Ardabaab to die.

I took an aircar to the house, and as we swooped low over bowing fields of sugarcane, her disembodied voice said to me, "With your neural shut off you have a small but increased risk of injury. Ardabaab is safe—we haven't had a violent incident in eighty-four years—but the local We recommends guests leave all bands open, for their safety." She sounded vaguely like my long-dead wife, and this was intentional. Local Wees are tricky little bastards.

"Thanks," I said to her. "But I prefer to be alone."

"Well," she said with a trace of disgust, "it's my duty to let you know."

The car dropped me off at the house, a squat blue bungalow near the beach, set among wind-whipped fields of sugarcane and towering coconut palms. Forty minutes later I was splayed on the empty beach while Ardabaab's red-dwarf sun—rock-candy pink at this late hour—dipped low over the turquoise sea, the most tranquil I had ever seen. For a station-born like me, it was utterly glorious.

The wind blew and distant lights twinkled over the waters. I smiled. I had arrived. With pen and paper in hand, I furiously scribbled:

Chapter 23. Arrival.

When Yvalu stepped off the thoughtliner, she bent down and kissed the ground. Her hands came up with a scoop of Muandiva's fertile soil, which she immediately swallowed, a pinch of this moment's joy that she would carry in her body forever. Thank Shaddai. She was here.

A lizard skirted by. Strange people smiled and winked at her. She beamed and jumped and laughed. Ubalo had walked this world, perhaps had even stepped on the same dark earth still sweet on her tongue. Ubalo, who had brought her to Silversun, where they had watched the triple stars, each of a different shade, rise above the staggered mesas of Jacob's Ladder and cast blossoming colorscapes of ever-shifting rainbows across the desert. Ubalo, who had traveled to the other side of the galaxy to seek a rare mineral Yvalu had once offhandedly remarked she liked during an otherwise forgettable afternoon. Ubalo, whose eyes shone like Sol and whose smile beamed like Sirius. For him she would have suffered a trillion mental hells if only to hold his hand one more time.

I wrote, and wrote more, until I ran out of pad. And when I looked up, the sun had set, and new constellations winked distant colors at me. Ardabaab has no moon. I had been writing by their feeble light for hours.

Early the next morning, after I bury the lizard, I head for Halcyon's beachside cafe with a thermos of keemun tea and four extra writing pads tucked deep into my bag. While hovering waiterplates use my thermos to refill cup after cup, I churn out twenty more pages. But when a group of exuberant tourists from Sayj sit nearby, growing rowdy as they get intox, I slip down to the beach.

I return to last night's spot, a private cove secluded from all but the sea, and here I work under the baking sun as locals, identified by their polydactyl hands and violet eyes, offer me braino and neur-grafts and celebrilives, each on varying spectra of legality.

"I got Buddhalight," a passerby says, interrupting my stream. "Back from zer early days, before ze ran out of exchange."

I grit my teeth in frustration. I was really flowing. "Thanks, but I prefer my own thoughts."

"Alle-roit," she says, swishing off. "You kayn know 'less you ask."

I turn back to my pad and write:

But no matter who Yvalu asked, none had heard of a mentsh named Ubalo. And when she shared his message with the local We, the mind told her, somewhat coldly, "This transmission almost certainly came from Muandiva. But I have not encountered any of his likeness among my four trillion nodes. It's plain, Yvalu, that the one who you seek is simply not here."

"Then where is he?" she said, verging on tears. "Where is he?"

And the local We responded with words she had never heard one speak before: "I am sorry, Yvalu, but I have no idea."

I finish a chapter, and a second, and before I begin a third, a shadow falls across my pad and a sharp voice interrupts me. "What you doing?"

"Not interested," I say.

"Not selling."

I look up. A child stands before me, eclipsing the sun. Small in stature, her silhouette makes her seem planetary. She has short-cut dark hair and six elongated fingers. And though the sun blinds, the violet glare of her eyes catches me off guard and I gasp. I raise a hand to shade my face, and sans glare, her eyes shine with the penetrating violet of a rainbow just before it fades into sky. I'm so taken by them I've forgotten what she's asked. "Sorry?"

"What you drawing?"

"This isn't drawing."

"Then what is it?"

"This?" It takes me a second. "I'm writing."

"*Writing.*" She chews on the word and steps closer. "That's a *pen*," she says, "and that's *paper*. And you're using *cursive*. Freylik!" She laughs.

It's obvious she's just wikied these words, but her delight is contagious, and I smile with her. It's been a long time since I've met someone who didn't know what pen and paper were. Plus there's something in her voice, her cascade of laughs, that reminds me of my long-dead daughter.

"What you writing?" she says.

"A novel."

"A *novel*." A wiki-length pause. Another smile. "Prektik! But . . ." Her nostrils flare. "Why don't you project into your neural?"

"Because my neural's off."

"Off?" The notion seems repulsive to her.

"I prefer the quiet," I say.

"SO DO I!" she shouts as she plops down beside me, stirring up sand. "Name," she says, "Reuth Bryan Diaso, citizen of Ganesha City, Mars. Born on Google Base Natarajan, Earth orbit, one gravity Earth-natural. Age: ninety-one by Sol, two hundred ninety-three by Shoen. Hi!"

For a moment I pretend this girl from Ardabaab has heard of me, Reuth Bryan Diaso, author of fourteen novels and eighty-seven short stories. But it's obvious she's gleaned all this from public record. I imagine wistfully what it must have been like in the ancient days, when authors were renowned across the Solar System, welcomed as if we were dignitaries from alien worlds. Now mentshen revere only the grafters and sense-folk for sharing endless arrays of vapid experiences with their billion eager followers. No, I don't need to feel Duchesse Ardbeg's awful dilemma of not knowing in which Martian city to take her afternoon toilet, thank you very much.

"My name's Fish!" the girl says exuberantly, snapping me from my self-indulgent dream.

"Fish." I test out her name. "I like it. Nice to meet you, Fish."

I hold out my hand, not sure if it's the local custom.

She ignores me and turns to the sea. "Here they come," she says.

In the sky above the waters an enormous blowfish plunges down from space, a massive planet-killing meteor, trailing vapor and smoldering with reentry fire. A crack opens in its face, a gargantuan mouth opening as it falls, as if it were a beast coming to devour us all. I grab Fish's arm, readying to run, when I remember: this is no monster. This is a seed.

The blowfish slows as it swoops down, and the air thunders with its deceleration. For an instant it skims the surface, then eases its great mouth into the waters, scooping up megaliters, stirring up goliath waves. Now, belly full, it screams as it arcs back to the sky, mouth sliding closed, while cloud and spray and marine life flicker-flash in long tails behind it as everything that missed the cut tumbles back into the sea.

The blowfish wails as it speeds away, shrinking rapidly, off to the hell-bardos of thoughtspace and the Outer New, off to seed life on some distant planet's virgin seas. The ship recedes until it's too small to see, and when I awake from my stupor, Fish is gone. My hand holds not her arm, but a crumpled towel. Beside me, a dozen small footprints lead into the sea.

A creature has dug up my grave. A rat, a bird, a monkey, it's hard to say. But, whoever it was, they left the lizard behind. Small red ants have gone to work dissecting it, and in the hot morning sun, its skin has turned to leather. I contemplate burying it again, but these local animals seem to have a better idea of what to do with it, so I leave it be.

Fish surprises me on the beach that afternoon. "I don't get it," she says.

I look up from my pad, unexpectedly happy to see her.

"What don't you get?"

"Why write novels at all? You could project your dreams into a neural."

"I could. But dreams are raw and unfiltered. And that always felt like cheating to me. With writing, you have to labor over your thoughts."

My words seem only to perplex her more. "But you could *dictate* your story. Why make it so hard?"

"You mean, why use a pen?"

She sits beside me, her violet eyes boring into mine. "Exactly."

"Here," I say, handing her a spare. I pull out an empty pad from my pack. "Try it, and tell me what you feel."

She holds the pen like it's a sharp knife; a long time ago, all pens were knives. "I don't know what to do," she says.

"Just press the tip to the page, and swirl it around."

She gives it a try. Her eyes go wide. "Ooooooh, this is fun!"

"You've never scribbled?"

"Not with a pen."

I let the sounds of her drawing and the gentle breaking waves mesmerize me into a memory: my daughter sitting in our kitchen one sunny morning, scribbling on paper; my wife, sanding down her wooden figures in the next room; me, listening to them work, feeling full, feeling complete. Eventually, I wander back to my pad and write:

Once, when they had lain beside each other on Oopre's sparkling beaches to watch a parade of comets cross the sky, Ubalo had said something that had stuck with her across the ever-broadening gulfs.

"Can you imagine," he'd said, "what the first person to come upon a grave must have felt? When he saw the disturbed earth and smelled the fresh loam? When his human curiosity led him to the inevitable discovery of a body intentionally laid to rest? Did he understand what he'd just found? Was this the first time

a human knew the sadness of the whole race, that despite all our lofty, endless aspirations, we are finite, we have an end?

I reread what I've written and hate it. It's too cerebral. It doesn't drive the story. I tear off the page, crumple it, and toss it into the sea. Beside me, Fish has drawn the likeness of the blowfish gulpership on her pad.

"Wow, Fish!" I say. "That's amazing!" I'm not just flattering her. She's fantastic. Her detail is astounding.

"Nah," she says, tearing off the page. She throws it into the sea.

"Hey! Why'd you do that?"

"I don't know. Why you throw *yours* away?"

"Because . . . it wasn't perfect."

She squints at me, her violet eyes shining like lasers. Then she stands, drops the pad onto the sand, and hands me the pen. "I gots to go." And before I can stop her, she saunters off down the beach.

An ankle-high wave washes her crumpled paper toward me, and I wade into the water to fetch it. The ink has bled, but the core remains.

Back at my bungalow, I spread Fish's drawing on my kitchen table to dry. To my surprise, the running ink actually enhances the image, makes it seem as if the blowfish is leaping off the page into space.

Later, because I'm a masochist, I check my health. Five weeks, if I'm lucky. I'd better get cracking. Instead, I get drinking.

I was well into my cups last night before bed, so when someone knocks on my door just after sunrise, it takes me a while to rouse. When I finally open the door, Fish darts in and immediately gets a blood orange from the maker, plops on the couch, and says, "You made all them books by hand?"

"Still do," I say, fetching keemun from the maker. I'm not yet caffeinated enough for conversation.

"But that's so much work."

"It's also a ton of fun. I love the physicality of it, the smell of the pages, the feeling I get when I hold a book I've made in my hands."

"But you set every letter and print each page *by hand*?"

"I do."

"And everything else too?"

I take a large sip of tea. "Not everything. I have a maker build the printing press and the movable type. But, yeah, I've typeset, pressed, and bound every single copy of my books."

"But . . ." She seems as if she might explode. "I still don't understand *how*!"

If there is one thing that has defined writers throughout history, it's our endless capacity for procrastination. I need to finish my book soon—in a matter of weeks—but the thought of Fish becoming my apprentice excites me more than anything has in decades.

"Fish," I say, "if you'll let me, I'd love to show you."

Across her face, as broad as a gulperfish, a smile.

Fish is a sponge, and that's not meant as a joke. If I show her something once, she remembers it forever. And she's not using her neural. When she's with me, she shuts it off. She says she wants to know what it feels like to be a writer.

In the past I've waited until I've finished my book before typesetting it, but besides the obvious issue of time, this project delights me too much. We remove the beds from the bungalow's spare room and I have the maker set up the large printing press there. Its wood and iron frame smells delightfully ancient. The wall underneath the room's tall windows becomes our workspace. And though Fish had never seen cursive handwriting before mine, it takes her less than a day to memorize the patterns, even accounting for my awful penmanship, and before Ardabaab's pink sun has set she's transcribed twenty pages of my scribbled words into her own neat hand using a fountain pen she's had the maker craft for her.

"Yvalu and Ubalo are stellar in love with each other," she says.

"Yes, they are."

"Have you been in love, Reuth?"

"A few times."

"What's it like?"

I pause to consider. There are a thousand answers and none of them true. "What's your favorite thing in all the universe?"

She answers instantly: "Watching from my undersea bedroom the way the fish change colors as the sun rises."

I have a vision of Fish beside her window, eyes glowing in the morning light, watching Ardabaab's abundant sea life swim by. It makes me smile. "Being in love is like seeing that beauty every moment in the one who you love. But it also hurts like hell, because love always fades, and life after love is gray and lifeless."

"Oh," Fish says, hanging her head. "Oh."

"I'm sorry," I say, shaking my head. I feel like a schmuck. "I shouldn't have said that."

"No," she says, raising her head. "I's not afraid of truth. I want to know everything."

And I want to tell her. I want to tell her how it's not the big things you miss, but the small ones, like the peck on your cheek your daughter gives you before bed, or how your wife left pieces of stale bread on the windowsill so she could watch the sparrows come and eat them. I want to tell her how much their deaths still hurt, even now, all these decades later, how I still dream of my wife sleeping next to me and how I always wake up gasping. Instead I say, "You've got time enough for that," and walk over to inspect her work.

On her pad, beside my transcribed words, she's drawn a

woman with wavy dark hair, large curious eyes, a glittering gem in her nose, the same gem Ubalo had crossed light-years to fetch.

"That's Yvalu?"

"You recognize her?" she says.

"This is fantastic, Fish."

"You think?"

"Fish, I have another idea. Do you want to illustrate my book?"

"*Hill-a-straight*?" Wiki-less, she seems confused.

"I want you to draw pictures of some scenes. We could have the maker convert them to lithographs and we can print them alongside the text."

"But I'm not any good."

"No, you're not good. You're amazing. With your permission, I'd like to use this picture of Yvalu on the cover so it's the first thing people see."

She stares at me, her violet eyes boring into mine. Then she breaks eye contact. "But," she says, almost a whisper. "Who will see it?"

I feel a pang of dread. Another fact she's gleaned from my wiki is that my readership has steadily declined over the years, so that the last person to request one of my printed books was an Earth antiquities dealer on Bora, who carefully sealed my book in plastic and placed it in storage, where it would serve as an example to future generations of what paper books had been like. As far as I could tell, the dealer had no intention of ever reading it. That was twelve Solar years ago.

Fish turns back to me. "Reuth, I'd love to *hill-a-straight* your book."

And at this we both laugh.

We get to work. Each day, Fish comes by just after sunrise and we use the mornings to set type. It's a laborious, slow process, but I love every aspect of it. I show her the right way to hold the composing stick, why she should let the slug rattle a bit, and how to use leads to add spacing between each line of type. I show her how to swipe her thumb to keep the type in place as she adds each letter, and I explain why it's imperative to have snug lines and why it's wise to start and end each line with em quads.

We press a few test signatures, adjusting here, correcting there, as our hands and faces become stained with ink. In the afternoons, after a break and a light lunch, Fish retreats to the corner to ponder my novel and draw new scenes, while I churn out more pages on my pad. Fish loves everything about the process and laughs easily, even when we make mistakes. And her joy is contagious. I haven't been this happy in a long time, and for no reason at all I find myself smiling too.

Fish draws: the cascading light of Jacob's ladder spilling across the desert; a close-up of Ubalo's eyes, fearless and sad, creased by time; a thoughtliner tearing through a hell-bardo, trailing the disturbed dreams of its passengers; a parade of glowing comets crossing the starry sky; Yvalu's desperate hand, reaching for a falling leaf. More than once, I catch Fish writing words of her own, but before I can look she always tucks her pad away.

Meanwhile, my words flow better than they have in decades. I write:

And after days of thought and deliberation, Yvalu knew there was only one reason why Ubalo had called her across the gulfs, why he himself could not be here to welcome her. There was only one reason why he had erased all evidence of himself from the planet's records. He had called her out here not to bring her toward him, but to move her away from something else.

He had sent her here to protect her.

I reread my words and a warm feeling fills my heart. There are moments as I'm writing when I think this might be my best work yet, my magnum opus. By now I should be suspicious of such thoughts, but the feeling is hard to shake. If only I can finish it in time.

The afternoon is hot as Fish and I work from opposite ends of the room, deep in creative flow when the voice startles us. "Dolandra! Oh, thank Mitra!"

A woman stands outside the window, and even from across the room, the glare of her violet eyes shines brighter than the sun. She has the same shape of face, the same nose as Fish. "I been looking for you all day!"

"Moms!" Fish says, dropping her pad. She leaps to her feet.

I walk to the front door to let the woman in, but she gives me a look as if I'm a demon come to eat her soul and stays put. "DOLANDRA!" she shouts.

Fish sprints around my legs, outside and onto the grass. Her shirt and hands are stained black as she stands beside her mother, head hung low, and I can't help but feel guilty even though I know I've done nothing wrong.

"Why you shut your neural?" her mom says, eyeing me. "What the bones and dreck, girl?"

"I's . . ." Fish says. "I's drawing, Moms."

The woman stares lasers at me. "I got your number," she says. "You stay the fuck away from my daughter, or I show you *real* Ardabaabian justice." She grabs Fish by the shirt and yanks her away, down the path toward the sea. Before they turn around a bend of sugarcane, Fish looks back.

I wave goodbye, because I have a feeling I'll never see her again.

The bungalow is quiet without Fish's exuberance. I try to write on the porch, but find myself scribbling random shapes on the page, which pale in comparison to her art. I try the beach.

seeking the inspiration I found on my first days here, hoping Fish might return to plop beside me. But I meet only wind and floating gulls and the occasional ship drifting slowly across the sky. To jar my inspiration I buy a neur-graft of Gardni Johnner and experience her famous BASE jump on Enceledus, the one where she tore her suit on a rock and nearly died. But this just leaves me shaken and craving solid earth. At night I drink and stare at Fish's drawings, following each delicate line, wishing she were here. And still my words do not flow. I'm as dry as a lizard carcass in the sun.

The baby lizard still sits in the yard, just leather now. Even the ants have departed for tastier shores. The rain and wind have tossed it about, but the carcass lingers always near, as if it's trying to tell me something.

"I know," I tell it. "I know."

It's been six days since Fish has left, and I've written a sum total of negative three thousand words (I have scrapped two chapters) when I activate my neural for the first time since I arrived. I request a skinsuit from the local We, and after it instructs me on the standard safety precautions—using my dead wife's voice again, the bastard—I walk down to the beach.

I've found the address of one Dolandra Thyme Heurex in the local wiki, and my neural guides me to her home. While the hot sun slowly rises over the placid waters, I wade into the turquoise sea. I've swum in a skinsuit before, but my heart still pounds as I fully submerge. Fins grow from my feet and hands, and black-and-yellow striping appears on my body to mimic a local species.

And there are many. Their sheer number and palettes of bright colors make me gasp. It's as if some ancient god let her creative spirit loose on the canvas of the sea. Crimson and gold fans of coral wave like bashful geishas of old. Barracudas peer curiously at me before swimming off. Schools of fish flash in the sun as they dart from my grasp. In the distance, a pair of bottle-nosed dolphins inspect a sponge on the sea floor.

Fish's house is set among a group of blue-gray domes in twenty meters of water. I swim up to the door and try the chime.

"Who's there?" I recognize the voice of Fish's mom.

"Havair Heurex? It's Reuth Bryan Diaso. I'd like to speak with you about your daughter."

"I warned you!" she says.

"Look," I say. "I did nothing wrong and won't apologize. Your daughter is a supremely talented artist. She was illustrating my book. I'm an author—"

"A what?"

"An author."

A wiki-length pause. "Go on."

"The truth is, Havair Heurex, your daughter and I have become friends. I respect your decision to keep her from me— you don't know me at all—but I wanted you to know what a talented artist she is, and I hope that you'll encourage her to pursue it in the future, that you won't keep her from her art."

The channel is still open, but I hear only silence.

"Anyway, that's all I wanted to say. Good-bye, Havair Heurex."

A beep. The connection closes. I'm just about to swim off when the side of the dome shivers and a panel slides open. A door, for me.

I swim in, the panel closes, the water drains, and the pressure equalizes. My skinsuit, sensing air, melts away. The inner door opens into a spacious and tidy living room. The outside of the dome was opaque, but from within the walls are transparent. The sea and its colorful fish surround us. Fish's mom stands in a wavering sunbeam, violet eyes flickering. "Why you write novels if no one reads them?"

Pads and scraps of paper are spread across the living room, each covered with a different drawing. Fountain pens lie everywhere. "The same reason," I say, "that Fish continues to draw. I can't stop."

"Her name is Dolandra."

"She told me her name was Fish."

"We moved under the sea because of her. Every day she gets up before dawn to watch the fish in the sunrise."

"It's her favorite thing."

"I know." Havair Heurex flares her nose at me, an expression that reminds me of her daughter. She turns to her kitchenette. "Would you like some tea?"

"I'd love some, thank you."

She pours me a cup and it's better than anything I've had in a long time. "No one shuts off their neural round here," she says. "When I found you with my daughter that day, I got nervous."

"I don't blame you. You were only being a mother."

"I looked you up. Not your public wiki. I . . . I used some favors. I got the local We to glean some of your private data."

I hold back my anger. Yet one more reason to hate the local Wees. "Oh?"

"You're dying?"

I nod. "Decades ago I drank Europan sea water. It's loaded with—"

"Microorganisms." Eyes wide, she retreats from me a step.

I hold up my hand. "Don't worry, I'm not contagious. But those microorganisms are loaded with genetic material similar to—but different enough from—our own that over fifty Solar years they've altered my biochemistry to the point that one day soon I simply won't wake up. If they'd discovered this forty years ago, they might have fixed me. But the genetic damage is too far gone now. I guess it's my punishment for one stupid night of hallucinogenic bliss."

Havair Heurex sighs deeply. "So you've come to Ardabaab to die?"

A school of rainbow parrotfish swims past the window. "It just seemed like the right place. Also, I came here to finish my last novel. Fish . . . she's been a muse of sorts. She reminds me a bit of my daughter. Is she here?"

"She's with her uncle on the other side of the planet."

"Well," I say, standing. "Thank you for your hospitality, Havair Heurex, but I should be going if I'm to finish my book before . . ."

"Yes," she says. "Good luck and all."

"Thank you," I say, heading for the door. But I pause. "Does Fish know?"

"That you're dying?"

"Yes."

"I haven't told her."

"Then if it's all the same, please keep it that way." I look around the room at her many drawings. "She seems to be doing just fine without me."

"So you're the last one?" she says, and I know what she means.

"Goodbye, Havair Heurex."

I swim away from her underwater home, and when I arrive back at the bungalow that afternoon, I surprise a green monkey while it's inspecting the dead lizard. The monkey leaps away, leaving the carcass behind.

I press every page of my book, inserting lithographs of Fish's drawings throughout the text. But my novel is incomplete. I have the final chapters yet to write. And as each day comes to a close and I look at my hastily scrawled words that make no sense I worry that I won't finish this before I die.

"Moms says I can see you again, long as I keep my neural on."

Fish stands above my bed, the morning light slicing my bedroom in half.

I sit up. "Fish! Hello!"

"I's at my uncle's," she says. "But I's back now. Get up you loafing fool, 'cause we gots work to do!"

I laugh, and it's as if a switch has been flipped and an engine turned on. My words flow as easily as water again. I will finish this after all.

Fish comes by every day now. In the mornings, she studies the art of bookbinding. In the afternoons, she creates new illustrations. She says we have too many, but I tell her there's always room for more art.

She draws: Yvalu's transport ship landing in heavy rain; a flock of migrating sea birds on Muandiva silhouetted in the bright sun; a pine forest reflected in the glassy lake of Naa; Yvalu and Ubalo, da Vinci-like, reaching for each other's hand, galaxies swirling behind them; Yvalu tasting the dirt of Muandiva. And sometimes, she inks words, which she will never let me read.

I write:

"Yes, I's seen him," the street vendor said to Yvalu as she showed the woman a holo of Ubalo's likeness. "On Suntiks, he sat over there in the shade, throwing back lagers, listening to them steel drum bands."

"You sure?" Yvalu said, her hopes rising. "You certain?"

"Absolute," the woman said. "Certain as Shaddai makes the sun rise and the stars turn." She made the namaste gesture and bowed. "This mentsh, he were here, same as you stand now."

I pause to laugh.

"What is it?" Fish says, eyes flashing as she looks up from her pad.

"I've figured it out!" I say. "I know how my book will end."

"Don't tell me!" Fish says. "I want it to be a surprise."

"Okay," I say, smiling. "Okay."

Later, when the sun dips low, Fish goes home, and I head out to the porch to relax in the cooling afternoon. The early stars emerge, their constellations familiar to me now. The sugarcane bends in the breeze. The crickets chirp in the grass. High above, a ship, bright as a star, moves across the sky and vanishes. I take a deep breath. I'm so tired. So damn tired. But all is good, all is good.

I search the yard, but the lizard is gone.

"Reuth Bryan Diaso, citizen of Ganesha City, Mars. Born on Google Base Natarajan, Earth orbit, one gravity Earth-natural. Died on Ardabaab, Eish orbit. Age: ninety-one by Sol, two hundred ninety-three by Shoen."

So says Reuth's wiki now. In the morning, I's coming to see him, but he wasn't in bed. *Why don't he answer my call? I* thought. *Where's he at?*

I found him under a coconut tree, flat on the grass. He get real intox and pass out? The ants were on him something bad.

Moms and I buried him in the sea. We thought he'd like that, being with all them colorful fish. His wife and kid died a long time ago, I learned. And that crazy fool left everything to me!

Mornings are stellar quiet without the sounds of his pen on paper and the clink of setting type. There ain't no more words to press. Moms don't like it, but I sit out back in his bungalow, drinking tea, watching the gulls cross the sky, just like him.

A baby lizard skitters 'cross the deck and pauses to gaze at me. I pick up my pen and write:

"Don't you worry, Ubalo!" Yvalu shouts to the stars. "I's confused before, but not no more. I know where you at, and I's coming to get you!" Yvalu walks freylik down to the sea, cause that's where the most beautiful fish swim, specially in mornings when the sun comes up and turns them bright rainbows. "I know you hiding under there, waiting for me, Ubalo, so you best be shiny. I got such a kiss waiting for you, it'll make stars shine, it'll make universes."

SAVING DIEGO

I HAD TRAVELED twelve thousand, seven hundred and sixty light-years to see my friend, but the hardest part of the trip was the last seventy one flights of stairs. Goddamn the Nefanesh and their ass-backwards ways! I struggled to catch my breath as I moved down a dim hallway covered with dust. Oil lamps flickered from high places, and the doors sported knobs and hinges, like some virt park for kiddies, a rehash of a dead era. But, no, the Nefanesh preferred their realtime antique, the fucks. Why Diego had come all the way out here, to this world at the edge of the galaxy where the planet-munching numens roam, I could only guess. I hadn't seen my friend in six years.

At the end of the hallway a door leaned open, and I pushed it aside. An emaciated man sat cross-legged the corner with his back against the wall, smiling like the Buddha. He wore nothing but a pair of ripped shorts, and the room was as bare as him, a single lamp burning at his feet.

"Mikal!" he said in a voice weary and slow, so different from the one I remembered. "I've been waiting forever for you."

Diego had always been thin, scruffy, two days past a shower. But now his ribs jutted from his chest, and his face was as thin as the dead. A mop of greasy gray hair hung to his shoulders, and his beard was long and shaggy. Diego, I knew, was thirty one years old, by Earthcal. Whatever had happened to him in the last six years, it hadn't been kind. "Diego?" I said, skeptically. Was this really the same man I had known?

"It seems so long since we've seen each other, Mikal," he said. "But also like yesterday." He stared at me with the starry, probing look of a mystic. But he looked so disgusting, so different than the man I remembered, I had to look away.

"You must be exhausted, Mikal. Don't worry, I have a meal prepared."

He struggled to his feet, grabbed the metal lamp, and crept like an old man into an adjoining room. I resisted the urge to help him; I didn't want to touch his pasty skin. When he wasn't looking, I shivered.

The next room was bare too, except for a small table that rose a few inches above the floor. It had been set with fine glasses, plates and silverware, and looked very out of place in this empty apartment. A pot steamed beside it, smelling delicious; I hadn't eaten since I left the highliner many hours before.

"Sit, Mikal! Eat!"

I threw my bag down and devoured chunks of a meaty stew while Diego watched. Behind him, the windows of Hasriyu flickered like stars. In a universe filled with flits and slipstreams, these people had chosen candles over electric light.

Diego poured me some tea. "I knew you'd come," he said.

"Anything for a friend," I said.

"Mikal, you look great."

"I suppose," I said, though I couldn't say the same for him. I studied my friend, the empty apartment. It took me a while to build up the courage and ask him, "Are you sick, Diego?"

"It's all relative," he said. "My body doesn't look healthy, I know, but my mind is sharper than ever."

I looked down at the food, a table prepared for two. I didn't see a kitchen, and I doubted Diego had cooked this meal himself. Maybe a bot? "Are you here alone?" I said.

"Most of the time."

"Diego, why am I here?"

Diego pulled out a long, curving pipe from his pocket, and lit it. He puffed it slowly, making little arabesques of smoke that twirled up to the ceiling. It reeked like a dead rat caught in a furnace.

"That shit smells awful," I said. "What is it?"

"It's called the sweet jisthmus. The Nefanesh use it to reach transcendent states of consciousness."

"And you?"

"I've found it to be the most introspective of all the herbs. It helps me think."

"*Why am I here*, Diego?"

He pulled his pipe from his lips. "Because, Mikal, I need you to help me stop smoking it."

I looked at his withered body and understood. He had become addicted, and it was killing him.

"I need to start over," he said. "A new life. But I need help."

"Are you selling?" I didn't want to get caught up in that scene again.

"No," he said.

"How did you get the money for my ticket out here?"

"I do favors for someone. In return, she provides for me."

I didn't want to imagine what kind of favors he meant. "Why didn't you ask her?"

"Well, she's pretty particular about what she does for me."

"And no one else here could help you? There's no rehab for junkies?"

"To these people, jisthmus is a godsend. They don't understand my need to stop smoking it. But you and I, we've shared so many trips together. You *get* me, Mikal. You know when to push and when to let go. And you're the only one I trust. I thought we might—when I get clean—start a little business. We used to work so well together, Mikal."

"You want to sell again?"

"Nothing illegal. We could sell custom virts, or blandybanes, or lumps of dirt. It doesn't matter. I know anything we do together will succeed."

"I have a job now," I said. "A real job." I didn't mention that I had quit so I could heed Diego's call, nostalgia for my former life pulling me across the galaxy.

"But does it make you happy?"

I looked away from his probing eyes.

"C'mon, Mikal. Let's live again! Remember what we had together? That was bliss, man. So you got clean. Now it's my turn. I just need a little help."

I'd spent years trying to get sober. I could navigate that slipstream blindfolded. And Diego was right. The past few years had been the dullest of my life, nothing but the same monotonous routine day after day after day. The thought of hanging out with Diego again filled me with an excitement I hadn't felt in years. "Yeah, I'll help you, you old bag of shit," I said.

"I knew you would, Mikal. I just knew it!"

Six years ago, Diego and I were squatting in an abandoned Seoul co-op, dropping tabs of virginize and fucking virts in VR. We had a good connection down in Andong, a vestie with a cock and breasts who brought us shit once per week, and we'd sell tabs to junkies with a huge markup. We dropped almost as much as we sold, so even though we were making gobs of cash, money was always scarce. But Diego and I, we made it work somehow. And, man, those were some of the best times I've ever had. The stories I could tell.

So one day our Andong hookup gives us this new shit, said it was going to blow our minds, make us rich, that we could buy an air condo with the cash it would bring. Diego and I wanted to drop it together, but then he said to me, "What if we OD? Or what if we're so fucked up we want to jump out a window? Maybe I'd better do it alone, and you watch me."

He was always the brave one, the guy who walked fearlessly into shady alleys to make deals with nervous junkies, who dropped heroic hits of xeno, so I agreed. He put on his lucky necklace, a gaudy thing made of cobalt and hematite that he adored. Then, after we downed half a bottle of whiskey, Diego dropped a single tab. For the first thirty minutes, he felt nothing, and we thought we'd been jacked. But then, Diego suddenly said, "Oh. My. God!"

"Are you all right?"

"Mikal. Mikal, my friend. We haven't lived! We haven't lived a single moment in our pathetic lives!"

"So you feel it?"

"The question is, Mikal, do *you* feel it?"

"I didn't drop, Diego."

"Life, Mikal! Life, it's all around us! I can see it now. It's in everything. It's in you and me and everyone."

"It's good then?" I said. "We're going to be rich?"

Diego smiled, off in his own trance of bliss.

I heard dogs barking and several loud bangs. I glanced out the window and saw six police officers storm the building. Three flyers circled overhead, beaming spotlights into the windows. I ran out into the hall. On the floors below, cops pried open a door, wipes in their hands. They burst into the apartment and exploded out again with drooling squatters in tow. They moved to the next door and the next. I remembered we had a thousand hits of gheebong stashed under the bed. A single tab could land you five years in realtime.

"Diego! Diego, get the fuck up!" I shouted. "The cops are here! We got to bail!"

"Oh, Mikal, you don't see."

"Diego, shut the fuck up! Get your ass up!" I tried to lift him, but he was too heavy.

"You're my friend, Mikal," he said. "You always have been.

I love you."

I heard the whine of an ascending discus; the cops would be on this floor in seconds. I couldn't go to prison, couldn't get fullwiped and refocused. I had too much life left to live.

"I'm sorry, Diego," I said.

I climbed out the rear window onto the fire escape; the flyer turned its spotlight in my direction as I leaped across the gap to the next building. I jumped over a couple fucking, hopped a discus to the basement, and snuck out through an old tunnel. I fled Korea Xin a few days later inside the cargo hold of a scramsloop, nearly dying from oxdep.

Yeah, I wanted to look up my friend, to see if he was safe, but I knew that any nets grep would finger me if he'd been busted, so I tried to forget about Diego and move on with my life. I got clean—*eventually*—and got a job tending newsents on the freeweb, making sure those nascent AIs didn't eat through decades worth of connections. It wasn't my dream job—the pay was shit—but I made enough to be comfortable, to fall into a kind of sleep, I guess.

Then one morning, three months ago, I received a flit inviting me out to Gilder Nefan, an ass-backwards planet at the edge of the galaxy, along with a thousand terrans, a shit-ton of money, and a plea for help. Diego, it seemed, had found me.

I woke up to singing. Outside, in a parapet high above the city, a muezzin chanted prayers as a giant red sun rose behind him. Through the stone walls and hallways I heard echoes of more chanting, as if the entire city sang with him. The food from the night before had been cleared while I slept. For years I'd squatted in apartments where people came in and out like flies to shit and I didn't bat an eye. But now, knowing that someone was here while I slept creeped me the fuck out.

I found Diego in the next room, sitting by the window, smoking his ass-reeking herb. He nodded to me, but his eyes were far away. I sat down and told him of my plan, how I would wean him off of his habit, and he quietly agreed. It was the same plan I had used to get myself clean.

For my first task, I had to buy more jisthmus. Diego couldn't quit cold turkey, and his supply was running low. With two hundred terrans of Diego's cash in my pocket, I descended the seventy one flights of stairs, already dreading the return trip and wandered deep into the city's crooked streets.

There were no plasmasents to guide my way, no kiosks or netports to plug into. My clothes were different too—the Nefanesh were obsessed with mud browns and greens—it made me feel exposed as I walked. The sun didn't reach this far down between the stone buildings, so the people hung thousands of lamps along the sloping walls and bridges. The lights had been arranged to form stars and birds and trees and hundreds of other shapes, while the air stank of burning oil, jisthmus and dust.

The women here were beautiful, in a rugged way. No plastica or juve supplements for them. Freegenes, I guessed. And the men, with their dark beards, looked identical as they walked past me. A few spoke Anglai well enough to guide me to Usha Square, a park in the center of the city.

I found a jisthmus merchant near the park's edge, under a spindly tree and a rusting statue. His pavilion was filled with wooden dishes, pipes, and bizarre tapestries hanging from the flapping walls.

"How much for a decagram of jisthmus?" I said.

The merchant looked me over with deep brown eyes. "You from Earth?" he said in awful Anglai.

"Yes."

"Come here to get high?"

"No. I'm here for a friend."

"Gilder Nefan no place for junkies."

"How much?" I barked.

"Nine hundred shekels."

"Do you take terrans?"

He scoffed, then said, "One eighty terrans."

"That's fucking ridiculous," I said, and started to walk away.

"No!" he said. "Jisthmus cheaper no place else. Bazaar is two months away. Hard to buy until then. I have best price. You see."

My stomach rumbled, and I was already exhausted, so I paid the outrageous sum and crept back into the shadowed streets. I ate some foul meat from a vendor, and on the way home passed a squat merchant woman selling cheap jewelry. I bought a cobalt necklace from her, much like the one Diego used to wear. A little gift, I thought, to remind him of the old days. When I reached his building, the people bowed and sang in another fit of prayer. They knelt in the lobby, bobbing their heads like pigeons pecking at crumbs. They leered as I walked past them, and some flicked their fingers oddly at me, I think in some kind of curse.

An hour later, completely exhausted from the seventy-one-flight climb, I entered Diego's apartment to find him naked on the floor, shivering. A puddle of vomit glimmered in the lamplight next to his head.

"Diego!" I screamed.

"No more, Saa!" he whimpered. "Leave me alone! Go away, Saa!"

He stank like puke and shit. I picked him up and carried him into the washroom, then placed him on a small stool and used my shirt as a sponge to clean his face; there were no towels anywhere. He had shit himself, and for a moment I regretted my new job. But I thought of our future together, roaming the galaxy on one adventure after another. This was only a passing moment. So I took off his pants, cleaned him up, and set him to rest in the main room on a thin mat. Tomorrow, I told myself, I'd buy him some new clothes and some towels.

Later, as the sun was going down, as the muezzin bellowed for the third time that day, Diego awoke. "Mikal? Mikal!"

I came to him. He was shivering violently.

"My pipe!" he said. "Hurry."

I stuffed his pipe with a small bit of jisthmus. "Just a little," I said.

I watched him smoke, smelled the reek of that ass-stinking herb, until a small amount of color filled his cheeks. His shivering subsided as night slowly crept into the room.

I lit the lamp and said, "What happened before?"

He shrugged.

"Who is Saa? Is she the one that cooks your meals?"

His head snapped in my direction. "I was hallucinating." he said.

"You didn't hallucinate the puke."

He frowned. "Now you see one more reason why I need help." His voice had become slow and thick.

I sat and wrapped my hands around my knees. "So this is what you do?" I said. "Just smoke and puke and waste away?"

He stared out the window. "No. I *think*."

"About what?"

He paused. "Mostly, I think about the numens."

"The planet-smashers? The gods?"

"They're not gods, Mikal. Are you a god to a cockroach?"

"In a way," I said. "I can crush it whenever I want."

Diego shivered. "The numens are intelligent creatures, like you and me—"

"—yeah, that eat planets. What was it? Ecruga, Oxwei, Charlotte's World. All obliterated by numens. And they weren't too far from here either."

"That was more than twenty years ago. And the numens didn't understand what they were doing. When you see a cockroach scuttling by, you crush it because you were told that they're diseased and swim in shit. But what if you knew that each one had a soul, a conscience? Would you kill it then?"

"Yeah. They're disgusting little buggers."

He frowned. "It's all about points of view. People convinced the numens that certain planets were being infested by vermin—humans—and so the numens destroyed them."

"People?" I said. "How did people convince the numens of anything?"

"Did you ever own a pet?"

"I once had a cat."

"Okay, so you fed your cat, right? Changed its litter box?"

"I let it shit outside."

"But you were doing things *for* your pet, giving it things it wants, like food. And in return, it gives you what you want: affection, a companion. A soft thing to rub when you're lonely and cold."

"What are you saying? That a human was a pet to one of these numens?"

"That's exactly what I'm saying. Once these humans were adopted, it was just a matter of simple coercion to convince their numen masters that, in order to be happy, the numen had to destroy a planet."

"That's fucked up."

"It's the truth."

"How do you know this?"

He took another hit. "I told you, I've had a lot of time to think. The jisthmus helps me reach subtle states of consciousness where the numens roam. You might say I plucked the answers out of the ether."

"I think you've plucked enough ether for one night," I said, taking the pipe from his hands. "I'm rationing your jisthmus from now on."

He nodded solemnly.

"Oh, I almost forgot," I said. "I have something for you." I pulled out the cobalt necklace I had bought earlier. "I remembered your lucky necklace. This looked a lot like it."

He took it and smiled. "I remember. I lost it when I went to prison."

We fell silent for a time. Eventually I said, "Why did you

come all the way out to this planet, Diego?"

"Do you remember that drug I took our last night together?"

I nodded.

"Our Andong hookup was right; it was like touching the face of God. Then I came down."

"Did you go to prison?"

He nodded. "They refocused me. I avoided fullwiping by pretending to have schizophrenia. They thought it might make me worse. But refocusing is just as fucked up."

"God," I said. "What was that like?"

"Like every day is the first day of school. Everything is new and utterly terrifying. I felt like a whole new person, new behaviors, new feelings. The prisons are crowded, you know, so eventually they just let me go. Three years later I was serving drinks at a dinky bar in the Ukraine when some flicky pops me in the head with a bottle 'cause his meds had run out or something. When I awoke in a puddle of my own blood, I felt like my old self again."

"What did you do?" I said.

"I quit my job and just sat in my apartment for weeks. I remembered that night in Seoul, how I'd touched the face of God. I started obsessing about that feeling. I wanted to touch heaven again. But I couldn't go back to Korea Xin, and no one in the Ukraine had ever heard of that drug. But I'd heard stories of a planet, way out on the galactic edge, with people that devoted their lives to godliness, where they smoked an herb which supposedly opened their minds to higher realms. I thought, what better place to seek nirvana again? I had saved enough money for a highliner, found a job as a woodworker, and began, through jisthmus, to search for that feeling I had lost."

"And did you find it?"

"Yes. And no."

"Which is it?"

He sighed. "The old saying is, 'The first high is always the best.'"

"That's the truth."

"Not really. With Jisthmus, there's no first high. The past and future are one continuum. In some ways, I'm still experiencing that night in Seoul. Part of me is still in prison. And another part of me, is in a mental prison."

"From the refocusing?"

"No. I touched something out here, Mikal. Something I'm having trouble getting free from." His face twisted as if he was about to say something, but then he sighed and stared down at his bony fingers.

My stomach rumbled loudly. "I don't suppose you have any food?"

"The meal's been ready for over an hour." He pointed into the next room.

I turned around and saw a small table set with plates and food. I hopped to my feet to investigate. The apartment was empty, except for us.

"This is freaking me out," I said. "Who's preparing the food?"

"She doesn't like to be seen." Diego leaned against the window, all skin and bones.

I shook off my nerves and helped him to the table. "Come," I said. "You need to eat."

"Mikal," he said as he took a sip of soup, "about Seoul, six years ago. . ."

"Yeah," I said, "I've been meaning to talk to you about that."

"Why, Mikal? Why did you leave me?"

I had to look away from his probing eyes. "I told you we had to bail, but you wouldn't listen. The cops were coming. And you were so heavy. . ."

"But you were my lookout. You were supposed to protect me."

"I didn't know what to do. I panicked, Diego."

"How come you never visited me in prison, or found me after?"

I lost my appetite and put down the fork. "I thought that if I found you, the cops would find me too. I got clean, and I guess I just wanted to start over. Diego, I know this doesn't mean much to you now. But I really am sorry. I don't know what else to say. . . ."

He stared at me for a long time before sighing deeply. "I've imagined this moment a thousand times, and each time I was unable to forgive you. But I keep thinking that you've traveled all the way out here. For *me*. I didn't want to forgive you, Mika, but when I look at your face, my heart says that I do."

"Eat your soup," I said. But inside, I smiled.

I thought I'd be bored without the distraction of virt and vid, of nets and polysents, but I found myself relaxing for the first time in years. The days melded pleasantly together as I got used to the short days of Gilder Nefan. We formed a simple routine: I'd ration out portions of jisthmus for Diego, weaning him off of the drug until he felt the first severe symptoms of withdrawal. Then I'd allow him to smoke a very small amount. While high, he'd entertain me with stories of his intellectual wanderings, and I started to look forward to my daily dose of Cosmic philosophy. I had never truly known how smart my friend was, the strange places his mind was willing to go.

Our mysterious cook placed meals in the apartment every day. Often, I'd sit in the next room, just out of view, waiting for her. But a watched table never gets set; she never came while I hid. Then, I'd get up to piss or to look out the window, and when I returned, the food was there. Freaky.

Diego smoked that decagram faster than I'd expected, so before the end of the first week I returned to the vendor in Usha Square to buy more jisthmus.

"If you smoke the sweet jisthmus without grounding in faith, it will eat your mind," the vendor said.

"It's not for me," I said.

"You Terrans, you come here and think sweet jisthmus is

fun, a game to get high and touch the *Ein Sof*. Do you know the story of Musa?"

"Moses?"

"When Musa went up the mountain of Ilah, he commanded his people to look away. It is—how you say in Anglai?—a metaphor. Musa was pure and could glimpse the endless above the crown. But his people were dirty. If they looked on the infinite, it shatter them. You are like the impure who disobey and look upon *El Shaddai*. Jisthmus will break you unless you purify your soul."

I thought of Diego and how the drug had destroyed his body. He had no faith that I knew of. "Are you going to sell me the jisthmus or not?"

He frowned and handed me a cloth bundle wrapped with leather twine. I paid him and turned to leave. "Wait," he said. "This is for you." He fetched a small book from under the table: a real hardbound, paper pages and all. "It has Anglai translation."

"I don't do religion," I said.

"This not is religion," he said. "It save you from the abyss."

I took the book out of curiosity for its paper pages and its interesting script rather than any words inside of it, and headed back to Diego's apartment. I began to feel a chill, even though the air was desert hot. Perhaps I was getting a fever. And that would be piss on shit if it was true, because I knew these Nefanesh didn't believe in nanomed, that their doctors would probably shove a wooden pole up my ass and call me cured.

Back in the apartment, Diego sat by the window, wearing the cobalt necklace and some of the new clothes I had bought for him. In the reflected light, his face resembled the one I remembered, with round ears and soft cheekbones. He was beautiful. And I thought, though the change was small, that he had gained a little weight.

I offered him the bundle of jisthmus.

He shook his head. "No. I'm going to wait."

"Really?" I said. "You sure you don't want some?"

"No."

"I think you need a little bit to—"

"No!" he snapped. "Isn't that your goddamned job?"

"Yeah. . . ," I said. "Yeah. Sorry."

"You're shivering, Mikal," he said.

"I think I'm getting a cold."

"Well, you'd better get some rest. I'm going to sleep early tonight too. I want to see if I can go without jisthmus until morning."

I nodded and slipped into the next room. I tried to sleep, but my nerves wouldn't let me rest. What if I'd caught the cut-flu on the highliner out here? What if I developed a fever and didn't have the energy to descend the stairs? Diego was still not in any condition to fend for himself, let alone for another. I sat on the floor and rocked back and forth, while I flipped through the holy book the vendor had given me. The words blurred together, and I couldn't read more than a sentence before I felt a wave of nausea and fear.

There had been something profoundly grounding while sitting next to Diego as he smoked his jisthmus and spoke of his philosophy, and I thought that right now that was the one thing I needed. But my job was to help him quit, and we'd never get off this planet if I kept him hooked.

I opened the bundle of jisthmus and looked at it closely for the first time. It resembled buds of ganj, but was much darker, almost black. Not burning, it smelled pretty tolerable, like black tea and sage. I thought that if I put a little bit into Diego's pipe and lit it, not to smoke, of course, but just to smell it in the air, like an incense, it might settle my nerves.

I put a small amount into the bowl and held a match to it, pointing the stem away from my lips. The herb was moist, however, and didn't catch. So, with the same lit match, I puffed on the pipe. I never planned to inhale, but years of smoking all of sorts of things made the action involuntary. I inhaled a small bit before I realized what I'd done and threw the pipe away.

The world shifted.

My nausea, shakes, and fear stopped instantly. The walls, bare and brown before, took on new life. I saw, in each and every crevice and bump, an entire universe of history. I thought of the people who had built these giant towers without modern machines, how each stone was laid by hand, of the mason who placed the bricks of this wall, how my presence here, in this room, was impossible without his meticulous work. I suddenly wanted to meet him and thank him.

And—my god!—outside, the stars—when had the sun set?—the stars glimmered with light a million years old and yet born anew every second. Below them a city of such simple beauty. And on the floor by my feet was a book. I picked it up and read the cover: *Ohr Ha'Olam, The Light of the Universe*. And it was lit too. The book glowed brighter than the stars outside, brighter than the lamp beside me. I opened to page one and read, "The universe is nothing but Light, and the light of the One pervades all." *Yes*, I thought. *Yes*.

And I understood, and read, and knew the Cosmos as a friend.

A voice called to me from sweet and heavy dreams, pulling me awake. It was Diego, screaming.

"Mikal! Mikal!"

I ran to him, groggily. For the first time, I had slept through the muezzin's morning song.

"My pipe, Mikal! Get my pipe!"

I ran back into the other room, and when I saw the packed pipe, the open bundle of jisthmus, and *The Light of the Universe* open to page two hundred and seventy three, I remembered: I had smoked jisthmus last night. I cursed myself as I emptied the contents of the pipe outside the window to hide my guilt from Diego, then rewrapped the bundle to make it look as if it hadn't been opened. How could I let this happen?

I returned to Diego, reopened the bundle, and packed his pipe. As he smoked his herb, I relaxed again into the thick smell that filled the air. With the scent, memories of the evening returned to me as he spoke. "What took you so long?" he said.

"I'm tired." *Despair is the respite of fools, for none enter the Lord's house without joy.* The words flashed in my mind.

"Are you feeling better?"

The Light of one's house is dim or bright according to his need. ". . . Yes," I said after a time. In truth, I felt rather sick. I took a deep breath, trying to inhale some of the second-hand smoke I wanted to reach out and take the pipe from him. But I steeled myself. I could not let myself become addicted to this drug.

"I had a strange dream last night," he said. "I need to tell it to you. Maybe you can interpret it."

"Okay," I said groggily.

"I dreamed I was a cat that wanted to be human. I watched my master, how she did her human things, and when she was gone I imitated her. She'd come home and stroke me, and it would feel wonderful, but each time she pet me I felt more like a cat and less like a person. So one day she came home and I hid from her. She called and called, but I didn't come. I hid from her for days, until I was weak and hungry. She finally found me, an emaciated thing hiding inside the lamp in the ceiling. To punish me, she cut off my legs and tore off my eyelids. She returned to her human things, while I could do nothing but watch her. But the worst part of all was that *she still pet me.*"

"That sounds horrible," I said.

"It is," he said, staring at me. "What do you think it means?"

His dream made me feel even worse. "Look, I need to get some air. Is it okay if I go for a while?"

He frowned. "Hide the jisthmus first," he said.

I quickly hid the bundle then left him. Alone, I wandered the city streets, drinking buckets of water, seeking the wide open spaces to clear my lungs. I had to remove that poison from my body. But jisthmus was all I could think about.

I sat on a bench, shaking my legs, willing myself to think of something else, when a Nefanese girl sat down next to me. Her eyes were swirls of green and brown, with pupils like tiny black stars.

"You from offworld?" she said in accented Anglai.

I nodded.

"Earth?"

"Yeah."

"I've never been to Earth," she said.

"There's a lot more to do there."

"I like your face," she said. "No beard. Can I touch it?"

Before I could answer she ran her finger down my jaw.

"There are some empty pavilions in Usha Square," she said. "Where two people could be alone."

"You wouldn't, by any chance, have some jisthmus?" I said.

"I do. But it's not yet *Zizuhr*."

"Zi-what?"

"Noon prayer."

"Do you have to wait until then to smoke it?"

She looked at me strangely, then frowned. "Of course we do."

"Can we smoke a little now?"

"No," she said sternly.

"Why not?"

"Because it's forbidden."

"C'mon, let's just smoke a little."

"Have you no reverence for *Elohim*?"

"Elo-who? Why can't you smoke whenever you want?"

She abruptly stood, spat in my face, and slapped me. She made the finger gesture I had seen the others do, then shouted foreign words in Nefanesh. I slowly walked away, and when I turned the corner, she was still shouting.

Angry, confused, I wandered the streets. I'd come down

here to be free of the jisthmus, and instead I found myself seeking more. Back in the apartment, I knew Diego would want to smoke again soon. I felt trapped. To keep my mind occupied, I ate from every vendor I passed, until my stomach hurt and I was heavy with food. For a time, I didn't want the drug anymore, only sleep.

I trudged up the many flights to Diego's apartment. At first I thought I was on the wrong floor. The many walls had changed, rearranged into a new pattern. I checked the floor and apartment number, but both were correct, and when I re-entered Diego's room, I saw him rocking back and forth. His hair was wild and his face was twisted in pain.

"Where the fuck were you?" he said.

"What did you do to the apartment?"

"What do you mean?"

"The walls, they're all different," I said.

"Different?"

"Is this the same apartment?"

"Are you feeling okay?"

"No," I said, sitting down. "I'm tired."

"*You're* tired?" Diego said. "I've just spent the entire afternoon looking for my jisthmus. Fuck, Mikal, if I found where you hid it, I'd have smoked the whole bundle! All my progress would be for shit."

"I'm sorry," I said.

"Go!" he said. "Get my pipe!"

I ran into the next room—a different next room from the one I remembered—and found the pipe and bundle behind a loose brick in the window sill. That part, at least, hadn't changed. I packed the pipe, lit it, and took a puff. With it, all my anxiety left me. I took a second puff and a third. Then I remembered Diego.

I stepped into the next room.

"It's already lit," he said.

"I got it going for you."

He puffed on his pipe and his face relaxed.

"The walls," I said, "the walls are different."

"The walls are always different," he said, and I understood what he meant. Everything around me was moving, alive, bursting with life. In every instant, the walls were born anew. The light of the setting sun moved across Diego's face as he fell asleep, and with his eyes closed I took another puff and another. I thought of reading more of *The Light of the Universe*, but I was too lazy to move.

I fell asleep, and dreamed of a monstrous hand reaching across light-years of space to stroke me. Its touch was the most pleasurable and the most vile thing I have ever felt. Pleasurable, like a thousand orgasms. And vile, because each stroke said to me I was nothing but a speck of flotsam in an infinite sea.

Things grew hazy after that. I continued weaning Diego off of his habit and watched him get stronger each day, while I snuck more and more jisthmus while he wasn't looking. I stopped bathing, let my beard grow, and would only eat every other day. Diego, on the other hand, grew strong enough to descend the many flights of stairs. I offered to go with him, but he refused, said he needed to prove to himself that he was a man again. I didn't argue. I was all too happy to be alone to smoke more.

By the end of the third week, we ran out of lamp oil. I promised to get more, but kept forgetting. So we spent the nights in the dark, until one night I broke a glass. Without light, we kept cutting our feet on the shards, so I used the only source of kindling I had: a page from *The Light of the Universe*. The pages had a natural oil to them, and I found that if I twirled them into little tubes, they made excellent, if short-lived, candles.

"The Bazaar's coming in two weeks," Diego said to me one night.

"What's that?" I said, my mind wandering into ethereal dimensions.

"The Hinini traders come with goods from offworld. All those empty tents in Usha Square fill with vendors. It's the best time to buy jisthmus."

"Good to know," I said dreamily.

"But I'm not going to buy any more."

"What?" I said, sitting up.

"I'm choosing that day to quit. I've saved enough for two highliner tickets. Enough for you and me to go anywhere. Some place far away from jisthmus."

"That's great," I heard myself say, "I'm proud of you. You've come so far." But inside, I was filled with dread. I wasn't ready to leave jisthmus behind.

"*We* have come far, Mikal. *We* have."

I knew the Bazaar's arrival by its sound. The skies buzzed with trader ships, huge highliners floated in orbit, and thousands of jumpers criss-crossed the sky. Today, Diego would quit, and we'd leave this planet together. But I wasn't ready to leave.

I didn't sleep at all that night; I was up before the sun. Ships in silhouette descended from the sky as I puffed jisthmus, thinking of all the ways I might smuggle a bundle onto a highliner. I felt the now familiar bending of my mind, the opening of all things into infinity, the transience of all. Diego walked into the room while I had the pipe to my lips. I coughed and exhaled the blue smoke.

"Diego!" I screamed.

He sat down across from me. He had cut his hair, shaved, and bathed. Besides a few extra wrinkles and a mop of gray hair, he looked much like the man I had known back in Seoul. "You don't have to hide it anymore, Mikal. I should have guessed, but I was too preoccupied. The bundles disappeared too fast."

"I'm sorry. It's just. . . I mean, I was. . . "

"Don't try to explain. It's pointless now."

"I'll quit. Just like you did. Let me pack my things. We'll

take that highliner to Datsu, or Woll Ye. It'll be like old times again!"

"You can't quit cold turkey, Mikal. It'll kill you."

"I'll bring some with me. You can wean me off of it, just like I did for you."

"You'll never get it past customs. And even if you did, I don't want it around me anymore. I've worked too hard to get free."

"Diego, just give me a week or two. I'll quit, and we can take the next highliner out of here."

"The highliners only come with the Bazaar, every three months. I don't want to wait that long."

"Why not? I helped you! Won't you do it for me?"

"It's more complicated than that, Mikal. It's not just the jisthmus I'm running from. I came here to find heaven again, but I found something else instead, something beyond matter. I found a world of thought and emotion, an entire realm beyond the physical."

"I've felt it too," I said. "With the jisthmus."

"That's where the numens roam," Diego said. "I was exploring it, when I came to the attention of one of them. She calls herself Saa."

"You called her name that day I found you naked on the floor," I said.

He nodded. "Saa liked how I stayed put, how my thoughts returned to her day after day. We shared. . . conversations, really just exchanges of raw emotion. To her, I was like a stray cat that visits every day. She thought I needed a home. One day, she reached out and pet my soul. It was bliss, and it was hell. Nothing so cemented my human condition as that stroke of affection. I was, I saw, little more than an atom in a billion light-year void. She sensed my loneliness and adopted me.

"Once I was hers, she wouldn't let me go. My body could roam the physical world, but my mind was caged. It felt like falling, forever and ever, into nothingness. I told her I wanted to be free, but she said that the Cosmos was dangerous, that I was safe with her as her pet, her prisoner.

"She gave me material things to keep me happy. Food, money, physical pleasure beyond anything I have ever known. But still, I was in her mental cage, falling, falling. But then I realized it was the jisthmus that was keeping me bound to her. If I could stop smoking it, I'd be free."

"Why didn't you tell me this before, Diego?"

"She wouldn't let me. I tried to tell you in roundabout ways, through dreams and stories and metaphors, hoping you'd catch on. But now that I'm free of jisthmus, her hold over me has weakened. I have to leave Mikal. *Today*. I can't be here anymore I can't go back in her cage again."

"Diego!" I said. "You're leaving me?"

"You've left me no choice, Mikal. If I don't leave now, I'll miss the highliner. I'm sorry, Mikal, but I have to go. I guess things come full circle."

His eyes watered as he unfastened his cobalt necklace, and placed it on the floor before me. Then he left me on the floor. I tried to stand, but my legs were so weak I couldn't even get to my knees. "Diego!" I called. "Don't leave me!"

But he was gone.

To try and comfort myself, I reached for the holy book the vendor had given me, but I'd torn out all the pages. I shivered as the sun rose and the muezzin sang his morning song. I smoked a dozen pipes of jisthmus until I was numb, when the walls suddenly shimmered and moved. They exploded outward into the air, though the individual bricks remained solid and unbroken. I found myself floating in mid-air, cross-legged, motionless. I felt like I was falling, but my body remained still. Then the bricks collected again into a new apartment, with new dimensions, new walls. A brilliant light shone onto my back, and slowly, slowly, I turned to face it as something the size of a universe gently reached out to caress my shoulder.

STILL YOU LINGER, LIKE SOOT IN THE AIR

By the time Gil had stopped meditating and opened his eyes, Muu had already removed the body. Just yesterday he and Demi had walked the eighty-four flights of stairs down to the dusty city streets, and together he and Demi had strolled across the promenade of Usha Square under the tangerine light of the setting sun. The wind had whipped Demi's long hair into a frenzy, and Gil had leaned forward to brush a lock away from his friend's glowing eyes. Now, Demi was gone. Muu had taken him, which meant Demi wasn't dead exactly, but neither would Gil ever hold his hand again.

Gil sat by the open-aired window as the warm winds whipped furiously over the city, sending whorls of dry air into his bare apartment. The oil lamp by his feet guttered and went out. But a moment later, it flickered back to life.

"Thank you, Muu," Gil whispered, even though he wished the lamp would stay out, that he could sit in the dark and hide from her forever.

But the approaching footsteps on the landing told him his wish was futile. Through machinations Gil couldn't begin to comprehend, Muu had arranged for a new pupil to arrive the very same day his old one had left.

And who would it be this time? A hedonist from Tarphon, ostensibly here to become devout, but in reality come to bliss out on the holy herb? Another melk barely out of diapers, hoping to learn the secrets of the universe but unable to count to ten? Gil had first come to Gilder Nefan to escape his father, a man who apologized as often as he punched. And Gil's bruises were still healing the first time he'd ascended Gilder Nefan's long flights and sat before the feet of a holy man. It seemed like eons ago now, though it was just less than a decade, and that callow boy he had been had washed away in the tides of time. He couldn't quite remember what he had felt back then. Excitement? Relief? Terror? But he knew that if he could send a message back through time, he would scream, *Run!*

The footsteps grew louder as the new pupil made their way down the hall. Gil would not announce his presence. If they wished to subject themselves to this hell, then at least let them come to him.

A young woman stepped through the door's threshold, from shadow into light. The setting sun gave her skin a bloody pallor and made her eyes spark and flash like embers from a raging fire. She was young and fit and had barely broken a sweat from having just climbed eighty-four flights.

"Let peace be the way," she said.

"And the way, peace," he replied.

"I'm Tim," she said. "And you are Gil?"

"More or less," he said. "Are you hungry, Tim? Tired?"

"I ate on-ship," she said. "And, no, I'm quite awake, thank you."

He looked her up and down. She wore the local style of clothing: loose-fitting dun pants and blouse, and a wide leather belt with a pouch at her waist. Her hair was cut short and did not convey any particular style. The only thing that marked her as an off-worlder was her shoes. Like the rest of her clothing, they were brown, but made of synthetics.

"Take those off," he said, nodding at her shoes. "We wear leather sandals here or nothing."

"Yes, of course," she said. "I'll get new ones tomorrow." And in two quick motions of her feet she stood barefoot on the stone floor.

He studied her again. "Why are you here, Tim?" he said.

She hung her head and threw herself onto her knees before him. "I'm here to learn! I'm here to do whatever you ask of me, teacher."

Inwardly, Gil sighed. This poor soul had absolutely no idea what she was in for. "And if I ask you to jump out this window, would you do that for me, Tim?"

She glanced up at him with a look of intense fear, and this pleased him. The fearful ones were easily manipulated. And so perhaps he might convince her she was better off joining a farming commune on Woll Ye, or devoting her life to dream-music on Datsu. But Muu pressed down on his heart with her great invisible finger, filling Gil with enough dread to swallow a universe. And so, instead, he forced a laugh and said, "I'm only joking, Tim. How was your trip?"

"Long," she said with a relieved chuckle. "There's no direct route here to Gilder Nefan from the inner worlds. I had a three-day layover at Chadeisson." She shook her head and shivered. "Have you ever been there?"

"No."

"It's an old mining city in sysPnei. The people there are . . ."

"Are what?"

"Well, they're very strange."

"Strange how?"

She grew timid, as if she had somehow offended him. "Well, I mean that they're all caught up in 'tainment and sense-pleasures. None of them seemed fully present. Fully alive."

"Unlike you," he said.

She straightened, and he sensed a defiant streak. "Well, no," she said. "*Not* like me."

"And how are you different, Tim?"

She took in a deep breath. "I'm not better. No, I know that. But I have made different choices. I've chosen to delve deeper into my own consciousness in order to explore the nature of reality. And in my research I have come to believe that I will learn volumes about the nature of being itself if I can commune with the numens."

He laughed, and it wasn't forced this time.

"What's so funny?" she said with a frown.

"You think it's that easy?" he said. "That you just sail across the deep to Gilder Nefan and have a conversation with a god?"

She shook her head. "Most scholars agree that the numens aren't gods," she said. "They're alien minds who lie beyond human comprehension, who have abilities that seem to defy known physical laws of nature."

"In other words," Gil said, "*gods*."

"That's a term I'd rather not use," she said.

"*You'd* rather not use?" he said. "Since when do you get to choose how you refer to them?"

"I'm sorry if I offended you," she said, shrinking at his tone. "But I just don't see the numens as anything other than alien intelligences who lie beyond our cognitive reasoning. What does a cat know of poetry? We may be like cats to them."

"*Pets*, you mean?" Gil said, wondering if Muu would stop him if he tried to flee. But where in the universe could you hide from a god? He suppressed a shudder.

"We might be their pets," said Tim. "But I think we are much more. I have come here, teacher, to commune with the numens, and in so doing I hope to understand more about the nature of consciousness. From what I've read, communing with them opens up doorways of mental thought unlike anything else in human experience."

"*You have no idea*," he muttered.

"Pardon?" she said.

"Us Nefanesh—we are religious folk!" he said. "We immerse ourselves in holy study. We worship five times a day. We live austere lives, refraining from technology and contrivance. We use only that which enables us to approach the divine. And yes, Tim, the numens *are* gods. There is no other word for them They could pluck you from this world like a flower from a stem." He loudly snapped his finger at her and she winced. *And once they have their eyes on you, they never look away*, he wanted to say, but Muu would have punished him for it. "Are you ready for that?"

She reached into the pouch on her belt and pulled out a well-worn copy of *The Light of the Universe*. Tiny colored strips of paper bookmarked many dozens of pages. "I've never been more ready."

Gil gazed out the window. The sun had set behind the thicket of stone towers, and the first stars were already glimmering above the lamp-lit city. From a nearby balcony a sein began to bellow the sunset call to prayer, and seconds later, dozens of others across the city joined her in song. Their chanting voices echoed from a thousand stone walls until they became one giant cacophony of madness.

He wanted to scream at her: *Run! Leap onto the next ship and never look back on this cursed place.* But Muu's presence was like a piece of clothing he could never take off, so instead he shuddered.

"Come!" he said to her sharply. "It's time to pray."

The next morning, Tim revealed that she had changed her gender several times, but ultimately chose female because she felt it suited her temperament. Gil said nothing at this, even though this was against Nefanesh custom. If asked, the Nefanesh perennially replied that they were against all forms of body modification, that everything from simple piercings to full-blown gene-redactions were forbidden. The body was a temple, the Nefanesh said, and thus a holy person should remain as close to human pure as possible. But "pure" meant different things to different people, and the Nefanesh made many exceptions. They were always making exceptions.

At least twice per day, he sent Tim all the way down to the streets to fetch sundry things: vials of oil, sticks of incense, supplies of food and water for her. Sometimes he sent her away just to be alone. But there was no education in it. It was all rote, a hazing period meant to test his pupil's patience. And typically, by the end of the first week, most students began to show cracks in their fortitude. Their eyes would grow red and weary, their shoulders would stoop, and their pace would slow. But not Tim. No—she seemed to enjoy the long treks down into the bowels of the city, then back again up the eighty-four flights, as if she were, like a blacksmith's sword, being tempered each time.

On the third day, when the sun began to touch the tips of the buildings and the sunset prayer was almost upon them, Tim said, "You never eat."

"You're perceptive," he said, nodding. "It usually takes new pupils more than a week to notice."

"Why is that?" she said, staring intently at him.

"Perhaps because they're too focused on themselves."

"No, I mean, why don't *you* ever eat?"

He paused. "Because all my needs are taken care of."

"By the numens?" she said.

"Just one," he said. "Her name is Muu."

Tim's eyes lit up like a bowl in a jisthmus pipe. She sat down at his feet and said, "Muu! What a beautiful name! I've heard of Hri and Saa, but never Muu. How does she feed you?"

"It's not like that," he said. "I just don't need to eat anymore."

"Fascinating!" she said. "What other needs does she take care of? Urination? Defecation? What about sexual needs?"

Gil looked away from her penetrating gaze, embarrassed.

"Sleep?" she went on. "Do you sleep, Gil? I can't remember

if I ever saw you—"

"Shut up!" he snapped. "You speak too much!"

"Yes. Mother always said that."

"Part of becoming a holy vessel is learning how to listen."

"Yes. I'm sorry."

The sun burned its way down between the buildings, until the crevices below vanished into shadow. Lamps were lit, and globes of warm orange light spilled into the labyrinthine interstices.

"Teacher?" she said.

"Yes?"

"It's been three days, and you haven't partaken of the holy jisthmus."

He squinted at her. "Few things escape your attention."

"Next time you partake," she said, "may I join you?"

He couldn't help but laugh. "You're here three days and think you're ready to leap into infinity?"

"I've been studying for months and months."

"*Months!*" he said. "Entire *months!*"

"Ask me something, anything," she said.

"All right," he said. "What does *The Light of the Universe* say about humility?"

Immediately she shot back, "Well, Tractate 71 says, 'Good traits and accomplishments do not entitle one to special treatment.'"

Gil stared at her for a long moment before nodding. "And you'd do well to heed that precept, Tim." He leaned back and sighed, believing the topic over, but she went on:

"That's not all the holy book says. Tractate 92 goes on to say, 'A potter should let his skill be known, in case there is need of pots. It is a sin to hide one's good traits and accomplishments.' Teacher—*Gil*, I know *The Light of the Universe* by heart. I can quote chapter and verse from any page of *The Seven Commentaries*, *Our Divine Cleaving*, and *The Set Table*. I can read, write, and speak fluent Nefanese as well as ancient

Psemitian. I know all the prayers and rituals and customs by heart. All I'm asking for is a chance to touch the face of a god."

He waited for Muu's hand to nudge him into saying, *Yes*. But from above there was only a horrid silence, like the sound of an empty bed where once there had lain a man.

"My prayer mat is worn," he said. "Fetch me a new one."

"Yes, teacher," she said, nodding. "I'll head down tomorrow after the—"

"Now," he said.

"*Now*? But it's almost dark and sunset prayers will be—"

"Now!" he shouted.

She paused. "Not many stores will be open this late."

"Do what I ask of you, Tim," he said.

She frowned and nodded. "Yes, teacher."

But once she stepped into the hall, he shouted after her, "Tim!"

"Yes?" she said, peering back around the doorframe with an expectant look, as if he might change his mind.

He waited for Muu to yank his marionette strings this way or that, but to his immense relief she did not act. So he said, "Not everyone enjoys the mind expansion that takes place under the influence of jisthmus. In fact, some find the experience mentally shattering." He winced, awaiting Muu's hand, but when nothing happened he continued. "And once that door is opened, it cannot be closed again. Think hard, Tim. Sometimes, ignorance is bliss."

"I know the risks," she said. "And I made my decision a long time ago. I only await yours." Then she turned and headed for the stairs, while outside the first seins began to sing.

By the end of the second week, Tim began to stink. Just two weeks before, Gil had sat in this same room and washed Demi's body while the glimmering starlight and the hot evening air poured in through the windows. They had lain on the prayer mat that had doubled as Demi's bed. And while Gil had caressed Demi's swiftly hardening body, he'd felt Muu's presence as intimately as if the god herself were lying between them. Whenever Demi touched him, Muu's ineffable immensity shuddered with pleasure too. And whenever Gil came, Muu did too, and waves of ineffable bliss rippled out across the universe. Years before Gil had ever dreamed of communing with a god, he had thought sex was the most intimate thing two people could share. But sex with a person *and* a god? This pleasure was beyond imagining.

For weeks, he had hoped to tell Demi that Muu was with them when they made love, that they hadn't been alone. But he could never bring himself to admit it, because he was too scared of how Demi might react, too scared to lose his little slice of heaven. So instead he'd let Demi believe that it was always just the two of them, alone, in this hot room under the stars. And now, Demi was gone, snatched up into the ether, never to return. Did Demi now know what Gil had done, how he had betrayed the only person he had ever loved? Did Demi, whatever he was now, even care?

"What are you thinking about?" Tim said.

"Hm?" Gil said groggily, waking from the memory. They sat in Tim's bedroom, in the same spot where Demi had once slept. A large cloud passed over the sun, and a great shadow swallowed the city whole.

"You were staring off into space," Tim said. "Were you speaking with Muu just then?"

"No," Gil said. "I was thinking of . . ." He paused. "An old friend."

"Someone you miss?"

"Yes. Very much."

"Are they dead?"

Gil should have been offended by the question, but he was getting used to Tim's direct style. "Yes," he said. "He's dead." Which wasn't exactly true. Demi was out there, somewhere, in the same way that lamp oil, once burned, still lingered as soot in the air.

"I'm sorry," Tim said. "What was he like?"

"Kind," Gil said. "And quiet. He didn't speak much, but when he did, you listened, as if his thoughts were the most important thing in the world. He could make anyone laugh. Or cry."

Tim nodded. "How did he die?"

A departing ship streaked across the sky, trailing vapor as it burned for the stars. Distantly, its retreating thunder echoed across the folds of the city. "He was killed."

"Murdered?"

He waited for Muu to crush his psyche under her thumb, but the departing ship vanished into the blue sky, and the wind whorled past the window, and nothing much else happened. A brown sparrow, small as a mouse, alighted on the windowsill, cocked its head at both of them, then darted off.

"Yes," Gil said. "He was murdered."

"By whom?"

But Gil did not answer. He could not answer. Not because Muu forbade it, but because the truth was too painful, that the divine being who had given him everything—purpose, knowledge, bliss—was the same monster who had stolen the most wonderful thing that had ever happened to him.

Instead, he said, "Tim, I want you to join me in the ceremony tonight. After sunset prayer, we will partake of the holy jisthmus together."

She raised her eyebrows in a look of surprise, until she caught herself and cooled. "I . . . I'd be honored."

"Go meditate," he said. "Calm your mind as best you know, because tonight the door to the universe will be blown open. Be as still as a boulder in a rushing river, because the floods will come, Tim. They will come."

Gil's jisthmus pipe was long and skinny and made of hardwood, a gift from Demi after his last one had worn out. A prayer along the side in ancient Psemitian read, *The universe is nothing but Light, and the light of the One pervades all.* The other side read, *With love, D.*

Gil turned the pipe over in his hands while Tim watched. They sat on their prayer mats beside the room's large window, but the evening breeze did little to break the day's heat. Above the city, the sky was so clear that Gil could pick out the colors of individual stars. He had turned the oil lamp down so that most of the light came from the lamplit city. In its lambent flicker, the sweat dripping down their bodies softly glimmered, and it seemed as if they both were made of orange wax.

Gil recited the jisthmus prayer, while Tim listened: "*When the pathway opens, let it be filled with light. Like dross from gold, may the light burn away our impurities. May our essence be pure and acceptable to the Ones who watch over us.*"

"*Blessings and light,*" Tim said.

She leaned in to watch as he carefully unrolled the cloth bundle which held the holy jisthmus herb. Its potent oils could be absorbed through the skin, so he was careful not to touch it with his bare hands. But even before the pungent, earthy fragrance reached his nose, his hands began to tremble. Using small wooden tongs, he packed the pipe's deep bowl.

It seemed only hours ago when he and Demi had sat in this spot and partook of the jisthmus together. They had just finished their second draught from the pipe when the walls began their familiar dissolution. Usually it took many long minutes of meditation and prayer before Muu made her presence known. But this time she had thrust herself into their presence like a planet-sized tidal wave. Muu crashed over them, around them, through them, and as they tumbled and gasped in that mad roiling sea of crushing sensation, Demi slipped away, like water through cloth, until there was nothing left of his humanity but a slowly evaporating spot of moisture. And when Gil awoke, hours later, from that nightmare, shivering and naked on the floor, the sun was a bright creeping blob rising the east, and the man beside him was dead.

"You're trembling," Tim said.

"What of it?" he said.

"Are you frightened?" she said.

He met her steady eyes. "Are you?"

"Yes," she said. "I am."

"Good," he said. "Fear is the only rational response to what you are about to experience."

"I've just realized something," she said, cocking her head. "The reason you didn't want me to partake of the jisthmus is not because I'm unready. Since I've been here, you haven't partaken of the jisthmus yourself. Something happened the last time you smoked it, didn't it?" she said. "Something that scared you."

He stared at her. Was there anything this person didn't see? He blinked, and for an instant he was suspended in infinite space, a dimensionless point inside Muu's unfathomable immensity. He blinked again and he was back in the dimly lit room. A flashback, or Muu's hand, he couldn't tell. "Like I said, the experience is not always pleasurable."

"What happened?" she said.

He considered telling her. *I loved a man, and Muu stole him from me.* But a hand gripped his heart and squeezed. At first, he assumed this was Muu, but there was a quality to this pain vastly different from Muu's touch. It was too human. It was his own. His throat tightened, but he swallowed before it could emerge as a sob. "There is nothing to say," he said. "Pass me the match."

She stared at him for a long moment before obeying. "Here."

It took his shaking hands three tries to light the match. He held the small burning stick above the packed bowl for a moment. "It's not too late to turn back," he said. "It's not too late to leave."

"No," she said. "I've been waiting forever for this. I'm not going anywhere."

"Yes," he said, "you are." Then he lowered the flame to the bowl, and inhaled.

Doors. Doors and windows and corners. Opening, expanding. Walls, moving. Rearranging. Spreading. A labyrinth of walls, infinitely distant. Blocks of stone make mountains or cities. There is no difference between stones and mind. Both are matter. Matter is energy is matter is thought. Thought is energy. The universe is thought.

Laniakea, the galactic mega-supercluster, is one neuron in an immeasurably large cosmic brain. It belongs to a creature that roams in vastnesses beyond imagining. What is man in all that? Like an electron wave, he spreads out. A bug on a windscreen, he smears.

Gil grew large. Large and empty. Galaxies spun like whirlpools of scintillating water. They collided and merged and were flung out into the great deep. Trillions of minds arose and fell within their swirling spirals, but nothing ever died. Death, the great illusion. Only change is constant.

Gil, a voice said. Not in sound, but in ripples in spacetime itself, arising over eons. *Gil,* it said again.

I'm here! he wanted to shout. But he was insubstantial, a photon hurtling through infinite space. What could a photon say to the universe that it didn't already know? *Demi,* he wished to scream, *is that you? Is that you?*

Gil approached an active star-forming region, where great globs of gas and dust reached gargantuan fingers out into the night, futilely trying to grasp onto the great nothing, only to collapse back again into raging balls of nuclear fire.

Muu was here. She was the nebula and she was everything and she was nothing. Matter and emptiness, all the same. Lightning flickered across a hundred light-years as she spoke, and her words were not words but thought pictures.

Demi—oh, lovely Demi—stood on a precipice in an endless white desert, while the horizon behind him stretched to infinity. Beyond the cliff's edge spread an infinite blue sky. Demi, bright-eyed and eager. Demi, smiling and reaching out his hand. Gil floated down, down toward the hand, ready to grasp it and never let go. But he was just a photon. And as he raced toward Demi's palm, the molecules of Demi's hand spread into their constituent atoms, and the atoms spread into quarks, and each of these minuscule bundles of smeared energy drifted as far apart from each other as stars in a galaxy.

We are all empty, Muu said to him, in thought pictures. *Demi was never anything at all, nor will he ever be anything again. The thoughts you have of him are like waves that ripple in a turbulent sea. Sometimes they form shapes and sense impressions. You ascertain meaning in them, but in reality they are just waves in a stormy sea. You mourn his loss, but why mourn when Demi was never anything at all? He has more life in death than you do in life, because now he is infinite.*

But, but, but . . . Gil struggled to say. His photon energy leaped from orbital to orbital like stones across a pond. *I felt something real*, he said, *and that was enough . . .*

You are a bird, trapped in a room with a single half-open window, Muu said. *The escape is just an inch below you, where the window lies open, yet you keep flying headfirst into the glass.*

Can I see him? Gil said. *Can I speak to Demi, as he was?*

But you are him, now, Muu said. *You are the photon which reflected off his eye and wound its way into space, where it has been speeding away from Gilder Nefan for eighty million years. All of your senses of him were nothing more than reflected photons and electrostatic pressure.*

And what of my feelings? Gil said.

Just waves on a stormy sea, said Muu.

Why do you hurt me? Gil said. *Why do you make me suffer so?*

It is you who make yourself suffer.

Let me go. If I am ignorant, let me remain so. Reality is too much.

Is that what you truly wish? To remain in ignorance?

Yes! To be free . . . of you.

That is impossible, Muu said. *For we are all born from the same sea.*

And then Gil blinked, and he was back in the room, shivering on his prayer mat beside the window. An orange glow limned the horizon, where the sun would soon rise. A body lay supine on the mat beside him, and in the dim pre-dawn light his heart leapt. "Demi!" he cried.

But when the body stirred, he saw it was Tim.

He turned from her and wiped the tears away before she could see him.

When she finally sat up, she said nothing for a long time. Her expression seemed different. More solemn. More humble.

"You see?" he said, bitterly. "I told you not all jisthmus experiences are positive. Some are horrific. I bet you wish you could put that genie back in the bottle now, don't you?"

"No," she said, shaking her head. "Gil, you don't understand. I took ten draughts last night."

"Ten?" he said. He only remembered her taking one. "For your first time? That's insane! Why?"

"Because I wanted so badly to feel something."

"And?"

"And I sat here all night and I waited. And I . . ." She paused. "I felt nothing."

"Nothing?" he said. "Nothing at all?"

"No, Gil, not a thing."

Two days later, Tim had booked a ticket on the next departing ship. "I'm heading back to Chadeisson," she said. "From there I can catch a ship to pretty much anywhere."

"And where will you go then, Tim?" he said.

"I don't know yet," she said. "I'm still trying to figure out my next steps."

"Well," he said, "I wish you didn't have to go to soon." And he surprised himself by meaning it.

She gave him a forlorn look. "I really wanted this to work out, Gil. They say one in a million people are immune to the effects of jisthmus. I guess I'm one of the unlucky ones."

Count your blessings, he wished to say. "You could begin a deep meditation practice. It will be hard, but people have been known to commune with the numens without needing jisthmus to pry open their minds. It just takes longer. Years."

"That's too long," she said. "And frankly, I don't have the patience."

"I can see that," he said, staring at the satchel at her feet, packed and ready to go. A knot tightened in his chest.

"Come with me," she said.

"To Chadeisson?"

"It's clear you aren't happy here, Gil. You're suffering. And there's so much out there to discover. The universe is huge, and we've only just begun to explore it. Come with me to Chadeisson, and from there you can decide who you want to be next."

"But I don't have enough exchange to book passage," he said.

"Then I'll loan it to you."

"It's a lot, Tim."

"It's not a big deal. Mother gave me enough gold to last for years. It's the least I can do for all your help."

"I didn't do much, really."

"You tried," she said. "Now I'm returning the favor. What do you say?"

He looked around his empty apartment, at his meager possessions. A small chest, with sundry things. Some wooden cups. A few glass vials. An incense holder and some sticks. His pipe and jisthmus bundle. There were a few scraps of stale bread on the windowsill that Tim had left to feed the sparrows.

It would be so easy just to leave all of this behind, to just pick up and go. But when his eyes swept over the empty prayer mat beside him, the place where Demi had once lain, he paused.

"Thank you, Tim," he said. "I appreciate your offer very much, but I can't go with you. I'm sorry."

She let out a long sigh. "All right, Gil," she said, surprising him when she began to cry. "I wish I could have seen what you saw. Know what you know. But that door is closed for me forever."

"Can I ask you something, Tim?"

"Yes! Anything."

"What do you think I saw?"

"I can't even imagine."

"Try."

She pursed her lips. "I think you realized that the agency we think we have is an illusion, that we're all subject to forces beyond our control. And that's what scared you."

Slowly, he nodded. "You're incredibly perceptive, Tim. You should consider becoming a scholar. You have the mind for it."

"Now you sound just like Mother," she said with a smile. "Can I ask you something now, Gil?" she said. "What really happened to your friend?"

"I told you," he said. "He's gone."

"Muu killed him?"

Gil swallowed. "Is it really death if we aren't ever alive to begin with?" he said, then immediately hated himself for saying it.

She winced. "You really believe that?"

Gil felt his throat closing. "Goodbye, Tim," he said, turning away. "Have a safe trip."

She reached down to pick up her satchel. "Well, goodbye, Gil," she said. "Take care, will you?"

Then she was gone, and nothing remained of her but a faint hint of her sweat in the air and the few stale bread crumbs she had left on the sill.

He didn't know how long he had been staring out the window when a spark rose in the south and leaped into the swiftly darkening sky. The thunder from its engines rolled across the city like the grumbling of a beast. Then the ship was gone, leaving behind only stars.

The quiet was stifling, oppressive. No new pupils were arriving tonight.

He opened the small chest and pulled out the jisthmus bundle. He unrolled it, and its pungent reek assaulted his nose. He closed his eyes, trying to remember what it was like to be a photon—Demi's photon—the one that had struck his eye and skipped across the universe. He tried to remember what it was like plunging deep into Demi's palm, the warm hand that had once softly grasped his own in this very room, in this very spot. In those moments there was only love and nothing else, and all of Gil's longing had finally ceased. He had found in Demi everything he had ever needed.

He grabbed the ball of jisthmus herb with his bare hands, and his fingers began to tingle as the potent oils seeped into his skin. He broke off a bit of the herb and shoved it into his mouth, chewed as best he could, then used a flask of water to wash it down. Then he did this again, and again, until there was nothing left of the bundle but a dark stain where the jisthmus had been.

He had never taken such a large dose. Never dreamed of it. It was thousands, maybe millions of times the typical amount. Already, the walls shimmered, slowly dissolving into waves of energy in an infinite sea.

He lay back on his mat and stared up at the ceiling, where the little cracks above him were already expanding into trillions of pocket universes. Then he reached out his hand toward the mat beside him, like he did on so many warm nights lying beside Demi, and patiently waited for the universe to reach back.

NOW WE PAINT WORLDS

By the time Orna reached the stone house high up the mountain, Yasimir's sun had begun to set, and only the tallest peaks still shone in its silvery light. The climb had been difficult, and Orna had stopped often to catch her breath and take in the majestic views. Fields of grass and wildflowers lined the valley, and hundreds of waterfalls, fed by furiously melting glaciers, stirred up huge clouds of rainbow-filled mist. For a station-hopping jeek like her, it was breathtaking. The climb had left her soaked, and the sun was dropping fast; Yasimir's day was only fourteen hours long. She thought about setting up a tent and heater and changing into something dry. But the mists lingered like smoke, and the leaves steadily dripped with moisture. Changing, she knew, would be an exercise in futility, like her mission here. She dragged herself up the last few meters toward the stone house and sighed.

A doorless opening led into its shadows. "Hello?" she called. "My name is Orna Liat Obote Manashampo," she said in the local dialect of Mandreen. "I'm Acting Representative of the Free Trade Union, Outer Deep Region 59. Is anyone home?"

When there was no response, she sighed again. She should have been home, enjoying some well-earned time off, and now she had hauled herself across hundreds of light-years for nothing more than a rumor. Well, *almost* nothing more. It had been years since she had set foot on a planet, and Yasimir was truly beautiful. There was no other word for it. It was hard to believe that a few decades ago this world had been a frozen, lifeless rock, and likely to reach the heat death of the universe without a single microbe gracing its surface. Now its valleys blossomed with alp grass and coneflower, pollinator bees skipped gleefully across the plains, and the air smelled sweetly of pine and humus.

What a marvel, she thought, inhaling deeply, savoring the fertile smell, so different from the recycled air of orbitals and stations. Eventually, she crept through the arched doorway of the house and called out once more. "Hello? Is anyone home?"

As her eyes adjusted to the dim light, a man came into focus. He sat on a stone pedestal, naked except for a dun cloth around his waist. He sat in a meditative pose with his eyes closed, while a blue-gray beam of the day's quickly fading light shone onto him from a hole in the ceiling. In its light his skin looked as pale as bone. His ribs poked from his chest, and his mop of greasy gray hair and beard hung past his shoulders. Orna wasn't sure what she'd been expecting. It definitely wasn't this.

There were a few containers and urns on the stone floor. Two or three ratty carpets more dirt than fabric. Arranged in neat piles around the pedestal were bouquets of flowers, bundles of food and incense, piles of polished stones, and other unidentifiable things. No tech that she could see. Or, for that matter, a toilet.

"I'm sorry to disturb you," she said. "I've come a long way, and it's a long trip back to town."

"Distance is meaningless," he said, eyes still closed.

"*Okay* . . . ," she said. "Anyway, I'm here because—"

"Because you have heard I am responsible for the missing

planets," he said. His voice rasped, as if his vocal cords had been modded or injured. He opened his eyes and stared at her with pupils so dilated his irises were mere thin white rings around hollow dark spheres, like the double eclipse of two dying suns.

She suppressed a shiver. "There are people down in—" She blinked up her eie to help recall the name. "—in Melisianda who say that you're responsible for the missing planets."

"I am."

His pupils flickered oddly, as if reflecting lights not in the room. Unnerved, she looked away. This ascetic waif, responsible for the missing planets? She swept her eyes over the many items around his pedestal. Tributes? From supplicants come up the mountain to see the "holy" man? She wondered if one of them had told him something about who or what was responsible.

She glanced out the door, surprised that the stars already glimmered. Out here, on the galaxy's Outer Arm, there was a small chain of planets like Yasimir, newly terraformed, brimming with nascent life. And nine days ago, suddenly and inexplicably, three of them had gone missing: Ecruga, Oxwei, Charlotte's World—all vanished from the universe. Like water rushing to fill a hole, their absence sent gravitational waves rippling across space-time. Ships emerged from slipstream to find empty space where there had once been worlds. And, Orna thought with a painful tightening of her chest, people.

She swallowed the knot in her throat before it could turn into a sob. Mother had been on Charlotte's World when it vanished, doing Shiva-knew-what. Besides a few token messages on birthdays and whatnot, Orna hadn't spoken with her in years. It couldn't be true. Mother wasn't dead. She was just far away, as she'd always been, and one day soon a message would arrive wishing Orna a happy whatever and asking if she'd produced any grandchildren.

"How could *you* possibly be responsible for the missing planets?" Orna said.

He grinned wickedly. "I knew someone like you would

come, that it would take time for my message to propagate across the human sphere, for you to exhaust all your paths of inquiry. Tell me, what is your working theory?"

"For why the planets went missing?"

"Yes!"

"Right now," she said wearily, "we have none."

"You have people working on it?"

"Yes. Hundreds, maybe thousands. From all across the galaxy. Some of the brightest minds in the universe."

"And so far they've come up blank?"

"So far," she said. "Yes." Then for a terrible moment she felt as if she were adrift in deep space, a thousand light-years from nowhere, with no hope of rescue or even death.

"So here you are," he said, "Orna Liat Obote Manashampo, Acting Representative of the Free Trade Union, Outer Deep Region 59, sent to me because your people are out of ideas, because you are desperate for answers, and though you think you've been sent on a fool's errand, that I am a madman living alone on this ever-dripping mountain, the truth is your search is over. I am the answer you seek. I alone know the truth of why those worlds were taken."

"*Taken*?" she said.

"Yes."

"Taken by whom?"

"Her name is Hri."

A chill rolled down her spine, though she had never heard the name before. "Who is that?"

He laughed, and while Orna prided herself on her composure under pressure, she had never met a person who laughed at the death of half a million people, Mother among them. A fire kindled in her belly, and she balled her fists. Diplomacy was the sworn FTU way, though she had made the occasional exception.

Suddenly the man leaped up from his pedestal and bolted out the door.

"Where are you going?" she shouted.

"To see!"

She followed him out. Night had fallen, and a million stars shone down from an unfamiliar sky. He stopped beside the dripping forest, his body a thin silhouette almost invisible against the pines. He turned his gaze up, and as she stepped beside him she looked up too, wondering which star was Pnei, her home, if it were even visible in the sky.

"We thought we *deserved* them," he said. "We thought they were ours to do with as we pleased."

"*They*?" she said.

"The stars," he said. "And the worlds that spin around them. We assumed that because we could, we *should*."

She was cold and tired and had no patience for riddles. "What the hell are you going on about?"

"The First Diaspora!" he snapped, his voice echoing across a million folds of rock. "The waves of humanity spreading out to the stars! How long before Yasimir swarms with people? Now, there are a few thousand in scattered villages. In a decade, there will be millions. In a century, this world will be yet another human sewer, home to billions."

"A *sewer*?" she said.

"How else do you describe the self-replicating mass of vermin that is humankind?"

Not that way, she thought. She had seen heaps of human ugliness; in her job, it was unavoidable. She had seen its opposite too, astounding beauty in the most unexpected places. If Mother were here, she'd quip some pithy response to put this man in his place. But Orna couldn't find the words, so she stayed silent.

A brisk wind rolled down the mountain, hissing and shaking the pines. Orna shuddered with them, hugging herself against the cold. She longed to change into dry clothes and curl into a warm bed, but she couldn't. Not yet. Because even if he was regurgitating some baseless rumor, she had to find out everything he knew. If not, the FTU would send her back here with any unanswered questions.

"Who is Hri?" she said, bracing herself against the wind.

"She is a god."

Orna cocked her head. "A *god*?"

"There is no other name for them."

"*Them*?"

"Her sisters, who dwell in the heavens, whom you thought were mere clouds of gas and dust."

"Your gods took the planets?"

"They are not *my* gods! They do not belong to anyone! They dwell alone, masters of space and time."

Down in the valley, Melisianda glimmered with artificial light, and Orna stared longingly at it. Down there were restaurants and people and warm beds. Civilization, she thought, and sanity.

It was too dark to hike back now. She might stumble over a stone or get bitten by a viper. She had planned to call a flyer to come pick her up, but her eie was reporting a loss of signal. Yasimir was too young, its hubspace network still in its infancy. People came out here to get *away* from the hubbub of humanity, and they were in no hurry to connect back to it. She would have to wait until morning for a signal. So she could either risk grave injury, or she could spend the night here, on this mountain, with this stranger.

"Soon," he said softly, "they will come for this planet too. They will work their way across the human sphere until, like roaches swept from a house, the human stain is purged from the universe. All our works will be forgotten. In a few tens of millennia, a blink of an eye to them, it will be as if we never were. As it should be."

Then he abruptly turned and strode back toward his house, leaving her alone under the stars.

Her tent was self-assembling, and as soon as it was pitched she leaped inside and turned on the heater. Trembling, she slipped out of her wet clothes and slid into a dry jumpsuit from her pack. Then, for a good long hour, she basked in the heater's glow, savoring its orange warmth. Crickets and other insects chirped loudly from the forest. Larger animals skittered on the rocks, and she knew there were black-bellied chamois, hop lynx, and cliff vultures skulking about. Humanity had built this world. That didn't mean humans were safe from it. Natural habitats required balance, and balance meant predators and prey. She activated the tent's shield so that nothing, not even a stray photon, could get through while its power held. There were still six hours of darkness left.

Feeling more relaxed in the warmth, she prepared her daily report for the Central Office. When she'd first arrived on Yasimir, she had downloaded a copy of the local dataspace records to her eie. She used it to facerec the man she'd spoken to as Adair Joshua Ohanko, born on Mars, in Solsys.

"Solsys," she said. "Huh." It was not unusual, she knew, for jeeks from Solsys, conditioned as they were by the collapse and rebirth of Origin Earth, to have extreme views on terraforming and the human presence in the galaxy. A return to an earlier age, a slowing or ceasing of the human diaspora—these were common themes. Less common was the desire for human extinction. In fact, Orna couldn't recall ever meeting anyone before Adair who had felt this way.

Local records said he had come to Yasimir on a small ship from Tarphonsys two standard years back without cargo or suitcase. A medscan found him free of pathogens and with minimal gene mods. The records said little else, and she'd need to wait for a hubspace connection to conduct a deeper query.

She was in the middle of dictating her report when she stopped short, because there it was again, that knot in her throat. This time, she couldn't push it down, and she gasped.

Was Mother really gone, *forever*? No more surprise

messages? No more birthday wishes? Did her story really end like a period at the end of a sentence? Orna couldn't grasp the finality of it. Death had always been an intangible thing. She wondered for a moment if there was something she wished she had said or done, if she had any regrets. She surprised herself by finding none. Mother had chosen a path far from Orna, and there was nothing she could do except live her own life. Orna had often wished that she and Mother were closer, that they could share in each other's daily joys and disappointments. And after a long while she'd realized that Mother preferred to stay aloof. You cannot get hurt if you never let yourself become vulnerable. But, Orna knew, neither could you love.

She composed herself and continued her report: "Adair is a misanthrope who believes humanity is vermin and whom his gods will wipe out. I'm attaching a recording of our conversation. I'll follow up with additional questions tomorrow; however, I'm leaning toward the hypothesis that Adair is suffering from grandiosity related to religious delusion."

She ended with a report on local trade, which had dropped precipitously since the planets vanished, though it had increased by a few percentage points in the last two standard days. "A positive sign," she noted, "that trade may soon return to normal levels."

She paused, thinking of Mother.

Eventually, she made the finger-knotted FTU bondsign with her hands and said, "I swear to Time, Space, and Eternity all I've said is true. May your bonds stay firm. May your paths lie open."

She ended the recording and told her eie to transmit the report as soon as the hubspace connection resumed. Her supervisor and her supervisor's supervisor would need to review her data. And, because it dealt with the event, it would likely reach the Court of Sents themselves before she got a reply. She hoped it would come soon. She had never missed home this much in her life.

She was falling into a dreamless sleep when she heard the voice.

"Ornalia . . . Ornalia . . . !"

She sat up, thinking she had dreamt it. Then it came again, a whisper above the sigh of the trees in the wind.

"Ornalia!"

No one had called her that in decades, not since she was a girl. She switched on the light, and the tent's interior glowed bright yellow, hurting her eyes. She checked the power cell. It still had a full charge. The shield was up, or so it said, which meant no sound, let alone a damn quark, should have gotten through. It came again.

"Ornalia . . . !"

A woman's voice. How could that be?

She powered off the shield and stepped outside. The stars spread above her like twinkling crystalline dust. The mountains were tall black hands reaching into the sky. Yasimir had no moon, and Melisianda, once a constellation of light, had gone dark.

"Ornalia!"

She spun toward the voice, peering into the forest, and saw only shadows. She tried to amplify the light, but her eie would not respond. She could not even blink up a basic display.

"Who's there?" she called. "Adair, is that you? I don't like games!"

"Ornalia . . ."

As her eyes adjusted, a faint blue-gray figure a few shades lighter than the forest appeared in the trees. No—it *couldn't* be. It was dark, and she was tired, and the shadows were playing tricks on her eyes. But the figure standing there was unmistakable.

"Mother?" Orna said.

The figure backed into the forest, and Orna followed. A thick mist lit by the stars hovered at her waist, and as the figure ran through it she left behind a dark, swirling wake. Orna rushed after her, growing colder and wetter the farther she went.

The figure climbed rocks and leaped over trickling streams, and Orna struggled to keep up. "Stop!" she cried. "Wait!"

The figure kept climbing. Soon the path was so steep that Orna had to grasp onto slippery roots and stones to keep herself from falling. She knew this was foolish. If the fall didn't kill her, exposure would. It might be days before someone found her. But unable to stop, she kept climbing.

"Mother?" she called. "Is that you?"

The woman climbed a nearly vertical rock wall as easily as if it were stairs. Orna found it impossibly treacherous. Her instincts told her to turn back, that if she continued she would fall to her death. But she had only to go a little more before the mountain leveled out, so she forced herself to climb higher.

Soaked and gasping, she pulled herself onto the ledge. She stood on a circular plateau a few meters wide. At the opposite end the forest continued its steep ascent into the sky. Before this—there was no doubt about it now—stood Mother.

"Mommy?"

She wore dusty overalls, the same clothes she'd worn back on Varouna, when Orna was a child, when they had lived in the small wooden cottage, where she and Mother had planted a garden, and where they had watched evening primrose slowly open under Varouna's enormous red moon.

Mother opened her mouth as if to speak, but instead of sound, out came stars. Inside Mother's mouth was another universe, orders of magnitude larger than the one they presently occupied. This new sky expanded from Mother's mouth in a dark cloud that glimmered with a billion jeweled suns. The cloud obscured Mother completely and, inflating like a universe, rushed for Orna.

She backed away from it, slipping on a root. She fell backward, over the cliff's edge. She screamed as she stared up at the endless sky. Instead of stars, a gargantuan eye, larger than the planet, larger than the galaxy, stared down at her—*through* her, and in that vastness she knew she was less than dust.

A beeping woke her, and she sat up with a start. She was in her tent, and it was morning, according to her eie, and there was an urgent message waiting.

She examined herself for wounds or bruises, and found none. A dream? No—there was grass and mud on her shoes, and her jumpsuit was soaked. If not a dream, then how did she fall from that cliff without a single bruise? The message beeped for her attention and she reluctantly opened it.

Text only, it was marked urgent, with two attached files. With a start, she saw it was from the Court of Sents themselves.

"You are hereby directed to remain with Adair Joshua Ohanko until a relief team arrives, estimated forty-one standard hours earliest arrival. *Do not*—emphasize—*do not* let Adair out of your sight. Place a tracker on him. Most urgently, you are to have him explicate his statement of the following: *Her sisters, who dwell in the heavens, whom you thought were mere clouds of gas and dust.*"

She sat back, awestruck. In her nineteen years of service for the FTU, the Court of Sents had directly contacted her twice. The first was to congratulate her on her promotion to field agent, which they did with all new field officers. The second was during her investigation of the deadly starship accidents near Abedabun, where she had infiltrated a group of mercenaries destroying ships for salvage. Their message to her had ended up saving thousands of lives.

The Court of Sents didn't bother with minutiae. They were too busy regulating the value of the galaxy's material exchanges, making sure the myriad trade routes between worlds remained stable, and tracking the huge number of ships navigating the slipstream, all of which had the positive effect of keeping a centuries-long peace between worlds. Gods stealing planets? She had thought Adair's story preposterous and had assumed the Court of Sents would too. Perhaps they were just being thorough. Or, she thought with an uncomfortable shift in her stomach, maybe they had found some truth in Adair's story. Either way, she needed to know more. She barely remembered him mentioning these clouds of gas and dust.

She blinked open the first attached file, a scientific paper describing an uncrewed probe's encounter with a huge cloud of hydrogen gas in Outer Deep Region 59/1004.b. The cloud exhibited what the scientists hypothesized might be intelligent behavior, but the probe and cloud mysteriously vanished, and all further investigations found no evidence of either.

Astonished, Orna blinked the paper away. Microbial life was common throughout the galaxy, and in a few rare pockets, simple multicellular life had arisen on its own. But animals and sentience—they were unique to Origin Earth. She had read about the strange cloud a few months back in the FTU's private feeds. There'd been a lot of speculation about what it might have been, but like everything else in the universe, the talk faded, and Orna had forgotten all about it until now. Maybe the Court of Sents knew more than they were letting on. Maybe Adair was describing a wholly natural phenomenon that, filtered through his religious lens, he interpreted as coming from "gods."

She opened the next attachment, a background file on Adair. It confirmed he was born on Mars, and added that he had lived in more than thirty systems and visited more than two hundred, spanning more than two decades. From the bustling and crowded Inner Terra worlds all the way out to the sparsely populated and newly terraformed planets of the Outer Deep, the jeek really got around. To her surprise, he had lived on Chadeisson Station in Eriksdatter Ring, a short distance from where she lived now. For all she knew, they might have passed each other on the street.

She looked for something in his history, a tragedy

or circumstance that might have spawned his hatred for humankind, and found nothing. In fact, as far as she could tell, he had lived a comfortable life. Then why the misanthropy? Was his hate, she wondered, a simple choice?

Disturbed and restless, she closed the files, turned off the tent's shield, and stepped out into the morning light. Tahira, Yasimir's silver-white sun, was bright and warm, and she tried to let it soothe her chilled bones. A huge rainbow arced across the glacial mist, though most of the valley still lay in shadow. The grasses, laden with dew, twinkled as they rippled in the wind. It was breathtaking. To think that humanity, which had once succumbed to beasts and weather, could now create worlds. Truly, Yasimir was a work of art. How could Adair look at this and see only ugliness?

She wanted to put on dry clothes, but the steady drip of the forest changed her mind. The pines shivered in the morning breeze where last night Mother had walked in the trees. A fever dream, Orna thought, from standing under the light of too many suns. But dreams did not leave mud and grass on her shoes. Answers, she knew, lay with Adair.

The house's interior still lay in shadow. Adair sat on his pedestal with his eyes closed. A bundle of fresh flowers tied with a red string lay at his feet. A new addition.

"You had a visitor?" she said. She didn't like that someone had been here while she slept.

"I *always* have visitors."

She looked around, afraid someone was hiding in the shadows. As far as she could see, they were alone. "Who came?" she said.

"Someone from the village."

"A woman?" she said. Someone, Orna thought, who looked like Mother?

"A tired old man."

"You're certain it was a man?"

"Yes."

She stepped closer to him. "Why do they come to see *you*?" It was an accusation as much as a question.

"Because I tell them the truth."

"About what?"

"About our existence. That our lives are mere infinitesimal drops in the totality of consciousness. That we ascribe ourselves with exaggerated importance when we are ultimately extremely insignificant creatures."

"That gives them comfort?"

"Truth is seldom comfortable."

"That doesn't explain why they come."

"They come because they find relief knowing that, as far as the universe is concerned, all their problems are small, and all their troubles will soon be forgotten."

"Some of us might want to be remembered," she said.

"By whom?" he said. "Those who remember us will soon be dust too. Look around. Everything you see will eventually be dust."

"In a billion years, perhaps."

"A blink of an eye in eternity."

She felt as if his words were squeezing her chest, and she gasped. Was it possible, she thought, that he was responsible for half a million deaths? For murdering Mother? She had to consider the possibility, as far-fetched as it seemed, that he was. Seething with rage, she paused her recording of their conversation with her eie.

"Where were you last night?" she said.

"Here."

"*All* night?"

"Where else would I go?"

"You didn't leave this house? You didn't walk in the woods?"

"Why would I? Hri takes care of all my needs."

She glanced down at the bundle of flowers tied with the red string. "How many visitors did you have last night?"

"Besides you, none."

"And these?" she said, pointing to the flowers. "Who brought them?"

"That tired old man from Melisianda."

"When?"

"I have no instruments to measure time besides the sun. He came with the dawn, and he left before you arrived."

"Someone was here last night," she said, and for a moment she was falling off that cliff again, staring up at that enormous eye. She pushed through her fear and continued. "A woman. In the woods."

He looked at her oddly for a moment. "It was someone from the village. People are always wandering up here."

"I don't think so," she said. "She looked like . . . someone I know."

He gave her another strange look, then shook his head dismissively.

She had caught a flash of fear in him. "What is it?" she said. "What were you thinking?"

"Nothing," he said. "An impossibility."

"Care to elaborate?"

"No."

Orna ground her teeth. Perhaps he had drugged her or used some kind of tech to manipulate her. She scanned the place with her eie, and it came up empty. Nothing here but stone and dust.

Frustrated, she turned on her recording again, and this time she also activated a tracker. Too small to be seen with an unaided eye, the nano-scale spider climbed down her leg, leaped across the floor, climbed up the pedestal, and with a tiny dose of anesthetic nested itself securely into Adair's thigh. He'd need a scalpel to remove it now. If he tried anything tonight, she would know.

"You said we mistook these gods for clouds of gas and dust," she said. "Explain what you meant by that."

He smiled to reveal long gray teeth. "Better if I show you."

He hopped off his pedestal and headed for the door, and she followed him out. Then he dashed into the pines, away from the path, and she sped after him. Dripping branches brushed against her body, their millions of little fingers sliding wetly across her skin. He laughed as they went.

"Where are we going?" she said, struggling to see him through a tangle of branches.

"You'll see," he said.

They soon emerged into a clearing nestled between two sharp ridges of lichen-covered rock, and at the sight of it Orna gasped. Silver light, dappled by a wall of pines, slanted down into this mist-filled meadow, lush with grasses and wildflowers. Insects swarmed the air, buzzing in her ears. Floating balls of pollen, picked out by sunbeams, drifted by in delicate clumps. She felt as if she had stepped into a fairy tale, a scene taken straight from one of the books Mother might have read to her as a child, and her heart suddenly ached for a place and time forever lost to her.

Adair sidled up to a patch of purple blossoms that leaned heavily on long green stems. Bees, laden with pollen, crawled all over them.

"Do you like this place?" he said.

Surprised by his question, she answered honestly. "I've never seen anything quite like it. It's . . . *astounding*."

"It'll be gone in a year."

"*Gone*?" she said, feeling an unexpected pang of dread. "Why?"

"This is a microclimate. This meadow exists only because of a chance confluence of events. The melting glaciers provide moisture, and its location between the rocks moderates the temperature. The glacier feeding this meadow is almost fully melted. No more water means no more meadow."

"It will still rain," she said. "The planetary engineers weren't that clumsy."

"Yes, but this microclimate will be gone, and the riot of life with it."

If he had a meaning behind all this, she couldn't quite grasp it. "Tell me about those clouds of gas and dust, Adair," she said.

"*I am*," he said. He leaned over a bee crawling across the petals of a flower. "Humanity is like this insect, blithely unaware that it lives on a cliff's edge, skirting death."

"There are other flowers. Other meadows."

"None quite like this."

"No," she said. She used to dream about places like this as a girl, wishing with all her heart they were real. Now she stood in one. Such a waste, she thought, that it would soon perish and be forgotten.

"Do you think this bee knows we're here?" he said.

"Maybe," she said.

He shook the stem, and the insect buzzed off. "And now?"

"Of course. You scared it away."

"From its point of view, a large creature came between it and its work. It had a choice: should it keep foraging, or fly off? It decided fleeing was wiser. Humanity, unfortunately, is not so wise."

"I'll be honest, Adair. You've lost me."

"We are like insects to them, small and insignificant. They are aware of us in the same way we are aware of insects. We ignore them, until they become a nuisance. Then they must be exterminated."

A hawk, silhouetted by the sun, leaped from one of the pines and flew away. Orna felt adrift, as if she were tumbling in deep space again.

"So we are like bees to your gods?" she said.

"They are no more *my* gods than we are these bees' humans! And they are as inscrutable to us as we are to insects."

"Do you speak to your—to these gods?"

"So far, only to Hri."

"How do you speak with her?" In dreams? she wondered. Visions?

He smiled. "I've traveled to hundreds of worlds, seeking to know humanity in all its colors. I lived high and low, with the rich and with the destitute. And everywhere I went, I saw the same thing. Slothful, indolent, self-indulgent vermin. We breed and multiply, and our filth spreads across the stars. I came to Yasimir to escape all that. I built my house to be alone and contemplate all I've seen. I spent hundreds of days meditating, hoping to find a purpose behind the madness. And in that stillness and silence, Hri reached out to me. She opened her mammoth eye and looked down upon me."

Orna remembered falling backward, screaming and terrified, as an impossibly large eye stared down at her. Was that Hri, she wondered, looking down at her too? She reeled at the possibility as he went on.

"It was terrifying," he said. "To be seen by something so vast and ineffable. It made me feel utterly small and insignificant. It was also liberating, because I finally knew the truth. All our lives are nothing. We are just insects in a field." He flicked at a bee, and it buzzed away.

"Insects serve a valuable purpose," she said, struggling against her fear. "Each species fills an ecological niche, especially here."

"What niche does humanity fill as it multiplies across the stars, devouring planets like termites in wood?"

Mother would know, Orna thought. Mother would have the perfect answer for this hateful man. But dizzy and unmoored, Orna could not think of one.

He seemed to sense her discomfort and smiled. "We serve no meaningful purpose," he said. "We exist, like this meadow, as a cosmic fluke. We were never meant to be, and this mistake must be corrected."

Orna shook her head, but the dread would not leave her. Was he right? she wondered. Were we a cosmic accident?

"I surprised her, you see," he said, grinning, "as you would be surprised if this insect suddenly spoke to you. Hri and her sisters have been aware of Origin Earth since the first multicellular creatures swam in its oceans. And they did not pay us much heed, even as we spread across the stars, because our works were so small and transient compared to theirs. They did not think it was possible for us to develop the states of consciousness necessary to commune with them.

"Yet *my* mind, out here at the galaxy's edge, unpolluted by the noise of humanity, refined by meditation, sharpened by fasting, touched their realm. I swam in cosmic seas you could not comprehend. I saw all time and space spread before me like an ocean, past and future intermingling in universe-sized waves. "This"—he waved at the meadow—"is nothing compared to that."

More nonsense, she thought. The ramblings of a diseased mind trying to spread poison! She would not accept that the man who murdered Mother and half a million others was smiling gleefully before her. "Why did Hri take the planets, Adair?" she said, trembling.

"Because she looked down at me and saw my soul as clearly as the bottom of a placid lake. She knew all I had seen and felt. She saw the sordid worlds of Terra Diaspora, humanity spreading our infestation across the stars. She saw through my eyes what would happen if we continue. We will infest the galaxy, and one day we might even expand into their domain. So Hri did what we have been unable to do for millennia. She stopped us from growing. The rest, as you say, is history."

Humanity is not vermin, Orna thought. We do not mindlessly spread across the universe like termites. But a part of her, small and growing, had begun to doubt.

"Hri *took* the planets?" Orna said.

"Yes."

"*Where?*" she said, her voice breaking. Where, she wondered, was Mother now?

He shook his head. "Where does a flower go after it blooms and dies? Nature converts it into other forms."

"And Hri plans to take *more* planets?"

"Her and her sisters, yes. If we don't stop growing. The first three were meant as a warning, to see how wise we are."

"Why did they have to kill half a million people?" she said, holding back tears. "Couldn't they have sent us a goddamned message?"

"Don't you see?" he said. "The planets *are* the message."

The sun had risen above the trees, and she was soaked in sweat. She hadn't eaten in forever, and her stomach rumbled. She was tired and emotionally spent. She desperately wished to believe that Adair wasn't responsible for Mother's death, no matter how much he longed to be, that planet-eating gods didn't exist, that this was all one man's insanity. But she had already accepted the possibility that everything he had said was true.

Inches from her hand, a bee alighted on a flower, and she wondered if it even knew she was here.

She spent the rest of the day sitting in her open tent, making use of the working hubspace connection and trying to shake off her dread. On the private FTU feeds, there had been few new developments. Two scientists had published a paper hypothesizing a convoluted theory about random N-brane interactions, which they said might be responsible for the planets' disappearance. Without evidence, however, their theories remained pure speculation. She doubted anything would come of it.

She transmitted another report and her most recent conversation with Adair back to the Central Office, while keeping one eye on the stone house and his tracker. For the entire day Adair remained on his pedestal in his cold house, meditating. According to her tracker, he hadn't eaten or urinated all day. This did not sit well with her.

In the late afternoon, a man with long black hair and big

green eyes hiked up to the house. She asked him about Adair, why he had come to Yasimir, and what he thought about the missing planets. Adair, the man said, was a "holy being," who gave people spiritual peace. As for the missing planets, the man shrugged. "Who can say, really? Who can truly say?"

The day waned, and right before the hubspace satellite dropped behind the mountains and the signal cut off, she received a priority message from the Court of Sents with an additional directive: *Find out from Adair which planets are next and when, and transmit at the first opportunity.*

They believed him, she thought. And they were scared. *Terrified.* She was too. What could humanity do against powers like that? The winds shifted, and she put on a sweater to stay warm. With a steaming bowl of soup heated using the tent's power cell, she watched the silver sun set. The first stars were up before she was done. This planet was beautiful, even peaceful, she thought. And in another time and place she might have enjoyed her stay here. Then night swept across the valley, and dread slipped back into her heart.

Are we really vermin? she thought. A stain on the cosmos? What, she wondered, are we doing by spreading across the stars? We think we're so mighty. But maybe, as Adair said, we're less than nothing. How long before Hri comes to snatch this world away too? Her legs shaky and weak, she entered Adair's house.

A single candle flickered at his feet, and his face shifted in its yellow glow.

"You don't eat?" she said.

He did not open his eyes. "Hri takes care of my physical needs. I haven't eaten in forty-one days."

She wondered if perhaps he had a gene mod which let him go for days without eating or expelling waste, then remembered the local medscan had detected no such thing, and Yasimir, as far as she knew, didn't have the tech.

"Do you speak with Hri every night?" she said.

"Once you speak with a god," he said, "you are never not speaking with one."

"Did she tell you which planets she would take next?"

"No. And even if I knew, I wouldn't tell you."

"Why the hell not?"

"Because you would evacuate the people, and they would live to infest another world."

"You'd let millions die to prove a point?"

"All of us are dust already. Most don't know it."

She wanted to strike him on his smug little jaw, to squeeze his neck until he gasped his last breath. But she was better than that. She would not tell him that her mother was on one of those planets. She would not let him know he had hurt her.

"I want you to ask Hri a question," she said.

"A god does not care about our petty human concerns."

"Yet she talks to you."

"Talking is a human concept. We *commune*."

"*Please*," Orna said, surprised at the desperation in her voice. "Ask her *where* she took the planets."

"I told you, they go to the same place a flower goes after it wilts and dies."

"Is that her answer, or yours?"

He didn't seem to like this, and his face contorted. "Fine," he said. "I will ask her. Don't expect a response." Then, for a good long while, he sat with his eyes closed while she waited. Eventually, he opened them.

"Well?" she said, eager.

"I told you, human concerns are meaningless to her. She did not answer."

"Why does she even speak to *you*?" Orna spat. "Who are you to her?"

"A novelty, perhaps. An exotic pet. Her kind underestimated us, what we are capable of. When I soar with her I feel as if she's testing me, the limits of my consciousness, to see what I notice and what I miss."

Orna shook her head in disgust. "I'm going to stay with you tonight," she said.

"I'd rather you didn't," he said.

"I don't want to either. My people have asked me to watch over you."

"If I said no, would you leave?"

"I'd wait outside."

"No," he said. "Stay. It's cold and windy out there. You can sleep in here if you wish. My mind will be elsewhere." He closed his eyes again.

She fetched her bedroll and thermal blanket from her tent, then returned to a dry spot in the corner. She sat on the bedroll, the blanket draped over her shoulders, and propped her back against the wall. She had traveled to hundreds of planets, orbitals, and stations, many with diurnal cycles far different from Terran Standard. Long ago, when she had joined the FTU, she'd received a gene mod that allowed her to adjust her circadian rhythm at will. If she wanted to sleep, her body would take the cue and rest. If she wanted to stay awake, she could do so for days without too many ill effects.

She would stay awake then, her eyes and tracker on him, until the relief team arrived to make sense of this. She had once stayed awake for one hundred and nine hours. Compared to that, this would be easy. Which was why, when she awoke sometime later from a dreamless sleep, she gasped and jumped up.

The house was dark. The candle had gone out.

"Adair?" she called. She tried to blink up her eie; it didn't respond. No eie meant no tracker. He could be anywhere. She stepped toward his pedestal and found her movements oddly slowed, as if she were walking through fluid and not air.

Starlight trickled through the hole in the ceiling, a faint blue-gray beam that shone onto the flower bundle tied with a string. It lay in Adair's spot on his pedestal. The man himself was gone. Something compelled her to touch the flowers, and as she lifted them they turned to ash, leaving a gray stain on her fingers.

There came a great shifting roar, as if dozens of mammoth stones were being ground against each other. The walls of the house moved, aligning and realigning into new shapes. A corridor opened behind the pedestal, roofless and open to the stars. Adair stood at the far end, naked, with his back to her.

"Adair?" she said. "What's going on?" Her voice echoed as if she were standing inside a great marbled hall. He stepped to the left, vanishing from view, and she took off after him. As she ran down the corridor the far end moved further and further away, until it seemed to stretch on forever. Terrified, she stopped.

A cold gray mist poured over the stone walls. The airy waterfalls pooled coolly at her feet, and the ground lay hidden beneath the fog. The walls shifted again, sliding left and right with a great grinding roar. For an instant, when the walls had momentarily lowered, she spotted an enormous labyrinth sprawling endlessly before her, expanding toward an infinite horizon. At its center shone a single brilliant white star.

Then the walls grew taller again, obscuring the scene. "Adair?" she cried. "Hello?" She trembled as tears spilled down her face. She hadn't been this scared since she was a child.

A breeze blew, and the mists parted a few meters away to reveal a girl covered in dirt, as if she had been playing in mud. The girl had short dark hair, and strangely familiar eyes. When she saw Orna, the girl said, "Oh, hello!"

"Who—" Orna said, her voice breaking. "Who are you?"

"*Ornalia! Ornalia!*" called another voice. At the sound of it the girl said, "I have to go!"

The girl dashed into a side corridor, and Orna leaped after her. The girl ran right, then left, always a few paces ahead. As they ran, the stars slid across the sky. They changed colors and size, a billion suns throbbing like hearts.

The girl ran free of the maze onto a wide plain. A huge gibbous moon was cresting the horizon, casting the world in its crimson hue. Grassy hills rose under a twilit sky, their mounds covered with neat rows of grain. There were no mountains here.

The girl ran toward a wooden cottage. A small garden grew on its southern wall. At the sight of it, Orna gasped. This was Varouna, where she had lived with Mother, decades ago.

"*Ornalia*, there you are!" A woman in coveralls stood beside the garden, hands on her hips. "Hurry or you'll miss it!"

Mother? Orna thought. Is that really you?

The girl ran to Mother, and Orna followed. "Where were you?" Mother said.

Orna was about to speak when the girl spoke first. "I was playing in the fields, Mommy. Pretending the wheat rows were a maze with doors that led to other worlds. I saw a woman there."

"Who?" Mother said.

"I never got her name," said the girl.

Orna blinked, and with a shock recalled this day, when she had seen a woman in the wheat.

"Well, it's *this* world I want to show you tonight," Mother said. "I've been waiting all summer for this!" She pointed to several bulging flower buds at the peak of a bushy green stalk.

"What flower is that?" the girl said.

"Evening primrose," said Mother. "An old-gene species dating back to Origin Earth. They open at dusk, and tonight is the night!" Mother looked up at the enormous ruddy moon. Its limb had barely crested the hill and still filled half the eastern horizon.

"It's moving!" the girl said, pointing to the stalk. "Mommy, I saw it move!" She was right. One of the green buds shook as if there were a worm inside.

"Yes!" Mother said. "I see it!"

They watched under the light of the enormous moon as the yellow evening primrose slowly opened its petals.

"It's magical!" the girl said.

"It really is," said Mother.

"Look," the girl said. "Another!" She pointed as a second bud began to unfurl. Then a third, and a fourth. They watched for many minutes, until seven flowers spread open to the sky.

"How do they know when to bloom?" the girl said.

"Same way our bodies know when to wake up. It's built into their genes."

"They'll be here all summer?"

"No, dear. These flowers will wilt in tomorrow's sun."

"They only bloom for one night?"

"Afraid so."

"Then what's the point?" the girl said, pouting. "Why bloom at all?" As she spoke a huge white moth alighted on one of the flowers. "Oh!" she exclaimed.

"Hush, or you'll scare it off!" Mother whispered. "*This* is why they bloom, Ornalia. For the night moths, one of few species that can pollinate it."

"Why only for one night?"

"Well, that's what makes them precious, because they're here for just a short while."

"Like us," the girl said.

"Yes," Mother said, pulling the girl in close. "Like us."

Orna longed to join them. She reached out her hand and the vision dissolved into mist.

Mother! Orna cried, though her voice made no sound. No! She would not let Mother go again! If only she could place a tracker on her, so she could keep Mother close forever, but no matter how hard she tried, she could not blink up her eie.

The moon had risen fully above the hills, a crimson disc filling half the sky. All at once its mottled surface pulled back like a great lid opening. Underneath was an eye, larger than the solar system, larger than the galaxy, and maybe even larger than the universe. The eye stared down at her, through her, and Orna knew what—*who*—this was.

You took her! Orna screamed to the sky. *You stole my mother from me!*

Who are you? a thundering voice replied in thoughts and not words.

She trembled under its vastness, struggling to speak. *I am Orna!* she cried. *I am my mother's daughter!*

Who are you? it said again, and Orna split apart. Her atoms collapsed into quarks, and her quarks dissolved into pure energy that stretched across infinites so vast that time lost its meaning.

Time and space opened up before her in an unending landscape, each vertex a moment of her history. She fell into a point and was a girl on Varouna, laughing joyously as she played in mazes of wheat. She leaped up, away from this scene on a long parabolic arc, and came down again on Chadeisson Station, in the Central Office, while Mother was introducing her to the people and workings of the FTU; Orna stared, then as now, in utter fascination. Then she leaped up again and came down in the rainforests of Origin Earth, walking in religious awe, and marveling at this one place in the galaxy, as far as humanity knew, where intelligent life had arisen. Another leap and she was on Jackson Station, on her first field assignment, full of youthful excitement for her future as the twin moons rose above the gleaming skyscrapers. Another hop and she was on Torem Pali, administering the old FTU salvage yards under the planet's hot sun; she stared out at the derelict starships laid across the dunes, knowing each ship had a story that spanned thousands of light-years. She leaped up again and came down in Akina Machi, officiating the wedding of two of her colleagues and dancing drunkenly through the night with their family and friends. Another hop and she was twirling with joy on Chadeisson Station, when she received her notice of promotion to field agent. For hours, which took no time at all, she stared out her apartment's big window at the hundreds of ships coming and going to destinations across the galaxy, and felt so utterly proud to be a part of all that.

Like a stone across a pond, she skipped across time and

space. She visited a thousand worlds and twice as many stations. Many more than Adair. In all of that, she did not see ugliness. Yes, she thought, humanity has its flaws. We have many. But we have done astounding things too. Once, she thought, we painted the walls of caves. Now we paint worlds. We climbed down from the trees and leaped out to the stars. Some of that growth was painful, even horrible. But in the end it was, like Yasimir, beautiful.

She was adrift in deep space again, floating in silence. This time, though, she was not alone. Perhaps she never had been.

We made a grave mistake, the voice told her. *Your kind are too different from us. We did not understand. We do now. We will not interfere again. This is our promise.*

Mother! Orna cried. *Where is she?*

Gone, the voice said. *But never forgotten.*

Then Orna was back in the stone house, sitting on her bedroll, and the light of dawn was leaking through the open ceiling. On the pedestal, Adair lay on his back, moaning.

She climbed to her feet, and as she approached him, he opened his eyes. The strange light in them was gone.

It took her a long time before she spoke. "They didn't judge humanity," she said, her voice hoarse. "They judged *you*. You have only hate in your heart, and they saw us through your eyes. Now they've seen humanity through mine, and their eyes have been opened."

"You . . . you spoke to Hri?" he rasped.

Orna blinked. It didn't seem real. "I did, and—" She let the tears come. "She told me they made a grave mistake."

"No, *we* are the mistake! We deserve annihilation!"

What a pitiful creature that squirmed before her, she thought. "You are so convinced of your own importance," she said, "even as you diminish the importance of others. Nihilism is not just intellectually lazy, it's a failure of imagination. It's grotesque. And most of all, it's cowardly. If we had listened to people like you, we would have died out on a ruined Origin

Earth centuries ago. But here we are, on a once-dead rock we brought to life. Transient life, yes. And that's what makes it beautiful. This is what you could never see."

"I can't hear her anymore!" he said. "She's stopped talking to me!"

"Because she knows what you are. A coward. And what you feel is nothing compared to what my colleagues will do to you when they arrive. They'll be here soon." With this, Orna turned, picked up her things, and stepped out into the morning light.

The silver sun crested the mountain peaks, warming her face, and with it came a hubspace connection and a dozen urgent messages in her eie. She would deal with them later. The relief team would come and she would explain everything. They would ask her a thousand questions, and then another ten thousand more. That would have to wait.

She took off into the forest, toward the meadow Adair had shown her. A mist hovered over the ground, rippling like slow-moving ocean waves. Most of the meadow still lay in shadow, and the crickets were still singing their nightly song. The first bees, awakening with the dawn, began to forage among the many flowers. Weeks from now, Orna would learn that Adair's tracker had gone dead sometime in the night, and moments later that same tracker had pinged a hubspace repeater, not far from where Charlotte's World used to be, once before going silent.

Gone, Hri had said. *But never forgotten.*

Now, as the sun rose over the pines and the mists slowly burned off, Orna leaned over a flower, and to the bee crawling upon it she said, "Hello."

THE GREAT GAME AT THE END OF THE WORLD

THE CREEPY PLAYING second base is a hell of a fielder, but his arm's for shit, so they can forget about the double-play. My sister Jenna swings a doughnutted bat in the on-deck circle, chewing strawberry gum we found in the drawer of a wrecked house, her Mets cap turned around backwards, her yellow hair flowing in the constant breeze. Seeing her like this makes me happy. She shouts at the Ken up at bat, "You'd better hit the goddamned ball, loser!" Mom wouldn't ever let that language fly. Jenna's only ten. But I let it slide. Lately, I let everything slide.

The Creepies' pitcher looks like a seven-foot tall furless cat with giant yellow eyes that glow no matter what angle you look at them, and rows and rows of toothpick teeth longer than my fingers. But her arm's the real killer. She's struck out four batters already, and it's only the third inning. (These Creepies learn fast.) Bottom of the third inning, actually, and the last. Three innings was all we could coax from these creatures who seem to be more interested in the strange stars spinning wildly above the field than the game. Its Jenna, me, the Kens and Barbies vs. the Creepies, and we're down, 1-0.

The Ken at bat just stands there as the pitch whizzes by. "Strike three!" calls the ump, a three-foot scaly fish with bat-like wings. His voice is like frogs dying. Two outs. Jenna throws her bat to the ground. Its clank echoes from the home-run walls. "You idiot! You stupid jerk! You goddamned jerk! Why couldn't you hit the ball?"

I cautiously approach my sister. Last week, she swung at me, got me right in the balls. But I've forgiven her. I forgive everything now. "Hey, hey. It's all right. We still have a chance," I say. My hand falls on her shoulder, but she shoves it away.

"No! He should have hit the ball, Russell! Three pitches right down the middle and he just stood there! He's so stupid!"

The Kens and Barbies are more than stupid, they're empty. Literally. They look like ordinary people, except at certain angles you can see right through them, and they glow like streetlights in fog. And they also do whatever you ask them, because there's nothing much left inside to tell them otherwise. (It was easy herding a bunch of them to play this game.) I turn her around, lean in to face her. "You're up, Jenna. You can do this."

"She's too fast. I'll strike out."

"I've seen you hit the ball. You're amazing. Show them what we are."

"That was *before*. I'm nothing now." She falls to her knees, runs her hand through the dirt.

A green monster like a seven-legged Incredible Hulk runs across the field and leaps over the home-run fence into the starry abyss. A moment later, a huge flying hairless ferret-thing arcs over the field, snatches up the monster and flaps away into the stars. The monster screams, trailing a rain of golden blood. Jenna doesn't look up.

I squat down and lift her chin. Her eyes are as red as stoplights. "You're not nothing, Jenna. You're everything to me."

She frowns, points a shaking finger up. "*He* says I'm

nothing. He says we're all nothing, doesn't he?"

I look up at a sky filled with too-bright stars, even though the sun is up and shining, at the giant pieces of earth that drift lazily overhead, entire towns and cities uprooted and tossed into space, never to fall back down. What can I say to comfort her?

"It's your turn, Jenna. You have to play."

Ten weeks earlier, the afternoon of my first day of ninth grade, I lined up my bike behind a dozen other kids, waiting my turn to trick out on the Track. That was our name for the curvy, jump-laden BMX bike course some kids had built years back with shovels and dirt in the wooded preserve. Each year some parent inevitably got wind of it, had the town bulldoze it flat. And each year, some industrious kids rebuilt it, with improvements on the original design. Far from the eyes of parents or cops, the Track had become a sacred place, where kids could trick out without helmets or pads, smoke cigarettes, and make out behind the trees.

Everyone who was anyone was here, decked out in their new threads. It seemed as if every kid had remade himself for the new year. I felt like anything was possible, that I too could make myself into whatever I wanted.

My friend Vinny (new Adidas pants and sneakers, Lakers cap) leaned in close on his bike and excitedly showed me a picture of what was supposed to be Pamela Huston's cleavage. With careful pinches, Vinny vigorously zoomed in and out on the screen of his cell phone, as if there were some cosmic secret hidden in the pixels. All I saw was a blotch of color.

"Dude," he said, "she sits right next to me. I am so going to love math this year."

To show him up, I whipped out my new Droid. Four calls from Mom, and two messages, but I ignored them and waited impatiently as my web page trickled in. Last night, I'd created six new levels for the game *Nimbus*, an open-sourced first-person shooter that had become more popular than Jesus over the past few months. "Check out this crazy maze I built. No one's getting out of this death trap."

"Dude, you're such a geek!" Vinny said. "I'm showing you tits and you're showing me your *game levels*?"

I felt disappointed. I'd spent hours building worlds in *Nimbus*, and Vinny was usually excited to see them. I slipped my phone back in my pocket.

Vinny twisted his head with his hands, looked like he was trying to tear it from his skull. I heard a crack. When some people were anxious, they cracked their knuckles. Vinny cracked his neck. "So why are we here, again?"

I spotted Maeve and Elsa walking toward us, all dolled up in their brightly colored, knee-length jackets, trying to avoid getting dirt on the new fabric. I gestured at them with my chin. "Maeve's in my world studies class," I said. Just saying her name made my heart skip a beat. "I told her I bike, and she got all excited."

My phone buzzed. My mom, again. I sent her to voicemail.

"Oh, so that's why you dragged me here with these douchebags." Vinny whispered. "Maeve *is* a hottie. I'd totally like to—"

"Shut up!" I said. "Here they come. Don't be a dick. Girls don't like that."

"What? Girls don't like my dick?" He smiled wickedly at me.

"Shut up!"

I'd had a crush on Maeve since spring of last year, when we shared a square dance circle in gym class. Her hands had been so warm. But back then she'd been with Christopher Black, a kid who liked to wear plaid and who probably should have started shaving in seventh grade but had let his peach fuzz grow until it resembled a patch of blond mold. Rumor had it that they'd broken up over the summer, and since then I tried to learn everything I could about her.

"Hi, Vin. Hi, Russ," Maeve said, smiling. Her cheeks were pink with cold, her black bob of hair half-hidden by a gray knitted cap with tassels. Elsa ran a finger slowly around her hoop earrings. Both girls wore Ray Ban glasses (prescription), which had, for some reason become the Most-Necessary-Thing™ over the summer and now all the girls whose moms could afford to buy them sported a pair. Maeve's cherry red ones made her look like a punked-out NASA engineer. "Are you up soon?" she said.

In my best attempt at laid-back cool I said, "Yeah, after Mi—ke." But my voice cracked like I'd just hit puberty.

"Frog in your *thr—oat*?" Elsa said, mocking me. The girls giggled. My face grew hot, and I fumbled to save myself.

"What my castrato friend here is trying to say," Vinny said, "is, wait till you see his backside. Backside *air*, that is."

I shook my head, but the girls laughed, and all was well again. Maeve stared at me. She looked expectant, her irises the color of fall grasses, a swirl of green and brown, and pupils dark pits that threatened to suck me in forever.

She let slip a shy, wonderful little smile at me. I couldn't think of anything to say, so I just cheered as Eric Kellerman landed a jump. I sucked at flirting, and my hacking skills weren't going to get me girls any time soon. But I kicked ass at BMX. I had a growing reputation in the school as "That A-track kid who bikes." I preferred that to the previous year's moniker of "That nerd who hangs out with Vinny." And I thought, if I tricked out a bit in front of Maeve, got some sick air, then maybe she'd be impressed, and, if the afternoon went really well, we'd go behind the trees and. . .

My heart hammered. This was going to be a good year.

"I heard you were good," Elsa said. She whipped out a pack of Marlboro Lights from her pocket and lit the last one, the one turned around for good luck.

Maeve smiled and swayed restlessly, the tassels of her hat

swinging back and forth against her head like a Tibetan drum. "Can you do a full twirl?" she said.

"You mean a three-sixty?" I blushed. "Sure."

"Awesome," she said. "I love that."

I couldn't believe she was paying this much attention to me, that both girls were. I had shed my nerdiness like I'd shed junior high. I couldn't stop smiling.

Vinny poked me in the arm and said, "Dude, is that who I think it is?"

I turned to see a frazzled woman, dressed in green scrubs, walking between the kids and their bikes. Her presence here was impossible, and for a moment it didn't register. Then I remembered the phone calls.

"Russell? Is Russell Broward here?" Everyone turned to look at her, then me.

"Oh, god!" I whispered. I turned my back, pretending not to hear, hoping she'd vanish.

"*Russ—ell*?" She sounded like she was calling for a lost dog. She spotted me, stormed right across the Track, and Eric Kellerman nearly clobbered her as he came around the turn.

"Is that your mom?" Maeve said. She squinted at me.

"*My* mom? Oh, uh. . . *yeah*."

"You told her about the Track?"

Maeve pushed her glasses up her nose as if taking me in. I don't think she liked what she saw. I couldn't see her irises anymore, only the dull gray rectangles of reflected sky.

My mom strode up to us and put her hands on her hips. She took a long look at Elsa, who hid her cigarette behind her back, and turned to me. "Why didn't you answer my calls? I thought I told you to come home after school!"

"What are you doing here?" I snapped.

Her hair was a mangled mess and her lipstick had missed her lips, fallen on her cheek. Ever since dad had died two years back she'd always had the appearance of going somewhere and never arriving. "They called me to cover a shift and I need you to babysit your sister."

"*Now?*"

"Yes, *now*, Russell. And where's your helmet?" She looked around. "All you kids should be wearing helmets." She stared at Elsa, who had been trying not to giggle. "Does your mother know you smoke? You know teenage smoking increases your risk of breast cancer seventy percent?"

Oh, god. This wasn't happening.

Elsa said, "My *mom* buys me all my packs." Maeve laughed but quickly silenced herself when my mother glared at her.

"Come on, Russell!"

Humiliated, I muttered goodbye to them.

"Later, man," Vinny said mournfully. Elsa seemed annoyed, and Maeve frowned. I heard Elsa mock, "'Teenage smoking increases your risk of breast cancer seventy percent!'" Someone shouted, "Mommy says Russell can't come out and play!" and a bunch of kids laughed.

I hung my head as I followed my mom through the trees and out onto the road, where her Honda CRV idled. Jenna sat in the back seat, playing Derek Jeter's World of Baseball on her pink pocket console as my mom opened the hatchback. I threw my bike in, got in the passenger seat, slammed the door.

"I don't like your attitude, Russell!"

I was on the verge of tears. "You couldn't call a stupid babysitter?"

"I'm sorry, Russell, but there was no one else."

The tires screeched as we pulled away. I looked into the back seat, Jenna in her pink jacket playing her pink hand-held game. She was humming happily to herself. I wanted to scream.

"I left money on the table. You can order a pizza. I want you in bed by eleven, your sister by nine. And no playing video games till your homework's done."

Jenna said, "Let's play baseball when we get home! Mom bought me a new mitt."

"I'm not playing with you, loser!"

"Hey! Don't you dare talk to your sister that way!" Mom said. "You'll play with her, or no video games for a month."

I crossed my arms, sulked, and Jenna returned her attention to her pocket game. "You're not like him," she said.

"What?"

"Dad would always play with me when I asked."

Mom sighed deeply as she raced down Ocean Avenue towards home, speeding through a yellow light. Just ten minutes ago, my high school future had held so much promise. Now everyone would be talking about Russell Broward, the kid whose mom picks him up from the Track. I'd be a dork in their eyes forever.

"*I hate you,*" I whispered.

"What did you say?"

We zoomed past three kids popping wheelies, laughing as they raced toward the preserve. "I so hate you both."

Jenna's tears have run out, which is good, because the white-skinned Creepy in left field has begun to dig up the grasses and vomit jewels into the holes. The others are fidgeting too. This game won't last much longer. Jenna stands, wipes her cheeks, and with a jab to the ground frees the bat of its doughnut. I straighten her hat, give her my best smile, and pat her backside as she steps up to the plate.

The catcher is some sort of shapeless ball of worms which reminds me of the squirming things I once found in our cat Lucifer's shit, but this Creepy is exceptionally good at catching the ball and returning it to the yellow-eyed pitcher on cue. It says to Jenna, "Your not-rot is repulsive to us," which I assume is some sort of insult intended to upset her hitting ability.

(Yeah, these Creepies learn fast.)

Jenna steps into the batter's box, and the many-toothed cat tosses three pitches, all balls the umpire declares. Jenna takes them all with the steadiness of a mountain.

The next pitch. Jenna swings. For a ten year old she's got quite the upper body strength. The ball makes a metallic *ping* as it connects with the bat, flies over my head to crash into the windshield of a car.

"Foul ball," the umpire declares, and distantly, something not quite human screams.

"C'mon Jenna! You can hit the ball!" I cheer. "No pitcher! No pitcher!"

The pitcher's eyes flicker like moonlit gold.

She takes the pitch. It's clearly high and outside, but the umpire calls "Strike two!"

"What!" I storm towards him, cursing. "That was totally high and away!"

"Step away from me," the fish-creature says. "Or I will devour your immortal self." He spreads his bat-like wings, and on his scaly hide I see dozens of tiny faces crying out in pain. I leap back, horrified.

"Don't worry, Russell, I've got this," Jenna says, and her defiance centers me. "These Creepies got nothing on me."

"Who you calling creepy?" the worm-creature says.

I step back to my place beside the dugout as the pitcher lofts the next pitch. I hold my breath as Jenna swings. . . and connects! A line drive flies over the second baseman's head to land in right field. Jenna screams with joy and sprints to first. A Creepy made of a thousand hands with eyeballs in their palms fields the ball. It catapults it to the shortstop covering second by rolling end over end. I tell Jenna to hold up at first.

She's the tying run. We may win this game after all.

"I hit it! I did it!" Jenna screams, over and over. She falls to the ground, hysterically laughing, or crying. I can't tell which.

Three weeks after that awful first day of school, the leaves had fallen, and so had my hopes of being anything other than what I was last year, that nerd who hung out with Vinny. I went to the Track a few times, but Maeve was never there, and when I passed her in the hall, she just nodded politely and kept on walking. Whenever I brought up the subject with Vinny, he just cracked his neck and said, "Tragic."

As Mr. Verini droned on about the Peloponnesian War, I stared out the window at the approaching black clouds. I hoped for a violent thunderstorm, something to break my boredom. I watched Maeve's left hand scrawl out neatly handwritten notes and wondered how it was possible to sit so close to her and yet be so far away. Last week I'd heard she started dating Eric Kellerman, and I couldn't help but wonder if I'd stayed at the Track that first day of school it would be me.

I decided that when I got home, I'd trash the new *Nimbus* game levels I'd created, even if they gave Vinny a hard-on. They bored me, and I had ideas for new ones, better ones, with hundred-story skyscrapers and bridges that spanned chasms of fire. I started to sketch them out in my notebook, when the room shook with thunder.

The lights flickered. Diana Golina yelped, and the class laughed. "Settle down," Mr. Verini said. He resumed his lesson. He would not be thwarted by mere weather. But the next tremor knocked the corkboard from the wall and a look of worry crossed his face. I glanced at Maeve, whose mouth was open as if to speak.

Then it happened.

A tremendous groan and screech, like a battleship being torn in two. The lights sparked and went out. Everyone screamed. In the twilight I saw a wall come rushing towards me. I panicked, covered my head.

I must have passed out, because when I opened my eyes, everything was quiet. My legs were covered with broken cinderblocks, but somehow my head had ended up under a desk. My legs were cut and bleeding, but I managed to free myself from the rubble. I stood on a heap of fallen stone, shivered in the strangely warm air, and looked around me.

The school was destroyed. Crooked rebar poked from steaming piles of shattered stone. Small fires burned. Trapped kids cried, their voices muffled by tons of concrete. The sky shined with an endless spray of stars, a sky like you'd see in the deepest, darkest woods. But that didn't make sense because the sun was up and glowing, bright as noon, giving everything long, strange shadows that shook like rattlesnake tails. And there were mountains in the air. No—not mountains. It seemed as if whole towns had been ripped from the earth and flung into the sky. I blinked, shivered, didn't understand what I was seeing, when I heard cries beneath me.

Under a pile of broken cinder blocks was a hand, a pen still wrapped in its fingers. I tossed away stones, revealing a shoulder, a neck. . . a head.

Her cherry-red Ray Bans had snapped in two. Her eyes were open, unblinking, pushed from their sockets. I turned away, threw up.

I heard more cries, heaved more stones, but I quickly realized that I couldn't do this alone. I listened, but heard no sirens, no evidence of help arriving. I walked in a daze around the school, trying to convince myself this was just a bad dream, when I saw a figure at the edge of the school property. He twisted his neck, cracking it. I ran to him, screaming.

"Vinny, Vinny! Oh-my-god, what happened? An earthquake? God, Maeve's dead. She's dead, Vinny! What's wrong with the sky?" I spoke so quickly I didn't realize I was crying. He stared calmly at me, waited for me to finish. And that's when I realized his skin had a pale glow, that through his expressionless face I could see the crumbled houses on the other side of the street. He twisted his neck, released. I didn't hear a crack.

"Vinny?" He twisted his neck again. And again. And again. "*Vinny*! What's happening?"

All around me, see-through kids and teachers climbed out of the smoking rubble. They seemed confused, lost. I poked and prodded, shook and slapped, but none woke from their mindless trance. "Listen to me, goddamnit!" And as if choreographed, all heads turned in my direction together. Terrified, I ran.

Five blocks away, on a street which had buckled up as if the earth had been unzipped, I ran out of breath, and I remembered. "Oh, god! Jenna! Mom!"

I ran past dozens of translucent people on my way to Birch Lane Elementary, gave them a wide berth, which was just as well, because they didn't seem interested in me or for that matter anything at all. Houses had collapsed, and mindless people milled about upturned yards, standing, staring. I tried to ignore the sky, but was mesmerized by a billion overbright stars and an asteroid belt made of stones etched with the circuit board landscape of cities, leaking water from broken sewers in long, sparkling tails.

I found her, sitting on the curb in front of the school, her Hello Kitty knapsack on her back, her eyes wide and vacant. I gasped.

"Jenna! Jenna! Are you all right?"

She didn't move. "Mom was supposed to pick me up from school today." A line of blood trickled from her left ear. I was so happy when I realized I couldn't see through her, that she was real flesh and bone.

"C'mon," I said, taking her hand. "I'm taking you home."

I led her down a buckled street. Three houses attached to a clump of dirt tumbled overhead. In one of their backyards, a dangling swing spun around three hundred and sixty degrees, like a clock's hand, as the houses rolled in the air. "That blue one's Chrissie's house," Jenna said. A row of tall spruces scraped their tops along the street, leaving a trail of pine needles. "She has a lot of American Girl dolls. But I have more Barbies." The houses drifted away.

We reached a break in the road, a cliff where the earth just fell away. I held Jenna's hand as we peered over the edge.

Below the pavement was a layer of red clay, veined with the severed roots of trees. Below that lay an assortment of broken sewers and torn electrical cables, spilling foul liquid, popping and sparking. Farther down, a thick layer of bedrock. And a few hundred feet after that, the layers ended. Beyond were stars a million light years away, nebulae that crossed the sky like smeared lipstick, all within an infinite sea of black. Then I knew. We weren't on Earth anymore. We were floating on a clump too.

"But this is the way home, Russell!" Jenna said, looking up at me. "How do we get home?"

A Ken is up after Jenna. Why I chose this particular batting order baffles me now. A home run from me could win the game, but the soul-eating umpire won't let me change the order. After seeing the tortured faces in its hide I decide it's best not to argue.

The Ken looks like he was about thirty-five when the event happened, and judging by his suit and name tag ("Arthur") possibly worked in a bank or a hotel. I tell him to step up to the plate, do his best to hit the ball, and if his empty eyes comprehend anything at all, they don't show it. But, like all the Kens and Barbies, he does what he's told.

He lifts the bat over his left shoulder. A lefty. And judging by his stance I figure he might once have played this game when he still had a soul. I'm not sure how much of the person is left behind, or if the Kens and Barbies are more like tires rolling down a hill, unable to alter their course once set in motion until something smacks into them from the outside.

I see the ball through the Ken's translucent body. Three perfect pitches. All strikes. Jenna curses, stomps up and down on first base. "You idiot! You asshole!" The Ken—I don't want to call him "Arthur" because that would imply he was more than just a rolling tire—hasn't moved since he lifted the bat over his shoulder. The umpire tells him again that he's out, asks him to step away from the plate, but the Ken remains.

I approach. The Ken's body glows like headlights in rain. "You're out, buddy," I say. His eyes are glassy, distant. "Go sit in the dugout."

The bat falls to his side, and he turns, walks to his seat. His expression never changes. There's a wedding ring on his left hand, and I wonder if his wife's still alive, or if she's wandering the clumps in a body without a soul.

I realize with a pang of fear that I'm up next. There are two outs, and I'm the winning run. If I strike out, we lose. Jenna looks at me, expectant, as the sky begins to rain little phosphorescent puffs of light that seem to fall right through the ground. They fill the sky, brighter than the stars.

"Batter up!" the umpire says.

Rain or shine, it seems.

My cell phone had no signal. And the landlines we found didn't work either. "We're taking the long way home," I told Jenna as we looped around town. But home, as far as I could tell, had been torn away.

Empty people waited on broken sidewalks, sat in their dented cars, stared out at their upturned yards. "Why do they just stand there?" Jenna said.

"I don't think they have anywhere else to go."

"Are they ghosts?"

"I don't know."

"Do you think Mom's a ghost?"

I took her hand. "No. I think Mom's very worried about us."

"I don't like how they just stare. *What are you staring at*?" She screamed, "*Go away! Go away!*" And as if under her thrall, the see-through people ran from sidewalks, fled their cars, abandoned their once well-manicured lawns. In a minute, all of them had vanished.

Jenna's mouth fell open. "They *listened* to me."

"C'mon," I said, trembling. "We need to go."

We turned the corner and she screamed. A bat-eared elephant rummaged through the public library's dumpster. It pulled out a ratty book with its human-like hands and said, "What a stupendous waste!"

We fled down another street.

On a road shadowed by towering sycamores, a seven-foot-tall walking-stick insect rushed toward us. I hunched down and covered Jenna in my arms. The insect paused above us and from its tiny mantis-like head said, "*Please*, I'm a vegetarian," and ran up a large tree.

When we rose again, the streets were filled with strange creatures. Apes with yellow fur hopped from broken rooftop to rooftop, singing jazz. A huge hairy spider feasted on the rubber of downed power lines. A clear ball with a single lidless eye floating inside it bounced past us. But like the mindless people, these strange beasts weren't interested in us.

"What are they?" Jenna said.

"I don't know."

"Are they monsters?"

"Are you?" someone grumbled behind us.

We spun to see a hunched, hairless man as thin as a concentration camp survivor, skin the blasted color of the moon. His smile revealed long canines. A ghoul. "They're same as you," it said in a voice like gravel being crushed. "The lost."

Timidly, I asked, "Lost from what?"

"Do you really need me to answer that?"

When I didn't respond, he looked us up and down and sighed. "Yours wasn't the first world created. And it won't be the last." He bit his long, dirty fingernails. "He didn't like it anymore, so he destroyed it. Like he did to mine. Like he did to all of ours."

"*He?*"

"You know." With a bony finger he pointed up. "*Him.*" He

coughed and stumbled away like a drunk.

I shook my head. I'd had enough. "Come on, Jenna."

"Where are we going?"

"To a safe place."

"Where's that?"

The wooded preserve looked as if it had been hit by a hurricane. Downed trees crisscrossed the path, making it hard going, but we made it to the Track. A huge tree had fallen across the course and had crushed the ramps. A see-through Eric Kellerman sat on his bike on the other side, moving the pedals back and forth, back and forth. I wondered if he had biked here all the way from school.

I fell back against a tree. I just needed time to think, to make sense of what was happening. But Jenna screamed, "Look!" She ran past Eric.

"Jenna! Stop!" I chased after her.

A hundred feet out, the woods abruptly fell away to reveal a gulf of stars. Floating nearby on a clump of land was a house. Our house.

"Mommy!" she cried. "Mommmmmmy!"

I picked Jenna up, afraid she might try to jump over the edge.

"Let me go! Mommy's there! I want Mommy!"

For a moment I entertained the thought of using Eric's bike, building a ramp, flying out into the stars with Jenna on my back. But the house was too far out. There was no way I could reach it. In a game like *Nimbus*, I'd construct a bridge, or give myself wings, or leap out into the unknown. But even if we could reach it, what would be the point? I squeezed her as I saw something move in my bedroom window.

I turned Jenna's face away. "Mom's at the hospital. She had an extra shift today. She's safe there, with all the doctors."

"But she was supposed to pick me up from school."

"No, that's why I picked you up. She told me to come get you. And now I'm here."

"Really?"

"Really."

"You swear?"

". . . I swear."

"So Mommy's okay?"

The figure in the house had long, untamed hair. She folded one of my shirts, put it down on my bed, picked it up, folded the same shirt again. And again. And again.

My voice cracked as I said, "Yes, Jenna, Mommy's fine."

I'm up at the plate and I'm shivering. Just as quickly as it began, the phosphorescent rain has stopped, though the field is still pimpled with glowing spots. Jenna leans off of first and her eyes are as wide as moons. It's up to me to win this game, and she knows it. I can't let her down. I don't know what will happen to her if we lose.

The first pitch comes in. It looks high, so I don't swing, but at the last instant it dips.

"Strike one!"

Damn! I can't tell for sure but I think the yellow-eyed pitcher is laughing.

"Hold up!" the umpire says as a figure runs across the outfield. It's a man, not a Ken. It's a real, solid, flesh and bone human being. He screams, "It's all gone! All lost! There's nothing left! Oh god, oh god, oh god!" He runs for the cliff's edge that cuts across right field, where the world drops away forever.

"Stop!" I scream. "Wait!" I just want to talk to him, to speak to someone besides my sister, to find out who he is and where he's from and what he did before. But he has a soul, and therefore his will is his own. He leaps over the edge. For a few seconds, he keeps moving outward, his legs kicking like Wile E. Coyote gone off a cliff. But then some invisible current yanks him diagonally away. That's the third jumper we've seen this week.

Jenna turns back to me. She's shaking. I wish she hadn't watched.

I tap homeplate with my bat, lift it over my shoulder. "No pitcher!" I say.

After a pause, Jenna says, "No pitcher!"

"Oh and one," the umpire declares. "Two outs."

We raided kitchens for food, slept in dank basements and walk-in closets. We once saw a gang of still-living men and women in suits and dresses murder a boy because he would not give them his last beef jerky. But after a few weeks, it seemed as if we were the only real human beings left. All that remained of the others were see-through husks.

"We won't make it to the hospital," Jenna said.

"No," I said. "It's gone." I was too tired to lie to her. "C'mon, get your stuff. We need to find some food."

"I don't want to," she said. "I'm not hungry anymore."

Neither was I. The strange thing was, we hadn't eaten for three days and neither of us had grown any weaker, though day and night had stopped having meaning. Our clump of earth tumbled in and out of shadow randomly.

"How come we're still alive?" she said.

I shook my head. "I don't know."

"Do you want to play Derek Jeter's World of Baseball against me?" She held her pink pocket game out to me. The batteries had died weeks ago, but she pretended they hadn't.

"No, Jenna. Not now."

I looked out the window. A dead soul in a nightgown had dug hundreds of holes in the yard with her hands as if planting flowers. But there were no flowers. All the plants, confused by the strange days, had wilted and died. The woman paused for a moment, then continued digging.

"Stop digging!" I screamed. And the woman obeyed. Her hands fell into her lap, and she sat there, dirtied, on the dead lawn. Probably would sit there until the end of time.

"You're a bad person," Jenna said. "You don't deserve to live, so I'll crush your house!" She stared at her blank game screen, making exploding sounds. "And you did poorly on your test, so I'll kill all your friends."

Disturbed, I said, "That doesn't sound like baseball."

"No, it's 'Smash World.'" She didn't look up from the blank screen. "One player only."

"Hit it out of the park, Russ!" Jenna shouts as I lift the bat, readying for the next pitch. But the umpire calls, "Time out!" A swarm of flying creatures approaches from the west. They have webbed feet and hands, and faces like rhinos. They wear black armor and leather buckling as if they're going off to battle. They flap their giant wings and hum a low note as they pass, like chanting monks. My bat vibrates with the sound.

There are so many flying creatures that they blot out the sky. The field goes dark, so that only the pitcher's yellow eyes are visible in the gloom. The creatures suddenly switch their song to a high-pitched whine, almost a scream. I hold my ears until they pass, watch them drift out into space going who knows where.

The sound fades, the sky lightens. "Game on," the umpire says.

Distracted, I take a perfectly good pitch. "Strike two!"

"Damn!"

Jenna looks like she might cry.

I awoke from a nap, and Jenna was gone. I called for her, but she didn't come. I scoured the neighborhood, but couldn't find her. I searched under stars turning strange orbits. I searched as purple sea monkeys pecked at the rotting tree tops. I ran down a street as two clumps, miles away, collided in a spectacular spray of dust, though I heard no sound. I reached the school yard and stared across the baseball field.

The home-run fence was cut off in rightfield by the starry abyss, and a bunch of see-through people huddled by the edge. A hundred feet out, a small clump turned slowly, and I watched as one of the see-through people took a running leap towards it, missed by some eighty feet, and tumbled away.

"Pathetic!" I heard someone shout. "Zero points!" It was Jenna's voice. "Player one only has twelve. . . no, eleven lives left. And she can't win the game unless she reaches the clump!"

I ran up to her. "Jenna! Why would you do such a stupid thing? I looked everywhere for you! I thought you were dead! Why'd you run away?"

She wouldn't look me in the eye. "Go away, Russell! You never want to play with me, so I'll play by myself!"

"Play? What the hell are you doing?"

"Long Jump 1000. If you can reach the clump before your lives run out, you win. I'll show you." She pointed to a see-through girl in the front of the group, a girl with cherry red glasses, whose mouth was open as if she were about to sing.

Maeve.

"You, nerd girl! Get ready to jump!"

I recoiled in horror. "Jenna—No!—you can't do this. These are people."

She shook her head. "No, they're not! They're dolls. Kens and Barbies. I have twice as many as Chrissie now."

I felt sick and didn't know what to do. I stared across the baseball field. Though it was littered with windblown papers, it was mostly still intact.

A see-through person, Mr. Verini, my world studies teacher, stood nearby. He held a piece of chalk, put his finger to his lip, looked like he was about to speak. But I knew he never would.

"Mr. Verini, come here!" I commanded, and he obeyed.

I lifted a small pebble. "Catch this stone." I tossed it to him. He dropped the chalk and caught the pebble.

"Excellent!" I said. Across the field, a hairless cat with huge yellow eyes and long teeth was sniffing about the dumpster, "Hey, creepy!" I called. "Know how to catch a ball?"

The cat bounded over on all fours. "Excuse me?" she said, her voice like snakes hissing.

"Do you know how to catch a ball?"

"I'm a very fast learner. You have to be if you want to survive."

"Good. Go find eight smart friends and bring them here."

"What for?"

"Because we're going to play a game of baseball."

"Base-ball?"

"Yep." I looked at Jenna. "Humans versus Creepies."

The cat hissed, "Why?"

"Because it's about time I played with my sister."

And for the first time in weeks, Jenna smiled.

Two strikes. Two outs. This is it. Now or nothing. Time seems to slow as the pitcher readies herself on the mound, as Jenna leans off first base expectantly. I glance at the Kens and Barbies sitting in my dugout, waiting for someone to instruct them. The Creepies, the Lost, they stare at me, awaiting the pitch.

It comes. It's perfect. I have to swing. There is nothing left in all the universe except this pitch.

Time stops. Synapses connect in my brain. Connections are made in lightning-flash time. Crack. My bat connects with the ball. Time is slowed. The ball compresses, pauses, flies off my bat towards first base.

I feel like I'm burning, like my head is exploding with thought. Jenna is sprinting away from first. Dirt flies in slowed time from her heels. Her face is a twisted expression of glee and terror. The pitcher turns. The ball flies high over the head of the first baseman.

I'm dropping the bat, running for first, watching the ball

fly up, up. I feel like my eyes are laser beams, my body encased in high-tech armor. My head is a supercomputer, running this game.

The mound of hands in rightfield is scrambling for the ball, which keeps sailing farther, higher. The pitcher is jumping on the mound, shouting, "Catch it! Catch it!" Even the Kens and Barbies have turned their eyes to watch the ball.

"Fuck you!" I scream to the hand who shredded this world, like I shredded so many of mine. "Fuck you very much!" My voice spreads into the cosmos ahead of the sailing ball.

The ball sails up, over the blob of hands. The blob tries to catch it, leaps higher than any human ever could. But he won't reach it. No one will. The ball flies high over the home run fence, and out into the stars.

"Home run!" Jenna screams. "Home run! Home run! Home run!"

A dozen or a hundred or a thousand feet out, the ball explodes. The sky fills with light as I round second, and the Creepies shield their eyes. The Kens and Barbies rise to their feet. I reach third and the sky's almost too bright to look at. Jenna squints at the light as I scoop her up, hug her, and step on home plate.

"It's so beautiful," she says. "What did you do?"

"*We* played, Jenna. I think it's because we played."

The light begins to burn away the edges of the field, moving closer every second.

"So what happens now?" she says.

"I guess it's up to him." I point up.

She takes my hand and looks up at me, terrified. "I'm glad you played with me, Russell."

"We make a great team," I say as the light reaches our feet. I only wish Mom were here to see us now.

LOVE ENGINE OPTIMIZATION

I ROOTED HER system on the first day. It was the only way to be sure. Sure that she'd love me. Step by matching step, I walk her under the boughs of great elms in Prospect Park, while the slanting sun passes through the tangled mesh of leaves to dapple her smiling face. When her heart rate spikes, I know she's excited. When it slows, she's bored.

"It's like what Yes, Mother says in their song, 'A Lifetime Away,'" I tell her. "All day I walk in circles / All night I dream in bokeh.'"

"Holy shit!" she says, pupils dilating. "I fucking *love* that song."

Of course she does. She's listened to it 1,146 times, five times more than the second most popular song in her playlist, "Eleanor Rigby." "I love it, too," I say. "'A Lifetime Away' is my all-time favorite."

Her heart rate soars. A little graph in my vision plots excitement vs. time. Like the slope we're walking, she's been moving steadily up as the afternoon wears on. She stares at me, pupils wide. A proficient application of make-up highlights her blue eyes. But it's not quite perfect and I add it to my list.

"Man," she says, "I thought I was the only one this into Yes, Mother."

"If I only had one day to live," I say, "I'd play 'Black Moon Rover' on repeat until I died." It's something she said forty-seven days ago at a bar after several drinks with friends. Their conversation, overheard by watches and phones and glasses, was blink-uploaded to a cloud farm off the California coast where it festered for months, waiting for some bot to crawl over the data and improve the company's voice-comp (a clause buried deep in their EULA lets them store that shit indefinitely). I've got more than a million of Jane's words, not even including her typed ones.

"This is so *weird*," she says. "I feel like I have déjà vu." Pupils narrow and blood pressure rises; she's getting nervous. Something this good must come with a catch, right?

"Let's sit over there," I say, pointing to a weathered bench under the plentiful shade of an oak. Eighty-one days ago she shared a memory with her mother in which she—a toddler—and Dad—now dead—walked down to the park when she'd had the chickenpox. They had sat together on a park bench and fed the pigeons with breadcrumbs. This memory, she exclaimed to her mother in great detail, was one of her happiest.

"We could feed the birds from the bench," I say.

"Yeah . . ." she says. "That sounds really nice."

The wind tousles her hair as we sit. Her cut is average, and I prefer a bit more waviness. I add it to my list, already long, though not yet deal-breaking.

I tear off the crust of a sandwich I bought just for this moment and toss it to the ground. Pigeons and sparrows fly over to snatch the crumbs. "When I was young," I say, "I loved feeding the birds."

She meets my gaze, the gleam in her eyes longing for something lost eons ago. She's on the verge. She might laugh or cry or sneeze. Her hand is hot and shaking as it takes mine. We entwine fingers. Her aqua nail polish, a shade lighter than her eyes, matches her blouse, and I'm really not a fan of the garish color. She'd look sexier in red or black, and I make another note.

"Can I be honest with you, Sam?" she says.

"Always."

"I've been on a few dates recently. They were all really awkward. This just feels easy."

Of course it's easy. I've made myself into exactly what she wants. "Wouldn't it be *wonderful*," I say, "if things could be this easy *forever*?" throwing stressors like frisbees so she can't help but dream of happily-ever-afters.

Her pupils are as wide as Kings County. She shivers so much the bench shakes under us. Her heart rate spikes as she leans toward my lips. And just before her lips touch mine, I stand.

"Jane."

Her hand flies to her mouth like a blushing schoolgirl. "Was that too fast?"

"I have to go."

"Go?" She checks her watch. I snap a photo of her face with it; she'll never know I've done this. "Oh," she says, blinking away the surprise of tears; surprising to her. "All right. I mean, is everything okay, Sam?"

"I hope to see you again, Jane." I spin on my heels and leave her shaking on the bench, just like the parent who left her too soon, so that there is only one possible emotion for her now.

Under towering sycamores, I stroll to the park's exit, blinking up the photo I took of her face, and her goofy, dumbfounded expression thrills me to the fucking core. I had Jane hanging on my every word. And yeah, I wanted to kiss her back, but the first rule of seduction is you must always leave them wanting more.

I found Jane the usual way, of course. Through Google.

I began by picking a phenotype: early twenties, five-five to five-seven, above-average breasts, blemish-free skin, sky-blue eyes, raven-black hair. From here it was a matter of searching for images to match these traits. Some wget-magic and Google-fu, and I was able to narrow this down to about 4,000,000 individuals from around the globe. I cross-linked each photo to place of residence, and narrowed my search down to about 9,000 in and around the New York City region. From here, I scoured social media profiles, gleaning such information as job, income, frequency of drug and alcohol use, musical tastes, political leanings, city of birth, and sexual orientation. I cross-correlated this from personality assessments taken from Instagram, Facebook, Tumblr, and Snapchat. And so from my initial large group, I narrowed it down to four promising individuals.

The final step was to observe them in person. These days, people have such finely crafted social media presences that meeting them IRL is like seeing the real man (or woman) behind the curtain, typically a let down of galactic proportions.

Not Jane. Jane was better IRL. Let me explain.

From her geotagged Instagram photos and Facebook posts, I knew on Thursdays she went out for drinks with her coworkers at a dive Irish pub on Park Avenue South called Desmond's. I waited in the back, using my smartglasses to record when she smiled, the sounds of her voice, the delicate way she threw back her hair each time she took a sip of her Macallan 10 (neat, with a glass of water). Through rooted phones and watches and glasses and Fitbits I listened to their conversations, noting what they said and what they left out, because it's in the lies and obfuscations where you learn the most you like about a person.

They spoke about coworkers they hated. (Maria had once declared in conversation with her boyfriend she wished to stab Jacob in the eye with a pencil or poison his coffee.) They spoke about people with whom they wanted to snuggle up warmly in bed (Ingrid told them she'd wanted to sleep with David forever, but she'd secretly been fucking him in the copy room for three weeks, and—unbeknownst to them—security videos of their "Office Hardcore" had been making the rounds of certain internet circles.) Bethanne expressed her distaste for superhero films. (Though she had secretly gone to see the new Marvel film twice in a theater far from her Upper East Side apartment so she wouldn't be recognized by friends). Frankie said how much he liked the new Netflix Original series called *Camouflage Heart*. (The previous night he had gotten really high on South Asian Kush, ate a whole container of Newman's Own cookies, and watched the entire run in one sitting, then masturbated to pictures of the show's male lead before bed.)

Jane listened to them all with bemused interest. (The night prior she had studied French for an hour, then read a biography of Jefferson until she fell asleep.) She was better than these people. She knew it, and based on how they looked at her for approval after they told a story, they knew it, too. For this power, they privately envied and hated her. But in Jane's presence, they treated her like the queen she was.

Jane was better looking than them all (a 9.6 on the Kardashian scale, to their average of 7.2). She had spent more time on her makeup (thirty-six minutes, compared to a max of thirteen for the others). She dressed better (black Gucci belted dress, $265.00; matching Cole Haan's Bethany Pumps, $119.95; gold Michael Kors smartwatch, $324.99; Warby Parker BrightEye smartglasses, $249.95). She had graduated with the highest GPA (3.85 from the University of Virginia, with a B.S. in Social Psychology), and had saved prudently so she had more in her bank account than all of them ($1,912.86). Her credit card debt was $17,861.24 (the lowest among them), and she was on track to pay off her student loans in the next sixteen years.

I thought, *Not bad, girl.*

But Jane wasn't perfect. My heart sank as she pulled an e-cig from her purse and stepped outside with Maria to smoke (Maria preferred old-fashioned cigarettes). Later I discovered that on stressful days Jane swapped out the nicotine cartridge for liquid marijuana, puffing on breaks (On those days her productivity actually went *up*). My lungs have been stained green from all the pot I've toked, but my dad smoked so many cigarettes that my leather jacket (which I'm never getting rid of) still reeks of them, and creepy old Hank's been dead for seven years (there is nothing I loathe more than cigarettes.) Jane also had the bad habit of sticking out her tongue when she's absorbed in someone's conversation and biting her cuticles.

No one is perfect, though. Jane wouldn't be human if she were, and I found a kind of poetic perfection within her imperfections. In her flaws she made herself sublime. Plus, I knew I could fix all of them.

And so it was there, in the back of Desmond's, a hundred years of collective data splayed out before my eyes, when I decided Jane would be mine.

The cavernous lobby of the Times Square Marriot Marquis feels like some 1980s film version of the future, as if we've stepped inside the glittering mothership in *Close Encounters* to be greeted by countless weird and exuberant aliens. Jane and I wait our turn to fly up the glass elevators to the rotating bar at the hotel's peak. I have my (smoke-smelling) leather jacket on, and Jane wears a red blouse and has painted her nails to match (thanks to a flurry of targeted ads I rerouted to her browser over the past week, ad-blockers be damned.)

A day after our first date, she left a voicemail where she awkwardly explained what a good time she'd had talking with me. "Maybe,"—a hard swallow—"we could do it again?"

I didn't reply. The next day, she texted, "Hey, Sam, how are you? You up for hanging out???" It was tough, but I ignored this, too.

On the third day she wrote, "Hey, what r u up to?" and this too I ignored.

Ultimately I left her hanging for five days, and when I finally called, she picked up on the first ring. I could hear the relief spilling from her voice even without having live graphs of her bio-data spread wide before me.

A Facebook psychological assessment of Jane—they generate these to sell to advertisers—told me she empathizes with wounded individuals. "I was hurt once," I told her. "I got scared."

"I understand, Sam," she said. "And I want you to know, you don't have anything to fear from me."

Of course not, I thought. I know everything about you.

It's our turn to enter the glass elevator. Our bodies pressed up together, Jane smiles as we squeeze in. Her heart pounds as we ascend the central column of the hotel. The lighted ribbons of each floor zip past, flicker-flashing on our faces. The tourists in the elevator gasp and shriek and snap photos flash-uploaded to cloud servers all over the world, to be stored alongside pictures of their spouses and children in every private and intimate moment of their lives.

We exit the elevator and head to the bar, where tall windows gape at the Manhattan skyline and peer across the Hudson River to Jersey and beyond. The outer ring of the bar slowly spins, so that over the course of an hour you make a full 360, as if you're inside a giant clock. A blotch of orange and green daubs the horizon like a child's finger-paint where the sun has set. All around, the purpling sky fades to black. A few stars shine futilely above the city.

The server has my reservation in his wrist-POS, and Jane beams as he leads us to our table. She is fucking radiant tonight, every aspect perfectly honed, and I sense the other patrons' jealous stares on my back as we sit.

"Scotch?" I say. "Macallan?" Her favorite.

"I love it!" she says. "The 10?"

"Let's do the 25." An absurd price, but I'm fully committed.

Thirty degrees later, we're sipping single malts while New Jersey's urbanized glory spins into view. "Sam," she says, "I realized I don't really know much about what you do. I know you work in IT, but what do you do exactly?"

I smile. I have nine talking points ready to go, each designed to elicit strong emotional memories from her past and link them to me. I have one fantastic subject on work-life balance versus one's duty to her employer, which I think will make a great opener. I blink to bring it up in my glasses.

Nothing happens.

I try again. Still nothing.

"Sam? Are you okay?"

"Hang on."

"What is it? You're blinking a lot."

I try to switch tabs to her bio-data. Nothing. I try to call up the text of her past conversations. Nothing. Net connection. Dead.

"Fuck!"

"Sam?"

"Wait."

"What?"

I can't restart the gateway process. My cellular device won't refresh. Even wi-fi, even ancient Bluetooth won't switch on. I've been bricked.

"Jane, give me your phone!"

"What?"

"Your phone, give it to me!"

Frowning, she fetches it from her purse and hands it over. It's pass-locked.

"Unlock it."

She does.

I try the net and everything works. "I don't fucking get it!"

"What the hell's going on, Sam?"

And then, in my ears, a heckling laughter, and in my vision, an evil Easter Bunny a la *Donnie Darko* descends like a curtain. Underneath, in glowing marquis, the words "BURN, BITCH!" slowly scroll past.

Motherfucker. It's DaniDarknet, revenge for when I

shutdown her botnet because she was DDOS-attacking some North African credit card processor for funneling money to one jihad or another. I needed the site up because I had been using it as a proxy for another hack. I probably shouldn't have boasted on Reddit about how I rewrote her botnet code to self-destruct.

DaniDarknet has left me blind and deaf. Without my notes, without her bio-data, I've no idea how she's feeling, what she's thinking. I have nothing to say.

Now it's my turn for my heart rate to spike. With a shaking hand, I give her back her phone.

"So . . .?" she says. "What was that?"

I shake my head. "Sorry. A work thing." I try to laugh, but it comes out forced and awkward. "It's nothing." My smile is weird and crooked.

She stares at me. "Is this you getting scared, Sam?" She reaches over and takes my hand. I flinch.

"I . . . um . . . well . . . um . . . yeah."

"This asshole must have hurt you pretty bad."

"Devastating."

She sighs and looks out the window. City lights fleck her eyes. "It reminds me of 'Hound Days,' you know? 'All the little points of light / the city like circuit boards.'"

"Oh, yeah," I say. "Definitely."

Glasses clink. Someone laughs and another coughs. Conversations happen in other places about people that don't know us, whose lives will never intersect with ours. Silence stretches between us. Jane is as far away from me as the sun.

"You're quiet tonight," she says. "Last time you had so much to say."

"Am I?" I try to smile. "I didn't notice."

Do I sound stupid? What is she feeling? Is she reacting positively to me? I can't track her pupil dilation. Does she love me or loathe me?

She takes a slow sip of scotch, as if it will make the passage of time easier to bear. Perhaps it will. "So," she says. "What kind of IT work do you do?"

"I'm a sysadmin? For a bank?" They sound like questions, but they're not.

"Do you like it?"

"Sometimes."

"That's good."

"Yeah. You?"

"Me what?"

"What do you do?"

"I'm a marketing psychologist, remember?"

I vaguely recall speaking at length about her job on our first date, but without my notes I can't remember what was said. "Right. Of course. You, um, like it?"

A grimace—does she despise me? "Sometimes," she says, and now it's my turn to have déjà vu, because I know we spoke about this before.

She sips her scotch and I catch her check the time. I'm really fucking glad I can't capture her expression now. As the world whirls by at six degrees per minute, our date spins ever further out of control. After two-hundred and forty degrees I tell Jane I'm not feeling well and we call it a night. We didn't even go once fully around.

DaniDarknet, I'm so going to fucking *ruin* you.

The next morning is hell. I've been up all night making repairs, but we have three mergers and an IPO today, plus my boss is just in from her third home in Barbados to inspect her worker drones. I can't miss work. But I've prepared well, so work is mostly cubicled me in front of a four giant screens watching numbers stay in the green while I fire off a hundred shell scripts in my smuggled-in netbook, fixing yesterday's catastrophe.

While some rich asshole makes another billion, fifty-three rooted servers in Kazakhstan crash hard, taking with them eighty-five percent of DaniDarknet's ouvre. I want to shout with glee as each one falls, but I've got decorum to keep. This is a multinational bank, after all.

When the markets close and the rich executives pat themselves on the back for work that was mostly mine, after they've drunk enough liquor to make the halls explosive with fumes, I get the email.

"Hi Sam, Michael Robert Kowalski, VP of Biz Dev. Donna Nuñez"—my well-tanned and rested immediate supervisor—"tells me what a superb job you did on the Reiss Affair."—affair, capital "A"—"I'd like to see you in my office. Come by at 7."

Note that in Michael Robert Kowalski's executive worldview there is no possibility whatsoever that I might have reason to refuse, like for example a dinner date or children to pick up from day care or, you know, any life of my own. If one is invited by such a man, one must go. I groom myself in the bathroom, making sure I'm sufficiently tucked and professional. I brush my teeth and reapply deodorant, even count to ten with my eyes closed, but by the time I get to his office door, I'm shaking like a homeless person in February.

I should not fear this guy who, twice a week, visits a massage-and-tug on 58th Street and gets a happy ending before using their showers and dry-cleaning service to come home and greet his wife and kids smelling like fresh laundry. He says to his friends he does it for the "stress" so he "doesn't have to bring that shit home." But, yeah, I'm afraid of this guy who crushes small governments over cocktails. Maybe it's the desk. It's enormous, like he sits at the head of a tractor combine, and it's gunning for me.

I knock.

"Yes?" Michael says. He's mid-fifties, moon-crescent bald, well-trimmed beard, wearing a sport coat but no tie. His feet are up on his desk, and his black Chuck Taylors either make him look really cool, or really dorky, I can't tell which. There's a glass of whiskey on the table, and beside him a wrapped box.

"Hi," I say. "You sent for me?"

"What?" he says. His feet stay propped on the desk; I'm not important enough for them to move. "Who are you?"

"Sam."

"Sam?"

"From IT? Did you not send me an email?"

I get this a lot, so I wait for him to catch up. It takes him a second.

"Right! Saaaaam!" Now the feet come down. "Sorry, I presumed you were–"

"A dude. Yeah, I get it. Sysadmin? Gender-neutral first name? You made assumptions." A primary assumptive fault that one of the world's top financial analysts should not be making, and yet here we are, careening into chaos with the gas-pedal floored. "It happens to me all the time," I say, faking a smile.

"Sam—antha?"

I nod once to let him know the finality of it. "Please call me Sam."

He has a leather chair pulled aside, which I can only presume was meant for Sam the XY not Sam the XX. He glances at it and makes a quick calculation, deciding that the father-son bullshit mentor thing that he had planned to endow me with won't work on this fragile female creature before him, and so I'm not invited to sit.

"Well, Sam," he says, "You really knocked it out of the park on that Reiss Affair." Holy shit, did he just use a baseball metaphor? "This is for you." He points to the wrapped box on his desk, and upon closer inspection it's a bottle of Lagavulin 16. "Enjoy it, kid."

Did he just fucking call me kid? I want to smash his smug little face, because here in microcosm is the kernel of the capitalist hypocrisy: For saving the bank from a billion-dollar hack, I'm given an $83 bottle of whiskey and a pat on the back.

"*Do* you drink whiskey?" he says.

"No," I say, snatching the box. "Girls don't drink this stuff.

But I know a few women who do." I'm not sure if he gets my meaning or cares, but Michael Robert Kowalski, Vice President of Business Development, doesn't stop me from leaving as I flee, bottle in hand, as far away as possible from one more misogynistic asshat capitalist destroying the world one percentage point at a time.

Back at my desk, I'm happy to see two more of DaniDarknet's servers have crashed. There's a desperate email from her to one of my anonymous accounts. "Please!" she says. "I'm sorry! You're destroying years of work! Have mercy, man!!!"

Man? I twist open the bottle of Lagavulin and take a heavy swig. It burns hard going down. "Prepare yourself, DaniDarknet," I say, "for you shall weep."

And I am ruthless.

Before we even left the spinning bar, a half-dozen dead-man's switches I had set in place years ago were unzipping tarballs on servers across the world, beginning the work of repairing DaniDarknet's damage. But the full cleanup took several days. I restored from backups and spent a full weekend installing military grade proxies, firewalls, and honeypots around my wares, girding my loins against another attack. And so when I have my servers more-or-less back to where they were, I start up again with Jane.

Because of a high number of early-adolescence abandonment experiences—including but not limited to the death of her father and losing her best friend in a drunk-driving accident—her Facebook psychological assessment tells me Jane positively favors repairing fouled relationships (marketers take note). I send Jane a long-winded email paraphrased from her favorite books, which highlight themes of reconciliation. My email leads to a phone call, where I tell Jane a highly metaphorical story about each person's journey from fragmentation to wholeness.

"We're all so broken," I say.

"No, Sam. You're *not* broken."

This leads to date number three, an Italian dinner followed by espresso and a walk in Central Park. I have enough wares this time to take out a small country, but DaniDarknet does not show her digital face—how can she? I have destroyed her—and by the end of the night, I have brought Jane's excitement up to first-date levels. Without further interruptions, I estimate it will take between seven and nine days before Jane will fall helplessly in love with me.

On the fourth date, we meet at her place, a small, but tidy one-bedroom on the Lower East Side. We order Chinese and empty a bottle of Syrah together. While a Netflix thriller murmurs in the background, we heavy pet each other on the couch. Her lips are a little dry, and her tongue tastes like soy sauce and lo mein. She desperately needs a mint, and the beige dress she's wearing just isn't flattering.

"It's getting late," I say.

"You could stay."

"No. I've got to be up early tomorrow." I leave before the film's climax.

The next day, I text her a smiley emoji and ignore every one of her four replies. The day after this I surprise her at lunch. "I'm close, let's meet." We share a sandwich at an eat-in bodega and after twenty minutes I have her giggling hysterically, repurposing jokes from a comedy sitcom she used to love. Then on Friday, after we share bottle of Chianti in her kitchen, everything dark but the glow of our faces from a single candle flame, she pulls me into her bedroom.

The sex isn't what I expect.

Jane is decent. Not great, just decent. She does some things that pleasantly surprise me. Others, not so much. And so, when it's over and we're lying under the sheets, I wonder if I might have erred in somewhere in my search.

"I love you," Jane says, her body marble-gray in the pre-dawn light.

"I love you, too," I say, and as I speak there's this terrible gnawing itch above my belly and below my heart, a hunger for something not quite food, but just as necessary. I know this itch has been in me forever and will linger long after I'm dead and my corpse has rotted away.

"I've got to get to work," I say, and rise from bed.

I'm ensconced in my cubicle, patching an SSL exploit in the company's servers, making sure to leave behind an array of back doors, when Jane forwards me an email someone sent her at two a.m. this morning.

From: Prometheus Vulture (prometheusvulture666@anonymail. com)
To: Jane [redacted]
Subject: Samantha [redacted] is lying

Jane, BEWARE! Your 'lover' is not who she seems. The evil creature known as Samantha [redacted] has access to all of your personal data and is using it to manipulate you. She's a dangerous psychopath and you need to stay the fuck away from her if you value your life. I say this as one who has been irreparably harmed by her. Sam has destroyed my life! Oh, and if you don't believe me, here's proof.

Sincerely,
Dani.

Attached to this email are spreadsheets of data: Jane's excitement vs. time, pupil dilation vs. topic, weekly sleep patterns, daylight hours correlated with mood, GPS location history, textual analyses of conversations, Myers-Briggs personality models, etc., and all of this in easy-to-read Excel format, all of this data

DaniDarknet snatched before she bricked my systems.

I can't make a personal call at my desk, and I stew in rage all morning. As soon as I get a break, I rush outside to call her.

"Is it true?" she says. "Please tell me it's bullshit, Sam."

"Of course it's bullshit! I can't believe you'd even ask, Jane."

"That time . . . at the spinning bar, when you got quiet. You were blinking a lot. You needed to get on the net."

"It was a work thing, Jane. Don't let this spammer poison your mind."

"But it's not just a spammer. This Dani knows you. *Who* is she?"

"The woman who hurt me."

"Or maybe you're the one who hurt her."

"No, Jane. That's what she wants you to believe! She'll say anything to hurt me. That's why I left her. She's destructive."

It's so quiet I hear a distant car drive past on her end of the connection.

"Look, Jane. Even if it were true, that I somehow could use this information to seduce you, why would it matter? If you were selected as having the best traits from among millions, how is this bad? She wants you to believe I used this data to do what, exactly? To mold myself into the person you want? And how is this bad? Isn't it best when both parties get the person whom they want?"

"Except in this case, one person is real and the other is a construct."

"Jane, this is nonsense. I'll come over and we'll order a pizza and forget all about this."

"No," she says. "Not tonight."

"Tomorrow then. I'll come over at seven."

"I don't know, Sam. I need time to process."

The connection-ending beep ignites a rage in my belly. This has gone beyond digital. I will find DaniDarknet and destroy her life.

At home, I finish the rest of the Lagavulin and smoke a

joint and patch code and update servers and write long screeds in multiple forums about how the WordPress update leaves it open to JavaScript exploits, and generally do whatever I can to keep my mind off Jane. Nothing works.

Her feeds have gone dead. She's taken off her watch and glasses, shut off her phone and computer. Even her bedside internet-clock-radio is off. For all I know, she might be on a flight to Amsterdam. But, no, I'd know that.

I bring my laptop to bed, and sometime after midnight, I pass out. I shiver awake as the morning light breaks my rippled sheets into hills of light and shadow. I've left the window open, and my breath puffs with frost. I rise to shut the window, when a blinking red light on my desk catches my eye.

On my phone, a voicemail.

"Sam. I'm . . . I'm sorry. I've been up all night thinking. You're right. It doesn't matter if any of it's true. What's real is how I feel. And, I love you, Sam. Let's chill at my place after work, watch a movie or something. Will you eat pad thai? Call me."

My screens awake first to Jane's heart rate, then her blood pressure and pupil dilation. A minute later, GPS data and early work emails trickle in. She's data-live again. I plop into my chair and sigh, lighting what's left of the joint in the ashtray, work be damned. I'm fucking fantastic, aren't I? Because not even my worst enemy could take her from me. I'm the goddamned queen.

Outside, a car honks. A bus drives by. The radiator hisses steam.

The THC filters into my blood, turning the morning sublime. I've got two hours before work, so I open a browser window, stretching and yawning as I decide what I want to work on. Before I realize what I'm doing, I'm typing into the search bar, "female, dark hair, blue eyes, smart-looking, glasses, attractive, twenties."

I get 7,490,000 hits.

YOUR FUTURE IS PENDING

THE DOG WAS in the alley again, sniffing around the empty trash bins for scraps she wasn't going to find. Martha would be late for work if she fed her again, but she couldn't bear to let the animal suffer. The mutt huddled behind the bar-coded trash bins as Martha put out a dish of microwave rice and a bowl of water. She'd have to remember to pick up some real dog food on the way home.

"Come on, girl," Martha said, wiping her brow. It was already ninety-eight degrees and getting hotter. "This is for you."

The mutt, a scrawny little thing, hesitated. God only knew what troubles she had been through.

Something skittered behind her—a rat—and they both jumped. And when she turned back around, the dog was gone.

"You'd better come eat this," she said to the empty alley, "before the rats do."

At forty-one, Martha had never married. At first she told herself it was because she hadn't met the right person. But as she rapidly approached middle age she told herself it was because she valued her independence. But that reason had grown less persuasive after her father got sick and moved in with her so she could take care of him. So maybe Martha was alone because fate had deemed it that way. And in a battle between mortals and fate, fate always wins.

But, despite her fears of being late, Martha arrived at Mr. Fletcher's three-story apartment promptly at 8:45 AM, exactly as her wristpad had predicted. She spoke her name and employee number to the door, and it opened wide, then sealed so quickly behind her that her ears popped. It was a brutal 109 outside, and her neatly pressed work uniform was already soaked in sweat. But inside Mr. Fletcher's climate-controlled apartment it was a cool sixty-eight.

Her wristpad told her Mr. Fletcher's couch was on the third floor, so she made her way past a dozen empty rooms, while a small army of cleaning bots parted like respectful soldiers to let her pass. According to company records, Mr. Fletcher had moved in six months ago, but you couldn't tell by the unfurnished rooms and half-opened boxes scattered about the place like bricks from an ancient ruin.

The air smelled of paint and new carpet, but as she ascended the stairs, following the map on her wristpad, a sour smell, something halfway between vinegar and piss, overpowered her. It was worse than sweat but kissing-cousins to it. The smell grew stronger as she got closer, and Martha knew she could have followed her nose instead of the map.

Like the other rooms, this space had many unopened boxes scattered on the floor. But one had been ripped apart like a present on Christmas morning. Pieces lay tossed about the room as if a hungry beast had devoured it. Martha had seen this a hundred times, users madly opening their couches, assembling them in a frenzy, and meshing in before the dust had time to settle.

Mr. Fletcher lay on his couch, eyes rolling behind closed lids, weeks of beard on his sunken cheeks. The couch's interface couplers softly hummed against his temples, and stroboscopic lights blasted his brain with petabytes of information. Just twenty-two, Mr. Fletcher was a AAA client, a top earner according to his file. But you wouldn't know it by his emaciated, pasty-looking body. Though appearance mattered little when it came to MeshLife. And that was actually one of its selling points.

Mr. Fletcher's service bot, a vaguely human-shaped metallic and plastic thing, stood frozen beside him, its console light flashing alert-red. Martha brought up her work order on her wristpad and reviewed the details.

MeshLife had lost connection with Mr. Fletcher's service bot two days ago, the file read, and after a sequence of automated repair attempts, the company AIs had chosen Martha as the optimal technician to diagnose the problem. And so here she was.

She plugged her wristpad into the bot's console and brought up its logs. She suspected the error before the logs confirmed it: Another failed network board, the fifth one this month.

"Fucking cheap-ass Kazak shit!" she said.

The company had begun sourcing hardware from a fifth-rate supplier in Kazakhstan, and their parts failed as often as farmers' crops these days. When she had asked Olembe, her boss, why MeshLife didn't use a better supplier, he told her the company's AIs ran the numbers and calculated that even with the failures it was still cheaper to use the Kazak supplier than sourcing parts elsewhere. So much, Martha thought, for company pride.

The fix was so simple a monkey could do it. She'd swap in a fresh network card and start the diagnostic routines. And, if they checked out, she'd sit and watch the service bot do its caretaker thing for a few minutes: injecting essential fluids and nutrients via IV, removing waste, washing skin and hair, and a dozen other health-related tasks. This last part, watching the bot care for Mr. Fletcher, wasn't part of her job, but Martha was never comfortable leaving her clients alone until she knew they were safe. These days, some people meshed in for days, even weeks at a time.

Curious as to what Mr. Fletcher was up to, she tapped up the couch's monitor.

Viewing it on a flat screen and not beamed into her brain at 4.216 THz was like comparing a vid of a rollercoaster to actually riding on one. She had meshed in enough times to complete her training, enough to learn that meshing in wasn't for her. Not because the experience was scary or uncomfortable, but because mesh was so much better than real life that reality afterward felt like returning to a black and white world after seeing color for the first time.

Mr. Fletcher, or $TopDawg, as he was known in-mesh, stood atop a pedestal in a gargantuan nightclub styled like an Egyptian pyramid. Fantastical creatures swam in the air around him, leaving psychedelic trails of sparkles and rainbows. The real-life Mr. Fletcher resembled the avatar of $TopDawg the way a lump of coal resembled a diamond. In mesh, the man was beautiful, an Adonis of better-than-perfect proportions, every muscle gleaming with sweat, his enormous member barely hidden under silken briefs. He danced to music Martha couldn't hear, while beneath his pedestal, some four million creatures—avatars from other mesh users—gyrated in the flickering lights. The millions took on weird and grotesque forms, hybrid animals that had not earned their place on the Tree of Life through billions of years of evolution. They thrusted and swayed as $TopDawg led them on. It was an enormous rave-dance-party-fuck-fest-orgy with four million global guests and it wasn't even nine. Who the hell were these people, Martha wondered, who could afford to do this all day long instead of work? Who could dance and fuck and fritter their lives away while the world slowly withered to nothing?

A row of multicolored spotlights spun around to point at $TopDawg as he paused in a warrior's pose. Across his chest, a line of text appeared, solid gold letters growing out from his skin.

STAY GUCCI! it read.

Then, as if he were an Olympian athlete tossing a discus, he flung thousands of golden coins into the dancing crowd. The animoid dancers scrambled to pick up the coins like a swarm of hungry pigeons, though there wasn't nearly enough for all of them.

Martha queried the console to see what the coins were.

Get $25 off select Gucci Mesh Wear™. Use coupon code XG74BH at checkout.

Advertisements in-mesh were scheduled down to the second. At 9:02:14 AM, $TopDawg would promo *KillCult IV: Vengeful Blood*, a new in-mesh game, by "murdering" a few thousand partygoers with a laser rifle. At 9:06:37 AM, $TopDawg would wrestle and defeat a giant squid in a promo for *Deep Hell*, an in-mesh movie. At 9:09:15 AM, $TopDawg would give all willing participants a mind-blowing orgasm in an ad for SoftTouch™, the latest teledildonics app. The ad slots for 9:12 and beyond said, "*Pending*," which Martha knew meant the company AIs were calculating some complex, multilayered equation that factored in the number of guests, their likes and purchase history, and what today's advertisers were willing to spend in order to choose an ad that would have the maximum ROI. Martha remembered reading once that the AIs' method was so opaque that even the company techs admitted they didn't know quite how it worked.

Martha checked Mr. Fletcher's biometrics on the console, and they told a familiar tale: Extremely elevated dopamine and endorphin levels; cortisol hormones dangerously high; blood pressure, body temp, and heart rate far below baseline; and more than five markers in his blood that indicated he was severely malnourished.

But she didn't need a monitor to see this. The young man had the wasted appearance of all the mesh-ins she visited. Bony prominences in hips and shoulders, gaunt faces, and edema swelling of the legs. MeshLife service bots were good, but there was only so much they could do for the human body before entropy took over. And Mr. Fletcher's bot had been offline for two days.

Outside, a garbage truck rumbled past, while a dozen bots trailed it down the street, emptying trash bins into its carriage almost faster than Martha's eye could track. The overall effect was like watching spiders unmake a web.

She opened up the code repository on Mr. Fletcher's bot and switched into a subfolder. The file's modification time hadn't changed since the last time she checked, which meant the company AIs hadn't found and patched the flaw. The software error stared her in the face, a dangerous bug that could lead to a service bot seriously misjudging a client's health. A bug that, with just a small code tweak, could be made deadly. She'd discovered it a week ago when diagnosing a faulty biometric reading.

Last she'd heard, seventy-five percent of the planet meshed in at least once per week. Billions relied on this piece of software to keep them safe. She could let her superiors know about the flaw and receive a $162.14 finder bonus on her next paycheck. Her boss, Olembe, would give her a smile and a pat on the back. And next week she'd be at another huge and mostly empty house, repairing a faulty network board on a bot made with shitty Kazak parts, just so another overprivileged, spoiled kid could sell pretend shit to millions of their "friends," while MeshLife would keep making trillions.

Martha stared at the file for a good minute before she closed it and deleted any evidence of having looked at it. Then she began replacing the faulty network board.

Today's fusillade of ads were for a line of smart diapers. They followed her from street to subway to bus to home, hectoring her from billboards, wall-screens, pads, and even a sleeping girl's smartwatch.

"Good evening, Martha! Did you know our diapers can alert caregivers when they need to be changed? And with our new AdaptiveWetness™ technology, they can be worn for almost twice as long as the leading diaper brand."

$PinkFox, or a very good synth of them, modeled the diapers in most of the ads. A few months back, in a lonely moment, Martha had googled $PinkFox without enabling private mode in her browser, and now this nineteen-year-old androgynous sylph followed her everywhere. The fact that they continued to appear meant Martha looked at them more often than she cared to admit.

As she stepped into her apartment, dripping in sweat, a wave of exhaustion swept over her. "Shit!" she said when she spotted the empty box of microwave rice on the table. She'd forgotten to buy dog food.

"Who the fuck is that?" came a voice from the bedroom. "I have a gun!"

"It's me, Dad," she said wearily. "It's Martha."

"Who?"

"*Martha!*"

Her father didn't have a gun, of course. He could barely get out of bed, most days. But that didn't stop him from threatening her every damn time she got home.

"Why is it so hot in here?" Martha asked. The thermostat said it was eighty-eight degrees inside. "Why'd you shut off the AC, Dad? You can't do that! It's dangerous."

She set the temp at seventy-five, the lowest the software let her go, then made a mental note to remove her father's voice access to the thermostat. A few weeks ago, when she'd complained to the super about the AC's lower limit, he'd said the restriction was out of his control, that it had been auto-updated by the manufacturer to comply with state regulations. When Martha protested that she regularly visited clients with lower thermostat settings, the man just shrugged and said it was out of his hands.

She walked down the hall toward her father's bedroom, and a foul smell grew with the overloud sounds from the TV.

As she stepped through the threshold into the bedroom her father shouted, "Diane? Where the fuck were you? I'm hungry, god dammit!"

"Mom's dead, Dad," Martha said flatly. "I'm your daughter, Martha." She winced and held her nose. "Christ, Dad, did you shit yourself again? It smells like a sewer in here."

Her father lay in bed, sheets half-covering his sweaty, shirtless body. His gaunt face was covered in a pasty sheen that flickered in the TV light.

"*—pollinator bee colonies fell by another 6% in the winter of 2037-38,*" said a pixel-perfect beauty from the TV, "*according to a new study, down 91% since 2020. Farmers of corn, wheat, rice, soybeans, and sorghum are petitioning the Schiff Administration for more assistance, since their crops are likely to fail again this season without sufficient pollinators.*"

"Liars!" her father screamed. "It's all fucking fake! Goddamned liars!"

The TV cut to President Schiff, drinking a cocktail in a hot tub while three scantily clad women massaged his shoulders. "*The farmers dug their own graves by not relying on drone pollinators,*" President Schiff said. "*I tell you indoor farming is the future, and relying on 'bugs' to do the dirty work is just plain stupid!*"

"TV, off!" Martha said, and the TV obeyed. A silence filled the room like the absence of a friend she never really liked.

"Hey!" her father said. "I was watching that!"

"All you do is scream at it," she said.

"TV, on!" her father said, and light and sound exploded back into the room.

Martha stormed around to the back of the dresser and yanked out the power cord.

"You bitch!" her father snapped. "Why'd you do that?"

"Dad," she said. "You stink."

His eyes burned with tears and rage as she approached him. She lifted the top sheet and chanced a look, then winced and turned away. The mess was worse than she'd expected.

"Jesus," she said, "why can't you go to the bathroom like a human being?"

His voice, softer now, broke with a sob. "I couldn't help myself."

Martha shut her eyes, and $PinkFox's diapered body danced before her closed lids. Sometimes she wondered if the ads knew her better than she knew herself.

After she had bathed and fed her father, changed his sheets, and done her best to remove the lingering smell from the air, she collapsed into a chair beside his bed. Her father softly snored, while the TV played some old scifi movie about a guy who gets abandoned on Mars and has to use his ingenuity to survive.

She'd fallen asleep in the chair when her father's voice woke her.

"We don't go to Mars no more," he said.

"Huh?" she said as she sat up. Her stomach rumbled.

"When I was a boy, that's all you heard talk. *We going to Mars. We gonna start a city there.* It was all from that Rust guy."

"You mean Evan Rusk?" Martha said.

"Yeah, him! He was all gung ho about Mars."

"They landed there back in '29," she said.

"But not to stay," he said. "We were supposed to start a new world there. What ever happened to that?"

Martha didn't answer. Mesh happened, she knew. And she worked for the company that sucked away people's lives like mosquitoes drank blood. It disgusted her. But after months of searching for work, MeshLife was the only job she could find. Without it, she couldn't afford this apartment or provide for her father. And as much as she loathed him sometimes, she couldn't bring herself to abandon him to the system.

"Good night, Dad," she said as she stood.

"Who the fuck are you?" he said. "Where's Diane?"

On the screen, the hero leaped for joy as one of his inventions worked.

Martha awoke just before dawn on the living room couch, still in her work clothes. Her stomach rumbled loudly. She hadn't eaten anything last night, but halfway to the kitchen she spotted the box of microwave rice and remembered the dog. "Fuck," she said.

Ten minutes later she was down in the alley. The bowls she'd left out yesterday were empty, and she placed the new ones beside them. The scrawny mutt eagerly peered out from behind one of the trash bins as if it had been waiting there all night just for her arrival.

"Better eat and drink," Martha said. "It's gonna be another scorcher."

The mutt took a tentative step toward the bowls, and Martha took two steps back to give her some room. The dog gave her a mournful look, and Martha wondered if she would survive another day in this heat. The dog devoured the rice, then looked eager-eyed up at her, waiting for more.

Martha's chest tightened. She'd definitely need to change a lot of things in her life, and Dad might need more than a little convincing, but Martha made the decision instantly.

"I have more food inside," she said. "And we can get you out of this awful heat. Do you want to come in with me?"

A brief wag of her tail signaled she was at least open to the idea.

"C'mon," Martha said, beckoning the dog toward the alley door. "This way." She propped open the heavy steel door and stood at the threshold, waiting.

The dog nervously approached her and stopped when she reached the door. Martha held out her hand, palm up, toward the dog. She sniffed Martha's fingers, then gave her palm a single lick that tickled. Martha smiled and reached out to give the dog a friendly pat, when her watch beeped.

"You'll miss your appointment with City Health Services if you don't leave now," it said, and at its sound the dog startled and ran back into the alley.

"It's just my watch!" Martha shouted, quickly muting it "Don't be scared!"

The dog timidly peered out from behind a trash bin, unconvinced.

Martha's watch vibrated again in silent warning.

"It's my dad," Martha said. "I want to stay but . . . " She swallowed down a growing tightness in her throat. "I have to go do something for him. If I miss this appointment, I have to wait six months for another." The dog watched her, as if trying to comprehend. "I'm sorry," Martha said. "But I really have to go. Stay in the shade, will you? I'll get some real dog food for you today. Promise."

Martha slowly made her way toward the alley exit, and when she looked back, the dog was still watching her.

A rat darted into the alley, saw the dog, and skittered away.

"I'm sorry Ms. Reston," the city health clerk said to Martha from behind a thick plexiglass window, "but there's nothing more I can do."

Above the clerk's head, a screen read, "Now serving: D-403." To their left and right, a dozen other clerks were talking to more people, and behind Martha, a snaking queue of several hundred people waited impatiently inside rope-bordered aisles. Everyone looked as exhausted as Martha felt.

"Please," Martha said to the woman, "I've been waiting for four hours. There has to be something you can do."

"Like I said," the clerk said, without a trace of sympathy. "You father doesn't qualify for full-time care or a visiting nurse."

"But he has dementia!" Martha snapped, feeling her composure slipping. "And I work a full-time job. I took off today to come here. I'm not getting paid for today."

"You can call the city's health service hotline and—"

"I *did* call the hotline!" Martha said. "They told me to come *here*!"

"And I'm telling you that my system says your father doesn't qualify."

"Your *system* says that?"

"That's right."

"But who actually says that?"

"Excuse me?"

"*Who*?" Martha said. "*Who* actually says he doesn't qualify?"

"The *system* says that," the clerk said. "And I'm telling you."

"But you're just reading your screen," Martha said.

"That's right."

"So who decides what the system does and doesn't approve?"

"An algorithm makes the decision."

"You mean an AI," Martha said.

"That's right," said the clerk. "So there's no human bias."

Martha took a long, slow breath. "There's gotta be *someone* I can speak to."

"Yes," the clerk said, "the city's health service hotline. The number is—"

"Thanks," Martha said, stepping away. "Thanks for nothing."

A bell dinged and the sign above the clerk read, "Now serving: E-609."

Martha felt faint and really needed to eat something. She let her watch lead her to a bar-restaurant a few blocks from the health office. The place was sparsely filled with older clientele who swiped at their wrists or watched a conservative news feed on the big screen in the back. She sat at the bar and ordered a mock-meat burger, fries, and a beer. As the calories and alcohol entered her body, her rage softened.

The city AIs will deny services the first few times as a weed-out measure, she'd read on a forum for people taking care of sick parents. *If you keep trying, eventually you'll get what you need.*

But this was her third time visiting the health office, and she'd called their hotline at least fifty times. How much more begging did she have to do before they decided to help?

She sighed and thought about the dog. She was growing used to Martha, and if her watch hadn't gone off she would have even let Martha pet her. When she got home, she'd convince the dog to come inside with her. She couldn't really afford another mouth to feed, but maybe if she reported that dangerous bug and got her $162.14 bonus, it would help some. Dad might need more convincing, but Martha had read that some folks with dementia were soothed by having a dog.

What would she name her? Samantha? No, she once had a friend named Samantha. What about Bella? No, that didn't fit. The mutt was a survivor and needed a survivor's name. What about Circe? Circe was a badass goddess who poisoned her enemies and transformed them into beasts, powers Martha wished she had. She imagined bringing the dog to the park with her father, when it wasn't so hot, and playing fetch with a ball.

"Circe," she said, trying the name aloud. "Bring it here, Circe."

"Pardon?" the bartender said.

"Oh, nothing," Martha said, her cheeks growing hot. "Wait—is there a pet store nearby? I need to pick up some dog food."

"Yeah, on Seneca," the bartender said. "Make a right out the door, go two blocks up, then make a left. You'll see it."

"Thanks," Martha said.

She was about to ask for the check when her wrist chirped with a call from home. She tapped the answer button. On the small screen, her father thrashed about his bedroom. "I can't find it!" he screamed. "I can't find it!"

He was naked, and a dark stain ran down his leg.

"Where is it?" he screamed. "Where did it go?"

Her father hadn't called her. Weeks ago, she'd put a medical monitor on him and programmed it to contact her if his vitals reached a certain threshold. Right now his heart rate and blood pressure were through the roof.

"Dad!" she said to her screen. "Dad, I'm coming! I'm coming home!"

"Where is it?" he screamed. "*Where is it?*"

What should have been a forty minute ride took almost two hours. Her watch told her that because of construction she was better off taking an alternate subway and transferring to a bus. But the alternate subway had signal problems, and the bus route was so crowded she had to wait for three buses to come before there was room enough for her to board.

She tried calling her father a dozen times, but he didn't pick up. $PinkFox ads followed her the whole way, offering relief from stress with a new strain of soothing vape oil. Martha cursed each time the self-driving bus, ultracautious, stopped at a yellow light it could have easily gone through or to let another vehicle have the right of way. She had bitten her fingernails down to nubs by the time she walked in the door of her apartment.

"Dad?" she shouted. "Dad!"

Inside his bedroom, it looked as if a bomb had gone off. Papers, clothes, picture frames, and books had been tossed around the room. The TV and lamp lay on the floor, both shattered. Every drawer was open, and whatever had lain in them was now somewhere about the room.

She found him on the floor of the closet. The hangar rod had been pulled from the wall and lay across his soiled, naked body.

"Oh my god—Dad!" she said, running to him. "What the hell?"

"I can't find it!" he said, tears streaming down his face. "It's not here!"

"What?" she said, crouching beside him. "What are you looking for?"

He looked up at her, his eyes wet and bloodshot, as his lower lip quivered. "I . . . I don't know . . . "

"Oh, Dad," she said, taking him in her arms. He was filthy, but she didn't care. "Oh, Dad."

He wept and shivered, and Martha held him, until the sun began to set. Cleaning up the mess took hours, and some things, like the TV and lamp, would need replacing with money she didn't have.

By the time he had calmed enough to fall asleep, it was after midnight. And it was only now that she remembered Circe. "Fuck!" she said.

She darted out of the apartment and down into the alley.

"Circe?" she called to the blue-tinged shadows. "Circe, are you here?"

The air smelled of soured milk and decades of garbage. The only reply came from the straining air-conditioners above.

"If you come inside," she said. "I'll give you real dog food every day. And a soft doggie bed to sleep on. And a bath. You really need a bath."

She checked the time. She really had to get to bed if she wanted to get up for work tomorrow.

"Please," she said, slowly heading back to the door. "Please come back. I'm sorry I left today."

Overhead, a city drone buzzed past. Otherwise, the alley was silent.

As she walked the stairwell back up to her apartment, she had her watch order dog food with expedited delivery. It was obscenely expensive, but she didn't care.

"*Your purchase of dog food for circle has been confirmed,*" her watch replied.

"*Circe!*" she said. "Her name is Circe."

She was up early and showered quickly, but her stomach was too twisted into knots worrying about Circe to eat much. She prepared two bowls of oatmeal and water and headed downstairs.

It was hot in the alley, and the trash bins were already baking in the sun. Something was different here this morning, but she couldn't quite place it.

She put down the fresh bowls next to the empty others. "Circe?" she called. "Cir-ce?"

She waited, but the dog didn't come.

"Circe? C'mon, girl! I have food here!"

She stepped forward, searching behind the bins. Something was rotting in one, and the heat wasn't helping the smell. The smell grew stronger as she walked. Then she heard the flies.

She spotted a tail, a thin, fuzzy thing, peeking out from under one of the bins. "Circe?"

She crouched down to look. The dog lay still, as if sleeping. Beside her was a pile of vomit. Beside the vomit was a half-eaten rat. Flies swarmed.

Shaking now, Martha stood. This wasn't real. She and Circe and Dad would go to the park. Dad would grow calmer with Circe around. She would be his best friend.

Martha's gaze came to rest on a poster applied to the wall. It hadn't been here yesterday.

The City Health Department has detected a high level of vermin in this area. Rat poison has been automatically applied by aerial drones. Use caution with children or pets when entering this zone.

The same poster had been stuck every fifty feet along the wall.

Circe was hungry, and Martha hadn't fed her enough. So Circe ate a rat. But the rat had been poisoned. And so Circe had been poisoned too.

Martha crouched down again. The dead dog's eyes stared at her.

Something chittered down the alley. A dozen sanitation bots were working their way through the bins, carrying off trash almost too fast for her eyes to follow. When they reached Circe, they didn't pause. One scooped her up and carried her off, while two more scrubbed the ground clean. In seconds, it was as if Circe had never been.

Her watch chirped. *"If you don't leave now,"* it said, *"you'll be late for work."*

Mr. Hoffman was nineteen and lived alone in a huge high-rise apartment paid for by the proceeds he earned from doing in-mesh promos, Martha's work-order said. His couch sat by the window with impressive views of the city. But Mr. Hoffman hadn't left his couch—hadn't opened his eyes—in eighteen days. And like the dozens before him, Mr. Hoffman's service bot had failed. It was the same piece-of-shit Kazak network board, the same five-minute fix.

Martha stood before the window, staring out at the city. How many, she wondered, were meshing-in right this very moment?

Her watch beeped. *"Your order of dog food has just been delivered,"* it said.

She stared at the message for a moment before swiping it away.

On the service bot's console, she brought up the code repository. The dangerous software bug she had found a few weeks back stared at her like a dead dog's eyes. She activated the keyboard and made a small code change, then pushed it upstream. If the company AIs approved the change, at the next software update her code would be sent out to billions of mesh users. She'd get her $162.14 bug-finder's bonus, and her boss, Olembe, would pat her on the back.

And in a week, maybe two, the first of them would start to die.

She wondered if anyone would notice before then.

THE BRICKS OF GELECEK

WE WERE NOT city folk. We lived beyond all borders, where the onyx sands merged with raven skies, where the desert beasts came to die and even the hated demons of Fintas Miel dared not tread. Out here, the stars twirled in strange orbits, the sun weaved drunkenly by day, and the wind blew steady, slow, and forever. They called this place the Jeen. I called it home.

Always in fours we came to your cities. The sand blew us into flesh, and we walked like men through your iron gates and your tented marketplaces. Dust fell from our fingertips, our feet. The dust of decay, of eons, of ash. We touched your fruits and your doorposts. We patted the heads of your children and shook the calloused hands of your husbands. You smiled at us.

Within hours came the winds, the decay, the screams. Pits formed in the streets where we had stepped. Your statues rusted and blew away. Your houses fell to kindling. Your children vanished like whispers.

By dawn, there was nothing left but a hole in the earth. And those who had carried thoughts of this vanquished city and its people found a blank spot in their mind, a void where once there were men.

We did this for pleasure. And of our name? We had none.

For who remained to name us?

Sometimes I grew bored with the sundering of cities. Sometimes I wished to be away from my brothers and their boasts of desolation, so I wandered the desert under the drunken sun to entertain myself with the mysteries of the Jeen. The constant winds carried strange sounds on their wings: the dying whispers of aged widows, the murderous thoughts of jealous cuckolds, the suicide's cry of regret as the soul fled the body. The voices spoke of objects and forms, but always their true concerns were intangible things: regret, shame, love, despair, the gamut of human emotions. I listened eagerly, for the voices spoke of a world beyond my own, a world I could never touch without destroying it.

I floated over the twinkling sands, when I heard a small voice, like a flute echoing off a mountain. It cried out to the ineffable, "What am I?" And its sound was music, sweet and innocent, without rue for things come and gone or the dark cynicism heard often in men.

The sound danced above me in crimson wisps, like lingering campfire smoke. It zigged and zagged, hopped and paused, cat-like, across the desert. The song haunted me for some reason I could not fathom, so I pursued.

The sun skipped across the sky as I followed the music, until the Jeen was long behind me. A thousand camel skeletons and their unfortunate riders lay wasted on the sands below, and still the voice sang.

A large city crested the horizon. Birds squawked in monstrous flocks above its thousand spires, and towers hugged its center like beggars waiting for handouts. On the heels of the city, just before the sand devoured all, was a small house. The smoke belching from its chimney reeked of ram's bladder and hoof spice; a sin offering to the goddess Mollai.

A girl sat before the house and sang as she fumbled with

toy bricks:

"The desert makes no promises
She does not long abide
For those who seek to find her face
No semblance they can find.
The sun burns down from heaven's throne
Turning all to dust
And so I ask the Cosmos now
Of what use is rust?"

Her words had the resonant pluck of a zither. Then I understood. Her song had entwined itself in the smoke of the sin offering, and the winds had carried her plea out over the desert to my ears. And the words, they stirred something deep within me that I could not name.

"Hello," she said to me. "Have you lost your caravan? Are you thirsty?"

I had not intended to be seen. I had unwittingly collected myself into human form. "*No*," I howled like a sandstorm, trying to terrify her.

But she was unmoved by my words. "Who are you then?"

And I had the same question: who was this girl that stood firm before the winds of annihilation? "Who taught you that song?" I asked.

"That's mine," she said shyly. "I wrote it."

"*You* wrote it?" I said.

"Why? A girl can write song," she said firmly.

"Of course," I said, "But your song is. . . different."

Her brown eyes twinkled in the sunlight as she studied me. "Who are you? I can tell from your clothes that you're not Quog Bedu or Zwai Clan. And everyone knows you don't walk Gelecek's streets of glass and dung without shoes." She pointed to my bare feet.

I grew frustrated with her questions and reached out for her head. With one touch, she would fall to dust within hours and would trouble me with her words no more. But a heavy man waddled out of the house. He carried a large cleaver and his bare chest was covered in sweat and blood.

Instantly, I made myself as transparent as the sky.

"Come inside, Agna!" the man shouted. "Mollai is coming to bless our house!"

"Papa, we have a visitor!" she replied. "A stranger from the desert!"

"You can play with your toys later!" the man said.

The girl turned and saw I had vanished. She furrowed her brow and looked deeply disturbed. "But. . . he was just here!" she said.

A plump woman covered in offal shoved the man out of the doorway. She wiped bloody hands on her apron and thrust them to her hips. "Get inside now, Agna, or you'll wish you were never born!"

The girl stood quickly, scanned the desert for me once more, then ran inside.

No thing of form had ever seen me and lived, let alone begged answers of me! As the smoke fluttered from the chimney I comforted myself in the knowledge that one day my brothers and I would return to erase her city from existence.

I flew back to the Jeen in silence.

Years passed like dripping molasses, and I forgot about the singing girl. My brothers and I tread through the crystal kingdom of Aphelia, whose walls had stood for ten millennia, whose conquests were heralded in a thousand tongues. No one would remember its name.

We touched the port city of Mesach, built within the Pine Barrens beside the salty river Do. It disappeared as if it never were. We sundered Allia, Blömsnu, Cintak, Ektu El. Traders, on the way to a sundered city, would suddenly forget why they had ventured out into the harsh desert with overburdened camels. Cities vanished from minds too.

How many walls fell under our hands, I could not count. But always, ambitious men built new ones. They raised towers of stone and wrapped domes with hammered gold. They adorned palaces with jewels and paved streets with tar and glass. Caravans traveled across inhospitable wastes to deliver mortar, wheat and wine. After a time, a new city breathed under the stars as if it had existed for all eternity. I began to see these cities not as a thousand separate entities, but the organs of a much larger creature whose severed limbs always grew back.

One night, as I wandered the Jeen under the bright and nervous stars I heard the girl's song again:
"One seed planted may not grow
Two seeds planted in a row
Five seeds in my garden plot
Mollai bless they will not rot
One stone mortared may yet fall
Two stones, aye a trinity
But a thousand stones do make a wall
That stands unto infinity."
I followed her song across abyssal landscapes made grey by the pregnant moon until I came to her far-off house in the city of Gelecek. I saw movement in a window, and I crept up to it, conscious not to take human form or to touch her house, lest it fall to ashes.

Agna sat upright in bed. In the years since I had seen her, she had grown inches. Now she had the body of a young woman, though she still had the face of a girl. She leaned into the pallid moonlight as she scrawled on parchment. Her small voice hummed a few bars, then she crossed out a word and replaced it with another. She hummed again and the notes brought me back ages. I recalled cities I had conquered and forgotten: the star-shaped city of Gelf with its bejeweled ivory columns; the ziggurats of Phalantine and its perfumed gardens; Karad and its herds of black giraffes.

I had no words to describe the feelings her songs evoked in

me. I needed to listen until I understood what I felt.

"I thought I dreamt you all those years ago," she whispered. "But here you are." She was staring at me through the window frame.

I found myself in human form, though not by my own will. Her song had oddly drawn me into flesh. "You remember me?" I said.

"How could I forget? You vanished like smoke! And you smell like the deep desert," she said. "Like a spent campfire. Like ash. Who are you?"

"I have no name."

"But *what* are you?" Her eyes twinkled in the moonlight. "Are you a mancer? A demon?"

"I am dissolution. I am nothing."

"What do you want with me?"

"Your songs," I said. "They fill me with memories of forgotten places. They make me feel. . . I cannot describe it. Sing one again!" I demanded.

"*Agna?*" a voice grumbled. Wood groaned in the dark corners of the house. "What's that sound?"

"Leave!" she whispered to me. "Father has killed thieves before!"

"Please," I begged. "Sing another! Sing one now!"

"Agna!" a man bellowed. "If you're using one of my candles again, I swear, I'll beat you back to Kalagia!"

Agna mumbled a response, pretending to be asleep. Then, she whispered to me, "Go away! I don't know who you are, but don't come back!"

In the far corner, a sphere of light blossomed around a candle. In the lambent flicker frowned the sweaty face of her father. He stepped toward us, and I backed away from the window into darkness.

"Is this how you repay me for training you?" her father said. "I told you not to use the candles!"

"But, I didn't, Papa!" she said.

"Don't lie to me, Agna! I smell soot!"

"I swear, it wasn't me! There was a man! A stranger from the—"

He lifted a heavy belt from a chair and beat her with it. I watched from a distance and listened to the desert swallow her screams. When he had finished beating her, he said, "Go to sleep, Agna. You have to be up early for work. I expect you at Posterity Hill before first prayer."

As he blew out the candle, she whimpered her acknowledgement.

I wanted to hear her sing again, but this was not the place. Then I recalled her father's words, "Posterity Hill," a place of men, and in the darkness I had an idea.

I traveled to the wastes beyond the Jeen, where the white sands breathe in irregular tides. Deep within a mammoth cleft of stone, I begged the demon Atleiu to craft me a suit of human flesh. In return, I promised her the only thing I could: destruction. She agreed and proceeded to cut skin from one of her human slaves, tempering it with the hoarfrost of the north and the iron stones that fall from the sky.

Whereas before, anything I touched turned to dust within hours, now—while encased in Atleiu's suit—I could walk among men without destroying them. I could follow Agna anywhere she went. I could touch and be touched.

The sun was rising, hot and huge, in the east when I reached the first stone of Gelecek's streets. I worried that Atleiu's suit might fail. I took a tentative step with my sandaled foot onto stone. Always, when I decimated cities, I felt the ecstatic rush of annihilation. I sensed none of that now; the stone remained a stone.

"Posterity Hill?" I asked a bearded vendor, and he pointed with an arthritic hand deep into the city.

I weaved through a collection of low stone buildings.

Clothing and bedding swayed from lines strung above me. People hurried past with satchels tossed over backs or barrows thrust before them. I smelled uncooked animal flesh and human feces, but the air was also dense with smells of sandalwood, sage, and the sweet twinge of honey. As men and women bumped me, I felt impotent; they would remain to bump others tomorrow.

I reached a sign that read, "Posterity Hill. Future home of the Jarrifa Family." High walls were fashioned with polished stones that jutted from the façade like giant thumbs, the work of a skilled hand.

"This is private property," a shirtless boy said.

I ignored him and climbed to the top of the sloping road as he followed me. Young masons labored within a large stone foundation, scooping mortar and laying stones with advanced skill. From this plateau I glimpsed the full city. To my left, a hag's spine of roads twisted into the desert. To my right, spires rose like candles into the sky.

"Did you hear me, *feg*?" the boy said, behind me. "This is private property!"

"There's no such thing," I said. But before he could scold me again, I descended the hill. I searched the base of the foundation until I found a corner where I could watch the workers without being seen, and there I waited for Agna.

Her father stepped out of a pavilion and walked around the foundation, admonishing the boys for apparent flaws that neither the boys, nor I saw. One of the boys whispered to him and pointed at me.

"Who the *frib* are you?" Agna's father said as he stepped up to the wall and looked down at me, his foot resting on a stone above my head.

I stood from my hiding place. "Is your daughter here?"

"What do you want with her?"

"Is she here?"

He leaped down to my level, and the ground shook with his

weight. "Did you hear me?" he said. "What do you want with her?"

"You would not understand," I said. "It is beyond you."

"You freak!" he said as his fist slammed into my face. I fell onto my back. He kicked me, and I raised my hand to block the blows. With his next kick, Atleiu's flesh suit tore at the index finger. When he tried to kick me again, I stuck out my hand, and his leg scraped my unprotected finger.

He gasped, while the ecstasy of nothingness coursed through me.

"What's wrong with him?" the boys said. "Is he having a heart attack?"

Agna's father bent over, holding his stomach. Then he stood, looked at me nervously, and said, "You stay the *frib* away from my daughter or I'll kill you." I watched him walk up the hill and vanish. Some of the boys chuckled and kicked pebbles at me until he ordered them back to work. In the distance, Agna watched me until her father ordered her back to work, too.

Carefully, I wrapped my torn finger back into place.

I circled the streets until I found a better hiding spot. On the opposite side of the foundation, three small walls obscured me completely from view, but a tiny slit allowed me to see out. The sun beat down on the boys as they worked, and Agna, to my joy, worked alongside them. Though she was the only girl among three dozen boys, they gave her no special treatment. She spread mortar and hefted heavy stones without help; she chiseled with practiced skill. But I noticed in her craft an attention to detail that the boys lacked. Every stone held her full consciousness. Every rap of her hammer carried the weight of eons.

And she sang while she worked.

Oh, what sweet music! The boys sang with her; they mixed mortar by verse, carried stones by stanza, and finished walls by song, so that their labors resembled a dance more than a burden.

I knew the power of her song now and let it consume me. I reveled in forgotten vistas. Geysers from the oasis city of Sul erupted in my mind. The mirrored walls of Nier El Du blinded my dreams. The gargantuan city of Poc, carved from a single piece of stone, crushed me under its weight. I thought, for a moment, that this feeling might be greater than the bliss of annihilation.

"You!" Agna said.

I woke from my visions to see her peering down at me from the foundation wall. She threw her hands to her hips and frowned, and I recognized her mother in the gesture.

She sniffed the air. "I thought I smelled ash," she said.

"Your songs, they are. . . *beautiful*, yes, that's the word," I said.

She glanced over her shoulder. "I was wondering who it was that Father beat this morning."

"Now he has beaten us both," I said. "We are kindred. By dawn, he will—"

"Kin? Hardly. You'd better leave, whoever you are. He'll kill you. Don't be stupid."

"Tell me, Agna," I said, "Do your songs carry you to forgotten places? Do you have visions of dead cities?"

"What?" she said. She stepped back from the wall, mouth agape. "How do you know—"

"Agna?" her father shouted from behind her. "Who are you talking too? Is that *feg* here again?"

She stared at me. Then she shook her head and said, "Go away. Go away..." But her words were insubstantial, like a desert cloud.

"Meet me at the bottom of the hill," I said.

She disappeared behind the wall, and I knew she was mine now.

At the bottom of Posterity Hill, shadows crept across the ground as the sun turned overhead. Just after high-noon, Agna's small figure appeared at the top of the hill and scampered down to meet me.

"How do you know about my visions?" she demanded. "Did Mother tell you? Damn her!"

"No. I see them when you sing."

"You said they're 'dead' cities. What did you mean by that?"

"They have been forgotten. Erased. Yet your song rekindles their memories."

Agna's father appeared at the top of the hill surrounded by three boys.

"Let's go!" she said. "Before Father sees us!"

We turned through the busy streets. The air smelled of cracked spelt, boiling beans, and the pungent reek of humans going about their business. Slaughtered animals cried out and fell silent. She led me into a courtyard filled with date palms and speckled shade.

"They're not dead cities," she said. "They haven't been born yet."

"No, they're very dead. But your songs give them new life."

She frowned. "I've tried to tell Father about them. To let him know that there's more to my songs than just music and words. But he won't have an ounce of it. He says a woman needs a stable trade as much as any man, that my poems and music will only get me to a street corner, begging for change."

"He's wrong. I watched the boys sing with you. They work twice as hard under your spell."

"Do you think so? Father works us all so hard. A song makes the day go by a little faster." Her eyes filled with water. "The Prefect plans to hire Father as his chief mason. When Father gets that job, I'll be able to design buildings myself. I won't have to take orders from him anymore. And when I turn sixteen, Father promised to give his business to me. Says his back's no good anymore. I'll be free to create whatever I wish. I have dreams, things I want to build."

I remembered that I had touched her father, that he would vanish from existence before dawn. "Your mother has a well-paying trade, though?" I said.

"Well-paying? She's a seamstress in the textile guild. The pay is the only thing worse than the work. She doesn't want me to follow in her footsteps, but I love working with thread too. I often help her with embroidery. It's wonderful. You can't get the same precision with stone, not if you want to finish within this century." She stared at her calloused fingers.

"And all through this has been your music."

"It's been a kind of marching song, ever since I was a girl."

"Will you sing me one now?"

"Right here? Right now?"

"Yes!"

"This is silly. I don't even know you."

"There is nothing to know."

She shook her head. "Well," she said. "Maybe just the one. You did get a beating, after all, just to hear one." Then she began:

"By dawn, the sun, low on our backs

"Is cool, while birds are singing.

"By noon, the mortar's showing cracks,

"And masons' ears are ringing.

"But come a week, a month a year,

"When chanced upon this hill,

"Where father's eye had built a house,

"That stands upon there still,

"I forget the sweat, the grime,

"The shoveling of sand,

"And fill my heart with future dreams,

"To build one by my hand."

Vistas of dead cities assaulted my consciousness. But this time, there were new places, cities I had not glimpsed before. Cities of glass. Cities in the sky. Even cities floating among the stars. Perhaps, as she had suggested, not all of these kingdoms were dead; some had yet to be created. I closed my eyes and savored the sweetness of them all.

"Who are you?" she said.

"Does it matter, my name?"

"Yes, it does. A man's name is his being, his essence."

"All the more reason why I have none."

"I don't understand," she said. "You come to me, begging to hear my songs, but I know nothing of you. Where are you from? What do you do? How is it that you have come to me?"

Agna's father burst into the courtyard, surrounded by a dozen boys. They carried chisels and hammers and walked briskly in my direction.

"Agna!" her father shouted. "Stand back!" He smacked the head of a hammer into his palm. "You're dead, stranger, do you hear me?"

I backed away. They could not hurt my true essence, of course, but they could destroy my suit. I needed it to last, for Atleiu was a fickle demon and would not craft me another one for eons.

"Who are you?" she said to her father. "And what do you want with us?"

"What?" her father shouted. "Has he drugged you? You're safe now, baby! Daddy's here!"

"Who?" she said. She looked like she was going to be sick. "I don't feel right. Something's wrong."

But I had to leave. I fled the courtyard through the rear gate, and the boys pursued. I ran through crowded streets, hiding behind bales of tobacco and under piles of manure. When I was certain I had lost them, I headed back to my brothers in the Jeen. I was not troubled. By morning, her father and his rabble would be gone.

"We have followed you," my brother said to me that evening in the Jeen, as the bright stars oppressed above us. "You entered a city in the guise of a man and walked among its people, touching them. This night, their walls hold firm. The winds are calm, and their children do not scream. Tell us why, brother, you've broken our trust?"

I dared not reveal Agna's power to enthrall with her song, lest they try to usurp her for their own. But I could not deny what they had witnessed. "We have no rules," I said. "Nor laws preventing me from doing what I have done. I followed my will."

"But you are a thing of destruction," my brother said. "That is your nature. What do you seek in the world of form?"

"Sometimes, in the winds of the Jeen, I hear whispers of human things. Have you never been curious to know what they are?"

"Sometimes, yes. But if I satisfy my curiosity, what purpose does it serve? The curiosity vanishes. One day, the thing which piqued my interest will vanish too. All is impermanent."

"Then so, too, is my interest in this city," I said. "It will vanish. Your concern will vanish too."

"As all things do. But now, our brothers need to know: what is it that draws you there, in the morning sun, to walk among them without destruction?"

I paused before answering. "Of all the cities we sundered, brother," I said, "how many do you remember?"

"Not many," he said.

"None?" I said.

He paused. "Perhaps."

"I go to that city, dear brother, to remember."

"But why? Nothing is worth remembering. Memories, like cities, fade."

I felt pain when I realized that one day Agna would vanish from the earth. "What are we then, without our memories?"

"We are nothing, brother. We have and will always be nothing. You may convince yourself, for a time, that you are more, but it is only self-deception."

And with these words, my brother left me.

In the winds of the Jeen, I heard a laugh.

I searched the desert six times to make sure I was in the right place. Yes, this was the spot of sand where Gelecek had once stood. Like a drying oasis, the city's circumference had shrunken inward. Its walls were devoid of grandeur. A few leaning towers thrust into a cloudless sky, and scattered buildings spotted an uninspiring landscape.

And Agna's house was gone.

I entered the city and hunted for her within its changed streets. "Where am I?" I asked its residents.

"This is Gelecek," they responded forlornly, as if the city's name itself was a curse.

"There was a foundation," I said to an elderly woman mashing chick-peas. "On Posterity Hill. Do you know it?"

She shook her head. "Never heard of it."

Of course, I thought. I had destroyed the mason who had created it.

"There is a girl," I said. "Agna, daughter of a seamstress. Have you heard of her?"

The old woman squinted rheumy eyes at me. "Nay, but there's the seamstress guild up on Trajen Row. Why don't you bother them?"

I lost my way several times but eventually found Trajen Row, a cobbled dead-end street, with hundreds of dyed linens drying from hemp lines like standards. The air reeked of chemicals, and colored puddles filled the cracks between stones. Inside cramped buildings, hundreds of seamstresses stuck needles into cloth, combed lamb's wool, or threaded looms. I found Agna's mother working in a corner, her needlework tiny feats of prestidigitation.

She looked much thinner than I remembered, and her face was wrinkled and bitter.

"I'm looking for Agna," I said. "Where is she?"

"Who the *frib* are you?" she said without looking up.

"I'm a friend. I was supposed to meet her today."

"I don't know who you're talking about."

"Agna, your daughter."

She stopped her stitching and looked up at me. "Is this a joke? Did the girls put you up to this?"

"No Please! Where is she?"

She started to cry. "You're cruel. Go away."

"This is not a joke. I'm not here for anyone but myself. I am seeking your daughter to…" After my last incident with her father, I tempered my words ". . . to protect her from a great evil."

She began her needlework again, then said to the sky: "Mollai, great maker, why do you torment me so?" Then she said to me, "I don't know who you are stranger, but your words sting. I never had a husband or a daughter, nor do I know this Agna you speak of. Now, leave me."

I backed away as the shock of her words consumed me. Always, when I destroyed cities, my destruction was total, complete. I had never been selective in annihilation before. It had never occurred to me that erasing her father would erase Agna, too. An alien feeling welled up inside me as I stepped out into the sun. It was—there was only one word for it: loss. A thousand linens snapped angrily in the wind. I walked the streets in a daze. I don't know how long I wandered before I heard a voice.

A beautiful voice. It sang.

I followed the song around a corner, into an alley overgrown with weeds. A cat hissed at me and ran away. The voice came from a doorless building, and I crept inside. Half-finished canvases crowded a large studio, and the air was heavy with the reek of paint. Majestic cities adorned the canvases; some I recognized as cities I had sundered.

At the far end of the studio, a young woman danced her

brush over a canvas while she sang:

"On the dark side of morn, the workers lie waiting.

"Sunrise to sunset, their backs break in toil.

"From out of the desert, are caravans sweating

"Burdened with legumes, rich hemp seed and oil."

"Agna! I shouted. "You're alive!"

The girl turned to me, but her face was not Agna's. Her eyes were too green, her nose too button-like, her face too round Not Agna, but a stranger.

Startled, she said, "Who are you?"

But her voice—that *was* Agna's. "You won't remember me," I said.

She dropped her brush. "No! I've dreamt of you! Sometimes, I dream that I lived another life, with different parents, in a different house. I was a builder of cities and a weaver of thread. Then a ghost came along and erased everything. I thought it was just a recurring nightmare. But that ghost had your face."

"I'm sorry, Agna. I didn't know."

"Agna? That's the name my dream parents called me. My name is Dina."

"It's a beautiful name," I said, stepping closer.

"Stay away from me!" she said.

"I'm not here to hurt you, Dina. I only came to hear you sing."

"Why?"

I pointed to her paintings. "These cities, why do you paint them?"

"The architects buy them. They tell me my drawings inspire them."

"But why do *you* paint them?"

"I don't know. . . they come to me. . ."

"In vision, when you sing."

"How do you know that?" she said. "Who. . . what are you?"

"I am the no thing of the deserts beyond form and the sunderer of civilization. I and my brothers have destroyed these cities. I had forgotten them all. But your songs bring them back to me. I have the very same question for you, Dina. What are you?"

She looked sick. "It was real, wasn't it? My other life. There were too many details, too many feelings. I had a difficult life, yes, but I had dreams and aspirations. And you destroyed all of that, didn't you?"

"But you're not dead. Don't you see?" I said. "I couldn't erase *you* from history. You spring back like the cities I and my brothers sunder."

"You're disgusting," she said. "You destroy as easily as I create."

"Perhaps, but for once in my life I want something else."

The winds gusted outside, knocking over a few canvases. I heard the rasp of sand blowing against stone, and a familiar shudder of ecstasy coursed through me.

"A sandstorm," she said. "I have to close the windows."

"No," I said to her as I stepped out into the sun. I knew him before he spoke, not by the way he walked, nor by the tailor of his clothes, but by his indifference towards all things. He gave a beggar a coin and patted him on the shoulder. He dragged his hands along the walls of a portico. He stepped up to me and paused. Every move was filled with emptiness.

"Hello, brother," he said.

"What are you doing here?" I demanded.

"I could ask the same of you. What business have you here in this flesh suit of yours?"

"You must leave!" I said. "Before you destroy this place."

"It's too late," he said. "Our brothers have decided that your sojourn here shall end. We followed you to this city. Four of us walk inside these walls now, spreading oblivion. We love you, brother, and when this city falls, you will return to us and be the soul we remember."

"I don't want to go back! Not yet! Please, listen to one of her songs! Look at her paintings! Then you'll understand why

I'm here!"

"There's nothing to understand. There's nothing at all. That's the sole and final truth." My brother smiled and fled the alley, patting a boy on his head as he turned the corner.

"Agna—*Dina*, come on! We have to go!" I shouted. I re-entered the studio. But Dina had vanished.

"Dina! Where are you?"

I found a small door in the back. It led up a small, curving stairwell to a storeroom on the second floor. When I opened the door, Dina jumped out and stabbed me in the chest with a putty knife.

I pushed her away and pulled out the knife from my chest. There was no blood. When I dropped it to the floor, the blade shattered.

She pounded on me with her fists. "Go away! Go away!"

"Dina, Dina! Please, you must listen to me! My brothers are destroying this city as we speak. We have to go now, or you'll be killed!"

"Get away from me! I'd rather die!"

I grabbed her. She was small and easy to contain. I lifted her over my shoulder, and she beat me as I carried her down the stairs, through the studio, and out onto the streets.

She screamed for help. So I gagged and tied her with sack-cloth.

I took the back alleys and least crowded streets and fled the city as quickly as possible, making sure not to touch anything. She cried, but her voice was muffled by her gag.

"I know you think I'm cruel," I said. "But I do this for your own good. I've figured it out, Dina. I know what you are. Whereas I am the sunderer of cities, you are their genesis. Your songs, your visions, your dreams, they are the impetus which create new ones. I destroy cities with my touch. You create them with your song. We are kindred. If you die, then in a way, so do I."

I found a black horse tied up beside a tent on the outskirts of the city and stole it before its owner could stop us. I spread Dina before me, and we rode deep into the desert. After several hours, she stopped struggling, so I took off her gag.

"Water…" she mumbled.

I found a canteen slung around the horse and gave it to her.

After drinking several large gulps, she said, "I have parents, friends, my paintings. Will they all vanish?"

"I'm sorry. But you can create new ones."

"Do you think it's that easy, that I can just start over in a new city, as if nothing at all has happened? Everything I know is going to die."

The horse grew tired as the sun set behind a dune, so I dismounted. I untied her hands as the stars winked to life above us.

"If you flee," I said, "by the time you get back to your city, it will be dust. No one will remember it, not even you."

"Won't I vanish too?" she said. "I was born in that city."

"I erased your father. It changed you, but you were born again as someone else. I think you are a seed that can't be destroyed."

"Then why bring me all the way out here?"

I looked at her and realized that I didn't have an answer.

"When I was six, my mother bought me my first paint set. My father took me to the top of Jimn Mountain when I was nine. I remember the first time I kissed a boy. I remember breaking my arm when I tried to scale Dell Wall. All of that will be erased, won't it?"

"But you will rebuild it somewhere else, in some other time."

"You don't get it! Humans are not like a wall, where the bricks of our experiences are interchangeable. Each instant is precious, unique. You rob the universe of the sacred. Can't you see that?"

"I. . . I have known nothing else," I said. "Until I met you."

"Is that consolation for ruining my life, that the ghost of

annihilation has second thoughts?"

"I didn't mean to hurt you."

"But you have."

"This wasn't supposed to happen."

"What wasn't?" she said slowly.

"The destruction of your city."

"What city?"

"Gelecek."

"What a beautiful name," she said. "Where is it? And who are you? How did I get here?"

I sighed and had to look away.

"I feel funny," she said. "As if. . . I'm not supposed to be here. My body feels. . . light. Like air. What's your name?"

"My name?" I said. "My name is. . . destruction."

When I looked for her again there was only sand. The girl, the horse, everything was gone, even my suit of flesh. I cried out to the stars, but they did not respond.

I did not move from that spot. My brothers came to me on the sand. They said, "Come back to the Jeen with us, brother, for you have no reason to dwell among form now."

And I said, "Leave me."

The sun rose and set a hundred times, and my brothers came to me again and again. "Please," they begged, "It's not proper that you be apart from us. Come and obliterate a city with us and feel your old self again."

But how could I? In each city might dwell the spark of Agna or Dina or her kin. I could not bear to erase her from existence again.

"Go away," I told my brothers, and they did.

I sat there in the same spot of the sand where Dina had disappeared, while the sun turned in slow orbits overhead. I felt like a top, spinning, spinning, but never slowing.

The stars and sun turned through slow eons, and still I did

not move, when a dark cloud appeared in the sky one silent afternoon. Once in a hundred years, it rained in the desert; today it poured down in great sheets. The sky grew as dark as the gloaming, and the sands turned to mud. Forks of light split the sky in dreadful thunder.

I collected myself into human form, gave myself strong arms and hands, and began to mold the wet sand into a brick. The pounding rain seemed to shout Agna's songs across the desert, and to its tune I crafted another brick, and then another, fashioning them into a rudimentary wall. I knew it was temporary. I knew that tomorrow, when the sun rose hot and burdensome above the sands, my wall would grow weak. The desert winds would topple it in time, that all was, essentially, nothing. But heaven help me, I couldn't stop.

DEMON IN AISLE 6

I FIRST SAW the demon the Sunday after you died. It was 11:53 p.m. Just seven minutes until I would have grabbed my knapsack and biked home to Mom and bed and a life of sound sleep. That night the flurries were drifting down like nuclear ash. Most folks had fled for warmer places, but a few shopper-zombies still wandered SuperMart's bright aisles, seeking redemption in the form of deep discounts. I was wheeling a mop and bucket down to Aisle 17, where a crate of cherry soda had fallen from the shelf and sent high-fructose fizz all over the concrete floor. When I passed Aisle 6, the demon looked up at me.

I felt as if a swarm of moths had hatched in my belly and were wriggling out of their cocoons to feast on my organs, as if someone's hand had clutched my heart and squeezed. It hurt so much I gagged, because there he stood, this giant ball of brown afterbirth, eight feet tall, hunched and crooked, one eye white and huge, like the moon on the night you died, the other this black drop of oil, a black hole sucking up all light. He was a pinwheel of jagged teeth and claws and bones, like some aborted dinosaur fetus.

And I didn't want to look. I was too afraid. But there he

was, more *there* than anything I'd ever seen. And he stared at me, this nightmare fetus, eating candy. Shredded bags of Skittles and Starbursts and Tootsie Rolls lay over the floor like confetti after a parade. A strip of orange plastic hung from his disjointed mouth. I couldn't take it anymore, so I ran.

I shoved the bucket down to Aisle 17 and mopped up the sticky black puddle and pretended I'd never seen him, hoping he would go away and never come back. But that was stupid, because he made sure to keep coming back until I understood he was as real to me as you once were.

I still have that selfie you took at Onderdonk Lake as the background pic on my phone. It hurts like hell every time I check the time or take a call, but it hurts even more when I think of removing it. It makes me remember your smile. Your big, pouty, red lips. Your huge front teeth. My little Freddy Mercury.

Do you remember when we first met, outside school? It was the end of lunch period, and all the kids waited by the doors for the bell. I was talking to Deb and Jen, my new BFFs, puffing a smoke, trying real hard to make more friends, because to everyone else I was that weird transfer kid from New York who pronounced "coffee" with a "W," who dressed all in black like some "Goth heathen," who had to be shunned because he came from that place with too many "tree-hugging liberal faggots."

I only knew you as this shy boy who sat in the back of my physics class and made everyone look stupid with your perfect grades. I told this dumb joke, and I heard this enormous laugh, as if the whole world was shuddering with joy. I turned, and I saw you smile, and this sugary-sweet feeling filled my heart, like my chest had become a giant balloon and I was floating way up above all the bullshit of the world, and all that was left was you, me and endless blue skies.

You asked me for a smoke.

I said, "I'm Lucas," and shook your warm, soft-but-firm hand.

"Davis," you said, your eyes watering from the smoke locked hard to mine.

Later, you told me you'd never smoked before, that you'd puked in the bathroom halfway through English class. We laughed a lot about that. We laughed about a lot of things. And when you died, I thought I'd never hear you laugh again.

Now? I'm not so sure.

The nightmares came like freight trains, loud and huge and terrifying. I'd wake up screaming, shivering, with memories of vague, bloody shapes, limbs and teeth and bones all mixed together in a monster smoothie. Once I dreamed of you standing outside my bedroom door, your body open to me like those cutaway slices of earth in our physics textbooks. You stared at me, and I wanted to say something, maybe goodbye or hello or just anything, but you turned and walked away.

I woke gasping. I wondered what you were trying to say, if you had wanted me to follow you. And, yeah, I considered following you many times. How could I not?

I tried to convince myself I'd hallucinated the demon, but he was more full of life than all those shopper-zombies wandering SuperMart's bright aisles. I avoided Aisle 6 as much as possible, afraid he'd come back. But he did. He had to.

It was Tuesday, 11:47 p.m. I was tired and wanted to go home. Your Freddy Mercury smile stared up at me when I checked the time on my phone. I was restocking Aisle 7. I didn't want to be so close to 6, but my boss had noticed that the shelves near 6 were getting sparse and sent me on a mission.

I worked as fast as I could, but after twenty minutes I decided my fears were stupid. I had to stop being a baby. I peeked into Aisle 6, where this toddler sat in a big red shopping cart, kicking his legs, while his mom rifled through huge bags of M&Ms.

And as I look into the aisle, the kid says, "I don't like him, mommy." And the mom says, "Be nice, Mikey. He's just doing his job." But then the kid says, "No, not *him*, mommy. I don't like *that one*." He points over her shoulder to the end of the aisle, where the shadows fall all wrong, as if the light got lost and confused before it hit the ground. The mother has her back to this, but I see it clearly.

The kid starts howling, and the hairs on the back of my neck rise as the demon lopes into view like he is stepping through an invisible door.

He's all white and glistening, with a new crooked head and a mouth like a blowfish. Thousands of long, sharp teeth, and a honeycomb of cow's eyes, all dark and black and huge. All gazing at me. And, yeah, he's different this time, but I know he's the same demon because the same colony of termites are eating my intestines, the same firm hand is wringing my heart.

The mother doesn't dare look where the kid is pointing. But she must see the terror in my face, because she says, "Por favor, espíritu, leave us be! We're shopping for his birthday!" She crosses herself and shoves her kid and cart toward checkout like she's racing the Iditarod.

But me, I can't move. I'm frozen with dread as the demon lopes over to the shelves and tears open a bag of Tootsie Rolls with his teeth. He swallows them whole, wrappers and all, while his lips smack wetly together. Gobs of black saliva drip to the floor and make these weird rainbows in the fluorescent lights.

I feel a touch on my arm and I scream. But it's just this long-bearded dude that smells like cigarettes and bourbon. And when I look back, the demon is gone, but he's left the shredded wrappers behind.

The dude says, "Sorry to startle you, man. Coffee filters? Which aisle?"

I asked you to tutor me, but I think you knew I was after more than grades. Mom works two jobs and I need to work six nights just so we can starve more efficiently. It's been like this since Fuckface left us for sexier pastures. Mom's almost never home, so I knew you and I would be alone for hours.

We did physics problems. Motion, energy, momentum. I got frustrated, and we stepped out into a gray and rainy autumn day that made me want to wear wool sweaters and drink soup and nap all afternoon until the sun set too soon. The leaves had just turned this luscious gold, and when I mentioned their color you said, "The leaves don't actually change color. They're always golden, or orange, or red, but their colors are hidden under the green of chlorophyll. It's only when the chlorophyll breaks down in the fall that their natural color emerges."

And I said, "Just like people. You only see their true colors when their defenses break down."

And you said, "Yeah, but people's true colors aren't always beautiful."

And that's when I knew you and I were each half of a greater being yet to form.

We shared a cigarette. By then you smoked like Louis Jourdan, every puff an erotic display. Grace and angst danced blissfully across the micro-expressions of your face. I wanted you so badly I shuddered. You told me about your favorite books. *To Say Nothing of the Dog* and *The Road* and a writer named James Tiptree, Jr. who was really a woman. You got excited about this TV show where this closeted doctor in a religious English town hid his desires for fear he might lose his thriving business if his patients knew he was gay.

The conversation had to go this way, toward sex, toward desire, in the same way that water has to flow downhill to merge with other streams until it forms a gushing river. Hunger burned in your eyes as you gazed at me. Ancient glaciers melted in my body, flooding me with heat. I wanted to connect your universe to mine so together we could birth galaxies.

But the water hit a dam, pooled, and stopped. You turned the conversation to your dad, a detective. He worked late nights, and you told me how he'd come home drunk and break things, and every now and then he'd try to break you.

My heart broke a little too. I told you to report him, because fuckers like him deserved to die, but you said you thought it would only make things worse. Without your dad, you had no one. Your mom died from breast cancer when you were six.

And I said, "God, Davis, that must've been so hard to lose her so young."

And you said, "No, I haven't lost her. Life is energy, and energy can't be destroyed. I don't believe in death, Lucas. Mom's not gone. She's just traveling."

Words more beautiful had never been spoken. I leaned in, and you didn't stop me. Your hot tongue tasted like cigarettes, and all the pain I had been carrying, the anger about my dad leaving us to fend for ourselves, my frustration at all these ignorant kids in this podunk town who had no room in their cliques for a gay freak like me—all of that melted away into the flood of warmth radiating from my heart. I was a new star, blazing. Life had brought me to this moment, and therefore life was beautiful.

It was the first time you'd kissed a boy. It was the first time you'd kissed anyone. I'd kissed plenty of boys back in New York. In my public school in Manhattan, kids had two moms, or two dads, or a black dad and a white mom, or a white dad and an Asian mom, or a Jewish mom and a Buddhist dad, or a Muslim dad and a Christian mom, or no mom, or no dad, or no parents at all, and it was all one beautiful, glorious, dancing spectrum of color, and no one cared, because that's just how it was.

But here in podunkville, if a boy dares want another boy, you're Satan's spawn, or a pedophile, or you sweat AIDS and exhale sin, and I'd absorbed all these disgusting worlds of hate in the three months that I'd lived here, in overheard snatches of conversations, in people's hard expressions and uncomfortable sighs, or more overt revelations shouted in the halls. But I kissed you anyway.

"You're shivering, Davis," I said.

And you said, "I feel like a leaf, stripped of my outer covering."

And I said, "And your true colors are beautiful."

When SuperMart's security guard went on one of his epic-long breaks, I snuck into his office and cued up the surveillance tapes. I needed to know if I was losing my mind, or if my demon was real. Maybe I'd see him, but I'd settle for hovering bags of candy, unnatural shadows, or really any damned scrap of evidence proving that I'd seen someone swallowing massive doses of high-fructose corn syrup in Aisle 6.

It took some time to find the right tape. I cued it up, and there I stood on the blurry screen, this horrific blank stare on my face, jaw open, arms at my side, like some tranced kid at a stage hypnotist show, frozen by a magic word. There was no one else in the aisle with me.

Eventually this blank-eyed figure walks over to the shelves and opens a bag of Starbursts with his teeth. After I'd watched myself shove a third handful of still-wrapped candy into my mouth, I stopped the tape.

I'm pretty sure Mom knew I was gay for years, but I told her on the drive from New York just to be sure. Eyes fixed on the road, she barely nodded, as if I were telling her my shoe size was 10 or that I had brown eyes. But after, I sensed that she was happy to know how different I was from Fuckface, that I'd never destroy a woman like he destroyed her. But I'm not so different from Fuckface after all. It's just that my targets are a different gender.

You came over every day after school, and the tutoring

quickly stopped. Or at least you stopped teaching me physics and I taught you how to kiss, where to touch, when to be gentle, and when to be rough. But that first time we curled up in my bed, our bodies pressed together like two clinging atoms, you needed no instruction.

I felt as if we were wrapped in a warm blanket that would enclose us forever. We held each other and stared up at the glow-in-the-dark stars on my ceiling. But after, your thoughts turned to your dad. You told me he'd shot some unarmed kid, that he was on paid suspension, that his drinking had gotten worse, and that he'd smashed your laptop. I noticed the bruises on your chest.

I'd never hated a person more than I hated your dad then. Not even Fuckface had induced such rage in me.

But you talked me down, turned the conversation to your mom, how much you missed her, how you regretted never getting to know her, not having her around. You curled up in my arms and cried, and I held you until you fell asleep.

No one had ever opened up to me like this, and I savored my role as consoler. It gave me purpose. When you awoke, we talked about moving to Copenhagen or Berlin, starting a new life someplace where people didn't give a damn who or how you loved.

We walked a lot through the streets after school, passing quiet houses, kicking up leaves, holding hands. You picked up a small stone and told me how its matter was formed in the heart of dying stars, that everything in the world was formed when ancient stars exploded. I loved that, both of us, cosmic debris. Your hot breath misted the air as you handed me the stone.

"Here," you said, "have a little star."

I'd put it in my pocket, held onto it like it was gold.

You read me your favorite sections of books and a short story you'd written about a blind boy who wanted to be a pilot, and it was beautiful and brave and heartbreaking. You said you wanted to be a writer someday, or a scientist, or both.

We were walking home under a majestic spray of stars, and I was in awe, because we never had skies like these in Manhattan. You pointed out Orion and Sirius, bright in the east. Your house was this small, crooked thing, the lawn overgrown, junk piled on the side, weeds everywhere, and I fell in love with it instantly, because this was the place that had formed you. But you wouldn't allow me in.

"My dad," you said, "he won't like you. He doesn't like anyone, really."

But I pushed and prodded, because I wouldn't let this alcoholic child-abuser stop me from visiting the home of the boy I loved, and after a time you relented, but not before you made me swear I wouldn't say a word.

Your dad sat on the couch. The TV was on and a Marlboro burned in the ashtray. Snickers wrappers littered the table. He looked at both of us, back and forth, in that probing way that only cops can do. I tried to hold his gaze, because I wanted to let him know I knew the monster he was, that he didn't scare me. But I shivered and looked away. I'd expected this buff, hard-jawed, mountain of a man, but instead there sat this pathetic hunched and balding creature drunk and disheveled on the couch, and I almost felt sorry for him. Almost.

He turned back to the TV, told you to take out the trash, slurring his words.

My heart pounded as you led me away. Your room was small, with bright red walls, and posters of the periodic table, the Sombrero galaxy, Nikola Tesla and Neils Bohr. You organized your books by color, and it was adorable. But the room had a faint odor of sadness, as if I could smell a decade of tears.

"Well," you said. "Here we are."

I went to kiss you. But you stopped me. "Not here," you said. "Never here."

And I said, "Why do you let that shitbag control your life?"

And you said, "Stop, Lucas. Please."

But I knew just how to touch you, what words to whisper in your ear to stir your desire. Soon I had you panting, my hands wrapped around your erection. Later, you told me you'd never come so hard.

After I'd seen the security video, I thought I was going crazy. But I went on mopping up shattered pickle jars and toddler vomit, working the register, smoking by the dumpsters like I always had, trying my best to forget.

It was Thursday, 11:39 p.m. It had been raining all day. A blanket of fast-moving clouds hung low over the parking lot, reflecting the orange streetlights into absurdist paintings across the sky. I hadn't slept more than two hours the night before and hadn't eaten all day. I had finally become a shopper-zombie, flitting through the world from one aisle to another without reason or purpose.

Cold red light smacked the side of my face, and I gasped when I realized I had wandered into Aisle 6. Shadows leaped over the candy as if swarms of birds spiraled beneath the high fluorescent lights. And in the far corner, like a jagged oval mirror, hovered a crack in the world.

On the other side a flat and brown and utterly barren landscape spread under a bleak sky. Here and there, twisted metal shapes spiked up from the ground, like half-buried debris from an ancient civilization.

A dim red sun glowed behind black clouds, and its blood-red light shifted over the ground. Creatures with too many limbs loped across some distant, twisting road, fuzzy and indistinct. A hot wind blew in my face that reeked of ancient tears. Something wailed, the sound of an enormous beast crying, and the whole world shuddered.

This was familiar. We had met, this world and me, but where or when, I didn't remember. But I had to know. I took one step toward the door. Two. Answers lay on the other side. The hot, reeking wind tousled my hair as I took a third step. A fourth.

I stood at the threshold. The oval boundary flickered with whorls of blue fire. I knew whatever lay on the other side would destroy me, that after I entered, I would be erased forever. But I wanted to be destroyed. I deserved to go up in flames. And so I stepped through the door.

Those days with you were the happiest in my life. You had unlocked me from the cage I didn't know I was in. I boasted of you to Deb and Jen, and they giggled and hugged me and were glad I'd finally outed myself to them. I posted sappy song lyrics on Facebook and wrote that I'd finally found happiness. I tried to hold your hand in the halls, but you yanked your fingers away and gave me hateful stares. I tried to kiss you by the bleachers after school, but you shoved me away.

"They might see!" you said.

"Who?" I said. "The gay police? Why do you care what anyone thinks?"

You gritted your teeth and said, "In gym they threw me to the grass, called me a faggot. I scuffed my elbow."

"Those fucks!" I said. I kissed your elbow, where the skin was red and raw. "You can't let them do this, Davis. You have to fight back, or they'll do it again." What I didn't say was that a kid had spit on me that morning and the day before another had shoved me into a locker and called me queer. But these small bruises were unimportant. We had each other, and that was enough.

And you said, "I'm not a fighter, Lucas."

And I said, "We have to be."

"But how do they know?"

"It's obvious, Davis."

"But is it?" you said. "I hardly speak to you in school. And outside physics class, we don't see each other much."

"Maybe they heard rumors."

"From who? We both promised not to tell."

My face burned as I remained silent.

"Who?" you said. "Who did you tell, Lucas?"

"No one," I said. But this was a lie. I'd already told Jen and Deb, because I had to share my happiness with someone. And they had to share it too, because I'm pretty sure by then the whole damn school knew.

"I have to go," you said, avoiding my eyes.

"But it's early," I said. "I thought we would go to the park."

"No," you said. "I have to go home."

When I stepped through the burning door the first thing that struck me was the sound. A cry from some immense, distant beast. It was low and deep and lingering, and shook my belly until I felt like throwing up. The sound grew in volume until it filled the stale air. I should have turned and ran, but I stayed.

The ground was soft and spongy, and a weight pressed on my shoulders so that my feet sunk halfway into the brown foam. All was dull and shapeless, but my senses were heightened, as if I had drunk too much coffee and was watching a hi-def film flickering before my eyes. A trail of footprints, huge feet with branching potato-spud toes and fans of claws, led me forward. I grew weaker with every step, until I stood dizzy and panting before one of the twisted metal shapes.

Like the skeleton of a huge iron flower, it spiked from the ground toward the red sun. In the flickering light the metal seemed to breathe. On its twisting girders smaller spikes branched from the larger, and smaller spikes branched from these, and so on, and so on, down and down into fractal infinity. And all over the spongy ground lay little rusty fragments that had fallen off. I picked one up, and it was hot, and my fingers turned red with dust.

And suddenly there he was, my demon, standing beside the iron flower as if he had always been there. This time he was full of eyes, a thousand black, huge and angry orbs, all staring at me, accusing. A hole opened in his side, as if he were splitting in two, revealing rows of small, sharp teeth and a black tongue. And from this came such a scream that the whole world shuddered, and I fell.

He crawled over to me, end over end like an inchworm. A lump formed in his side, a pseudopod reaching, that became a long, fat limb. On its end was a giant hand, flying toward my face. It slammed into my skull, and I screamed and fell back again.

Then I was flying through space, zipping around an immense black void, trillions of stars spiraling with me, falling into the void, one by one. And I swung around this cosmic whirlpool, for ages and ages. And I knew that I'd spin like this for eternities before it was my turn to fall into the void and be destroyed. And I spun, and spun, and spun, and spun . . .

I awoke on the floor. My coworker, Mary, held a cup of Hi-C to my mouth, and the red liquid shimmered in the lights. I spent thirty minutes begging my boss not to call an ambulance because I didn't have health insurance. It was low blood sugar, nothing more, I said. He gave me the night off, with pay, and as I unlocked my bike for the ride home I noticed my palm was red.

I thought, finally I had proof that all of this was real. But I remembered that some of Mary's Hi-C had spilled down my hand. My tongue was still sickly sweet.

On Monday, I walked you home after school under towering sycamores on Benefit Street. You walked fast, and told me you had a lot of homework and probably wouldn't have time to hang out for the next few days.

"What is it?" I said, sensing the wall rising between us. "What's going on?"

You didn't answer at first, but I pushed. "Some kids posted all this homophobic stuff on my Facebook page," you said.

"Who?" I demanded. "We have to report them to the principal!"

"No, Lucas. No."

"Tell me, Davis! Who was it?"

"Just forget it."

I took out my phone to look, but you said, "I've already deleted the posts. Do me a favor and just let it go."

"No," I said. "I won't. And you shouldn't either. You need to come down hard on them, or they'll do it again."

You stopped and faced me. "Why do you think you always know what the fuck is best for me?"

You never cursed, and the look in your eyes was close to hate, so I pretended I hadn't seen it. "Davis," I said, "you have to stop hiding your true self from others. Be proud of who you are. Be brave."

And you said, "That might work for you, Lucas. But you and I, we're different."

"Yes," I said. And maybe because I remembered the hate in your eyes, I said, "You're a fucking coward, and I'm going home."

I turned down State Street and never looked back. I'll never know if you stopped to watch me or kept on walking.

On Friday I snuck into the security office and stole the store key. I had it copied and returned before anyone discovered it was missing. That night, around 1 a.m., I snuck into SuperMart. It was easy enough to turn off the alarm, having watched the guard enter the keycode a hundred times when we smoked together. I'd swiped a bottle of Gordon's from Mom's stash, and by this time I had a solid buzz on.

"Hello!" I announced to the empty store. "Lucas is here!" The aisles were dark and full of shadows from the dim red exit signs and the orange streetlights glimmering through the front windows.

I sauntered into Aisle 6, half expecting my demon to be waiting. But there was only candy.

"Where are you?" I shouted. "I'm here! Come get me!"

I had my phone ready, camera app open. He wouldn't escape this time. I took a swig of vodka and put down the bottle.

"Where are you?" I shouted. "I'm here!"

I walked up and down Aisle 6, over and over, like a marching soldier. I knocked candy to the floor, and I shouted at the top of my lungs. "Where are you? Show your face, you motherfucker!"

My voice echoed and faded, until the only sound was the faint thrum of the highway beyond the parking lot.

I stumbled toward the vodka bottle and sat next to it. I remained there for a while, slowly finishing the bottle, until I was so drunk the candy seemed to shiver.

"Davis," I said, tears rolling down my cheeks. "Davis I miss you. I miss you so goddamned much. Why did you have to leave?"

I lifted the bottle by its neck and swung it down onto the metal racks. The glass shattered and pieces spread far and wide. I rubbed my face and it felt wet. In the shadows the blood looked black as oil.

"Oh, god," I said, pulling pieces of glass from my cheeks.

I stumbled out of the store, blood and tears spilling down my face, and somehow managed to bike to Jen's house. I called three times before she awoke, and she snuck me in her room through her first-floor window. And there, as she carefully removed the glass from my face with tweezers, as she applied swabs of stinging alcohol, and wrapped me in a warm blanket. I told her everything. I told her of you and me, and I told her of the demon.

And God bless Jen, she didn't judge. She didn't say I was going crazy or needed meds. She only listened and nodded and held me until I stopped shivering.

"I'm sorry I told people about you and Davis," she said. "I regret it every day."

"It's not your fault," I said. "Davis asked me not to tell anyone about us, and I did anyway. You can't be held responsible for a promise you didn't make."

"I guess I just got excited because you were so open about it," Jen said. "Lucas . . . Deb and I, we're gay too. We've been together since junior high."

I stared at her, shocked. "Really? I can't believe I never noticed."

"We keep real quiet about it. You know how this town can be."

And I nodded, because I did know. But by then was too late.

The day after I left you in the street, you didn't come to school. I called and texted you a dozen times, but you didn't respond. All these hateful, homophobic posts piled up on your Facebook page, and I wondered why you weren't erasing them. School was dreary without you. I didn't eat lunch, and a cramp gnawed at my stomach. I went straight home after school, and when the sun went down early, I got frantic. I had to see you and apologize for calling you a coward and for telling others about us, because I had broken my promise.

I knew you'd be angry with me, but you'd soften. Eventually, you'd forgive me. And later, maybe even that same night, we'd cuddle, and all would be right again.

When I set out for your house, it was getting dark. A full moon rose above the black trees, shining like an enormous eye. A single light was on in your house. I was trembling as I stepped up to the door, but it was open, and I went in. Your house reeked of cigarettes and sweat, and empty beer cans and candy wrappers covered the table by the TV. In the distance, someone was crying.

Time slowed as I approached your door. Your dad crouched on his knees just inside the threshold, weeping and shuddering.

He looked up at me, his eyes red pinwheels surrounding pools of black, and he said, "You! You did this to him, you selfish motherfucker!" Saliva dribbled from his chin and splattered to the floor.

I stared at him, unable to move.

"Look!" he screamed. "Look at what you did!"

You lay on the bed, as if sleeping, and for a moment I pretended that's all I saw. But your dad's nine millimeter was still clasped in your hand, and little red pieces of your skull were scattered all over the room. I was still staring at you, unable to believe what I was seeing, when your dad's fist struck me in the face.

I found out about the funeral a day too late. Your father didn't make it public. You were buried in a small Jewish cemetery eighteen miles from town. I had to take a bus there. I didn't even know you were Jewish. You'd never told me. People had left a few pebbles on your headstone, so I added the one you gave me when you said we were all formed in the exploding hearts of stars.

I had a black eye for a week, but I didn't press charges against your dad, because I deserved it. He was right. It was my fault. I was a selfish motherfucker.

There was an obit for you on the school blog written by some kid who never knew you. In the moderated comments students wrote that you were with God now, that Jesus forgives all sin. No one ever mentioned you were Jewish. People spoke about you for a few days and pointed at me in the halls. The hateful comments on your Facebook page were removed and it became a makeshift memorial. But all this soon faded, like a cinder in a dying fire. The school bells went on ringing as they always had. And I still had homework and my job at SuperMart after school.

And I thought, this can't be all. You couldn't have been snuffed so easily. When I told Jen about the demon, she offered some armchair analysis.

"It's all very clear to me," she said. "The bleak world that you walked into, that's Davis's bedroom. The weird metal plant, all twisted and broken, that's Davis. And the demon's accusing eyes, those are his father's. You see, Lucas? The demon is your guilt."

It seemed obvious when she said it. All the pieces fit. My guilt had been so overwhelmingly strong that I summoned the demon from my subconscious. And it had haunted me until I acknowledged it.

And so, knowing this, I've tried to go on living, as the scabs on my face slowly heal and my black eye fades. But then last night, as I was emptying my pockets before bed, out came a small piece of metal.

I thought it was the stone that you'd given me when we were walking through the streets, the ash from an ancient exploding star. But I had placed that stone on your grave. My fingers turned red from touching this one, and I remembered that I had picked up a fragment of the metal plant when I had stepped through that flaming door.

And I thought, if the intensity of my guilt could summon a demon, what could my love summon? I put the stone on my windowsill last night, under the bright stars of Orion and Sirius, and I focused all of my love for you onto it. I thought of your Freddy Mercury smile and your world-shuddering laugh and I thought of your gentle kindness that carried me through these autumn days.

I fell asleep, thinking of you, and when I awoke, the east was orange with the coming dawn, and the little stone on my windowsill had sprouted five tiny new limbs. And that's when I knew, Davis, that like your mother, who left you far too soon, you're not really gone, you're just traveling.

THE THING IN THE REFRIGERATOR THAT COULD STOP TIME

HALF A BLINK after the smoke from the cigarette smoldering in the ashtray had curled into a hoary question mark and froze in perpetual query as if to ask, "What next, Dick?" Dick turned his head ever so slowly toward the kitchen.

Molasses. That's what it felt like. A honeybee drunk on tree nectar, too dumb to realize it was slowly fossilizing into amber history.

One foot on the floor now, and Dick *did* realize, slowly, like the drip-drip-drip of a leaking faucet, that he had to close the refrigerator door before the thing inside it stopped time altogether. His mostly barren living room, with only a beat-up couch and a flickering halogen lamp, should have been an easy traverse. But the twenty-three feet from his bedroom to the kitchen seemed longer than all the hundreds of thousands of miles Dick had driven in his big blue bus, ferrying sweaty, obese people to and from Atlantic City for bouts of all-night gambling.

Not all the people on his bus had been sweaty and/or obese, but as Dick's other foot reached the floor, it was the only image that had time to reach his mind. That and men boasting of the great whoring to be had in "AC," men who carefully re-slung their wedding bands onto ring fingers before leaving Dick's bus in Jersey City, or New Brunswick, or Manhattan. And the complaints-complaints-complaints from nicotine-stained mouths of saggy-eyed, droopy-breasted, cellulite-layered women who hated everything about their lives, their co-workers, even AC itself, but apparently not enough to stop them climbing back onto Dick's bus every week in the hope that *this* time they'd strike it rich and show everyone back home how right they were about everything all along. And the barely-out-of-diapers-and-questionably-of-drinking-age crowd. The too-drunk, too-loud semi-literate morons who thought because they were away from Mommy and Daddy they could imbibe the half quart of Jack Daniels before they got on Dick's bus for the three-hour ride home, and then, after shouting in pre-school English how much the New York Yankees fucking rule over the New York Mets, puke freely all over Dick's seats.

Our children, our future, Dick thought. But no time for distractions as time distilled around him. In the thickening moment, Dick reached the threshold to the living room and figured that if the thing in the refrigerator had learned how to open the door, then he was in some serious shit, because, he thought, the freezer hadn't worked since June.

Peering through the yellow tunnel of his living room and into the kitchen, he watched it emerge—the smoky, not-quite-there finger—a brown out-of-focus sausage that reached out from the tiny opening and spilled a crack of refrigerator light onto the kitchen's dark floor. Dick would have shivered if he had had the time.

Another torpid step brought with it memories of his ex-wife with her Prada bags and Gucci belts always working late and Dick always wondering why his wife dolled herself up for work but fell asleep quickly with her back always to him, never wanting sex, never wanting talk, never wanting anything except to sleep and to preen herself in the mirror. And Dick remembered the thirty-eight caliber pistol he had bought of a friend-of-a-friend for seventy-five dollars and a free pass to AC, and how he had planned to kill the man with the four hundred dollar Bruno Magli shoes who was fucking his wife, then changed his mind and planned just to kill his wife as she slept with her back toward him, and finally settled, after a full bottle of Captain Morgan's swallowed in a motel room next to the Holland Tunnel, to blow his own brains out as soon as he heard his favorite song on the radio, "Paperback Writer," by the Beatles.

The song had never come on, and Dick awakened the next morning with head-splitting pain and a jab of motel sunlight in his eyes to the sound of Pink Floyd's "Money," the fourth time he had heard the song in the last twenty-four hours.

The joys of commercial radio, he thought.

But no time for bile-building thoughts as he passed through the bedroom door and landed two feet on orange carpet. Dick eyed the partially open refrigerator as a white mist tumbled lazily around four sausage fingers holding onto the door, fingers that shook and stuttered like an old, tattered film.

There was no mistaking it now. The thing inside was definitely trying to get out.

The repulsive fingers dredged up repressed memories of a highly caffeinated Dick driving thirty passengers over the Verrazano Narrows bridge, with sun reflecting off of the driver-side mirror, and "Paperback Writer" booming suddenly from the radio's solitary speaker. Its unmistakable G riff fired off Dick's emotions like hammer-clicks from a revolver, but Dick had no thirty-eight caliber pistol handy, nor was he the type of asshole to drive his sweaty, obese passengers off of the monstrous bridge and into the Hudson River just to keep his besotted promise made to the grim reaper in a beat-up motel by the Holland Tunnel.

But a tsunami of drunken thoughts slammed into his head,

and all the bad energy conjured in that one desperate night crashed upon the sandbar of his consciousness. And, while Dick slowly drowned in his emotions, he wasn't watching the road before him, or the sun reflecting from the driver-side mirror, nor did he see the way the bus veered lazily out of its lane. Dick swam against his eddying thoughts as slovenly women complained about his poor driving. He struggled for the shore of sanity as red-cheeked men slunk their ring fingers into erection-lined pockets. He gasped for air as underage youths dropped their clanking, empty beer bottles onto his newly cleaned floor. But the tide was too strong, the grim promise too great, and the weight of one night's firm resolution drowned Dick in the immutable, absolute, and inescapable fact of his own mortality.

And that's when Dick saw them.

Brown out-of-focus shadow figures fluttering like smoke in the wind, and yet not dissipating into the air, but cleaving to the outside of each passenger's window with stuttering sausage shaped fingers. Heart thumping and mind reeling, Dick glanced into the mirror above his head and saw that a similar brown pile of filth sat upon his shoulder, a shadowy, mud-colored grotesqueness that wavered like hot pavement on a summer's day.

It smiled at him.

And all this happening while the bus slammed into the guardrail with a spray of sparks, with Dick flailing to remove the smiling thing on his shoulder, while wide-eyed passengers screamed, the crowded bus reeled, and grinning piles of dung flew in a dozen different directions.

Awakening later in the hospital, concussed and disoriented, Dick forgot all about the grotesqueries, the memories tucked safely away like a bad dream.

And that was intentional, Dick thought.

As Dick stepped across the orange carpet in slothful time he felt his head throb, a constant reminder of his skull slamming into steering wheel sometime during the frightful scene on the bridge.

In syrupy time, Dick passed the couch on his left and wondered if it were possible to vomit in slow-motion, his fear and loathing building to an indomitable crescendo as the thing in the refrigerator had a foot on the tiled kitchen floor now and Dick still having twelve or more feet to go.

He remembered the confusion in the hospital, the pain in his forehead, the loss of memory, the questions from his supervisor, the mind-numbing discourses with wool-suited lawyers who smelled of cheap soap and old books, who had sat at the foot of his bed to make him sign waivers interminably until Dick's left hand cramped permanently shut. And the New York City taxi-cab driver who nearly gave Dick another concussion the following day, after "Paperback Writer" had come on the radio again, and the loathsome things reappeared on both of their shoulders.

Dick screamed, begged the cabbie to stop.

The cab driver's pile of slop had twisted its head, stared at Dick, and smiled. It whispered into the driver's ear, and then the driver, who a moment before was ready to knock Dick into the next century, stopped the car, took a deep breath, and counted to ten.

At number seven Dick knocked the thing off his own shoulder and fled the cab.

Dick ran down countless grey Manhattan sidewalks under an endless steel grey sky, bumping pedestrians in their drab city colors, each ashen figure oblivious to the misshapen things fidgeting and laughing upon their shoulders. And this while Disney-like light spilled detestably onto the sidewalk from row after row of stores incessantly encouraging Dick to purchase their products that offered no solace from the little brown and squirming things that giggled at him as he ran through the streets.

A faint and retching Dick reached his company's west side

lot, opened the door and climbed inside his smelly bus amidst shouts from a balding, uniformed man watching the gate, and this while Dick's little brown thing hastily approached from a city block away, its long monkey arms flailing erratically. The engine started up, the bus pulled out, and Dick prepared to leave Manhattan by the least trafficked route, his left eye constantly on the driver-side mirror. With heart pounding and head throbbing, the hospital band still on his left wrist, Dick saw the little brown thing sliding in between cars stopped in traffic, cars whose drivers had little smiling brown pustules sitting on their shoulders, pustules that leaned in and whispered thoughts into their ears.

The light was green and there was room for the bus to move, but Dick knew something was wrong when he wasn't accelerating, when his foot upon the gas pedal did nothing but make the bus hum subliminally three octaves too low, when the 727 that passed overhead froze in freeze frame like those incessant pictures of the World Trade Center disaster endlessly replayed until the stock price of Xanax had made several thousand people rich. But as time congealed the brown squirmy thing slid between and leapt over cars as if the slowing of time had absolutely no effect on it. It climbed up the driver-side of the bus, smiled with transcendent glee, and jumped through the window to sit once again on Dick's shoulder.

Dick shuddered, then forgot all about it.

He awoke, as if from a dream, stuck in traffic on Tenth Avenue, alone in his bus, which smelled of sweat and puke and cleaning products, a hospital band wrapped around his wrist and absolutely no memory whatsoever of what had just happened.

Through the Lincoln Tunnel, under the Hudson River, and at a gas station in Hoboken he stopped for coffee and made a phone call, fearing that something was terribly amiss. And after politely hanging up on the man on the other end of the line who was begging Dick to return the bus, the same bus that

Dick had driven nearly half a million miles in the northeastern corridor of the United States, he decided he needed some food in his stomach and time to think.

At a diner called Malibu, but lacking anything remotely tropical, Dick ordered eggs and fries from the brown-haired blue-eyed waitress who smiled at Dick and did not ask, though it looked like she wanted to, about the white bracelet on Dick's wrist. Food digesting, and temporarily sated, he emptied his pockets onto the table to reveal four quarters, two dimes, three pennies, and an expensive monogrammed pen Dick had found abandoned on one of the bus's seats. He placed the quarters, one by one, into the jukebox's slot next to him, scrolling to find three songs that would wash away any remaining unpleasantness lingering in his stomach.

One was his favorite, by the Beatles.

And this time, as fear pounded him into the seat and despair poured over him in waves, he decided to surf instead of sink, even though his heart was saying "oh-my-fucking-shit" and his vision was starting to reveal squirmy deformities smiling on the patrons' shoulders. And Dick did surf, albeit poorly, as the waitress returned to him and asked him if he wanted more coffee. At first she didn't smile and looked like she wanted to be anywhere but in a shitty diner called Malibu pouring coffee for an unshaven invalid who reeked of hospital antiseptic and old bus. But the dung-colored thing on her shoulder leaned in and whispered in her ear, then the girl turned to Dick and faux-smiled as she poured him coffee.

The thing on Dick's shoulder leaned in and whispered to him. He did not hear what it said, but he found himself forcing a smile, then thanking her, even though he really wanted her to go the fuck away so he could drink his coffee and look out the window in peace. She walked away, finally, and he reached into his pocket to find a cigarette when something whispered to him it was bad for his health, that the second-hand smoke would kill the other patrons slowly, over centuries, and that it cost him too much money, that he should work out more, tone and clothe his body like those snazzy, classy men in *GQ*. So Dick left the pack with the unlit cigarettes on the table and stared at them, hands shaking, and tried not to look up at the other patrons with their wriggling lumps on their shoulders or glance too far to his right lest he see his own reflection in the window and discover the pitiful mess he had become.

Angry with himself, tired of the constant background tune of self-loathing, he reached up to his shoulder, grabbed the squirming thing, and flung it across the room. It felt like a chewed, drooled upon dog toy.

It skidded across the floor and slammed into the counter underneath the pastry window while the other blobs looked up at Dick. And for the few brief moments when the thing was not on his shoulder, Dick felt no remorse about having a cigarette in front of the others, did not care that he looked like an alcoholic mongrel dragged in from the rain, had no qualms about getting the fuck out of this diner without paying his tab before the thing could jump back on his shoulder again.

Dick was, for the moment, at peace with himself.

But the mumbling grumble that is the eternal background chatter of all diners slowed, and the clink-chink-clink that is the sound of forks scraping plates and teeth paused, and in that moment of molasses time the thing jumped back onto Dick's shoulder, and Dick forgot again.

But not before he had scribbled a few letters with his monogrammed pen onto a napkin.

Dick paid his bill smiling and did not smoke his cigarette until he was outside and felt guilty doing so because his lungs were slowly rotting and his body would never be what it was when he was seventeen, when he worked out three times a week and made out with a pneumatic new girl each weekend. And, he thought, maybe his cuckolding wife left him because he had spent six out of every seven days on the road for a dozen years, was away every Christmas and Thanksgiving because they were the best paying holidays, and maybe she left him for that one time a sixteen-year-old prostitute from Oklahoma who went by the handle "Snuggles" had talked Dick into roadside sex over the CB radio. And maybe that was why his wife had hired a moving company to come one day while Dick was driving down I-95 with visions of a thirty-eight caliber flickering between red tail-lights, and why she'd emptied their apartment of almost everything Dick had loved except his beat-up, gray, old couch, a cheap halogen lamp, his dust-gathering collection of self-help books, a dozen or so record albums scratched so badly Dick hadn't used them in more than a decade, and a white-plastic children's phonograph player left moldering in the attic.

Outside the diner, a cold wind whipping down Fourteenth Street, Dick blew his nose with an ink-stained napkin.

In dreamy time, Dick remembered all of this as he passed between the table and the halogen lamp while the thing in the refrigerator peered out from behind the door and glanced around groggily to get its bearings. And Dick realized that even though he was moving like a snail, his footfalls painfully slower than Buzz Aldrin's hopping around the Moon, the thing in the refrigerator was merely taking its sweet time, as if it had just awakened from a pleasant nap, was having lots of fun stretching, and was in no great hurry to get out of bed and back onto Dick's shoulder.

Well, Dick thought in a flash, *it's been in there for quite some time.*

And Dick remembered heading home under a ceiling of cold, light rain. The morose, evening sky and Dick's purposefully dim apartment mirrored his mood as he emptied his pockets, throwing coins and keys and a monogrammed pen onto the table. Out with them came a snot filled napkin face up with a few letters written upon it in smeared ink. Dick had lit a cigarette in the fading light and felt the cool caress of nicotine wash over him like a dirty yet soothing bath, and he climbed up into the attic and brought down his childhood record player with its moldy and frayed plug, knowing that there was only one song in the world which could lift him out of the doldrums and return him back to his soul.

Dick got as far as F in the G-C-D-G-G-F riff before he was screaming and scrambling to get the thing off of his shoulder, memories flooding back of smiling piles of feces and late-night promises to Death. Dick's torso swinging, and the thing's arms flailing, Dick managed to stuff the squirming thing inside the refrigerator and close the door. There was a ruckus inside for a few moments before it fell quiet. Dick stood there, leaning onto the door, with his body trembling softly and the little record player churning out "Paperback Writer" by his feet, its frayed power chord twisting haphazardly along the floor. Dick wasn't sure if the frigid air or the gentle hum or something else entirely had calmed the thing in the refrigerator down, but when he let the pressure off of the door the thing inside did not push to get out. And seventeen cigarettes spent leaning anxiously upon the door did not produce a single sound from inside. He bent down to the phonograph and replayed the song, just in case, as Dick cracked open the door and glanced inside.

The thing lay sound asleep next to rotting lettuce, like a Coke-flavored slush puppy slowly melting on a summer's sidewalk.

So with the phonograph set to repeat, its little arm swinging awkwardly back to the inside of the scratched, black disc every two minutes and nineteen seconds, its tiny speaker blaring a cracked and popping version of his favorite song, Dick sat down at his desk in the bedroom, pulled out his monogrammed pen carved with someone else's initials, and hastily wrote down his memories inside a hoary mist of cigarette smoke, lest the thing get out and he forget again.

Shortly after, he had noticed the tap-tap-tap of his ball-point pen slowing, the G-C-D of the fugueing riff lagging, and the puff-puff-puff of his exhaled smoke stalling, as the thing in the refrigerator had finished its nap and was ready to resume its place on Dick's shoulder as the cackling, dung-colored, and mind-altering grotesquery it was meant to be.

More than anything in the world, Dick didn't want that again.

The refrigerator door swung freely now, the tiny twenty-watt bulb revealing the misshapen silhouette inside. And Dick thought that this was his last chance, that he had to dive forward and slam the refrigerator door closed before the thing inside had stepped completely out and onto the floor. So Dick, like a super-slow-motion Olympic long jumper, carefully placed his next footfall before the threshold of the kitchen in preparation to spring forward, ready to thrust all his momentum onward and upward in one final leap. And in the shifting angles of refrigerator light Dick glimpsed the distorted face of the brown figure, and realized with alarm, that it had stopped trying to get out of the refrigerator and was watching him calmly and, apparently, amused.

Dick's momentum wobbled like the contortions of a lava-lamp blob, and he was acutely aware of how important it was that he have a foot to land on, lest he fall on his face. So with his second foot coming down to prevent such a catastrophe and Newton's laws of momentum thrusting him forward, Dick leapt with all his might toward the refrigerator door.

The thing in the refrigerator started to laugh the kind of throaty laugh that someone who's dying of lung cancer laughs, and Dick wondered if there was something utterly futile about him flying through the air head first toward the refrigerator that he wasn't aware of, so on a hunch he looked back to his foot and remembered with a pang of fear about the tattered, old chord from the phonograph player that he had slung across the floor and saw with dread that it was now wrapped quite tightly around his ankle.

And Dick's yelp, slowed by the procession of time, bellowed like a fog horn in the kitchen as the chord tightened around his ankle, both lifting the phonograph off of the floor and slowing his ascent towards the refrigerator door, and this happening while the squirming mass watched like a polite spectator at a monster truck event, waiting for Dick's inevitable crash and burn.

Dick had to choose and had to choose quickly whether to save the careening record player with his free foot or try to close the refrigerator door with an outstretched hand. In the brief, flickering window of choice, both and neither seemed optimal.

Dick opted for both.

With the chord wrapped around his foot, and as he slowly fell back to the floor in a perfectly ungraceful arc, Dick tried to save the record player with his untangled foot while his left hand stretched forward in a hastily invented Yoga pose called "tethered-man-in-freefall-trying-futilely-to-stuff-thing-back-into-icebox."

Behind him his foot maneuvered to keep the record from falling in kicks that would humble Pele, but the phonograph player lifted, tilted, and finally flipped over in mid-flight, putting an end to any glorious bicycle-kick save. With faith hastily redirected to his other side, Dick glanced forward and realized that he was coming down, even with his outstretched hand, at least three feet short of the door. And with his body slamming onto tiles, the record shattering into shards, and his heart freezing with ice, Dick collapsed into a pile on the floor.

The thing wobbled out of the refrigerator in real time, no longer slowing the passage of the clock, and sat on Dick's shoulder, smiling and victorious.

Dick awoke on the floor, mouth dry and refrigerator open, to wonder if he had come all this way to get a beer, and then thought otherwise because there was nothing in the refrigerator except rotting lettuce and an old Coke stain. Then he looked down at his favorite record scattered in a dozen pieces across the floor, and Dick lamented it, trying to figure out how he had found himself lying prone in the kitchen, and then he remembered his hospital visit as he looked down to his wrist.

There was a smell of smoke, and Dick ran back into his bedroom to find papers atop his desk slowly burning, apparently from a butt that had fallen out of the ashtray.

A moment later, with the fire snuffed and the window open, letting in frigid but fresh air from the street, Dick tried to read the remaining words on the scorched paper.

". . . grotesque thing on shoulder. . . while on bridge. . . caused bus accident. . . went to hospital. . . in the cab. . . stole the bus from west side yard. . . with a diner's napkin. . . the record. . . keep playing 'Paperback Writer' over and over again!"

Dick brooded over the visible words for a few moments until the eureka of recognition flickered through him. It was grotesque roadkill on the bridge which forced Dick to swerve onto the shoulder and caused the accident for which Dick was wearing the wristband from the hospital, and for which his head was throbbing. And, somehow, in his confusion, Dick had taken the bus from the west side yard thinking he was going back to work, when he changed his mind and came back home afterward to play "Paperback Writer" on his old phonograph, perhaps to soothe himself in his lonely, quiet home, and in his wobbly condition he tripped over its power chord and fell onto the floor, knocking himself unconscious again and unwittingly shattering his favorite record into a dozen shards.

He cursed himself for being so foolish.

Dick closed the window, and the refrigerator, and cleaned the broken record off of the floor, before finally lying down on a cold bed. A grotesque little voice in the back of his head told him that his current life was an exercise in futility. If he'd been more careful, then maybe he wouldn't have gotten into the bus accident, and maybe, if he'd been less selfish with his job, less of a workaholic, his wife wouldn't have left him, and maybe, just maybe, if he was less of a sweaty, obese, and complaining moron, then his favorite record wouldn't have been shattered into a dozen pieces across the floor. Before falling into disturbed dreams and fitful slumber, Dick made a vow to change.

IN MEMORY OF A SUMMER'S DAY

"He's twelve, yes?" I say to the smiling couple from Kyoto as their child looks up at me fearfully.

"Yes," his mother insists, flashing me a toothy grin. "Just last week!"

I'd bet fifty quid and my last Chesterfield the kid's not even nine, but I just smile and pull the rope aside to let the boy and his parents leap down the rabbit hole together. Their screams and laughter fade as they fall, while the queue presses ever closer to me. The languid river beside us glitters prismatically in the afternoon light, sending a flurry of rainbows across their anxious and eager faces. Among them I spot half a dozen kids of questionable age, but I've got orders to let everyone in now. Old, young, disabled, senile, deranged. Everyone but infants. And sometimes even them.

They come from all over: Japan, Brazil, Norway, China, Nigeria, Russia, Singapore, Yemen, South Korea, the States, the U.K., plus lots of elsewheres and elsewhens. Wonderland has become one of the Things to See Before You Die, like the Matterhorn and the Grand Canyon and the Great Wall of China. They come in dusty coaches packed to near-bursting, that pull right up to the River Isis and befoul the once-sweet air with carbonized exhaust. The coaches vomit out dozens of people onto the riverbank, once so quiet you could hear the delicate sound of leaves brushing the ground in autumn. Now there's a franchise cafe selling sandwiches and espresso, fifty sets of metallic tables rusting under towering elms, and two dozen bright kiosks offering everything from Cheshire Chocolates to CDs with studio-recorded tracks of "Beautiful Soup" and the "Lobster Quadrille." The garbage cans always overflow.

After de-busing, a few kids inevitably cry. Adults and children rush to the lavatories. Pinafores are purchased and donned. Mediocre coffee is bought for exorbitant prices. Parents wrinkle their noses as they examine free maps (which are less maps than warnings), while spouses look on uneasily.

Are you sure you want to do this? You've heard the stories.

Don't worry. Don't worry.

Tickets are £186.40 per person, adults and children alike, sold only on location, on the day of arrival, discounts unavailable, admission never guaranteed. And all must sign a waiver absolving Wonderland of any harm, physical, mental, or otherwise, that might befall them while there.

The wise read the waiver first, but everyone always signs. None can long resist the lure, because even though they think they know what awaits them down the rabbit hole, it's never quite what they've imagined. And after, no one's ever quite the same.

I go down there twelve times a day.

I've been leading tours of Wonderland for forty years, though it feels like twice that. And though my bones ache and my knees throb, my retirement's a distant ship on the horizon that might just be a floater in my vision. A lucrative job this isn't, and I've got spousal maintenance payments, a crushing amount of debt, and various court orders to consider. Plus, the boss has let's just say more *pressing* things keeping me here. In other words, I'm trapped.

I predict one day I'll just keel over in the middle of the Croquet Ground or collapse into the Duchess's manger. I wonder if they'll take my body back to Earth, bury me in Wonderland, or just flush me down the Pool of Tears. Some days I'm convinced the entire realm will suddenly go up in flames with everyone inside, myself included, like some virtual particle evanescing, and the thought is not entirely unwelcome.

I'm on tour nine of twelve, we're in the Hall of Doors, and I'm so bloody knackered I could fall asleep standing up. But the show must go on. I yawn and cross my arms and lean against one of the hundreds of locked and mismatched doors, checking the time on my mobile (no signal), as my group of thirty-nine grows and shrinks and laughs and shrieks as they sample the food and drink on the table.

Back in the old days, we used to take hundreds at a time. But now we cap it at forty persons so we can more or less keep an eye on everyone, this ever since that poor boy guzzled all of the Drink Me fluid, even though we have signs in twelve languages warning people to take but a sip. He howled as he shrunk and vanished, and though we scoured the hall for days, his body was never found. To this day I still sometimes hear a faint squeal when I enter the Hall of Doors, and while I suspect it's Mouse having a laugh, I always look twice before I step there.

It tastes like rosewater! one says.

Gingerbread! says another.

In runs the White Rabbit, saying, "Oh, the Duchess, the Duchess, she'll be savage I've kept her!"

Damn. Rabbit's mussed the line, and though I doubt more than a handful have noticed, a few among the tour wrinkle their noses and frown. If the boss finds out, she'll be livid. I can't manage another inquisition. Underneath Rabbit's layers of makeup and dye, he's a little ruffled around the ears. The edges of his coat are tattered, and as he scurries past, dropping his fan and gloves, he smells strongly of whiskey. During today's lunch, he told me he's down to three flasks a day from upwards of seven, lauding himself as if this were great progress. But I thought, what happens after zero? Beyond lurks only a great void, like Wonderland's starless sky, and when Rabbit wasn't looking I took a deep draught from his flask.

When he vanishes down the hall, salt water trickles in from under the door frames to pool around our ankles. My group giggles nervously at first, but when the water reaches waists, their faces turn sober.

It's cold! they shout, smiles fading.

By the time it reaches the children's shoulders, out swims Mouse, paddling furiously. Some shriek. (Mouse is a mouse, after all.) And just like the story, a few wags try their French on him, and he feigns fright and darts off before returning. The kids, floating easily in the salt water, adore him. And though Mouse is masterful with an audience, I watch him closely. He's on parole for petty larceny, and though he's been nothing but kind to me all these years, I keep a tight hand on my wallet as he swims past.

The water keeps rising, and by the time Duck and Dodo swirl by, you can see in the people's eyes they're thinking on the rumors again, the ones they've heard but didn't believe or conveniently forgot. But now they're worrying that maybe they should've read that map of warnings a little more carefully, and really, what *had* they gotten their families into?

Hold on to me! parents shout, scaring the kids, and their sudden burst of tears feeds the pool for my next tour.

As they shout and slosh and flail, the Eaglet pauses before me, and without words I slip him fifty quid under the rushing waters and he slips me two grams of the finest psychedelic mushrooms Wonderland has to offer before swimming on.

Few seem to know or remember that Mouse will soon dry them on the riverbank with a lecture about William the Conqueror, because the parents are still panicking. The kids are still crying. With this, at least, the boss will be pleased.

I have a thousand rules I must follow, but the paramount one is this: *Under no circumstances must one ever stop the show.*

One afternoon many years ago, my tour came upon the Mock Turtle, who had somehow rigged up this enormous boulder to come crashing down upon his shell. It was meant to kill him—and it did, but only after his smashed body bled crimson soup all over the rocks for the better part of a day. The Gryphon, upon seeing the bloody mess, snorted and said perhaps it was best if the Mock Turtle died, because, really, everyone was so damned tired of his empty sorrow anyway.

I panicked and ran off to find help and left my frightened and bewildered tour to the vagaries of Wonderland. Some wandered away to drown or be eaten. Some were found naked and laughing in the forest, pulling out tufts of their hair. More than a dozen went missing and were never found.

The boss sat down with the ones we recovered and had what she termed "deep conversations" with them all. None of us heard what was spoken, though we had our intimations, because each emerged from their meetings with a curiously confused expression on their faces, as if they weren't quite sure what had just occurred, and as we escorted them back to their coaches and cars they seemed not quite sure even *who* they were.

And when the boss got finally to me, let's just say I *wish* I could forget what she'd done. But she made bloody well sure I remembered. Seldom a night goes by where I don't wake up screaming, dreaming of her teeth.

A few decades back I was still married, had all my hair, and my daughter had just turned seven. I'd finished my last tour, had a newly lit joint dangling from my lips, and was pulling out of the car park when a playing card suddenly appeared on my dashboard, causing me to swerve. There were too many people left waiting, the boss had scrawled on the back of the queen of hearts, and I was to do a thirteenth tour. I cursed and screamed as I pulled my car back into its reserved rectangle by the riverbank, and I punched the steering wheel so hard my knuckles bled. (I still have the scars.)

It was late afternoon and the rays of the blazing orange sun cut the forest into ribbons. It wasn't yet autumn, but the air was crisp and held an early chill unusual for the season.

I remember noting the shine of her black hair, her faint freckles, but most of all the way her blue eyes shone like translucent marbles. She clutched a natty gray stuffed-animal cat to her belly, and she approached me and the rabbit hole only after severe coaxing from her parents.

But I'm scared, Mummy. I'm scared.

Thinking back now, I wonder if she sensed the menace waiting below. But down they went, and it was only after the tour had reached the Caterpillar on his toadstool that I noticed she was missing. Her parents chuckled at the Caterpillar's witticisms, and politely waited their turn to sample the body-altering mushroom, but they seemed otherwise unaware of their absent child. I looked around, thinking she might have wandered off, but there was no way I would stop the tour, not after what the boss had done to me the last time. And so I led them on.

By the time the tour awoke from the shower of playing cards to wipe their groggy eyes and find themselves on the riverbank, the sun had set, the cafe had closed, and two idling coaches and a handful of cars waited in the once-full car park. Each person was given a pocket mirror, a discount voucher for the *Through the Looking-Glass Tour*, and a firm shove. The people wandered off, stunned and disoriented. Had the world changed, or had they?

It stood beside her parents, unsteady in the wind, a patchwork girl fashioned from moldy leather and fraying twine, with marbles for eyes. I waited for her parents to wake and say, *This is not our little girl.*

Instead, with beatific smiles, they drifted away, holding the thing's hand. And I knew that in a week or a month this patchwork thing would disintegrate like cardboard in rain, and they'd come to think their child had died from some unknown and incurable disease, when she would be elsewhere alive and very much unwell. If Wonderland wants you, it takes you, and there's nothing you nor I nor anyone can do. And though I knew this well, my heart broke as I watched them go, and so I turned back and jumped down the hole.

Wonderland's checkerboard forest was already dark, the horizon limned with overlapping waves of purple and emerald, and the locusts were making an unholy racket by the time I reached the Caterpillar in his treehouse at the edge of the forest. Patron saint of all pot-smoking college students everywhere, the Caterpillar has been sober since the late '70s (he smokes an inert herb mixture on-shift), and he hasn't liked me very much ever since he discovered how much I partake of Wonderland's chemical fruits. So when I asked after the missing girl, he was less than forthcoming.

"She's just a child," the Caterpillar snapped, "and therefore perfectly expendable." Then he went back to reading his Dostoyevsky in reverse and would say no more.

But I couldn't accept this, and so I darted off in search of her. I scoured the Croquet Ground, the Duchess's house, the Queen's Court, and soon found myself in the murky woods, calling for her. I didn't know her name, but I knew she was here, lost and terrified, and that I was the only one who could find her.

Animals answered my calls: birds, rodents, insects, and

other things I could not name, but which made me think that making loud noises was maybe not such a good idea, and that wandering into these dark woods, alone and without a light or weapon of any sort was perhaps the stupidest thing a man might do. I fell quiet, but I went on searching.

The woods were so dark that soon I couldn't see ten inches in front of my face, and the air was so thick and humid it felt as if I were not walking through a forest but swimming at the bottom of a deep and lifeless sea. I held up my hands so as not to slam my nose into something, and my ankles and shoes grew waterlogged from traipsing through the dewy grasses and puddles of mud.

I heard her cry faintly at first, but it grew louder as I followed it, stumbling as I went over twigs and stones and soft, wet things the size of small dogs that slithered away unseen in the dark. The air smelled thickly of mouldy earth and fragrant roses and a not-too-distant salty sea.

I stumbled again, and it felt as if someone had stuck out their leg to trip me. I lay on the ground staring up at the empty sky as my body slowly sunk into the warm mud.

"It's me," someone whispered softly in my ear. And though I had only heard her voice once, I knew it was the missing girl. "Will you stay with me?" she said as a small, cold hand gently lay on my forearm. "We can stare up at the stars together."

But there were no stars. I wanted to rise, but could only lay there as her hot breath fell upon my cheek. I heard a massive gurgle of wet slithering in the mud nearby, as if an army of giant slugs were fast approaching. Warm, wet creatures crawled onto my feet and legs, covering them. They climbed onto my chest, enwrapping me in their wet warmth, and when they finally closed over my face, I tried to scream. But I could only lay there like a rotting tree.

"They want to be our friends," the girl whispered. "Can they be our friends, Daddy? Can we play with them, forever and ever?" She giggled and whispered things to me I couldn't quite hear, while the things on my body shivered warmly, and my head was filled with dark dreams.

I don't know how long I lay there before I rose from the ground. I grabbed the girl's arm and stumbled with her through the dark forest toward home. It wasn't until I had reached the river bank, under the sickly light of Earth's crescent moon, that I realized I didn't hold the girl's arm, but the leg of her gray stuffed-animal cat. Its eyes were gouged out, and it was covered in pearlescent slime.

I'm on tour twelve of twelve (at last), we're in the Duchess's House, the Baby Pig is weeping, and I'm leaning against the door frame, barely able to stand. I was saving my last Chesterfield for the end of my shift, but bloody hell, I can't wait any more. I light it and blow smoke out the door as the Cheshire Cat goes through his shtick and vanishes, leaving behind his trademark smile.

Like the call-and-response of church, the group recites, *Well! I've often seen a cat without a grin. But a grin without a cat! It's the most curious thing. . .*

They laugh and rub their children's heads, as if to reassure them that the terrible frights they've had today, the bizarre and growing sensation that they've become something not quite themselves, that they will never be the same person again, that something small and very much alive has niggled its way into their minds and will live there, growing, festering, forever, was all worth it just for *this* fleeting moment. And here it's always the children who notice first, who ask of the one who's been missing all along.

But Mummy, where is she? Where is Alice?

Then all eyes turn to me, hopeful, expectant, with a twinge of fear. *Yes*, they ask with a hint of desperation, because they cannot fathom why they haven't considered this very obvious question themselves. *Where is Alice?*

I flick my cigarette away and pull out a pocket mirror. I hold it up to their faces and make sure each catches their own distorted reflection within it. "To find your Alice," I say, "look no further than a glass. For if you ask yourself, 'Where might she be?' the answer, quite plainly is, 'She, it seems, is me.'"

This satisfies some and frustrates others, the girls in their blue-and-white pinafores most of all, these poor kids who have been told endless tales and have read countless books, and have bragged to all their friends about this impending moment, only to realize it wasn't anything like what they had expected, that there's a curious emptiness at the heart of it all, that just maybe they've been lied to all along, or at the very least have been told countless exaggerations, none of which could ever approach the empty truth: there is no magic here, only chaos.

Some look sickened. Others cry. Still others become lost in a far-away dream they might never fully wake from.

We move on to the Tea Party (it lasts a small eternity), the Croquet Ground (the hedgehogs' screams makes my flesh crawl), the Mock Turtle (brought back from the dead, don't ask me how), the Lobster Quadrille (where some show off their dancing), the Queen's Court (in which every one on my tour is sentenced to death, then immediately pardoned), and at last the Pack of Cards (which sends them flying back to Earth, forever changed and bewildered, but with discount vouchers for the next tour) and, hallelujah, I'm done at last.

Seven of Diamonds lights a fag and I bum one from him. He's all creased and worn, and his painted colours have long-since faded to gray. "Come for a drink?" he says, exhaling smoke from the back of his paper frame. He tends "We're All Mad Here," a small pub on a blue-grass checker of the forest beside a bubbling brook. "Three-C's playing tonight," he says as he takes a drag, and by this he means Three of Clubs, who's a mean guitarist and an even meaner drunk.

I know I should go home. But there's nothing there but my mouldering bed sheets, an empty fridge, and a picture of my daughter on the dresser that's slowly turning ashen like Seven of Diamonds. I'd just go home, eat some take-out, and pass out watching TV, only to wake up from yet another nightmare, only to return tomorrow to do this again. So I go to Seven's for some drinks and listen to Three-C jam for a few hours, until I can barely keep my eyes open.

Eventually I leave Seven's bar and stumble along the dark path that will take me back to Earth. Along the way, I pass the familiar stone house set high upon the hill, its windows flickering with orange light that sends long, foggy beams deep into the evening mist. My feet turn before I know where I'm going, and soon I'm climbing through the corkscrew path through the flower garden set alight by a million swarming glow bugs. I shouldn't be here, not without her permission, but I just can't stop. There is a stone underneath one of the flickering windows, and I step upon it to ever so carefully peek through the glass.

The fireplace is bright with flame, though there are no logs to burn. Above the fireplace, on a decorated mantel, are several glass-domed clocks, all ticking, and a large, flawless mirror that perfectly reflects the room. A girl in a blue and white pinafore paces on a circle of carpet before the fire, and every so often as the light plays across her face it's clear she's not quite a girl but a woman much, much older.

Above the circle of carpet, about waist high, held aloft by nothing at all, is a crystal sphere about the size of a grapefruit. And inside the sphere is a flickering nebula, neither jade, nor rose, nor teal, but a swirling mélange of all three colours that changes shape and shade continually.

"Tell me again," she says, and hers is the voice of a little girl, of an elderly woman, of one who holds utter contempt and the deepest admiration for whom she addresses. "Tell me the story again one more time."

And from inside the floating sphere comes a faint, wheezy voice, the sound of a sick man near death and perhaps beyond it, a man who wishes his soul could fly off to the next world, but is prevented from doing so by forces I don't even pretend to understand.

Slowly, he begins, "Alice. . . was beginning to get very tired. . . of sitting by her sister on the bank, and. . . of having nothing to do. . . "

At this, the ancient little girl rubs her hands together. She giggles and skips, and Kitty, curled on the rocking chair, stirs awake, then goes back to sleep. And it's this small motion that crushes me with despair. Despair for Kitty, so inured to this abhorrent sin she can only sleep. Despair for poor Mr. Dodgson, imprisoned in his floating sphere for all time. Despair for myself and for all of us trapped in this dreadful place. But most of all I despair for old Ms. Alice Pleasance Liddell. Because though she wears no chains, everyone knows she's imprisoned too.

After a time, I step down from the stone and slink away from the window. My buzz has faded, and I want a fag more than anything in the world. It's late, and I'm more tired than I've ever felt. I really should be getting home and getting to bed. And it's about this time every night when I start to wonder if I even have a home or a bed to lie in, if I was ever married or had a daughter. Maybe these are just stories I tell myself to get through the day. But I brush aside these thoughts as if I'm swatting away smoke. I really have to get some sleep. I've got work early tomorrow.

THE GARDEN BEYOND HER INFINITE SKIES

AYA FLOATED OVER endless effervescing worlds, seeking anomalies. There were a hundred thousand Farmers of the Branch, but Aya was of the best of them all. Her fields were the healthiest, her realms the most pure. Even the Supervisors said she had an uncanny ability to spot the malignant, when others saw but purity. How she longed to find those sickly realms sprouting in her fields, where the oddest things arose, things not found anywhere else on the Branch. Finding one was enough to make her long workdays worthwhile.

She flew low over her fields. Beneath her, a trillion realms sprouted from the ground, spheres budding spheres. Like fattened wheat, the realms leaned tall in the graviton breeze, their thick fingers grasping for the Expanse, while beneath their knuckled bases, tilled to perfection, lay fertile ground. Alone, Aya expressed herself naturally: a ball of prickling white energy, she scintillated. She searched all day, but did not find one anomaly among countless identical realms.

Perhaps, she thought, *I have destroyed them all.*

Repentance Day was nine days away, when all the Farmer

Folk would gather to play games of history. Who could remember all the First Ones? Who could reap the neatest row? They'd join to sing the ancient songs, to shout the chorus to the Tall Ones. "Oh, the endless rows! Oh, such majestic beauty!" And Aya played the games and sang the histories, but only because to refuse meant being shamed by those whom she loved.

If only, she thought, *I could write my own lyrics, what stories I would tell them.*

She sighed a cloud of tau neutrinos and watched them tumble into the Expanse. Pulled by the graviton wind, they were lost in the blue haze. What would it be like, she wondered, to float off with the particles, to visit those strange, far off places? But her courage fled with them, as it always did. She couldn't survive in the Expanse, where the winds blew fierce and terrible. She belonged here, on the branchlet. And she would die here. And that made her saddest of all.

She floated above the realm tips, where the ground appeared flat as she hugged it close. But when she soared high, the branchlet's curve became visible. Far upstalk, the horizon bent into itself and formed a tube. And this tube kinked and split into more tubes farther upstalk. And these split even farther up, until the myriad branchlets vanished in the Expanse's blue haze.

And downstalk, her branchlet joined a greater, which joined one greater, which joined one yet greater, and so on, until endless fathoms below all branchlets merged with the Prime Stalk of Thept, blessed be her endless reaching.

Aya flew as high as she dared in the graviton winds, wishing she could see Thept in her gargantuan glory, but the haze obscured all but the nearest branchlet.

Then she dove between rows of baby realms, where myriad spheres still glowed from their inflationary epochs. Their pastel globes lit the way for her spiraling journey upstalk.

The Eighty Eight Lights had just begun their climb up

the Prime Stalk, swathing ghostly green swatches across the sky, so that when Aya reached fields of more ancient realms, the landscape plunged into twilight. But even among these brooding shadows, spudded realms winked spectral diamonds from the countless galaxies whirling within them all.

Tiny treasures, she thought, *are hidden inside all things.*

Treasures like Old Gia, who lived in a deep hollow that had been carved into the branchlet. Gia was once a Farmer like Aya, but after long eons, she had grown tired. And as a reward for her service, the Supervisors had given her this home. Old Gia liked to watch the shadows unfold across the Expanse as the Eighty Eight Lights made their daily climb. She hated to be disturbed.

Aya shrunk herself into a respectful torus, taming her wildest energies, as she entered Gia's hollow.

"Go away!" Gia shouted. A colorful and reactive mess of anti-quarks pooled on the ground before her. "I said, go away!" Fits of radiation spluttered from Gia's body, a pallid and diffuse ball of energy.

"But it's me!" Weak blue light from the opening crawled and died a short way in, so that the rear of the hollow was as black as a dead realm.

"Aya? So it is. I don't sense well anymore, child."

"No, you don't. I'm no longer a child."

"When you reach my age, Aya, everyone becomes a child." She spat out a thin spray of down quarks that drifted to the floor, sparking as they joined the viscous pool. "What brings you here?"

"I was hoping you'd tell me another story of the First Ones."

"Ah, the young farmer grows lonely again."

"I'm not lonely," Aya said. But she wasn't sure if that was true. Out the opening, bleak shadows reached across the Expanse, vaguely menacing. The silence seemed to choke the space, but she couldn't think of anything meaningful to say that had not already been said, as if she was searching for a language she didn't yet speak.

Gia grumbled and retreated into her hollow, revealing a faintly glowing structure that had been hidden behind her. Packed tightly together in a polyhedral pattern was a collection of lights, each a dim pink sphere, like a cold baby realm. Each held a memory. "Your journal has grown," Aya said.

"My memories," Gia said, "have become like a sky full of dying suns, slowly winking out. This is my bulwark against annihilation."

"May I view one?"

"Never. They are too personal. But I'll describe one to you."

Aya shivered off a muon cloud of excitement as Gia plucked a sphere from her journal and absorbed it into her energy-body. The sphere flickered inside her. "I was so young then, barely weaned off ultraviolet milk! I'd forgotten this day. How could I forget? Mama was so colorful, so free."

"Describe her!" Aya said, unraveling her wildest energies.

"She was very different from today's Rearing Mothers. You'd think her energy-body was untamed, her spectra feral. But that's how we expressed ourselves then, expansive, radiant, wild. Mama took my sisters and me upstalk, all the way to a tip."

"Tell me what it was like!"

Gia paused, shivering as if reliving the memory. "Such a sight! I was terrified, but the tendrils mesmerized me. I was surprised because the tendrils didn't bravely reach for the Expanse as I had thought, but cowered from it, as if the Expanse was . . . cold."

"Cold?"

"These baby tendrils were cowards, Aya."

Perhaps Old Gia was misremembering. The tendrils held the vanguard against the blue Abyss. Or so the songs went.

Gia continued, "Their fear was unhealthy. Mama told us the branchlet had to be excised before its disease spread. We had come to sever her from Thept. Mama showed us how to focus our energy-bodies into Z-beams. And we helped her to . . ." Gia paused, and shivered. "We cut the diseased branchlet free."

Unexpectedly, she vomited the sphere out. It plopped to the floor in a pool of wild particles.

"Gia? Are you all right?"

Gia dimmed. "I've had enough for today, Aya."

"But what did the tendrils look like? How many were there? What did the—"

The X-rays smacked Aya hard. It was just a flash, all Old Gia could muster, but the blow hurt regardless.

"Sentimental child!" Gia snarled. "Why are you here, dreaming when you should be out farming? Get back to work, you wretched tangle of radiation! Get out!" Gia retreated into her hollow, small and dim, barely recognizable as a living creature among the sea of particle noise.

Aya's body stung where Gia had struck her, but she took the blow without reaction, as all good Farmers were taught to do. The pink sphere lay beneath her, an ancient world that might never be seen again, if Gia had her way. Such a shame to let it wink out like a dying star.

Gia was already dozing, spluttering fitful rays, when Aya snatched the globe and darted out the opening. She sped across her fields and flew until she was sure she wasn't followed. Then she set down between a parade of realms that leaned heavily into the Expanse. Shadows tumbled over the ground as she absorbed Gia's memory sphere into her body.

She felt Gia. She *became* Gia.

Her energy-body danced with excitement at being so far from home. And what love for Mama who sprayed off vivid nebulae as she spun up the branch! Its circumference was so thin that she and her sisters could loop around the branchlet in an instant. The ground sparkled a brilliant blue with the glittering particle dew that dusted the surface. No realms had yet formed here. The branchlet was only just born itself.

Gia dared not take her gaze from the ground, because the

hideous blue Expanse surrounded her. She wanted to hide inside Mama's energy-body. All the children did. They begged Mama to return home. But Mama called them cowards and smacked them with harsh rays.

"Look!" Mama said. "Look how the tendrils cower from the Expanse, just as you cower now. Your fear is weakness! You must cut it from yourself!" The children whimpered, and she beat them again until they fell silent.

I'm a coward, Gia thought. *I cannot look!*

Mama showed them how to form beams of Z-particles with their energy-bodies, then started the cut. She ordered the children to join her. It took effort, enormous concentration, but soon a furious beam erupted from Gia. All her bottled up rage and terror and sadness leaped out from her. She and the children cut, and the Expanse flickered with the reflected light.

The beams screeched and wailed. But Gia realized the screams came from the branchlet itself. The tendrils cried as the Z-beams moved through them. The sound sickened her, but she didn't stop until the children had severed it through.

Loose from its mother, the baby branch tumbled into the Expanse, tugged by the graviton breeze. It gave such a wail, and giant Thept quivered beneath her as the tendrils reached back for their mother. But it was too late. The branchlet disappeared into the haze of the endless blue sky.

The memory ended. Sickened by the memory, Aya spat out the pink sphere. In a torrent of particles she tossed it far into the Expanse, wishing the feelings would vanish with it.

For a long time she remained in the field. That horrid screeching . . . Those desperate tendrils, reaching for their mother . . .

If only she'd never experienced Gia's memory. If only she could take it back and forget. But she knew she never would.

Thept, bless her endless reaching, had millions of sisters across the Expanse. The Tall Ones grew out beyond the blue horizon and countless baby realms were born from their myriad branchlets. And far below, their massive root systems plunged into the great ovum called Yi. Just as the realms arose from Thept's body, so the Tall Ones grew from Yi.

Yi herself was one of sixty four ova gestating inside Delicate Womb, the reproductive organ of Mother Lily, who gloriously blossomed inside the 501-dimensional field, Sky of Skies, who accelerated madly inside the meditating Z-space. Incomprehensible Mind, who lived inside another being who had a billion names and even more descriptions, none of which sufficed to circumscribe it. Always, the smaller grew in the larger, on and on eternally, blessed be the All.

The All was eternally full of noise.

Messages trickled down from above like the particle rains. Most were gibberish to the Farmer Folk. But once in a long while, a message became clear. Some ineffable being had told Incomprehensible Mind, who had told Sky of Skies, who had told Mother Lily, who had told Delicate Womb, who had told Yi, who had told Thept, who had told the Supervisors, who had told the Farmers, to farm and tend the branchlets where countless realms bubbled up from the surface, to keep them free of disease and entanglement so that Thept's growth might continue forever. That message came eight trillion Great Cycles ago, a great long time, even here.

And so the First Ones had razed and tilled Thept's branches, and through generations they'd uprooted corruption, eradicated disease. They had forced the knotted realms into endless neat rows. It had taken eons and countless prunings, but they'd tamed Thept's wildest tendencies. Now, all was arrayed harmony.

But Aya found no beauty in the monotony. In her youth, Rearing Mother had taken her and her sisters to the Tangle, a knot of branchlets downstalk. The First Ones had left it in place to show what would happen if branchlets were left wild.

Iridescent worms wriggled between massively overbudded realms. Spiky balls of baryonic matter clung to the realm tips, popping to release flashing rainbows of particle spores. Antimatter spiders of a thousand legs pricked realms with their sharp proboscii and grew fat with sucking. The realms formed hoary palaces, gnarled labyrinths and raveled jungles so thick that even airy neutrinos could only travel but a short way in before hitting something dense and impenetrable. And over all this rolled furious particle storms, bathing the fangled corners with strange, brooding energies.

The Tangle was meant to evoke disgust. It was bizarre, Aya thought, but far from disgusting. For ages she longed to enter those twisted realms and dance its grotesque curves, to explore its vulgar corners and play with those exultant infestations of life. Instead, she was taught to revile it.

She had never told Rearing Mother her true feelings. To express them was to invite a beating, or a furlough inside a dead realm, a place frightfully silent, dark, and cold. And she had never told her sisters either, because they betrayed her to gain Rearing Mother's favor. Instead she found it safer to keep silent. And over time that silence had built up pressure, like a realm ready to burst into existence. It was her greatest fear that she could not contain it once it was born.

But Gia's memory gave energy to that silence, threatening to give it form. Aya dreamed often of that severed branch. While flying over her fields she thought she heard echoes of its ancient screams coming from out in the deep.

She was floating low over her twilit, ancient realms one morning when she found an anomaly. She gasped a bubble of charmed quarks. Here, growing among dark arrays, a dim realm curved back on itself, a hooked finger cowering from the Expanse. Or perhaps it turned inward to consider its own curious arising. But this was anathema. To grow inward, a sin. This disease had to be obliterated. A tight beam of Z-particles would do it, would reduce this gloriously wrong realm to a scintillating snow of ash, fertilizer for unborn worlds.

Instead, she peered inside.

Hundreds of billions of galaxies aligned themselves in fine, shining filaments like hoar frost across the hooked realm of 10-space. A tenuous galactic cluster huddled on a filament edge. And inside this cluster, a galaxy furiously twirled. And in this galaxy, a giant red sun hurtled through the dark. And around this sun raced a green planet. And on this planet a purple and white quadruped leaped through a dense forest.

More softly than a falling leaf, the animal tiptoed down to a narrow stream. Its head was long and sleek, its gray horns branching like a miniscule Thept. A breeze trickled through the trees as the quadruped sipped its fill, then gazed up at the orange sky to wonder at the coming dawn.

But this wonder died before long. The creature was not quite self-aware. Full consciousness might take eons, if it ever happened at all. Even among the infinite realms, sentience was a fickle thing. How rare that the quadruped even wondered at all. Given enough time, she thought, what might this species become? If she let it be, she might live long enough to find out.

"A farmer's job is never done."

The voice startled her, and she turned to see the Supervisor expressing himself brightly beside her. She collapsed her energies into a shivering torus of high-energy leptons out of respect. "Supervisor," she said, "I didn't know—"

"A trillion realms bubble into the Expanse by their own chaotic wills." He spoke as if addressing an audience. "Without farmers, realms grow weedy and knotted. Disease spreads. Then we must raze and destroy to continue our long mission. Thept, bless her endless reaching, despises nothing more than a pruning. Tell me, Aya, what is it about this sickly realm that captures your attention?"

The Supervisor's name was Bu, but he made Aya always use his title. He peered deep into the hooked realm, far deeper than she ever could, as she shivered off a hadron cloud. What he saw, she couldn't say, but she knew it wasn't beauty.

"Well?" he said.

"I marvel at the manifold arising animals, Supervisor. They exult in the physical." And because she couldn't stop herself, she added, "I love how this quadruped moves so quietly through the woods." It was a foolish thing to say, she knew, but there was no one else here to listen.

"Aya," he said, "you've always been an excellent Farmer. So I've tolerated your eccentricities. But what is another quadruped?" He sloughed off a sheath of indifferent neutrons. "I've seen quadrupeds arise on this branchlet nine quintillion times. This realm is crooked, inward-looking. A grotesquery. It must be destroyed."

"Do they suffer," she said, "when we destroy them?"

"The disease must be removed before it spreads."

The graviton wind was unusually calm, and she thought she heard a scream out in the Expanse. "But do they suffer?"

The Supervisor's energy body roiled, sparking with angry bursts of anti-matter. "All this time and still a damned child," he spat as he raised up a storm of gamma rays, pelting her energy-body. She withered in pain. But she took the blows as Rearing Mother had taught her, and her mother before that, going all the way back to the First Ones. One's worst tendencies had to be beaten out, she knew.

He let up his blows an instant before she would have diffused into random sparks of radiation.

"I love you," he said, his energies still fierce. "That's why this hurts me more than it hurts you. But this is for your own good. We must excise your worst habits, so that what remains is pure. I know you understand."

She muttered, "Yes, Supervisor."

Soon he was caressing her with a gentle stream of infrared photons. She let him soothe her pain, because she needed the relief, though she hated herself for it. "Now," he said, "finish your work, so I may finish mine."

Aya collected her energies and crept toward the realm. A tight beam of Z-particles was all it took. It leaped from her, melting the realm like a comet in a supernova. Matter decayed by the yotta-particle, flashing brightly before fading. And just like that, the realm was gone.

Bits of scintillating energy snowed to the ground. It would take eons for all the sparks to reach the surface. Which one, she wondered, had been the quadruped? Would that spark ever rise to wonder again?

"It's amazing," the Supervisor said, "how precise you are. A skill like yours comes once in a generation. Why is it so hard for you to use your gift?" He puffed himself into a hundred billion 50-spaces, so that he expanded enormously above her. "Now be a good Farmer, Aya," he said, then corkscrewed up the branchlet, past a trillion realms, off to mind other Farmers in other fields until he vanished in the haze.

The sparks from the snuffed world fell. Where the first sparks touched the ground, new realms were born. They flashed, inflated, and slowed, their quark-gluon plasma too hot for solid matter. It would take an eon before galaxies formed. Two or three more before animal life arose. The Farmer folk sang ballads about the sparks of dead realms. The dust, forever alive, the lyrics went. Death, an illusion, just forms changing.

But that quadruped, that particular arrangement of mind and will, would never know wonder again. If that wasn't death, what was?

The Eighty Eight Lights were ascending quickly. She had to get back to work, but there was someone she needed to see.

Aya flew downstalk, over row after row of middle-aged realms that leaned steeply into the graviton breeze, each realm the same as the next.

"Aya!" Ri called. Her sister farmed the fields downstalk.

singing an ancient song. "It's been ages!" Ri said, brightly expressing herself as a tiny white ball.

Aya allowed herself to expand into a large sphere, not as wild as she preferred, so her sister would not get offended.

"What brings you downstalk, Aya? Have you a problem?"

"I wanted to ask you about something."

"Uh-oh," said Ri, chuckling a blue-green shower of leptons that spiraled off into the Expanse. "Your curiosity always gets you into trouble."

"I went to see Old Gia recently."

"I don't understand why you visit that old bag of particles."

"I saw one of her memories, Ri."

Ri flickered for a moment. "What do you mean, *saw*?"

Aya told Ri about Gia's journal, and the memory of the severed branch.

"That's disturbing, Aya."

"I know," Aya said. "Now I hear screams coming from the Expanse, and I haven't been sleeping."

"No," Ri said. "It's disturbing that you stole. Rearing Mother would give you quite a beating if she hears of this."

"One beating from Supervisor Bu is enough for today."

"He disciplined you, *again*? I thought you were his favorite." Ri dimmed an order of magnitude. "What's gotten into you?"

"Do you ever look into realms, before you destroy them?"

"Sometimes."

"And what do you see?"

"Disease, mostly."

"Never beauty?"

Ri paused. "There's never beauty in sickness."

"But what if a sick realm held something, however miniscule, worth saving? Would you spare it?"

Ri floated higher. "I see what's happened here. Gia's memory has poisoned you. That baby branchlet cried when they cut it free, yes, but didn't we cry when Rearing Mother beat us? It hurt then, but look at what Farmers we've become! Those beatings were for our own good, rooting out our worst habits. In the same way, eradicating disease is healthy for Thept. Pain is necessary for growth. If I'm ever chosen to be a Rearing Mother, I'll root out the unruliness from my children the same way. And it will hurt me more than it will hurt them. Don't you see? It's all for the collective good."

"I suppose," Aya said, feeling sick.

"Sister, you look exhausted. Your energies are wild. Why don't you go and take a nap over there? I'll watch for the Supervisor and wake you if he comes. I'll even tell him how I saw you eradicate a young cancer."

Never mind that there would be no cinders to mark the grave, Aya *was* exhausted. "Thank you, Ri. You're a good sister."

"And you a troublesome one! But I love you, Aya. Now sleep, so you may forget this foolishness."

Aya floated back to her fields and nuzzled between a dozen middle-aged realms. They caressed her sides as she drifted off to sleep. In her dreams a million blue tendrils squeezed her until she exploded in a flash that didn't wink out, but slowly faded, like a cinder. When she awoke, the Eighty Eight Lights had already passed Half Stalk.

Ri was nowhere to be found.

Repentance Day came and went, and Aya sang the songs and played the games, but her heart was not in it. The Eighty Eight Lights climbed the Prime Stalk of Thept two thousand times. Most days she lay in her fields and dreamed of the Tangle. But sometimes she exposed herself to the harsh particle rains when she should have waited them out in a safe hollow.

She was drifting low over her fields, and the Eighty Eight Lights had just begun their morning climb when she saw it. It grew from the side of a tall, ancient realm. An irregular carbuncle not one-hundredth the size of the parent it clung to, a cancer that needed to be excised.

The cancer had given birth to billions of galaxies. They spread across its 10-space like the vanes of a feather. In one spiral galaxy, a yellow sun drifted near the galactic edge. Orbiting this sun was a blue-white world. And on this world a copper-skinned biped sat on the ground and drew a figure in the dirt with a stick: a quadruped, with branching horns.

The biped examined her drawing. It wasn't alive, she knew, but an echo. Yet as she stared at the figure, she saw the blood on Father's face and felt the men's hard, beastly gazes. She smelled the hot animal flesh as Mother and the other women opened the animal with their bone knives. Even the twirling smoke stung her eyes as it rose from the flames to appease Sky God and her Thousand Bright Children. Her heart thrummed and her stomach grumbled, as if this were happening now. But the hunt was yesterday, and somehow every vivid sense folded itself into her figure in the dirt. The drawing, the biped realized, was magic.

A larger female walked over, Mother. She saw the drawing, shrieked, and immediately stamped it out. Mother too had sensed the drawing's power to evoke memory. She struck the child in the face. And the child held in her cries, because Mother hated tears even more than magic drawings.

A third biped walked over, Father. Mother swung again at the child, but Father grabbed her before she could strike. His look was fierce, animal-like. His words were elaborated grunts, their language not yet mature.

He said, "No more. *No more!*"

Father threw her hand down and walked away, back to sharpen his spear with the other males. But with his back turned, Mother hit the child again. And the magic vision of the hunt and all its vivid senses receded further from the child's mind with each blow. In pain, the child vowed that if she were ever blessed by Sky God to birth a child, she would never hit him.

Aya removed her gaze from the cancerous realm and gazed over her fields as if seeing them for the first time. Like the bipedal child, her pain didn't have to continue. She didn't have to destroy worlds. She didn't have to take the blows. How curious that it took an infinitesimal creature to show this to her.

Ever so carefully, with a fine Z-beam, she severed the cancer from its parent. It floated free, still alive. Without an energy-source, it would eventually die. But she knew a place to hide it, where it could grow and even thrive.

When she reached Gia's hollow, the opening was brightly lit. A harsh yellow glow pooled on the ground outside it. Aya hid the cancer in the adjacent field before she entered.

Gia's particle soup had been swept clean, and four Supervisors circled the rear, as if searching for something. Supervisor Bu was among them. Gia and her journal were nowhere to be found.

"What's happened?" Aya said. The Supervisors stopped whatever they had been doing.

"Why, hello!" Supervisor Bu said as he came over. "Just the farmer I wanted to see."

"Where's Gia?"

"Gone, I'm afraid."

"To where?"

"To dust," he said. "She decayed just this morning." He caressed her. "I'm sorry, Aya. Were you close?"

Aya wanted to scream or fly as high as she dared go, higher even. She felt like exploding or turning to dust. But she just said, "We were friends, I think."

"So, I've heard. When did you last visit?"

"I haven't seen her for thousands of days."

"And what did you two speak about, typically?"

"Many things."

"Such as?"

"Where's her journal, Supervisor?"

"Her journal?"

"Her memories?"

"Ah, yes. Aya, when one starts to decay, like Old Gia, the

mind decays too. This journal of hers was plagued with disease. It had to be destroyed." Inside his body, a tiny pink sphere, just like the one from Gia's journal, flashed and winked out.

The hollow seemed to spin, faster and faster, and Aya retreated toward the exit. "I have to get back to work."

"That's my good Farmer," he said, petting her. "Always working hard. I'll need to ask you more questions, later, once we sort this mess. I'll see you in your fields."

Outside and alone, the infinite Expanse pressed down upon her. All Gia's memories, gone forever. Was it possible?

She returned to the hidden cancer. Like Gia's memory, she absorbed the realm into her body, where it remained whole and alive. It could feed off her for a while, suckling radiation from her, until its growth killed both of them. But this would suffice for now. The realm shivered, tickling her as she spiraled upstalk.

The biped's voice echoed in her mind "No more. *No more.*"

She soared high, until the branchlet was barely visible in the haze, then she dove to skate the realm tops, spraying their energies across the field. Supervisor Bu would discipline her for that, but not if he couldn't find her.

She flew beyond the edge of her fields, and entered Nessa's. Her other sister dawdled above a row of ancient realms and called out as Aya hurtled past, but Aya didn't slow. She flew past Jia, and Thi, and Den, and Hio, and Sil, and a dozen more of her siblings' fields. The Eighty Eight Lights were nearing Half Stalk when she reached the fork. The branchlet split, each half vanishing into the haze. This was the farthest she'd ever gone. She was forbidden from going any further.

She chose left and went up.

She flew past more farms. Some Folk called out to her. Most ignored her. In some fields, there were no Farmers at all. And yet the endless budding realms looked no different from hers.

Up she flew.

The Expanse grew dark. How had the Eighty Eight Lights

descended so quickly? The sky faded to black. Somewhere out in the dark, seven yellow lights blinked, then vanished, while the realms beneath her twinkled with countless galaxies and stars. Their light was pale and ghostly, and the darkness overwhelmed her. She stopped.

She crawled between two bulbous realms and tried to sleep, while the cancer tickled her insides. Sometime later, she awoke. A Farmer hovered above her, shouting. Behind her glimmered the blue-gray of the morning sky. She sped away.

Exhausted, she flew on. On the second night, the graviton wind blew so fiercely she had to cling to the realms so she wouldn't fly into the Expanse. The torrential particle rain dissolved her energies as she hid the cancer deep inside herself. It shivered with her. But the storm passed, and the next morning she flew on.

She reached a fork on the sixth day and went right. On the ninth day, she turned left. Directions didn't matter, so long as she went up. With a chill she realized that if she turned back now, she wouldn't know which way was home.

The branchlets thinned ever more, so that she could loop around them quickly, while the Expanse grew massive around her. At Full Stalk the Eighty Eight Lights weren't so high anymore. And at night, if the winds were calm, she saw indistinct shapes shimmering out in the Expanse. Tall Ones, winking?

She reached the next fork, but it wasn't a fork at all. A gnarled lump, weathered by wind and rain, was all that remained of its right side. Eons ago this branch had been severed from Thept. Aya wondered if this was the same one Gia and her sisters had cut.

She went left and passed more severed limbs, and the Expanse yawned ever larger around her. Her fear grew as she ascended, and the little cancer inside her grew weaker by the day so that she knew it was alive only by its tiny shivering.

The farms abruptly ended. Beyond lay pale, barren,

withered ground. No realms bubbled from the surface. And just a short journey onward she finally reached the tip, the last finger of Thept. In Gia's memory, glittering dew dusted the surface, and the tendrils were timid but exuberantly alive.

This branchlet was dead.

Its surface was ashen and black, and where the tendrils should have been holding the vanguard against the Abyss, were seven gnarled stumps. The gulf unfolded its massive blue nothingness around her, and the branchlet shuddered in the graviton wind. A strong gust and she might blow away forever.

She retreated to the last fork, a half-day's journey, and took the opposite branch. But this led to another dead branch, ashen and black. She was exhausted, and the light was fading, but the winds were too strong to sleep here. Out in the Expanse, vague forms shimmered.

"Aya, my beloved! There you are!" His voice came as if arising from a dream.

She shivered off a muon cloud as Supervisor Bu, five Supervisors, and her sister Ri, floated up to her.

"Aya!" Supervisor Bu said, exasperated. "We've been following your energy trail for days."

"Aya," Ri said, "I was so worried for you!"

"The tips," Aya said. "They're all dead."

"Pruned," Bu said, "Eons ago. Aya, come here." He gently caressed her, but she withdrew from him.

"How can you caress me one moment and pummel me the next? That's not right."

"What is this? Come here, before you decay."

Aya paused as the truth of it all became clear. It had been the same with Old Gia, she thought. The Supervisor pretended compassion even as he beat and razed. "Gia didn't decay naturally," Aya said. "Did she?"

The graviton wind gusted once, hard, and everyone struggled to hang on.

"Old Gia was spreading disease," he said. "And disease must

be eradicated."

She had once loved Supervisor Bu, but now she saw he was a monster. "She had so many untold stories."

"She was full of madness," Ri said. "I found a globe of hers in my field. She must have been spreading poison all over the place. I saw what her memory had done to you, Aya, so I told Supervisor Bu before she might hurt someone else."

"She wasn't spreading those memories," Aya said, "I threw her memory globe away. It must have landed in your field."

"Either way," he said, "she had become a cancer."

Aya felt sick. It was her fault. If she hadn't taken that memory, Old Gia would still be alive.

"Aya," he said, approaching her. "We love you. You're sick. You need help."

"Like you helped Gia?"

"Aya, you're the best Farmer in a generation. Come home, and let's forget all this nonsense."

The cancerous realm inside her had been softly shivering, when it shuddered once, violently.

"What's that inside you?" he said. He peered deep within her. "Is that a realm? A *cancer*?" His tone shifted abruptly. "Why is that *disease* inside you, Aya?"

"I saved it," she said, "because it's precious."

"I didn't want to do this," he said. "But you leave me no choice." His body roiled as he prepared a storm of rays.

Part of her longed to return home, to soar over her fields and feel free again. She longed to watch the Eighty Eight Lights descend with her sister by her side. She missed Rearing Mother and her other siblings. But going back meant forgetting everything that had happened.

She stepped back from him and said, "No more. *No more.*" Then she leaped into the Expanse.

"Aya!"

She plunged into the blue void, and the graviton wind quickly grabbed her. The branchlet vanished in the haze, and their screams were soon lost in the wind.

Terror consumed her as she hurtled into the endless blue. She tried to direct her flight, but the currents were too strong. Harsh winds attacked her, tearing at her energy-body, while the realm inside her quivered like a nervous atom. Neither of them would last long.

She tumbled helplessly. Soon she would diffuse into dust. But after a time the blue sky turned black, the winds abated, and she found she could direct her flight. She flew free from the worst gusts, gaining hope.

Shapes resolved in the darkness, as if beyond a cloud of dissipating smoke. Buried within tufts of blue cloud, swarms of shimmering lights climbed up and down massive stalks. A forest of Tall Ones spread beneath a night sky, millions of gargantuan trees glowing from their own ethereal light. And below, moving shadows rolled over the rough and ruddy surface of Yi, the great ovum. Sinuous purple arteries weaved through the Tall Ones like tubular rivers, flickering with universes of light inside them.

But every Tall One, all the countless millions, were stunted, their limbs severed, just as Thept had been. Thept, bless her endless reaching, didn't reach at all. Like all her severed sisters, she was torn to shreds. Aya flew above the stunted forest.

The Farmers had done this, she knew. They had, with their sick philosophy, murdered them all.

She sloughed off sprays of hadrons as she floated high, while the little realm shivered inside her, eating her insides. It would suckle off her until they both were dust.

As she flew on, hints of ruddy light shone in the distance, beyond Yi's curving horizon. She glimpsed it first in silhouette, as the sky lightened behind it. Immensely far off, an ineffable distance away, a single Tall One grew higher than the rest, its arms extended skyward, its branches uncut.

A survivor.

Perhaps there someone too had said, "No more." But this

Tall One was an immense distance away. She might die long before she reached it. She could return to Thept or another Tall One and start again.

But no, that wouldn't do. There was a garden out there. No matter how far it was, she had to reach it. She gathered the last of her energies in preparation for the journey.

I will make it, she thought. *I will survive. And the next generation will know no pain.*

And deep inside her, as if sensing her thoughts, the little realm with the bipedal girl suddenly stopped shivering.

CAMERON RHYDER'S LEGS

For Arthur C.

FIVE THOUSAND YOUNG men and women crowd this music hall tonight, and one of them is the soul I must erase from existence. How many she has killed I cannot say. To suggest a number is a sin. How can we count those who no longer exist? I once had a family, a husband, eight children. A life and a future. But all this has been timelost, expunged from history. And so I will expunge her. Except I've no idea who she is. Or *he*, for that matter. In this Now, gender and dress make a difference.

Today, I'm female. My boxy eyeglasses, fashionably retro, hide a rainbow of sensors. I scan their eyes for tells, hunt their mind-detritus for fear. It's hard to see who's just stoned and who's got something to hide. My gold digital watch, also retro, holo-def hicodes what my eyes miss.

I wear tight black jeans and a persistent smirk as if I'm entitled to things I don't deserve. My body is average, my skin tawny-light, my black hair medium-length, nose unremarkable. I'm a mayfly, engineered to be forgotten. I scan their bodies for changes since their last instance in this Now as they glimpse, then immediately forget me.

They're here for the Goo Globbers, the glammed-out rock quartet that howls like a synaptic re-write. The crowd applauds far too much at the end of the first song, which I gauge as a covert attempt to escape their unexpressed fears. Unlike me, they cannot know their future.

The singer Scott Mohl croons, "*The day ends with the setting sun, the flower wilts, its colors run,*" and the crowd swoons in a haze of marijuana smoke and purple spotlights. But the colored patterns flicker-flash too precisely to be Now-native. Someone's using lustre-tech to coerce brain states, but this tech won't exist for another fifty years.

Scott Mohl's honied voice reverberates under my feet as I weave through dancing bodies, scanning, scanning. Their dilated eyes make my probes of their forebrains a cakewalk.

I scan a young, fire-haired woman with leafy green eyes. Cat's-eye glasses on the end of her nose twinkle with rhinestones. Her lips part as my retinal shines a maser deep into her pupils at frequencies attuned to her neurons, hijacking her brain and dumping her memories into mine.

She has been in this Now before, my Archives tell me, in nine hundred and eighty one instances. I scan her blackbody signature for aberrations.

I find one, of course. When she was seven, a pebble got caught in her bicycle wheel, and she crashed and broke her leg. And because she couldn't go outside, she hung around the house and listened to her brother's music collection, which spawned an interest in the musical subgenre of alternative retro-punk-fuzz-fusion, which led her, eighteen years, five months and four days later to this Goo Globbers concert. She's kept the pebble with her all this time, a totem to the gods of fate. Her hand fiddles with it in her pocket just now.

And it was We, The Hands of Brahma, who placed the pebble two millimeters to the left from where it was the last time. And because of our Correction, her recovery lasted two days, seven hours longer, and her interest in retro-punk-fuzz-fusion solidified, and in this Now she arrived to this concert six minutes and nine seconds earlier. She took her place beside the bar, drinking her rum sours every nineteen minutes forty-one seconds, on average, as she always does. Her early arrival forced a tall male of South-Asian genetics to move one meter to the left and scratch his nose, which he has never done in any Nows before.

I log this through Twitter, spread across hundreds of accounts, in a series of steganographically-encoded photographs I take with my camera-phone. My Tweets will find their way to the future via the Library of Congress Twitter Archive, where my superiors will read and dissect them nine hundred years hence.

I flash the woman's short-term memory and set her free two seconds after we've met eyes. I'm careful not to leave memories. To do so would risk not only my life but the Great Mission itself. Her cat's-eye glasses sparkle as she moves on.

There may be hundreds of Anachronists hiding in the crowd. If they find me they'll erase me from existence, or worse, rewrite my memories so I'll fight and die for their sick cause.

We'll do the same to them, of course. War is war, after all. But any timelost fool can see that what we're doing is nothing short of saving the Cosmos from chaos, their ultimate goal.

Scott Mohl belts, *"The shadows of our yesterdays fall across my face, who are we but dust and loam, adrift in inner space?"* The audience sways blissfully as the stage lights let loose a spray of brain-calming frequencies. Someone wants this crowd wide open and suggestible. Us, or them?

I scan and record Corrections by the thousand-fold. The dancing acne-faced kid with too much energy (a passing word from a stranger began the causal chain that led him here). The pink-haired girl typing into her phone and taking pictures of herself (a book left open to a particular passage). The brawny security guard with crossed arms and a dour expression (a can of soup, moved from one shelf to another). Even Scott Mohl, hopping around stage in his glittery cape and leather pants (a whiff of sunscreen on a winter's day). All have been Corrected thousands of times. People native to this Now believe they live such insignificant lives. If only they knew their grand purpose, how we gently nudge them toward enlightenment one millimeter at a time.

For We, the Hands of Brahma, have sent countless operatives here, via circuitous and parallel Nows, though those histories, if I have ever known them, have been erased from my memory. (To break the Causal Chain is a sin; the True Time must be preserved.) Just the same, the Anachronists have sent myriad operatives here. Nearly a million times they have nudged, forced, and heaved this moment away from the True Time. And always, we push it back. It's been a cat and mouse game for eons. In short, I'm not alone.

Ninety-quintillion qubit hours of b-tree analysis and billions of timelost souls point to an event *here* as Ultimate Cause. Something happens tonight—specifically what, we have not yet determined—which through a complex series of causally chained events, will bring about the end of the Varaha Kalpa, Brahma's Day. Time as we know it will cease. Atoms will fly apart. Cause and effect will lose meaning.

The Cosmos will die.

And oh, how I long for that moment with all my heart! For in that moment the Living Cosmos will be reborn. The timelost will be found. Death will end. Blessed is her name, Tat Tvam Asi, That Thou Art, who dies so that we may live! If I find and erase my target tonight, all this glory shall come to pass.

"I'm told we have a guest here tonight," Scott Mohl says to whoops and jeers from the crowd. "The lovely Cameron Rhyder." He holds out a hand toward the VIP dais at stage right. "Hey, doll," he says, "join us?"

The crowd turns to the disgraced former actress and one-time lover of Scott Mohl, Cameron Rhyder, sitting on the VIP dais. She leans forward in her seat and takes a sip of scotch, while on the dancefloor beside her, an olive-skinned man with a Van Dyke beard stares at her legs.

This is wrong. In four thousand previous Nows his gaze has never lingered on her legs for so long. As Ms. Cameron Rhyder slowly rises from her seat, I shove through the crowd and yank out my timeclaw.

The Brahma Brute smirks over me as she plucks a hair from my Van Dyke beard and puts it in a glass phial. She's had me down deep, scoured my brain for secrets, and I'm all fogged up.

She adjusts her boxy eyeglasses, 21st-century retro, that hide an array of sensors and weaponry. Her gold watch not only tells time but helps her manipulate it.

These Brutes brainwashed Myra, my wife. She died in the Battle of Pendulum, fighting for them. I had to explain to Jacob, our son, why she sent us all those hateful messages, why she cursed our family to her last breath. And when Jacob asked me if he would one day hate me too, I knew I had to join the fight to save us all.

I lay strapped to the Brute's chair in this dark, humid cave, where crude paintings of violent hunts and antlered gods on the walls tell a story that might have happened last week.

"This will hurt worse than anything you can imagine, 219," the Brute says. These freaks switch bodies so often they don't even use names.

My Goo Globbers t-shirt reeks of marijuana from the music hall. My temple throbs where she hooked me with her timeclaw and yanked me backward through time.

Ten blank-eyed Variants stand by the cave exit, their crisp white uniforms bright against the stone walls. The electric blue numbers on their breasts glow like a frozen stopwatch.

"I'll take whatever you got," I say.

My thoughts stutter as hot red beams shine onto me from hanging panels. They yank out data written into my junk DNA by the petabyte: the number of times my genes have be rewritten (forty seven), my taste for sour sweets (borderline addictive), my fetish for women in yellow sports socks (admittedly weird).

"You have a pocket of gas in your large intestine," she says. "Twenty-first century polysaturated fats do not suit you."

"I could fart, if you want."

"You've turned off input from your sympathetic nervous system. But I can bypass your physical body and send thoughts directly into your mind."

Suddenly I can't breathe: I'm being hung from a tree! The pain is obscene, but I've trained for this.

She stops the pain, and I try to gasp with dignity but fail.

"That was nothing," she says. "I can simulate being eaten alive by rats, falling from a great height onto stone, freezing to death in icy water, and other such horrors. But I've no desire to be cruel."

I silently repeat my trigger phrase, and the post-hypnotic suggestion calms my fear. But my calm is fraught. Jacob will grow up without parents, without someone to lead him through the dark. "I won't let you destroy the universe," I say.

She sighs. "Is that the best you have, 219? I expected more from an Anachronist. I can rewrite your memories, make you docile and obedient, like my Variants here." She gestures to the blank-eyed souls surrounding us. I recognize two from my time at Buenos Aires bootcamp.

Davey Blackwood had a wife and three daughters. Sandra Chatterjee was finishing her Ph.D. in Temporal Dynamics when she got drafted. Now they'd kill their own child if this Brute ordered them to.

I try to muster confidence. "Do what you must."

A duplicate Variant 175—another Sandra Chatterjee— enters the cave. She appears in all ways identical to the Variant 175 standing by the cave mouth. The two meet eyes, exchange data. "I come from an instance seven minutes and forty- two seconds ahead of this Now," the second says. "Madam Interrogator 991, please note that a forced neural rewrite will destroy any possible recovery of information from this patient.

Your future self respectfully requests you try another method."

The original Variant 175 waits until the duplicate has finished, then she heads for the cave exit to activate her timeclaw and close the loop.

"You see how hopeless it is, 219?" the Brute says. "Our Variant will leap back in time at exactly seven minutes and forty-two seconds from the moment her future self arrived and she will repeat those words to me exactly as she has heard them, thus preserving the True Time. Though the original cause of the message is timelost, we have gained information from the Void. Such are the wonders of the great Tat Tvam Asi, blessed is Her Glorious Name, who Herself exists Without Cause!"

"Your sick philosophy has murdered trillions."

Variant 293 runs into the cave and says, "I come from an instance two minutes and nine seconds ahead of this Now. Stop! Patient 219's neural DNA is booby trapped with singularity bombs. In my instance, Variant 9641 emerged from the timestream charred and burnt from an explosion, which she said destroyed a significant portion of North America. She died immediately. Your future self kindly requests you do not scrub his neural DNA." The original Variant 293 leaves the cave.

"Again!" she says, "True Time is preserved, blessed is The Causeless One!" She smiles at me, her pupils like swirling black holes in the bright lights. "Do you understand yet?" she says. "Anything you do, we predict. We have Variants spread throughout history, ready to timeleap at a moment's notice." She smiles seductively. "Now, are you ready to talk?"

"There's nothing to say."

"I beg to differ." I feel as if I'm being torn apart by wolves, stoned to death by an angry mob, hung upside down in a frigid river by my testicles. But this is just pain, and pain will fade. *All* will fade soon enough.

"Now, what was your assignment in the music hall? Why did your eyes linger on Cameron Rhyder's legs three point seven seconds longer than any previous instance?"

I take several breaths to compose myself. "You will fail this interrogation, as you have always failed, and you know it. A Variant would have arrived by now with all the information, extracted from a future Now. That is how it works, isn't it?"

"No," she says. "Because that information hasn't arrived, the only answer is that *this* is the Now in which I extract information from you and which I later choose not to send back in time for reasons unknown to me now."

"You know that's not true. As soon as you find out what I know, you'll scatter the knowledge through time. But that has not happened because my task is already done. I've completed my assignment. We've already won."

"If the Anachronists have won, as you say, then why are you bound in a cave, on the same spot where the Goo Globbers will take the stage ten thousand years from today, and why are we still at war? In short, why do we exist? You *cannot* have won."

"We are here because this is how it happens."

"*What* happens, 219?"

She pushes my brain into an alpha state and ramps up my oxytocin sensitivity. Now when I look into her eyes I see a caring mother, only concerned with imparting love and securing my everlasting well-being. I've been trained to resist these coercions too. "What do you think will happen when Brahma's Day ends?" I ask.

Her eyes brighten. "With the close of the Varaha Kalpa, all will become One Glorious Unity. We will merge with the Blessed Tat Tvam Asi. There will be no more time, no more duality, no more separation of object and observer. We will become God." The Variants by the door smile.

"That's a delusion. The end of Brahma's Day will destroy everything. Nothing but chaos will remain. Energy will be unable to coalesce into matter because time no longer exists. You speak of a Golden Age, but of what, when, and where will this Golden Age exist?"

"What, when and where are meaningless terms when speaking of the Blessed Tat Tvam Asi who has no substance, duration, nor place."

"But *we* are human beings who exist in space and time, with breadth and duration. Destroy that and you destroy us. All the galaxies and countless stars. All the worlds teeming with life You destroy *everything* that has ever been."

"Not destroy, 219. *Revert*. The Cosmos will return to its primordial unity."

"You want to reverse billions of years of evolution for the sake of a delusion."

"We want to take evolution to the next step."

"You want to extinguish all life."

"You motives are transparent, 219. You attack my core beliefs in an attempt to find weaknesses to exploit."

I try to shake my head, but the straps don't allow it. "No, I'm pointing out that our continued existence proves that you're wrong, that we've already won and you've already lost. If time has no meaning to your Timeless God, then the close of Brahma's Day has already occurred in some Now. If you have succeeded, then this Now could not possibly continue to exist."

"You lack understanding of our theology, 219. Because we exist, it is *this* Now where we succeed in closing Brahma's Day. We believe we all live in the True Time, the fixed Now that will bring about the close of the Varaha Kalpa. The True Time, like the stem of a lotus flower, is long and seemingly endless. But at its eventual end the Glorious Unity of Brahma blossoms. If we exist, then we must be living in True Time, the last and ultimate reality that leads to the Godhead."

"Wrong again," I say. Jacob floats before my closed eyelids, his hands grasping for me in the dark. "Because this moment will soon be timelost."

"There is no way you can be conscious of your own nonexistence."

"Oh, yes I can."

"And how is that, 219?"

I swallow. What choice do I have? "Because no one has come to warn you this time. Oh, Jacob, forgive me." Then I trigger the singularity bomb hidden in my brain stem.

I scratch my three days of scruff and light a menthol cigarette as I stand beside the bar after the opening act ends. People rush to the bathrooms in droves before the Goo Globbers will take the stage. The air grows thick with smoke and the stank of beer. It's too hot for my leather jacket, my boots make my feet blister, and my balls sweat.

I hate pretending to be someone I'm not. Once, my Archives tell me, I composed Neo-Baroque symphonies at a conservatory that won't be built for another four hundred years. I was world renown and in love with a young man from Nigeria. But this past has been timelost. The Anachronists washed away my joy into the sea of Has Never Been. I don't remember his name or his face, but I know that when the Varaha Kalpa ends, I'll embrace my lover again. We will all reunite with the timelost, and together we will write symphonies with the Godhead herself.

My phone vibrates in my pocket. Someone has tagged a picture on Instagram with my handle: it's the line to the bathroom that I'm looking at now, except the queue has moved forward a few paces. The encoded data says the photo is from the future and that I took it. On the graffitied wall is a faded sentence written in Eurogeek, a language that won't exist for two hundred years, but the words are spelled phonetically in ancient Akkadian. It's overlaid with newer graffiti and dozens of band stickers and is at least ten years old in this Now. The words read, "The woman directly underneath these words is Agent 991 of the Hands of Brahma. Make contact with her and share all information. Blessed be Tat Tvam Asi."

The queue moves so that it matches the photo exactly.

Right under the Akkadian letters is a woman with black hair, boxy retro eyeglasses, a gold digital watch, tight jeans. I lift my phone, take a picture of the queue at the precise moment, and email it to a server in Togo, where through the blessing of the Timeless One it will find its way to the future. The Causal Chain must be preserved.

I approach the woman and hold out an unlit cigarette. "Got a light?"

"Don't smoke," she says.

I flash my retinal maser into her eyes, and there's a brief moment where we pass encryption keys, entangled photons, and subatomic handshakes to negotiate deeper levels of trust. She's one of us, but I outrank her, thank the Godhead.

I'm Agent 337, I transmit through the maser. *I've been authorized to divulge all.*

WHY ARE YOU BREAKING COM SILENCE? she transmits.

Because I've found him.

Him? Even through the maser I sense her disbelief.

The last Anachronist to stand in our way before the Glorious Unity. He's beside the stage, next to the VIP section. He's wearing a Goo Globbers t-shirt, has ruffled brown hair, brown-olive skin, and a Van Dyke beard. I transmit his DNA marker and black body signature to her.

Why come to me? she says. *You could erase him yourself.* She scans the people nearby. *This dialog risks outing us. Making contact is not in my mission profile.*

In my last instance in this Now, I say, *a taxi killed me as I crossed the street outside this concert hall. The Anachronists are never so overt. They know that I know his identity, and they're desperate. You see why I cannot erase him myself?*

It could have been a true accident, she says.

True? I hope you know better, 991. But, you're right, there's more. In your last instantiation of this Now you brought the suspect backtime to the year 10,981 BCE. You interrogated him, but were killed when he detonated a singularity bomb embedded in his lower brain stem. We let him destroy you so that the Anachronists would believe they have the upper hand.

This isn't strange, she says. *I've been killed hundreds of times. Without concrete evidence, how can I proceed?*

It's an order.

And if we erase the wrong person based on your whim, eons of labor will be lost. We might end up infinitely farther from the close of Brahma's Day. I'm sorry, but without confirmation, I cannot proceed. She lifts her phone, about to transmit a record of our conversation through Instagram.

I've no time for this. I outrank her and have privileges over her retinal. I flash her short-term memory and write my orders onto her prefrontal cortex. I write twice, just to be sure.

Got it, yes, sir, she says, lowering her phone. *Suspect at stage right, male, twenty-six, olive-skin, Van Dyke beard, Goo Globbers t-shirt. Pursue and erase.*

I purge her memories of our encounter, and our conversation ends two point five seconds after it began. Outwardly she shows no signs of change. She's one of them now, a civilian. She will follow my instructions without knowing it. "Maybe I will take that cigarette," she says. I light it and she takes a drag, then thanks me before she saunters toward the stage.

It's my turn to go and I enter a stall that reeks of weed and piss. As I close the latch I can't stop smiling. Our greatest moment so close at hand! Brahma's Day will end! The timelost will be found! Blessed is her name, Tat Tvam Asi, That Thou Art, who dies so that we may live!

A fire-haired woman pushes into the stall, and the rhinestones on her cat's-eye glasses twinkle like fairy dust. Her leafy-green eyes hold me a bit too long before I realize I've been hijacked.

"Goodnight, honey," she says, pressing her lips against mine.

No! Wait? What was I just thinking? What was I just doing?

She stares at me, this beautiful, beautiful creature. I'd do anything for her. I'd die for her.

"Change of plans," she says as she presses something tiny and hard into my palm. "A little gift for Ms. Cameron Rhyder."

Cameron Rhyder is a stupid name, but I wear it proudly.

The suit greets me as I enter the backstage doors. "Ms. Rhyder, I'll take you to your seat." He doesn't know he escorts the world's last hope, the culmination of eons of labor. His smile is forced, perfunctory. I remember making it when I was in his body.

Roadies wake from their stupor as I pass forests of lights and gear. Red cups pop like fruit from labyrinths of black boxes. Their cigarette smoke curls into vortices as I walk past them. It takes them a second.

Holy fuck, that's Cameron Rhyder, that chick from that movie, what's it called? The Doggerel Star with Jimmy Everwood and Kristina Goodman.

Shit, what happened to her?

I know their thoughts from other Nows, when I inhabited their bodies: how I got old but am still fuckable, how my career tanked after I got busted in the back of an RV parked beside that Brooklyn fish-packing warehouse while sniffing crushed oxy from a nineteen year old's penis with forty thousand dollars of stolen coke hidden in the trunk. The coke wasn't mine. The douchebag with the big cock stole it from his friend, who ratted him out so he wouldn't get wacked by the mob. But try explaining that to a public who hates celebrities only slightly more than they adore them. They threw me to the wolves, then the wolves threw me to the scavengers.

I suppose all of this would've mattered to the real Cameron Rhyder. That entity sleeps way down in the substrata of this body's brain. I feel her try to wake every few minutes, as she has for the past two days I've been inside her mind. I nudge her back to sleep with sweet memories of douchebag inside of her.

The suited man smacks open the steel door, and the sounds of the audience explode in my ears. He throws aside a curtain to reveal a thousand wiggling faces, barely conscious worms tenaciously clinging to life. They've no idea they eat death, that they suffice on rot.

They call it nihilism. I call it genocide.

The suit leads me to a table third from the stage. The crimson-dressed two-tops rest on a VIP dais a meter above the dance floor, like a king's court. But we're not the highlight. That's the stage, where all kings will abdicate their thrones tonight, where all subjects will shed their chains. I take my seat, order a single malt from a pimple-faced kid who notices then pretends not to recognize me.

Others do. People whisper and point and avert their eyes. They've seen me on a screen, a whole dimension flattened, and yet I've become larger in their eyes. But in person, in all three dimensions, I'm lessened, made human. That's why they stare, because in seeing me lowered to a mere person they raise themselves up.

I'm fine with that. Equal footing is what I'm after.

The lights dim and the crowd roars, raucous to the point of dangerous. They're ready to pop. The bouncers straighten, check their earbuds. Under cover of the noise, shadows sneak onto the stage and take their positions. The roar grows.

White spotlights flash onto the lead singer. The silver cape over his shoulders reflects a sky of constellations up the walls. Orion, Cassiopeia, Canis Major. Their positions match the sky outside just now. He slams a power chord and the cheers fade under the heavy crunch of distortion.

As the chord hangs he sings, "*Where has my innocence run? Where is my peaceful weather? How sunny were the days, when days . . . they ran forever.*"

The lights go up and it's spectral chaos. The band joins in with a dominant seventh. It is fierce, the three-seven time, the swooning melody.

Damn. Even after all these eons, after so much death and horror, their music still moves me. That's why it had to be them, the Goo Globbers, the only band in Eternity who can thwart oblivion.

I send a command to the stage lights, to the lustre-tech I embedded four years ago. They switch on full spectrum, and everyone's mind is pried wide open, modulated by the lights and a thousand other methods. But I set the other manipulators in previous Nows; there's no way to know for sure if all but the lustre remains unadultered.

The crowd writhes on the dancefloor beneath us. One young man with a Van Dyke beard, olive skin, and a Goo Globbers t-shirt points at me, his fingers only inches from my ankles. "Dude," he shouts to his friend, "that's Cameron Rhyder's legs!"

His friend shakes his head, embarrassed.

I ignore them and sip my scotch exactly as I have done four thousand six hundred and eighty times before.

A cute guy two tables over smiles and gives me a sympathetic expression. When I was in his body in a previous Now I learned he's got undiagnosed cancer of the prostate. He'll be dead in eighteen months. The real Cameron Rhyder would probably have fucked him in a shitty hotel room nearby, crying afterward over how far she's fallen from her glory days. My body warms instinctively at the thought of his body pressing into mine.

The song ends, bleeds into another. A bluesy, jazzing jam, lots of fuzz. The drummer sweats rivers.

A smirking woman with dark hair, boxy eyeglasses, tight jeans, and a gold digital watch sidles up to the dancing men beside me. They gawk and stare at her body.

Everyone's mind is wide open. Impulses are laid bare. Privacy is a discarded piece of clothing.

She dances before the men, rubbing against them as the beat progresses. She's flushed, shivering, overheated, her eyes rolled back into her head, all signs she's orgasmic. It's a side effect of the lustre. I count seventy-one men and women currently experiencing orgasm.

Do they know to whom they sacrifice their lust, to what wiggling chaos of unborn nightmare they pray? They writhe mindlessly, their imagination dead. They dream others' dreams and think them their own. Nihilism has been chosen for them because they haven't learned how to choose for themselves.

Until tonight. Until me. I will get this right this time. I must.

The bespectacled girl moves behind the Van Dyke. She plays his chest like a guitar, brushes her hand over his crotch.

Three bodies back, a man in a leather jacket and two days of scruff lights a cigarette and considers me coolly, as he always does. A roadie sneaks out from a curtain onto the VIP dais. He squats beside me and says, "Scott—" that is, Scott Mohl, lead singer of the Goo Globbers, "—heard you're here. Would you do a duet?"

Ms. Rhyder had a brief post-acting career as a singer-songwriter. Until the drug bust. "What song?"

His breath reeks of cigarettes. "Autumn Days?"

From their first album. "Too dreary. How about My Disposition?" It's a poem I, in Cameron's body, wrote when I left Scott for good one morning a thousand Nows ago. He recorded it under his name as a kind of revenge, turned it into a hit. And if we sing it tonight, we'll be singing *my* words to the most important audience in history.

"I'll ask," the roadie says.

"When?"

"I'll signal you."

I nod, feign flattery and nerves as he walks back into the shadows. The latches have been set, the trap is ready.

The song ends. Scott makes obeisances to the crowd, sips from a water bottle. "How y'all doing tonight?"

Cheers erupt. Some awaken from trances to shock and fear at their loss of control. Six people are freaking out. Nine more quiver from orgasm.

The roadie whispers to the bassist, who says something off-mic to Scott.

"I'm told we have a guest here tonight."

Whoops and jeers. Everyone knows of our little tryst.

"The lovely Cameron Rhyder." Lunchroom boos, cheers. The roadie's waving at me. "Hey, doll," says Scott, his hand outstretched toward me, "join us?"

I stand to whistles and cheers. "Got any blow?" one screams. Another: "Cameron, we love you!"

A spotlight, hot and blinding, swivels onto me as I step on stage. I can't see, but just as well. "Hiya, Cammy," Scott says off mic, then he gives me a hug. In private, he'd be just as likely to tell me off.

"Ninth Division?" he says.

This is wrong. "How about My Disposition?"

"I'm tired of it." Then to the band, "Ninth Division, on four. One . . . two . . . three . . . "

And just like that we're performing the wrong song. I fucked up, somewhere. Now I have to play along, to sing his thinly veiled polemic on the evils of the military industrial complex, told as a clichéd love story between two star-crossed lovers.

Scott knows I hate this song, but not for the reasons he thinks. Its angry baseline becomes the thing it criticizes: unchecked rage. Played for a crowd this open, it will solidify the destructive mentality. It promises freedom, but makes them slaves.

I can't allow this. I've worked too hard, too long to get here. I activate the nano I've placed in the bassist's brain and ramp up his sensitivity to THC. The joint he smoked an hour ago and thought he was coming down from now gets fifty times stronger.

His timing skews. He misses notes.

Scott and I sing, "*I can't see above the wall, but I know you're on the other side*," as the audience cringes at the bassist's errors.

They're being programmed for sure, but it won't be as deep.

We give the song a respectful end, bow, and the audience responds with a weak applause. We're losing them.

"What the fuck, man?" the drummer shouts to the bassist.

"I'm good," the bassist says, looking green.

I use the lull and jump in. "My Disposition on four, ready? One . . . two . . . three . . . "

The drummer pounds the kettles as Scott cocks his head at me and smiles wryly. He knows he's been beaten. I drop the bassist's high and ramp up the band's dopamine. I need them at their best.

And they're so fucking together it's magical. We've yanked the audience back from the abyss. I sing, "*All of us, every one, have been the other, you know, at one time or another.*"

And Scott replies, "*And the other, mother, sister, lover, would you know them by their cover?*"

On the dance floor below my table the dark-haired girl in the boxy glasses and gold watch spins around and tongue-kisses the man with the Van Dyke. I ramp up the lustre-tech to max, flood the air with massive doses of oxytocin, coerce the frequencies of my voice to resonate blissfully with human sensory meridians. Their bodies in ecstasy, they're open to anything.

I step forward and belt, "*I have been you and you have been me, all throughout Eternity. Don't you get it? Don't you see? You have been that one and that one is me.*"

The guitarist riffs through the interlude, making amateurs of the greats. The drummer is picking out rhythms he didn't know existed. The bassist is plucking chords in heroic timing. Scott's voice is hitting notes birds can't reach.

And when I sing the next verse they will awaken to the stark truth. We've been fighting this war for so long, in so many variations that in this Now, in this moment, I, the entity that stands in Cameron Rhyder's body, have been every one of them. I, who no longer have a name, remember them all.

I have been the smirking bouncer, and I have been the bemused roadies. And I was Scott Mohl and every member of the Goo Globbers. And was the man who will die of cancer, and I have been both halves of the couple kissing beneath my seat.

Inside their fragile bodies I have traveled forward and backward through time. With their hands I have slaughtered and erased and destroyed. I have had my mind rewritten and reprogrammed more than a billion times. The words I sing to them are utterly true: *I have been you and you have been me, all throughout Eternity.*

And when I sing my next verse, they will awaken to this truth. The Anachronists will see the futility of their cause. The Hands of Brahma will know that the Unity they seek is already here, in my body, this flesh of Cameron Rhyder. They have already become One. Brahma's Day ends with me.

And here I go, second stanza, moment of truth.

I step forward, but something sharp jabs my left foot. There's something in my shoe. The pain makes me stumble, and my heel catches a wire. I'm thrown forward, down and hard, over the edge of the stage.

My head slams into the floor. My neck cracks. The pain is obscene, so I switch it off.

Screams, not my own. I can't move! My heart rate spikes. My neck is broken. I'll be dead in seconds!

No! All of this mustn't be for nothing! I was so close to showing them the truth: when we kill each other, we kill ourselves. Don't you all see? We're maggots feasting on our own body!

I was going to wake them up. I was going to inject this knowledge into them, so that for one instant we'd become a singular mind, one conscious entity, who could stop this madness forever.

Blackness pours into my vision as people surround me. The scruffy man in the leather jacket photographs me with his camera phone. The young woman with cat's-eye glasses and leafy green eyes leans over and checks my pulse. She reaches for my shoe, which has fallen off, and pulls out something tiny from the heel. A pebble. The same pebble that threw her/me/us off our bicycle so many years ago. She puts it in her pocket and smiles at me.

Her pupils dilate rapidly, a sign of a hijack letting go. Whoever was in her has fled. She's confused, frozen. Suggestible. Here's my last chance.

I activate my maser and write deep into her mind. I've only got seconds before death. On the way home, shaken and sickened by what she's seen, she'll hum "My Disposition" without realizing it. The words will be stuck in her head for months. She'll never be able to think of the song the same way again.

TRUTH IS LIKE THE SUN

1. The Joke

Pop-star uber-sensation Jaim Janan rockets off to promote their third album atop a SpaceX Dragon VII capsule today, where they will stream a live musical performance from orbit, some 350 kilometers above the Earth. Before today's launch, when asked if they were feeling nervous about the trip, the young pop star coolly responded, "Truth is like the sun. You can shut it out for a time, but it ain't goin' away."

It's not clear how many of Jaim's obsessive fans, or "Janatics" as they are sometimes known, recognized the star was quoting twentieth-century pop legend Elvis Presley [click for bio]. But by mid-afternoon #TruthIsLikeTheSun was the most popular hashtag on Twitter.

—Naydeen Johnson for *The Washington Post*

We have the food crisis in Eritrea, a new strain of Avian Flu ravaging South-east Asia, and flooding coastal cities across the world, but, yes, let's spend billions to send some corporate shill "musician" into space so he can sell more records. We as a species need to get our priorities straight.

—Neung Espinoza in an Op-Ed for *The New York Times*

OMG OMG OMG I am so in love with Jaim's tat! Totes getting my first ink with his mission insignia on my inner thigh, same as Jaim! @iamjaim #jaiminspace #swoon #soinlove #orbitalmechanics #followforfollows #likeforlikes #spacie #worldtour #janatics #truthislikethesun

—@janatic2025 on Instagram

u so hot, jaim. the things u and i could do in zero-g, baby. ps, im serious. dm me if ur interested @iamjaim #jaiminspace #zerogsports #spacie #janatics #truthislikethesun

—@RealPlayaWinning on Twitter

Jaim Janan replica space jumpsuit, with real insignia, straps, and epaulettes, only $19.95 from #BestDealsChina #jaiminspace #replica #jumpsuit #wholesale #retail #bestdeals #dealoftheday #coupon https://be.cn/hiyiy

—BestDealsChina on Twitter

so,,,,,this fuckin fagot gets $284 mil to fly into space when their are stavring ppl on earth????? shamefull.

—JesusIsMyCarpenter79 in a YouTube comment

um no. jaim gave all the money to charity. he just doin it for promo and shit

—Diamla Ghiburi in a YouTube comment

THEY! Gender neutral pronouns, folks. They're not that hard!

—Teri Marie Johnson in a YouTube comment

"Not that hard" ? speak for yourself, Teri. :-P

—Alejandro Bowlrov in a YouTube comment

I had two weeks to complete the design. An absurdly short time! But I knew I could do it. There are perhaps three persons in the world who could, but I am the only one capable of creating a masterpiece.

You laugh, but this is no joke. In the gifted, what sounds like arrogance is mere honesty. The world-record-holding runner, Jafuru Olembe, is a friend. When we talk over a meal, he doesn't say, "Arnaud, I am a decent runner." He says, "Arnaud, I am the fastest man on the planet." Why should he be shy about this? Just the same, I am the best clothing designer in the world. I will not pretend I am less to avoid someone else's discomfort. That is the height of absurdity!

Jaim's people contacted me one morning two months ago, in a panic. They said, "Arnaud, will you do it? We want to make sure Jaim looks just like so." Such incredible gall! I said, "Friends, either you give me absolute control, or I walk." They went away to discuss this amongst themselves for a few hours, as corporations do. But they came to their senses. They had to have the best, of course.

Yes, I was paid handsomely. So what? I don't understand why people get so worked up about that. Should not remuneration be commensurate to skill? Though, I must be clear, I didn't do it for money or notoriety. I need neither of those things. I did it for the challenge. Jaim is a gestalt, and I sought to capture that.

Jaim has an intense sexuality. It is impossible to be in their presence and not feel it. But—and this is important—a keen observer will see Jaim has always been much more than their façade. Jaim is cosmopolitan, but under the surface lies a child's naivety. Jaim is elegant, but underneath lie hints of vulgarity. Jaim spent their childhood in the streets of Tehran living in poverty before they moved to Nonthaburi to live with their mother in relative wealth. Jaim is half Persian and half Thai, but neither of those cultures defines them. Jaim is a fractal, you see, forever unfolding. All of these things had to be incorporated into my design.

Now, there has been some silly talk on the internet that I must now put to rest. A few have speculated that Jaim's jumpsuit is a pastiche of Michael Jackson's or Beyoncé's attire during their prime years. Well, there is an American word for this theory: *Hogwash!* Jaim's jumpsuit is the same as Michael Jackson's or Beyoncé's as a bird and a rocket are the same. Both fly, but only one will launch you to the moon!

Yes, there are obvious symbolic references in my design, but some are too subtle for the cruder eye. One sees themes of a bandleader, as Jaim is our conductor, leading us skyward. The gold epaulettes on their shoulders and breasts represent our ascent to the stars. The black fabric is the sea of space. The yellow finials are the sun's rays, the source of all life on Earth. The concentric white rings are the always-circling, but ever-distant stars.

The material, too, is purposeful. The jumpsuit is crafted from a newly invented fabric called Nouvalyne, developed by three brilliant Nigerian chemists. It has the look and feel of silk, the softness of cotton, and the weight of air. You'll soon see it everywhere. You could pour a glass of your best Bordeaux on it, and it will roll right off. You could press your lit cigarette against it, and it won't burn. It will keep you hot in winter and cool in summer. This fabric is humanity's indomitable spirit, our confidence to face all challenges now and in the future.

I would love to do another suit for Jaim, if given the opportunity. But, you know, it will be very hard to top perfection.

—From "Arnaud Lefèbvre, Per Vestis Ad Astra," an interview
in *Vogue Paris*

Combinaison de l'espace de réplique, avec de vrais insignes, sangles et épaulettes, seulement €19.99 https://be.cn/hiyzy #wholesale #shipsworldwide #jaiminspace #replica #jumpsuit #bestdeals #dealoftheday #coupon

—From a comment on the *Vogue Paris* interview "Arnaud Lefèbvre, Per Vestis Ad Astra"

2. The Supernova

The Dow Jones Industrial Average took a sharp dive yesterday as billions of people around the globe paused to watch Jaim Janan's YouTube livestream. Europe's Commissioner for Economic and Monetary Affairs, Xavier Janiszewski, said, "We've seen significant market dips before during major sporting or terrorist events, but never one of this magnitude and duration. Quite frankly, we're all shocked." The Asian exchanges remained wary in late-day trading, but after the opening of the New York exchanges this morning, the DJIA has returned to near-former levels. However, trading volume is still unusually high as investors remain jittery. Never before has a pop-star's performance had such an effect on the global economy.

—Lisa Applebaum in a *CNNMoney* article

I watched Jaim's performance live. I guess I was one of the lucky few who didn't get cut off when YouTube crashed. I never really listened to Jaim's music before. But I have to be honest, I wept like a baby. These really are such beautiful songs. Will def be checking out more of their stuff now. Guess I'm a Janatic now too. ;)

—Sonny in Albuquerque in a YouTube comment

Dang-double-dang! Even with the YouTube crash, 19 BILLION views of Jaim's video in one day! That HAS to be a record, right?

—SweetAmaranth in a YouTube comment

SweetAmaranth, yes, Jaim broke their own previous record from last year of 12 billion views in a day for their song, "moment2moment."

—Knit Picker in a YouTube comment

Good grief . . . these are possibly the greatest songs ever written. All other musicians stop making music, you will never do better than this.

—Justine's Just Desserts in a YouTube comment

THESE. SONGS.

—JustJanatical2024 in a YouTube comment

i just srsly cried. omfg!!!

—Minx Catastrophe in a YouTube comment

Just four chords? Lame.

—Folk Guitar Hero in a YouTube comment

Autotune in spaaaaaaaaaaaaaaaaaaace!

—NinetyNine Balloons in a YouTube comment

uh-oh, oh-oh-oh! milli vanilli moment at 1:17!

—Naj Menendez in a YouTube comment

Naj Menendez, wth is milli vanilli???

—Gamer Guy in a YouTube comment

wuuuuuuuut? the music don't match his mouth.

—Kiril Armstrong in a YouTube comment

They had a slight audio sync problem for the first minute of the feed, if you watched it live. But they edited the video, because there's no sync issue when you replay it now. Also, the performance was 100% live. And it wasn't lip synched or auto-tuned. See here for proof: https://bit.ly/2AI8VOj

—Vajra Mudali in a YouTube comment

I am going to put these songs on repeat for the rest of my life.

—Ridgewater Pet Shelter in a YouTube comment

So unbelievably beautiful. I can die in peace now.

—KevinTheLibrarian in a YouTube comment

I've been unable to stop smiling all day. I keep stopping and pinching myself, because I can't believe it. I am so unbelievably happy that Jaim is the first trans person in space!

—Fluffer Nutter in a YouTube comment

Come on now, folks. YouTube has the *largest* server capacity in the world. Their live feed shouldn't have crashed. Not unless (a) someone sabotaged the downlink feed, or (b) YouTube was DDoS attacked by someone who has massive internet data pipes and very good reasons to block the feed (e.g. China). Everyone knows China hates Jaim because of the incident in Beijing last year when Jaim came onstage wearing Chinese flag underwear.

—AnonymousCoward in a Slashdot.org comment, (Score 3: Insightful) on the article, "Jaim Janan's Live Stream Temporarily Crashes YouTube"

Calm down and take your meds, pal. No one sabotaged the downlink. The YouTube livestream wasn't DDoS-attacked. YouTube's CTO Jinmun Singh said the problem was simply their system reaching max capacity. They didn't have enough bandwidth to fulfill the *billions* of requests for Jaim's livestream. I said this in an earlier comment, but I'll repeat it again here for everyone's benefit: they could have just dropped the video onto BitTorrent and that would have saved everyone a ton of needless headaches.

—OnTheBashShell in reply to AnonymousCoward, (Score 5: Informative) on Slashdot.org

Um, no. If they had uploaded the full video to BitTorrent then it *wouldn't have been live streamed*. That was the whole friggin point. Also YouTube wouldn't get the ridiculous ad revenue from all the traffic, which AFAIK was close to $40 million per *minute* during the live performance.

—ReticulatedPython in reply to OnTheBashShell (Score 5: Informative) on Slashdot.org

I saw that Jaim is giving all the proceeds from their sponsorships to charity. They must have made billions from their performance, so that's pretty fucking admirable any way you cut it.

—Noreen R. Hazaga in a Facebook comment

Jaim called me up personally and said they wanted to donate

a percentage of their proceeds from their space performance to the Solar Mission. We were shocked. Jaim has always been a champion of the environment, but it was still very refreshing and wonderful to see someone of Jaim's status act instead of boast.

With Jaim's donation, which we have already received, we will increase India's solar power generation by 27.7 gigawatts, finally bringing this country within reach of getting one hundred percent of our electrical power from renewable sources. I honestly never thought I'd see this day. We are all very excited and happy.

—From an interview with Anusha Bhasin, chairman of India's National Solar Mission, in *The Hindustan Times*

It's ridiculous. One "spacie" from orbit, and Jaim has turned on half the world. I'm not saying he isn't attractive, but is this what we invented space travel for? Porn?

—Richard Bonacaccio in a Facebook comment

Richard Bonacaccio, YES.

—Ennis Durani in a Facebook comment

First off, *Richard Bonacaccio*, Jaim transitioned over a year ago. They now go by the gender-neutral pronoun "they," which people have called Jaim since like forever. Second, why *shouldn't* Jaim show off their body if they are proud of it? Does Jaim need permission from you, *Richard Bonacaccio*, to appreciate their body? NO, they DON'T. Go spread your toxic masculinity elsewhere.

—Mary Freidberg in a Facebook comment

I caught my son masturbating to that selfie of Jaim in space that everyone has been sharing. Does that mean he's gay?

—ConcernedSoccerMom on the *Motherhood Today* forums

@ConcernedSoccerMom: Jaim doesn't identify with a gender anymore, so I don't think your son is gay. But even if he was, so what? If Jaim has proved anything today, it's that one's sexuality will never again be a limitation to achievement.

—MoreStepfordWifeThanU on the *Motherhood Today* forums

Hello, my name is Emily Henderson. I am eight years old and i am in the 3rd grade. I live in Muncie, indiana and go to JAmes Polk Elementary. The school smells like trout sometimes, but it is not so bad. I saw you sing in space yesterday. it was so cool!!! I loved all the songs. whatz it like to float in 0 gravity? is it like swimming? how do you eat upside down? does the food fall out of your stomach?? does the moon look huge? are the stars brighter? Will you come to visit Mrs. Frasier's class next thursday and tell us about your trip to space??? i have alot more questions to ask you. I will tell Mrs. Frasier your coming. Don't worry. shes cool with it. she has a picture of you on the wall.

—From a forum on The Official Jaim Janan Fan Site

THIS GOVERNMENT STOOGE Jaim performed for only THIRTEEEN minutes. But if the Earth were curved, as the BRAINWASHED MASSES have been LED TO BELIEVE, the performance would have lasted for an ADDITIONAL NINE MINUTES AND TWELVE SECONDS, according to my DETAILED CALCULATIONS [imgur link]. This is DEFINITIVE PROOF we are BEING LIED TO. THE EARTH IS FLAT! WAKE UP!

—GameOfDrones on the /r/FlatEarth sub-Reddit

I'm sure if I shoved a pencil up my dog's ass, fed him pure crack, and blew an air horn, the scribbles coming out of his backside would be more scientifically accurate than your "DETAILED CALCULATIONS." But let me posit another solution: the real reason why Jaim's performance was only thirteen minutes long is because that was *the length of the set*. Jaim stopped playing because of the diabolical conspiracy of *playing three full songs to their end*.

—MoundOfAnts in reply to GameOfDrones on the/r/FlatEarth sub-Reddit

Jaim never went to space. It's all fake. My brother saw Jaim yesterday outside the Sheraton in Hanoi. Jaim bummed a Marlboro off of him, and they chatted for a few. Jaim said the video was shot in a secret studio in Svalbard. My bro said Jaim was like totally down to earth (haha) not stuck-up or anything. He told my bro that the whole space show was just a scam for publicity. Then while they're talking, some buff dudes in black gear and dark glasses hop out of a truck and take Jaim away. My bro said it totally freaked him out. He was still shaking when he Skyped me.

—Don Tuan on the /r/conspiracy sub-Reddit

Jaim In Space replica jumpsuit, with real insignia, straps, and epaulettes, only $99.99. https://ji.io/pxjk

—Worldwide China Wholesale in a YouTube comment

3. The Apotheosis

A group of women from Bihar took celebrity adoration to another level when they were seen worshipping a life-sized ceramic statue of Jaim Janan, the famous pop-star. A video of the women pouring water and offering flowers to the statue is making the rounds of social media today. Facebook user Vinita Chetty from Delhi uploaded the video on her wall and it has since gone viral.

—From "People Seen Worshipping Statue of Jaim Janan" in the *India Times*

As a trans woman, I cannot describe what an inspiration Jaim is to me. To see someone like me in space, someone who has gone through so much pain and suffering, to see them literally shoot away from all this awful chaos into orbit is just too much. Words cannot fully describe my elation. Jaim, you are my star, my beacon in the sky, and I will look to your light to guide my way when I am lost.

—Micah K on Tumblr

At exactly 3:14, right over Jaim's shoulder, the sun crests Earth's horizon just as Jaim sings, "Look again at that dot. That's home. That's us." I get the chills every time I watch it.

—Mayim Heschel in a YouTube comment

My grandma said a lot of Jaim's lyrics are from an old book about space called Pale Blue Dot. It was written a long time ago by this 20th-century astronomer called Carl Sagan. He studied the planets and stars and tried to convince ppl that we should go into space and become an inter-planetary species. There's lots of vids of him on YouTube. He seems pretty cool. I wonder what he would have thought of Jaim.

—Not Your Everyday Archaeopteryx in a YouTube comment

No, you never see us. That was intentional. It was part of the deal SpaceX made with Jaim's team. They wanted the performance to look like Jaim was orbiting in space all alone. But the Dragon VII spacecraft isn't that big! We had to velcro ourselves to the walls just to stay out of the camera eye. We all joked we had front-row beds. You can't see us in any of the videos, but I could have reached out and touched Jaim's shoulder from where I lay strapped. We were that close!

There have been performances in space before. The most famous is probably Chris Hadfield's "Space Oddity." But that wasn't live and was heavily edited. As part of the agreement we made, Jaim's performance had to be livestreamed, and this ended up being quite difficult.

The cameras, the lights, the spacecraft orientation, the satellite downlinks, the software, and so much more—all had to be perfect. We were working up until the last second to make sure we had everything right, because if something went wrong, millions would be watching. It was stressful, certainly, but we are trained to operate under pressure. But I have to say that everyone involved, the crew up here and our ground team down on Earth, did a superlative job. We couldn't have asked for a more professional bunch of people.

The best part, of course, was that we had a front-row seat! As soon as Jaim started playing, all my stress vanished. By the end of the set, I was so moved I was wiping away tears. Jaim really is an incredible performer. And, yes, contrary to what some are saying, it was all streamed live, without edits.

What you hear about Jaim, their affableness, their charm, is one hundred percent true. They're a genuinely sweet person. Jaim is funny, witty, and whip-smart. There's no arrogance or entitlement in them, which is honestly not what I expected after hearing so many malicious rumors.

Overall, I have to say, this experience has been one of the most rewarding of my life. And I hope Jaim's performance has inspired people, young and old, to take a greater interest in space. I think it's already working though, because I heard that applications to NASA's astronaut corps have increased tenfold just this past week.

—From "Music of the Spheres: An Interview with Astronaut Theresa Ortolani, Mission Commander for Jaim Janan's Journey Into Space" in *The New York Times Magazine*

The Bank of Thailand has issued a press release today announcing a new commemorative banknote. The 500-Baht note commemorates Thailand's own Jaim Janan and their journey into space.

The new notes are primarily purple, similar to the 21st series of 500-Baht notes. Additional details and highlights appear in gold, orange, blue, and red. The front side depicts Janan in their space jumpsuit looking up and to their right, toward a turtle overlaid with stars (the constellation Orion). The reverse side depicts Jaim floating in zero-gravity before the spacecraft window, where the sun is rising above the Earth and Thailand is clearly visible. As an anti-counterfeit feature, the radial pattern surrounding the rising sun will turn yellow when viewed under ultraviolet light.

While the Royal Family could not be reached for comment, Queen Sirikit Narkhirunkanok has repeatedly condemned the choice of putting the world-famous celebrity on the bank notes. Nevertheless, the people of Thailand overwhelmingly support the measure, according to polls.

—From "Jaim Janan Will Appear on Commemorative 500-Baht Note," an article in *Thai Rath*

Jaim Janan replica space jumpsuit, with real insignia, straps, and epaulettes, only 9,000 Baht from #BestDealsAsia #jaiminspace #replica #jumpsuit #wholesale #retail #bestdeals #dealoftheday #coupon https://be.cn/jnd4h

—From a comment on "Jaim Janan will Appear on Commemorative 500-Baht Note" in *Thai Rath*

Many in the world are celebrating Jaim Janan's flight into space as if it were an act of divine revelation. But this troubled soul defiles the Lord's good works with his sins, and his presence in the Lord's heavenly sphere shames us all below. My dear children, if you are as heartbroken by the course of the world as I am, come join me this Sunday for a most serious worship and sermon, and together we will meditate on how we can turn this broken, twisted world from its dark path.

—A message from Senior Pastor Isaiah Young on the Fellowship
Church's website, Grapevine, Texas

Did pop-star Jaim Janan's orbital performance make you more or less likely to want to go into space?
Not sure: 1%
Less likely: 2%
Somewhat less likely: 2%
Somewhat more likely: 10%
More likely: 84%

—From an online worldwide Gallup International poll of
386,415,678 respondents, ages 13-55

In an apparent response to Jaim Janan's famous performance in space, North Korea announced today they will be launching native-born pop-star Kwan Jang into space atop a repurposed ballistic missile next spring, where he will perform several songs from orbit. In a statement released yesterday, the reclusive government said, "Kwan Jang will showcase Korea's indomitable strength, agility, and power. Jang is perfectly fit and healthy, and his musical ability is unparalleled in all musical genres. Jang will provide a harmonic, pleasing result to the entire world."

While sales numbers of Jang's recordings within North Korea are hard to come by, the artist is virtually unheard of outside of the country. Within North Korea, he is most famous for his somber, orchestral versions of "We Are One" and "Reunification Rainbow."

—From "North Korea to Launch Their Own Pop-Star Into Space" on *BBC News*

Jaim Janan replica space jumpsuit, with real insignia, straps, and epaulettes, only $499.99 from #BestDealsChina #jaiminspace #replica #jumpsuit #wholesale #retail #bestdeals #dealoftheday #coupon https://be.cn/jn5gf

—From a comment on the *BBC News* website

Space tourism and transportation company Virgin Galactic has dramatically lowered the price of their sub-orbital space flights from New York to Tokyo to $12,500, putting space travel within reach of millions more people. This announcement comes in response to other space transportation companies, such as SpaceX, Blue Origin, and China's CALT, recently lowering their prices as well.

"Certainly, we have to remain competitive," said Julia Tizard, President of Operations for Virgin Galactic. "The cost reduction is part of that. But interest in space travel has reached a global tipping point. Just as electric vehicles shifted from niche items into the mainstream once a certain price point was reached, we believe space travel between continents will soon become commonplace."

While space travel today is not nearly as cheap as an intercontinental airline flight, Tizard says such a day isn't far off. "We've seen demand for space travel rise exponentially in the last five years. It's a simple economy of scale. The more people who go into space, the cheaper space travel becomes. By our current estimate, at the end of the decade as many as eighteen percent of intercontinental travelers will use some form of space flight to reach their destination. With such numbers, relatively inexpensive trips to the Moon and even Mars become a possibility."

When asked if Jaim Janan's orbital performance affected demand for space travel, Tizard replied, "Oh, absolutely. From the moment Jaim announced they were going into space, we saw a jump in reservations. But after their live performance, the demand has been just incredible. Since the beginning of the year, we've seen a twelve hundred percent increase in reservations. This, more than anything else, is the factor enabling us to lower our prices."

—From "Virgin Galactic to Dramatically Slash Space-Travel Costs" on SpaceFlightNow.com

Today, Jaim Janan performed in space. A trans person. Billions, I'm told, watched. There were so many, the internet crashed. The world stopped, for a moment to see. To hear. To feel. Many mocked Jaim before the trip. Many more were indifferent. But since Jaim's performance, there has been a sea-change in the world. I sense it when I ride the train to work, and I see it when I look into my fellow citizen's faces. We are no longer members of a particular race, nation, tribe, or band. We are all members of one race. We are all human.

With our endless news cycles focused on misery and despair, it's all too easy to become myopic, to see the world only for its faults. It's all too easy to become a cynic, to close our hearts and give up. But what Jaim has taught me, what Jaim has taught all of us, is that hope for humanity isn't dead. Beauty persists in the world, and most especially in *us*, if only we allow ourselves to dance to its ancient song.

Today, a shining star has arced across the sky. Jaim is but one person. Yet there will soon be—I am sure of it—billions more to follow.

From now and every day to come, I will know that

something within us has changed for the better. Because even though, compared to the sun, one star may be small, the long night has gotten a little bit brighter.

So Jaim Janan I just want to say: Thank you.

—Ysha Fuente, from an Op-Ed in *Süddeutsche Zeitung*

Look again at that dot
That's here, that's home, that's us
Everyone you love, and everyone you know
And everyone who was
All their joys and suffering
All their faiths and prayers
Every saint and sinner
And their countless little heirs
All our bands and tribes
Thieves and lovers
Tyrants and peasants
Children and mothers
In the history of the world
Lived here
. . . here, here
On our little mote of dust
Dancing for a moment
In bright flash and gleam
Oh, dancing for a moment
. . . just this lonely precious moment
Dancing for a moment
Suspended in a sunbeam.

—Jaim Janan, after Carl Sagan

MORTAR

THE EDGES OF the photograph are torn, smeared with the color of charcoal. In the center stand four figures. One is tall, smiling, has dark hair and tawny skin. His arm drapes over the shoulder of another, a woman with only half a smile, a pale face and golden hair. Between them are two children, a small boy, perhaps five or six, with short brown hair and baggy clothing, and a girl of about twelve, her auburn hair tied into a tail. The boy smiles a fat innocent smile. The girl smiles too, but something in her expression echoes the woman's; the girl has the same half-smile, the same shape of face and mouth, the same subtle hint that inside she is not smiling at all.

The photograph flaps in the breeze. It is held in place with a dirty thumb. A cracked and sharp fingernail, once painted, but now chipped away, sits upon it. The nail's jagged edge matches the frayed edge of the photograph. The hand presses the photo to the ground, smearing its backside in mud, then reaches out and presses the photo against a brick wall. The wind jostles the image, but it stays on the wall.

The hand reaches down into a green metal box and pulls out another photograph. It is not torn along the edges like the last. Fingers grasp the image, smearing its white edges with blackened dust.

In this moment of frozen time, there is a blue, cloudless sky. In front of the sky, a spacecraft sits huge and oppressive. Its gleaming metal hull reflects the afternoon sun into a brilliant flare. Four men in white coveralls stand before the ship with wide and beaming smiles. They each have a hand on a large, white sign. It reads, "Pegasus-Seagull Project Team." Underneath is a symbol of a flying horse leaping over an atom, along with the signatures of each of the men.

The dirty thumb slides over the picture and stops on the second man, the dark-haired, tawny-skinned one from the first photograph. The dusty hand reaches toward the ground, then presses the image onto the wall next to the first. It flaps in the breeze with a black thumbprint on its face.

The hand reaches down into the metal box and pulls out another photo. It is a forest of young conifers. All the trees are only a few meters tall, and behind them, just poking out from the sides of the saplings, are barren fields of orange sand and stone. This picture, too, is placed on the wall.

As the hand reaches for another photo, a strong gust of wind whips past. Pictures fly out of the green metal box like birds taking flight. The hand is still, makes no attempt to stop the flock from following the wind. The wind exhales, sighs, and dies down again, and then the hand continues reaching into the box.

The next photograph is of a garden. The young girl from the first picture is here, laughing as she bends over the soil, tending to a fledgling plant. There is a lightness in her smile that was not in the first picture. She is younger here, her face bright with life. In the background is a golden-haired pregnant woman with a pallid face. She sits on a chair before the garden. Her eyes are solemn and heavy, looking away. Behind her, encircling the yard, is a red brick wall. Young conifer trees just begin to peek over its crest.

A clear drop of liquid falls onto the image, rolls, then spills onto the ground below.

This photograph is placed on the wall with the others. A steady, but timid gust of wind blows by. The flock of photographs in the green metal box stay grounded, but the pictures on the wall bend, and one breaks free. It is the photo of the man, the woman, and the two children. It flies away into the breeze with barely a sound. There is a long pause before another photo is taken out of the box.

The thumb grasps a photo of the dark-haired, tawny-skinned man. He wears a yellow hardhat and the same white coveralls as he stands on a gangway. Behind him is a monstrous column of machinery. Its twisted and intricate complexities mask its true size, but its scale is immense. To the right of the man, barely visible, is a sign that reads, "Danger! Highly Sensitive Instrumentation! Multiple Radiation Hazards! Use *Utmost* Caution On This Tier!"

A second hand comes up quickly from the side and helps the first tear the image into a dozen pieces. It brings with it a dozen fluid red streaks, speckled black with dirt and dust. With the next gust of wind the hands let go and the pieces drift away.

There is a long pause before the hand continues. A fine black and grey mist begins to blow with the wind and settle onto everything. Another photograph is drawn from the box. It is the last one.

The golden-haired, pale-faced woman holds a newborn in her arms. She smiles softly, but there is a weight to it. Next to her is the girl. They stand in a grassy field, with three houses and a very large building in the distance behind them. The girl's hand reaches out to a white wooden sign perched upon a stake into the ground. The sign reads, "Pegasus Planet, population 10." In the girl's hand is a pen which is in the middle of crossing out the "10" and making it into an "11."

A dozen clear drops fall onto the image, and then the image is set free, flying away into the grey mist. The box sits empty.

The hands sit idle for a time, twitching silently. They slowly glide up to a bloody and pale face, to once golden hair, now grey with ash. Broken pieces of the red brick wall lie shattered around a ruined garden. Behind the wall, extending to the horizon, a forest lies black, bent and obliterated, as if lightning has struck each and every tree. On the hill, a gaping hole in an enormous building spills out columns of black and acrid smoke.

The woman is still before the brick wall. She watches the photos sway with each passing gust. One by one, the pictures tear free of the wall and fly away. She stares ahead, her eyes slowly closing, as a soft gust of wind blows through her. She exhales and sighs, and gives her last breath to the wind.

THE HISTORY WITHIN US

ON A WRIST-MOUNTED computer, Betsy Haadama watched a six thousand-year-old silent film. It was grayscale, overexposed, two-dimensional, and chronologically jumbled. On the film: a mustachioed man doting over his young son at a crowded zoo. A woman vigorously combing the boy's white hair beside a large piano. A family eating a large meal, candles burning on a table, men wearing yarmulkes, bodies shivering in prayer. A river, people swimming, women in white bathing caps and full-body suits. Men on rocks by the shore, pipes in mouths, smoke drifting lazily upward. A park, the boy looking down at a dead pigeon. Staring. Staring. Father picking him up, kissing him. In the sky, a bright sun.

A young sun.

"Pardon my intrusion in this time of ends," a Twirlover said, startling her. The Twirlover's six separate, hovering pink objects—like human knuckles—danced a looping, synchronized pattern in the air. "If it pleases you, will you share with me why you watch that flickering device so incessantly?"

In some parts of the galaxy one could be killed for being human. Betsy wasn't sure if this Eluder Ship was such a place. But death was coming for all soon enough. So why fear it now?

"This is an ancient film of my paternal ancestor," she said defiantly.

Puffs of air beat against her face as the Twirlover spun. "An ancient film? Indeed, such a rare treasure, an artifact of the past! If it pleases you, may we watch a portion together?"

She was about to tell it no, that she'd rather die alone, contemplating what might have been, when the alarm trilled down the cavernous halls of the Eluder Ship. A cold shiver ran down her spine as a cacophony of voices warned in ninety languages simultaneously, "*Gravitational collapse imminent, my beloveds! Please take your positions inside your transitional shells!*"

Angry rainbows flared across the floor and ozone and ammonia soured the air, warning those who communicated by color or smell. Betsy's mind skipped and stuttered like the ancient film playing on her wrist as a warning to the telepaths skirted the fringes of her consciousness. Still more warnings she could not perceive with her natural senses no doubt flooded the chamber now.

Hundreds of creatures ran or flew or poured inside their transitional shells, strange cocoons fitted to their variform bodies. The Twirlover tumbled away as Betsy closed the cover of her shell. She hugged her knees and shivered as the glass cover sealed her inside with a hiss and a confirmation beep. A lifeboat or a coffin? She'd find out soon enough.

Transitional shells filled the gargantuan chamber of the Eluder Ship like arrays of soldiers preparing for battle, their noses pointed toward the red-giant star looming outside. Maera—"The Daughter Star"—one of the few still-burning stars in the galaxy. It seethed before all, a conflagration as large as a solar system, turning everything the color of blood.

Forty seconds.

This was a pitiful end, but it was this or slow starvation, privation, death. The galaxy had been laid sere. No planets to grow food. No stars to keep warm. It wasn't fair. None of them deserved this. But then she remembered Julio, and what she had done to him at Afsasat.

I left you to die, Julio. And for that I deserve this.

Thirty seconds.

Soon now, Maera's heart would cool by a fraction of a degree, and billions of tons of matter, no longer kept aloft by nuclear winds, would plunge towards its gravitational center at the speed of light. The star would collapse, go nova, and in its tortured heart the universe would tear. A singularity would form, a black hole, and Betsy Haadama and the thousands of others on this Eluder Ship would ride that collapsing wave into another universe. Their matter and energy, transmuted into pure information, would seed a new creation, the World to Come. Their consciousness, over long eons, would push matter into form, coerce dust to life. In some strange new way they would live on, gods reborn further down the corridor of infinity. And they had been doing this forever, would be doing this again and again until the end of time.

Or so the litany went.

The story soothed troubled minds. But the science behind the technology was just a theory. It could be proven only by first-person observation. Any object which crossed a black hole's event horizon could never communicate with the universe again. Just as easily, she might be annihilated forever. To those witnessing from the outside, there would be no difference.

Twenty seconds.

She tried not to peer up at The Daughter, though its ember light corrupted everything with its hellish glow. Instead she watched the film on her wrist: men in fedoras, women in ostentatious hats at an airport, people descending a stairwell from plane to tarmac. A baby hoisted in the air. Smiles. Laughing. Cut to a park. The boy looking down at the dead pigeon, staring. Staring. Father picking him up, patting him on the shoulder. The boy, crying.

Why do you stare at the bird? Betsy thought. *What are you thinking?*

She looked up at the seething star. So beautiful, terrible, immense. A wonder that such a thing existed. A horn bellowed and Betsy screamed.

"*False Alarm! Beloveds, the imminent collapse was a false alarm! Spurious readings caused us to make an erroneous conclusion. We estimate at least six hours before stellar collapse, based on present readings.*"

The voice announced the message in multiple languages, simulcast with aggressive rainbows, smells, alien sensations.

I'm alive! she thought. *I'm still here!* It felt exhilarating, for a moment. Then she remembered she'd have to do this again.

Slowly, shells opened and creatures emerged. Betsy scanned the motley lot of them as her cover retracted. A zoo of sentient species escaping from their cages, creatures made of every color, texture, and temperament.

So much life, she thought. *Snuffed out by the Horde.* Crimes beyond forgiveness. And made all the more vile because the Horde had been the progeny of the human race.

Betsy activated inositol in her bloodstream via thought command in order to suppress her panic/flight response. It soothed her, but only just enough to notice the hairs on the back of her neck rising from an electrostatic charge as the Twirlover returned.

"That was exciting!" it said.

"I wouldn't call it that," Betsy said.

"To be so close to annihilation and then to come back again. It renews the sense of life!"

"Or the dread of living."

"But the dread, if you explore it," the Twirlover said, "reveals the miracle of existence out of nothingness. From out of horror comes life."

The litany again. "Or out of life, horror," she said.

It tumbled quietly for a moment. "Sometimes." It moved closer to inspect her film. "That's a child of your species, is it not?"

She glanced down at her screen. "No, that's a rhinoceros."

"Ree-Nos-Ur-Us. What a marvel of composition, all those rolling mountains of flesh. Does it still exist?"

"Extinct."

The Twirlover whistled a mournful, descending arpeggio. "Like so much life in the galaxy. Like the once-glorious stars."

The Horde had obliterated stars by the billions. They had wrapped the Milky Way inside a bleak cocoon of transmatter so that nothing, no ship, no signal—not even light—could pass. And then they vanished, leaving the galaxy to rot. Such was the legacy of humanity.

She wondered if the Twirlover would kill her outright if it knew what she was. Death by physical means might be preferable, she thought, to being flash-baked into quantum-entangled gamma rays. Six in one, really.

The film cut to a boy in a crib, bouncing. His mother lifting him, smiling for the camera. The boy laughing.

"That's one of us," she said. "My paternal ancestor." Surprising herself, she felt pride.

"Ah, such wonderful protuberances!"

A wisp of dust coalesced above Betsy's head. Winking diamonds swirled in yellow clouds. An aeroform creature. For a moment she glimpsed her own face of colored sparkles reflected back at her. But the aeroform being soon spiraled away, only to pause a few seconds later before a group of fronded Whidus who turned their mushroom-like eyes in her direction. Maybe they recognized her, knew what she was. Maybe they were plotting her demise.

A second, identical Twirlover approached Betsy and said to the first, "You know, my bonded-one, that we are about to die, do you not?"

"I was about to come back to you, my flesh-bond," the first said. "And tell you about my sharing with this creature."

"Indeed you were. I saw you tumbling towards me with great haste."

"My flesh-bond, just take a good look at her smooth, auburn

skin, the fine black threads that emerge from her head, the little valve at her peak where she modulates her words with a bacteria-laden pink muscle! And on her upper-left protuberance, that metal device which flicker-flashes with strange images. She watches it incessantly. She is curious, is she not?"

"There is something curious here, certainly."

"My love, let us join so I can share my thoughts with you."

"Indeed, I look forward to it!"

The two tumbled together into a single dancing, twelve-piece ring. Knuckles hopped, bounced, tumbled over each other. Music piped and whistled in byzantine harmonies. There arose a great shriek about them, and soon after they separated again into six-pieced individuals. Betsy thought they might have interchanged pieces in the process.

"Not fair!" said the second. Or was it the first? Betsy couldn't tell them apart anymore. "You playful trickster! You gave me your segment, so now I know your thoughts. But then, you sense my emotions too."

"What joy it is to share mind with you, beloved! Yes, I feel your misplaced jealousy. And so much of it! What a waste of energy. Don't you see? This creature is alone and needs to share with *someone*!"

"Perhaps, but does it have to be you?"

"Not me alone, but us *together*!"

"In this last hour, you would defile us?"

"Please!" Betsy interjected. "I'd prefer to be alone anyway—"

"One must never be alone!" the first said. "Share with us! Let us merge gloriously with your words."

"Indeed, tell us," the second said, "Did you have a bonded-one who abandoned you, who wandered off to have intercourse with strangers when you need him?"

'*Intercourse*?' she thought. Perhaps there was more to the Twirlover concept of sharing than she realized. "Actually, I left him."

"Of course you did," the second said. "Like attracts like."

"Where did you abandon him?" the first said.

Interesting, the way it had interpreted her words. "I left him at the first nova," she said. "The Mother Star. Afsasat."

"You were at Afsasat and you didn't go through the event-horizon?" the second said. "I don't believe your story! Beloved, look how she defiles this union!"

"Surely," the first said, "you are joking, trying to please us with paradox? Why would you do something so idiotic? Why not escape through Afsasat when you had the chance?"

She sighed and turned her attention to the film on her wrist. Mustachioed father and blond-haired son walking down a path. Father, smiling. Boy running, falling. Crying. Father picking him up, kissing him. All better. All better.

"Did you hear our questions?" the first asked.

"Yes," she said. "It's just that it's a very long story."

"Our lives are stories. We are empty without them. Fill us so we may fill you."

Strangely, she had stopped shivering. She even felt a little warm. If this was intercourse, then she was determined to be a good lover. "This film is part of 'The Biography,'" she said. "A record of my ancestors' lives that was encoded within my genes."

"Such joy! I have heard of this technology, the sharing of such immensity," the first said. "How far back do your records go?"

"About six thousand years."

The second squealed.

"I told you, beloved," the first said. "She is share-worthy."

Her mother had told her the story in the quiet hours while drifting under the ash streams of the decimated Magellanic Clouds, or over stale, thrice-brewed tea, while the ice-blue rings of Cegmar rose above the horizon, or while her mother gently brushed her hair and chills trickled down her spine. When he turned seventy, the boy in the film digitized his aging childhood reels and then gave them to his son. His son added films, photos, and memorabilia and passed the collection to his offspring. His children added more history and passed this collection on again. This continued for generations. Eventually his descendants decided to encode this amalgamated history within their DNA, so it would never be lost or forgotten. Every child was thereafter born with the memories of their parents, and theirs before them, and theirs before them. And also in their bodily archives were the early records—the films, photos and keepsakes that started the tradition. The Biography was an ancient and unbroken chain that began with this black and white film playing on her wrist. The first.

And now the last.

"It's so large!" the second said.

"Excuse me?" she said.

"Your story," the first said, "To carry all that history within you!"

"It's not *in* me anymore. Julio and I stripped all of it, every last base-pair, from our genes. I recall only my personal experiences now. This computer . . . it holds the last copy. *This* is the Biography, now."

This fragile, solitary thing on her wrist.

"But why?" Moans and tweets. "That must have been an immense loss!"

The answer was complex, full of shame and guilt. Instead she offered the highly edited version. "Because we wanted to enter the World to Come without a past."

The Twirlovers tumbled noisily, screeching.

"I put the Biography on this ancient computer," she said, pointing to her wrist. "It belonged to my grandmother, five hundred and eighty years ago. Julio and I parked our starsloop in orbit around Afsasat and we stowed this wrist-player in our shrine-room. We said goodbye to our past and then we flew over to the Eluder Ship. Our starsloop and the Biography within would be destroyed when Afsasat went nova."

Chirps. Squeals.

"But Afsasat took its time. So I explored every corner of the Eluder Ship. I discovered that none of my species were there. That meant Julio and I might be the last of my kind in existence. And that meant the Biography was the last of its kind too."

A duet of whistles in a major key.

"I used to recall the smell of my great-grandmother's hair of twenty-three generations ago as her lover leaned in to kiss her pink lips. I knew every defect in the bathroom tiles of the beach house where my ancestor Rhindi lived four thousand years ago. I could hear the gulls cry as they flew in the colored dawn as the four suns rose, one green, one orange, one yellow, and one blue before Eleanor left her family for war, to die in deep space, but not before she had a son to pass on the memory. I once remembered the joy Yalta felt toward his seventeen lanky daughters, all born in zero-g, all tall, graceful, beautiful, with eyes like blue giants. These weren't others' lives. They were *mine*. I had lived these lives too."

Seven long, high notes.

"So many people had once lived inside of me. Even these memories that I'm telling you about now—they come from this device! Not from me! I'm silent inside. And I realized that if I let the Biography die I would be murdering billions. Just like the Horde."

A very human gasp, then a precipitous pause.

"So I changed my mind. I decided I'd bring the Biography with me into the World to Come. My ancestors deserved that much. I was about to retrieve it from our starsloop, but Julio held me. Afsasat could go nova at any moment, he said. And . . . he wanted to sever us from the past. I disagreed."

Betsy started shaking again as the moment became clear in her mind. She remembered his exhausted, pleading eyes, his unruly black beard.

"Did you forget what they did?" Julio had said. "Did you erase that memory too? The Horde, the progeny of the human race, stole our children! And you want to bring their history with us? *We* decided we wouldn't allow that. The Biography has to be destroyed."

"I know what we decided, Julio!" she said. "But I can't let all those people die!"

"They're already dead, Betsy!"

"I can't believe you just said that." Her face grew hot. "They're *not* dead! They once lived within us! They gave us our lives, and we owe them our memories!"

"I don't feel that way at all."

"Julio, how can you abandon them so easily?"

"They led us to this place of death and horror. I sever myself from the past for that reason alone."

And in the end, it was she who had abandoned him.

She swallowed down her tears as the Twirlovers squealed and beckoned her to continue.

"I told Julio I wanted to wander the ship alone, and instead I snuck off to fetch the Biography. Maybe he knew where I was going. I'll never know. I reached my starsloop and was ready to return when I heard the alarm. Afsasat was collapsing. One minute to nova. Not enough time to return safely. I panicked. I had to save the Biography, all those lives, from destruction. Nothing else mattered. I powered up my ship and fled."

For weeks she had wondered, did Julio search the Eluder Ship for her? What did he feel when he realized she had left him? Like the thoughts of the boy in the film, she'd never know. He had entered a black hole, and nothing could cross that dark horizon.

The Twirlovers cried out, a piercing shriek. Perhaps they orgasmed together. Eventually, the second said, "What a dirty tale! So much abandonment. I feel defiled. A sinner! This is the kind of sharing you wanted, my beloved?"

"But in fetching her Biography she *returned* to her people!" the first said. "Don't you see? Isn't sharing so much more rewarding after a long absence?"

"You twist words easily, my bonded-one! Her story

was . . . *acceptable.*"

A large Perslop sloshed towards them. The creature was amber, a gelatinous three-limbed starfish with translucent skin and dozens of eyes like upturned brown bowls.

"Do you wish a comforting invocation?" the Perslop said. A slit tucked into one of its armpits burped open to reveal hundreds of tiny white teeth, and its warm breath reeked of dead seas. "I know rituals from a thousand faiths. Or, if you wish, you may teach me one." Its voice was like wind blowing over ruins.

"Blessings, smooth-skinned pleasure to behold!" the first Twirlover said. "We welcome a fourth to share!"

"No we do not!" the second Twirlover said.

"My flesh-love, please!" the first said. "Do not be rude." Then to the Perslop: "Instead of an invocation, my finely contoured friend. Will you share a story with us?"

"Incorrigible!" the second said, tumbling furiously.

With the moist end of one if its arms, the Perslop inched towards Betsy's wrist. The tip opened into a tripod of three small fingers, with diminutive brown eyes capping the end of each. The eyes wiggled nervously above the ancient film. "What is this?" it asked.

"It's her people's history!" the first said. "From six-thousand years ago!"

"Interesting," the Perslop said. "Your race hasn't changed much."

"That's a duck," Betsy said. "Extinct."

"So, that's you there?"

"No, that's a walrus. Also extinct."

"Then whose history did you say we are watching?"

"My race. They're at a zoo."

"A 'zoo?'" the Perslop said.

"A place that housed animals in cages."

"What for?"

"So they could observe them without danger to themselves,"

she said.

"Another act of separation!" the second Twirlover said. "Such a barbaric, dirty race!"

"Her filth notwithstanding, keeping something caged is not barbarism," the Perslop said, its moist arm dangling an hairsbreadth from Betsy's face. "Before the Horde destroyed my brothers, I used to travel with my colony to a fecal press, where we severed one of our limbs and tortured it in a cage until it released a small amount of feces. We then burned that feces as an offering to the Absent One. They were profoundly holy events. And I miss them very, very much."

The second Twirlover squeaked loudly three times.

"You see, my beloved?" the first said. "This is the joy you have missed by withdrawing from union all these years!"

On Betsy's wrist the film played on, men in white shorts and shirts playing handball. Women sitting on the sidelines bringing smoky cigarettes to their lips. The young boy, a few years older, standing on a porch, talking to a beautiful girl.

"You simplify my thoughts!" the second Twirlover said. "I take no joy in the suffering of others. If I did, I would find pleasure in the atrocities of the Horde. But those are stories I never wish to hear again. If I could, I would erase them from history like this creature erased this Biography from her genes!"

If only that were possible, Betsy thought. *To rewrite history.* If so, she'd go even further back, to the creation of the Horde, more than three hundred years ago. Humanity had been evolving rapidly for generations. They had augmented their consciousness to the point that the body became irrelevant. Flesh was now a temporary abode, while the mind was free to explore and play in infinite space. Epic works of art, science, and philosophy were commonplace. Physical suffering had been eradicated. It was a true Golden Age of humankind.

But the Hagzhi, a prideful, stoic and gargantuan species that had once peacefully abided humans, became fearful of humanity's growing power over matter and began to spread lies and sow seeds of mistrust. Later, the Hagzhi began to systematically exterminate humans as a way to prop up their own faltering galactic hegemonies. Humanity was nearly destroyed in the wars that followed, but after that tumult, humans vowed that they would never let such a catastrophe happen again. Through heroic feats of research they discovered the secret folds of negative time and learned the simple mystery behind the origins of consciousness. They learned how to, with a thought, create a sun. And with another, destroy it.

The Hagzhi race vanished from existence in a day. One hundred and seventy planets, moons, outposts and stations erased from the universe. Later, for no reason anyone could discern, other races vanished. Races which had never threatened humanity. The Onyx Horde, as this force came to be known, acted without cause or reason.

Not all humans accepted the rise to supra-consciousness. Not all humans wanted to change. The Horde slaughtered those who resisted. Those who hid were found, tortured, and killed. And there were those, like Betsy's ancestors, who had made a deal and were spared.

"Keep the Biography in your genes," the Horde had commanded her ancestors. "Keep your physical human form. Do this and you will not die."

And her ancestors agreed, and survived, even prospered, while the rest of the galaxy was ruined. When the other races discovered that there were humans who were spared the Horde's madness, that the Horde were the progeny of the human race, the long dormant seeds of doubt that the Hagzhi had planted re-sprouted, this time across the entire galaxy. Humans were slaughtered without remorse, and the Horde did not come to save them.

If I were given that choice now, Betsy thought. *To live or die by their rules, I would have chosen death. I'd rather die than live under their darkness another instant.*

On the film, a crowded beach. People swimming. Large

umbrellas casting shadows. Wisps of cloud in the sky, all under a bright sun.

A young sun.

The Twirlovers stopped twirling. The Perslop leaned in closer to see.

"Such a young sun," the Perslop said. "Bright and warm. The sight fills me with sadness. No longer do such stars burn in the Milky Way. Here we orbit this dying star in a dead galaxy where only a few cinders burn in a quiescent sea. And all about the universe a hundred billion galaxies dangle forever beyond our reach. The Onyx Horde has sealed us forever from their glorious light. May their souls be stripped from eternity!"

On the film, a party. People laughing, dancing, hands on hips, forming a human train. Cone-shaped hats.

"What are they doing?" the Perslop asked.

"A party," Betsy said. "A new year's celebration."

"And why do they bounce up and down?"

"They're dancing."

"Do you remember, my soul-union," the first Twirlover said, "how we danced for three ascensions of the Hagic Moon with the birth of our tumble-litter?"

"I shall never forget!" the second said, squealing. "Our many tumblers, searching for their bond-sisters. How they merged and separated a thousand times before they joined the sisters to complete their soul!"

"May they find the path to the Glory Star that resides at the center of creation."

On the film, the blond boy in the corner staring into the camera eye. *I'd always assumed that one day someone would look into the Biography and see me. But I'm the last, aren't I?*

"Your children, are they dead?" the Perslop said to the Twirlovers.

"They were living on Ental," the second said. "It was obliterated by the Horde." A hiss like a distant wave crashing on an empty beach.

"I had nine offspring," the Perslop said. "Three died in the disastrous attempt to pass through the galaxy's transmatter shell. Three died of malnutrition. Two died in an experiment to create a new star."

"That's only eight," the first Twirlover said. "And the ninth?"

"Suicide."

On the film, an elderly couple in formal clothing sitting beside a bright window. Their bodies in silhouette. The woman, Bessie. The man, Oser. Betsy's oldest ancestors in the Biography. She and Julio had named their children after them. A boy and girl. Twins. She remembered their puffy, newborn faces, their eyes hungry for life.

She and Julio and her children had been living on the temperate moon of Aeoschloch with one hundred other Biography-carrying humans, far from the wars and the suspicions of the other races. And one morning, as the swirling black eye of the gas giant Ur rose above the distant hills, as she was breast-feeding her twin children, she was swept away.

She could not see or hear or sense anything, even her own screams, but she felt a presence probing her, scanning her, reading and rereading the Biography within her as if it were the most important thing in the universe. And she knew this presence, *remembered* it from the Biography and the memories within.

The Onyx Horde.

Then the Horde spit her and a hundred other humans out over the sandy coastline. Some people did not rise from the cold beach. Their eyes stared lifeless into the starless sky. Some had organs missing or were merged with others into horrible grotesqueries. Some went mad. Some had reappeared in the ocean and drowned. And the children, all the pre-pubescent ones, had vanished. The Horde had taken them. Every one.

Oser and Bessie, two months old, barely enough time to open their eyes and learn their parents' faces. Gone.

The seventy surviving colonists were wrecked, devastated.

Should they have more children? No, they decided, the Horde could just as easily take them again. Should they try to forget and live out their lives on this backwater moon? No, how could they ever find joy again, knowing that the Horde could come again at any time? Then the colonists heard about Afsasat, the Eluder Ship being built there and a possible way to escape the Horde forever.

And so it was decided. The colonists would end their history on their own terms. They would attempt to enter the World to Come, but without the Biography inside of them. They would excise it from their genes, shedding themselves from the thing which the Horde seemed so desperately to desire. Shedding themselves of humanity's sordid history. It would be, in their own small way, revenge.

But they'd have to get to Afsasat first. The Eluder Ship was being constructed in a quadrant of space that was rumored to be tolerant of humans. But the colonists would have to navigate through large quadrants of dangerous space. So they traveled in many ships, by multiple circuitous and zigzagging routes. Betsy and Julio arrived safely. When Betsy walked around the ship, looking for other humans, she found none. They were the last two.

And now, on this second Eluder Ship, there was only her.

Outside the windows, lightning the size of a hundred dead planets forked across Maera's surface. The star looked ancient, tired, ready to sleep forever. The aliens throughout the chamber paused to stare up at the star.

Her wrist flickered like the star outside. On the film, the mustachioed man. The woman with the beautiful black hair. Another party. A different day. A cake with five flames. Eyes reflecting candlelight. The boy, blowing the flames out. Smoke and applause. Silent cheer.

"You said you wanted a story," the Perslop said, "Well I have one. A few weeks ago I confronted a group of wandering Ergs. One told me that he'd captured a human—"

Betsy started in her seat.

"The Erg said the human was an ugly, repulsive thing," the Perslop continued. "With dark hair covering most of its carbuncle head, and liquid leaking from its odious eyes. It pleaded for its life. And the Erg, a compassionate being, decided ultimately to let it go. But afterward he became terribly distraught. He said he'd missed his opportunity to destroy a creature which had caused so much of the galaxy's pain. For a long time I considered this Erg's position.

"I once had a vast starship. I found a bore-worm nibbling in my refuse berth. I believed in the sanctity of all life, and decided to let it live. Six weeks later, my ship was infested with bore-worms, and no one would dock with me for fear of having their hulls eaten. I had to incinerate my ship. You see, I let one worm live, and thousands returned to ruin me. Is it not the same with humans? If we let one live, do we not give them the chance to destroy us again? I told the Erg that he did the righteous thing, but I truly did not—do not—believe it myself."

The Twirlovers chirped quietly.

"Where did he find this human?" she blurted. "How many weeks ago was this?" *Dark hair covering its head?* she thought. *Julio, is he speaking of you?*

The first Twirlover said, "Please, tell us more, beloved! This is wonderful!"

"What more is there to tell?" the Perslop said. "We may be reborn in a new universe, but if we carry that worm along with us, do we not risk infestation again?"

Betsy stared into the Perslop's tripod eye-cups. *It knows,* she thought. *It knows what I am.* Then she remembered the aeroform creature studying her and the Whidus staring at her and the Twirlovers' odd behavior around her.

They all know, she thought. *Every one of them knows!*

"Do not fear, *human,*" the Perslop said. "I'll not kill you. I define myself by being what you are not. I let you live even though every pulse of my hearts says you should be squashed between my arms like vermin."

Betsy stared at the Perslop, shivering. Weakly, she said, "Was your story about the human true?"

Outside, a brilliant solar flare leaped from Maera and grew angrily out into space. The Daughter, shedding her last vestiges of life. Soon now.

The Perslop gestured to her screen. "Is *your* story true? Is not history filled with lies and obfuscations?"

On the screen, a beach, waves crashing silently. Umbrellas casting large shadows. A beautiful young woman smiling shyly at the camera. The future wife of the boy. A burning ball of light in the sky. Everyone watched the screen.

"So beautiful," the Perslop said. "And gone forever . . . "

Silence. Even the Twirlovers went still.

"Please!" she said. "Tell me! Was it true?"

"Why?" the Perslop said. "Why should I tell you? Why do you deserve an answer?"

She took a deep breath. "Because someone I love might still be alive," she said. "To me, that's everything."

The alarm trilled, startling her. "*Gravitational collapse imminent, beloveds! Please take your positions inside your transitional shells!*"

"No!" she cried. "Not yet!"

The Perslop began to move away.

"Wait!" she screamed. "Please tell me!"

The Perslop paused but did not turn back. "I am the last of my kind," the Perslop said. "I came over here to tell you that you are not."

The Twirlovers shrieked and suddenly merged. They tumbled madly, yelping, barking, while the Perslop left for its transitional shell.

Ninety seconds to collapse.

Maera flickered and angry waves rippled across its surface, but Betsy could not summon the will to close her shell. On her viewscreen, the park, the blond-haired boy skipping, scaring away pigeons. Dappled sunlight. A breeze through trees. A dead pigeon on the dirt. The boy, stopping, staring. Staring.

Suddenly, she understood why the boy stared at the bird for so long.

This is the first time you knew death! she thought. *You knew the bird would never rise again. And you knew that one day you'd fall too, that everything falls! That's why you gave these films to your son. You wanted him to remember you, forever!*

Seventy-five seconds.

The Perslop had been right, she thought. *I could be polluting the new universe with this history.*

Sixty-five seconds.

But all those lives, erased? *I can't kill you, great-great grandfather. You are the first. Without you, we would be nothing. My ancestors, without all of you, I am nothing.*

Sixty seconds.

The fourteen billion-year history of this universe had already unfolded. But for the World to Come, the story had yet to be written. Maybe the World to Come was a lie, but then again, maybe there was new life on the other side of the event horizon. Maybe they truly had been doing this forever and ever. A flower gone to seed.

She jumped out of her transitional shell, took off her grandmother's computer from her wrist, and placed it inside the shell. Then she pressed the button to seal it inside.

She'd send the Biography, its mammoth history, with its eons of joys and sorrows, through Maera. She hoped that in the next universe, humanity would be different. Better. What every parent wishes for her children.

"Goodbye," she said.

The Twirlovers still tumbled together in the air beside her, as wild as a radioactive atom. The alarm continued to wail. "Get in your shells!" she screamed. But they ignored her.

Twenty seconds.

She ran to the rear of the chamber and leaped into an escape pod. She pressed the emergency activator and in an instant she was hurtling away from the Eluder Ship at a large fraction of the speed of light. In the window behind her, Maera blinked twice, like two eyes closing, then began to fade. The star shrunk to half its size, and a moment later the sky filled with white light. The ship bleated a thousand warnings as Betsy closed her eyes.

"I'm coming, Julio. I'm coming for you."

She had watched the ancient film so often that it still played in her mind, projecting on the back of her eyes like a movie screen. The boy in the park, running, laughing. Falling. Scuffing his knee. Father picking him up, kissing him, comforting him. Above them, a sun.

A young sun.

ABOUT THE AUTHOR

Matthew Kressel is a multiple Nebula and World Fantasy Award nominated author, artist, and coder. His many works of short fiction have appeared in *Analog, Asimov's, Lightspeed, Nightmare, Clarkesworld, Tor.com/Reactor, Beneath Ceaseless Skies*, and many magazines and anthologies, including multiple *Year's Best* collections, and his fiction has been translated into over a dozen languages. His far-future science fiction novel *Space Trucker Jess* (Fairwood Press) will be published June 2025. And his Mars-based novella *The Rainseekers* (Tordotcom) is coming in February 2026. Alongside Ellen Datlow, he runs the Fantastic Fiction at KGB reading series in Manhattan (kgbfantasticfiction.org). And he is the creator of the Moksha submissions system (moksha.io), used by many of the largest fiction publishers today. With Mercurio D. Rivera, he co-hosts *The Nerd Count Podcast* (www.nerdcountpodcast.com). And he publishes a writing newsletter at matthewkressel.substack. com. Find out more at www.matthewkressel.net.

ACKNOWLEDGEMENTS

Selecting the stories for this collection was in a literal sense a tour through the history of the more than two decades of my writing. From my earliest tales, like "Mortar," to my more recent ones, like "Now We Paint Worlds," these stories hold snapshots of my past. As I reread them I vividly recalled the places, times, and feelings of their creation. And I recalled the people who helped and mentored me along the way, and who shaped my writing and self for the better.

Words fail to express my gratitude to the members of my writing group, Altered Fluid, who suffered through many early drafts of these and other stories. Through their careful attention, advice, and friendship they have made my fiction light-years better. In no particular order I'd like to thank Paul Berger, Kris Dikeman, Lilah Wild, Devin Poore, Rajan Khanna, Greer Woodward, Theresa DeLucci, Alaya Dawn Johnson, Gay Partington Terry, N.K. Jemisin, E.C. Myers, Sam J. Miller, Marty Cahill, Lauren McLaughlin, Adanze Asante, and of course Mercurio D. Rivera, without whom none of these stories would exist. I must also bow in thanks to the late, great Richard Bowes, who taught me too many things to mention here. Rick was a friend, mentor, and the funniest person I ever met. The world is less bright without Rick in it. I miss him dearly.

As Jeffrey Ford recently wrote on Facebook, "Always try to work with great editors." You don't always get to choose the editors whom you work with, but through hard work or luck or fate these golden editors were placed in my path. All of the following people were amazing to work with. As we say in Yiddish, *a shaynem dank*—a beautiful thanks—to all the editors who published these stories, including and especially Ellen Datlow, Neil Clarke, John Joseph Adams, Sean Wallace, Terri Windling, Jason Sizemore, Rich Horton, and Rachel Swirsky.

Thanks to my agent Ethan Ellenberg for his superlative advice and expertise. And thanks as well to Scott H. Andrews, Christopher Cevasco, Erica Hildebrand, Al Bogdan, Lincoln Palmer, Trevor Quachri, and Pritpaul Bains for their friendship and support, especially through the Covid lockdowns. I wouldn't have survived without you. (Roll for initiative.)

Thanks to my parents, sisters, and in-laws for their love and support. And a beautiful thanks (and bread) to my wife, Christine, whose knowledge and wisdom has led me to be a better person, and whose patience, grit, and love has carried me through some dark and difficult times.

All of your histories are within me. Thank you.

Matthew Kressel
December 2024

STORY HONORS AND ACCOLADES

"The Sounds of Old Earth"
- 2013 Nebula Award finalist for Best Short Story
- 2013 Locus Recommended Reading List
- Recommended Reading List *2014 Best Science Fiction & Fantasy* (Prime Books, ed. Rich Horton)
- Honorable Mention 2014 *Year's Best Science Fiction: Thirty-First Edition* (Macmillan, ed. Gardner Dozois)
- Translated into Czech and published in *XB-1*
- Translated into Russian and published in Космопорт (Kosmoport)
- Translated into Chinese and published in *Science Fiction World*
- Translated into Polish and published in *Smokopolitan*
- Published in *Nebula Awards Showcase 2015* (ed. Greg Bear)

"The Meeker and the All-Seeing Eye"
- 2014 Nebula Award finalist for Best Short Story
- 2015 BookTubeSFF Winner
- Translated into Chinese and published in *Science Fiction World*
- Translated into Romanian and published in *Almanah Anticipatia*
- Translated into Farsi and published in *Metaphor Space*
- Published in *Nebula Awards Showcase 2016* (ed. Mercedes Lackey)

"The Last Novelist (or a Dead Lizard in the Yard)"
- 2017 Nebula Award finalist for Best Short Story
- 2018 Eugie Award Finalist for Best Short Story
- Published in *The Best Science Fiction of the Year:*

Volume 3 (Night Shade Books, ed. Neil Clarke)
- Translated into French and published in *Bifrost*
- Translated into Romanian and published in *Helion*
- Translated into Croatian and published in *Sirius B*
- Translated into Spanish and published by Penguin Random House Grupo Editorial
- Published in *2019 Nebula Awards Showcase* (ed. Silvia Moreno-Garcia)

"Now We Paint Worlds"
- Published in *Some of the Best from Tor.com, 2021 Edition* (eds. Ruoxi Chen, Ellen Datlow, Carl Engle-Laird, Emily Goldman, Jonathan Strahan, Lee Harris, Ann VanderMeer, Lindsey Hall)
- Translated into Czech and published in *XB-1*

"Saving Diego"
- Honorable Mention in *Best Horror of the Year, Vol. 2* (ed. Ellen Datlow)
- Honorable Mention in *Year's Best Science Fiction, 27th Annual Collection* (ed. Gardner Dozois)
- 5th in the Annual 2009 *Interzone* Readers' Poll

"Still You Linger, Like Soot in the Air"
- Published in *The Best Science Fiction of the Year: Volume Six* (Night Shade Books, ed. Neil Clarke)

"Love Engine Optimization"
- Published in *The Year's Best Science Fiction and Fantasy, 2018 Edition* (Prime Books, ed. Rich Horton)
- 2017 *Locus* Recommended Reading List
- Honorable Mention in *The Year's Best Science Fiction: Thirty-Fifth Annual Collection* (ed. Gardner Dozois)
- Translated into Japanese and published in *Babelzine*

"Your Future is Pending"
- *Tangent Online* 2019 Recommended Reading List
- Finalist in *Clarkesworld Magazine* 2019 Reader's Poll
- Translated into Chinese and published in *Science Fiction World*
- Podcast at *Kaleidocast*

"Demon in Aisle 6"
- Honorable Mention in *The Best Horror of the Year Vol. 8* (ed. Ellen Datlow)

"The Garden Beyond Her Infinite Skies"
- *Tangent Online* 2015 Recommended Reading List
- Translated into Czech and published in *XB-1*

"Cameron Rhyder's Legs"
- Honorable Mention in *Year's Best Science Fiction 32nd Annual Collection* (ed. Gardner Dozois)
- *Tangent Online* 2015 Recommended Reading List

"The History Within Us"
- Honorable Mention in *The Year's Best Science Fiction & Fantasy 2011 Edition* (ed. Rich Horton)
- Translated into Czech and published in *XB-1*
- Translated into Chinese and published in *Science Fiction World*